PRAISE FOR
Grace in Thine Eyes

"*Grace in Thine Eyes* was a joy to read! I savored every word of this tender and transcendent story of one young woman's journey from disgrace to *his* grace. Liz Curtis Higgs is a masterful storyteller whose eloquent pen has truly been blessed."
　—TERESA MEDEIROS, *New York Times* best-selling author

"If you've read Liz Curtis Higgs's earlier Scottish trilogy, you already know that she has an extraordinary gift for building a beautiful, elegant story around people thrust into crisis, people whose faith is severely tested in ways that hold us captive until the final page. *Grace in Thine Eyes* sings throughout with the pulsating rhythm of love—God's love for his people and our love for one another. Higgs manages to turn history and imagery and language into an unforgettable work of art. A timeless masterpiece."
　—B. J. HOFF, author of *A Distant Music*

"*Grace in Thine Eyes* is a phenomenal story that beautifully parallels its biblical counterpart. In a world where love has so often been replaced by lust, Liz Curtis Higgs reminds us that what the heart is truly seeking is the grace and mercy of God's forgiving love."
　—TRACIE PETERSON, best-selling author of *What She Left for Me*

PRAISE FOR
Thorn in My Heart
Fair Is the Rose
Whence Came a Prince

"A luminous sense of hope shines through this truly wrenching story of characters who are both larger than life and all too human. This unforgettable saga is as multilayered, mysterious, and joyous as love and faith can be."
　—SUSAN WIGGS, *New York Times* best-selling author

"Generously researched, heartily written, this grand stew of a novel is filled with meat, spice, and enough Scotch broth to satisfy the palate of the most finicky Scottish historical buffs. Compelling, shattering the barriers of time with frequently stunning imagery and always solid storytelling, *Thorn in My Heart* measures up against the finest historical fiction of our day."

—LISA SAMSON, author of *Women's Intuition*

"All the character portrayals are very authentic, as is the atmospheric setting. The dialogue is interspersed with plenty of Scottish words, whose meanings are thoughtfully provided in a glossary at the end of the book. The entire novel gently carries the message of faith in God and his mysterious ways. Simply put, the book leaves its readers with a satisfied feeling and teaches them to hope."

—THEBESTREVIEWS.COM

"A triumphant conclusion to a remarkable trilogy. Liz's impeccable research, sense of history, and love of her subject bring her characters' struggles and victories to life in a story you'll never forget."

—DONNA FLETCHER CROW, author of *The Fields of Bannockburn*

"A colorful tapestry woven from painstaking research, a rich, vivid setting, and compelling, wonderfully real characters. With excellent writing and a keen understanding of human nature, Liz Curtis Higgs delivers a first-rate, fascinating historical saga."

—B. J. HOFF, author of *An Emerald Ballad*

"An engrossing tale that transplants the Old Testament story of Jacob and Esau to eighteenth-century Scotland. Filled with Scottish history, lore, language, and geography, Higgs's first historical-fiction novel will delight her fans and anyone who enjoys tales of Scotland. It also shows a master storyteller's skill in shedding new light on a timeless story."

—CBA MARKETPLACE

Grace in Thine Eyes

Susie

Liz Curtis Higgs

Grace in Thine Eyes

LIZ CURTIS HIGGS

WaterBrook
PRESS

GRACE IN THINE EYES
PUBLISHED BY WATERBROOK PRESS
12265 Oracle Boulevard, Suite 200
Colorado Springs, Colorado 80921
A division of Random House, Inc.

All Scripture quotations are taken from the King James Version of the Bible.

The characters and events in this book are fictional, and any resemblance to actual persons or events is coincidental.

ISBN 1-57856-259-7

Library of Congress Cataloging-in-Publication Data
Higgs, Liz Curtis.
    Grace in thine eyes / Liz Curtis Higgs.—1st ed.
       p. cm.
    ISBN 1-57856-259-7
    1. Dinah (Biblical character)—Fiction. 2. Scotland—History—19th century—Fiction. I. Title.
PS3558.I36235G73 2006
813'.54—dc22
                                            2005033536

Printed in the United States of America
2006—First Edition

10 9 8 7 6 5 4 3 2 1

To Carol Bartley,
gifted editor
and precious friend.
Your patience,
encouragement,
thoughtful direction,
and unwavering faith
are blessings beyond measure.
Thank you, dear sister,
for taking this journey with me
again and again.

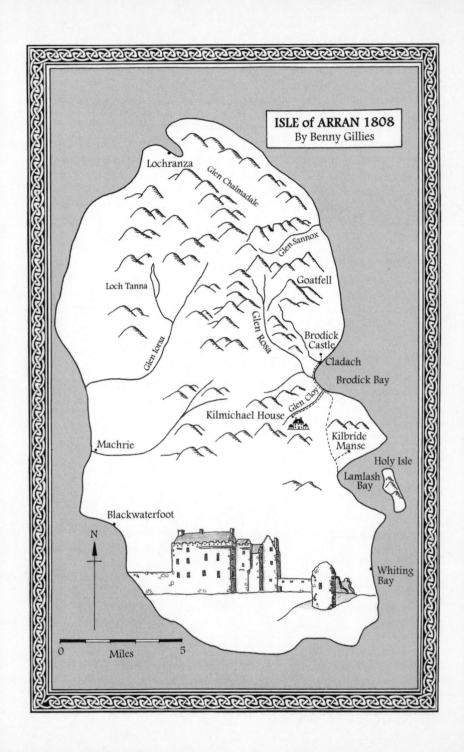

ISLE of ARRAN 1808
By Benny Gillies

Lochranza

Glen Chalmadale

Glen Sannox

Loch Tanna

Goatfell

Glen Rosa

Glen Iorsa

Brodick
Castle

Cladach

Brodick Bay

Glen Cloy

Kilmichael House

Kilbride
Manse

Holy Isle

Machrie

Lamlash
Bay

Blackwaterfoot

N

Whiting
Bay

0   Miles   5

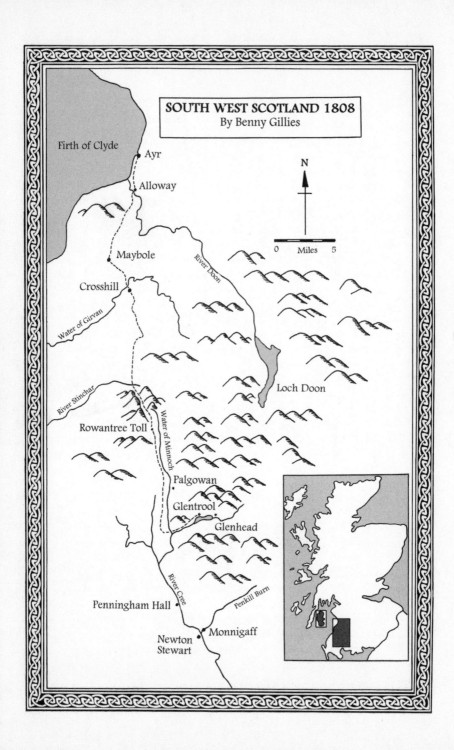

SOUTH WEST SCOTLAND 1808
By Benny Gillies

Firth of Clyde

Ayr

Alloway

N

0 Miles 5

Maybole

River Doon

Crosshill

Water of Girvan

Loch Doon

River Stinchar

Water of Minnoch

Rowantree Toll

Palgowan

Glentrool

Glenhead

River Cree

Penkill Burn

Penningham Hall

Newton Stewart

Monnigaff

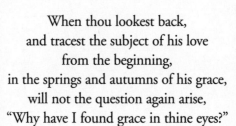

When thou lookest back,
and tracest the subject of his love
from the beginning,
in the springs and autumns of his grace,
will not the question again arise,
"Why have I found grace in thine eyes?"

ROBERT HAWKER

One

No doubt they rose up early to observe
The rite of May.
WILLIAM SHAKESPEARE

Glen of Loch Trool
Spring 1808

D avina McKie dropped to her knees on the grassy hillock, letting
her shawl slip past her shoulders despite the sharp chill in the air.
The silent glen stood draped in a pearl gray mist, the rugged peaks of
Mulldonach mere shadows edged in copper, hinting at dawn.

A smile stole across her face. Her brothers were nowhere to be seen.

Davina swept her fingers over the cool, wet grass, then lightly patted her cheeks and brow, touching her nose for good measure. If the
May dew banished her freckles, as the *auld* wives promised, she would
gladly wash her face out of doors every morning of the month. Never
mind that the ruddy spots matched her bright mane of hair; *ferntickles*
were better suited to a child's complexion. After seventeen years, Davina
was quite ready to be done with them.

She sat up and rearranged her drooping crown of daisies, meant to
safeguard her from brownies, *bogles,* and other uncanny creatures that
roamed the land on Beltane, then started to her feet when a familiar
voice rose from the fog.

"On May Day, in a fairy ring!" Her brother Will. There was no mis-
taking his baritone. His twin, Sandy—only their mother called him
Alexander—would not be far behind.

Ah well. Davina spun round to greet them.

Two shaggy heads, black as midnight, emerged from the mist. A
year younger than she, the twins were in every way identical, from their

dark brown eyes to their broad chests and muscular backs. "Like stags," their mother had once said, gently teasing them not to be seen on the moors during hunting season.

As the lads drew near, they finished the May Day rhyme. "We've seen them round Saint Anthon's spring."

Davina recognized the poet.

"Robert Ferguson," Will answered for her as if he'd read the name in her eyes. He tugged at her unbound hair, which spilled down her back, the scarlet ends brushing her waist. "Sandy, I told you we'd spot a fairy on the *braes* this morning. See how her ears come to a point?"

The McKie brothers never tired of comparing her to the wee folk since the crown of her head did not reach their shoulders, and her hands and feet were no bigger than a young girl's. She snatched her hair from Will's grasp, only to find his twin plucking at her skirts.

Sandy's eyes gleamed with mischief as he appraised her. "A light green gown, fair skin, and a wreath of flowers. She only lacks wings."

Will winked at her. "You've not looked hard enough, Brother."

She fluttered her eyelet shawl behind her, making them both laugh.

"I see by her wet cheek our fairy has been bathing in the dew." Sandy gently tweaked her nose. "Perhaps she thinks she's not bonny enough."

Davina knew he was teasing but turned on her heel nonetheless and flounced down the hill toward home, taking care not to lose her footing on the slippery grass and ruin her stageworthy exit. When her brothers called after her, she pretended not to hear them.

"Och!" Will shouted her name, the sharpness of his voice muted by the moist air. "Sandy meant no offense. You know how daft he is when it comes to the lasses."

She heard a soft groan as fist connected with flesh, then Sandy's voice, slightly winded. "He speaks the truth, Davina. You've no need of the May dew when you're already the fairest maid in Galloway."

An exaggerated claim. South West Scotland boasted dozens of young women far prettier than she. Still, she'd made her brothers grovel long enough. Davina slowed her steps, letting the lads catch up.

"There now." Will wrapped her right hand round the crook of his elbow, and Sandy the same on her left. "Let us cease any talk of your beauty. As it is, no gentleman in Monnigaff parish is worthy of you."

She could not clap her hands—her usual means of expressing amusement—so Davina simply shook her head at Will's foolishness as they continued downhill together. Perhaps that night when she took to the heath by the light of a gibbous moon, she'd evade her brothers altogether. The ritual required absolute silence—something she managed easily and the twins did not manage at all.

"We've a secret," Will confessed as the threesome reached level ground. "That's why we came looking for you." He led them away from the rushing waters of Buchan Burn and headed west toward the McKie mansion. "Father intends to make an announcement after breakfast. As usual, he's told us nothing."

"Aye." Sandy grimaced. "'Twill be a revelation to us all."

Davina searched each face in turn. Was it glad tidings or ill? She touched her lips, then her heart, knowing they would grasp her meaning: *Can you not tell me more? I will keep your secret.*

Will shook his head, stamping the grass a bit harder. "That's all we know, lass. Father demanded we arrive promptly at table. He wasn't smiling when he said it."

Bad news, then.

Her earlier joy began to dissipate, like the morning mist giving way to the sun. The trio walked on in silence broken only by the throaty cry of a raven gliding above the surface of Loch Trool. When the thick stand of pines along the loch made continuing arm in arm impossible, Davina followed behind Will, with Sandy close on her heels, her mind turning over the possibilities.

Was a wedding in the offing? The twins were only sixteen, far too young for marriage. Davina's steps slowed. Surely her father did not have a suitor in mind for her? Not likely, or her mother would have mentioned something. Was Ian to marry, then? Quite as *braw* as their handsome father, her brother would make a fine catch for any lass. Nineteen years of age come October, he was man enough to take a wife.

Ian was in every way her older brother. Responsible. Trustworthy. Intelligent. The twins used other words: Predictable. Unimaginative.

Dull. Davina suspected that envy fueled such sentiments: Ian would inherit all of Glentrool. Still, it was Will and Sandy who'd come looking for her on the hills, speculating about an announcement. Might their father not have some favorable word to share with his younger sons? If so, she would mark this day as a rare and welcome occasion.

As they neared Glentrool, Davina lifted her gaze to its square central tower and the round turret nestled in the heart of its L-shaped design. Built of rough granite from the glen, the house was rugged and imposing, like the Fell of Eschoncan that stood behind it; immovable and unshakable, like the faith of the great-grandfather who had built it.

After crossing the threshold, they started down the long entrance hall, the twins' boot heels loud against the hardwood floor. Davina paused at the mirror to smooth the muslin tucker round her neckline and pluck the flowers from her hair, now a tangled mess after her early morning ramble on the hills.

Drawing a steadying breath, she turned away from her reflection and walked into the dark-beamed dining room, where she was greeted by portraits of McKies from generations past. A single window did little to brighten the dim interior. The rest of the family was already seated, with Father at the head of the long table, Ian to his left and Mother on his right. Though Ian simply said, "Good morning," she saw the wariness in his gaze, heard his unspoken warning. *Something is amiss.* A slight furrow carved her father's brow. More cause for concern.

"I was about to send Rab off to find you." Their mother's tone was kind, without censure. "You see, my husband?" She touched his sleeve. "Your sons have joined you at table, just as you requested."

"So they have." Jamie rested his hand on hers, a slight smile softening his features.

Most marriages among the gentry were forged in silver, with little thought for romance; not so Davina's parents'. She thought they made a handsome couple: Leana, with her porcelain skin, silvery blond hair, and wide, blue gray eyes; and Jamie, his brown hair still thick but shot through with silver, his dark brows arched over moss green eyes that missed nothing. Her mother had quietly celebrated her fortieth year in March and her father the same a few years earlier.

"Dearest?" Leana's voice stirred Davina from her reverie. So did the sketchbook that she slid toward her. "I found this in your room and thought you might have need of it."

Davina opened the clothbound volume to a blank page, then fingered the attached charcoal pencil, carved to a fine point by her father's horn-handled knife. Whenever facial expressions or hand signals would not suffice to share her thoughts with others, she scribbled them along the margins of her sketches. Just now she felt a strong urge to draw something, to keep hand and mind occupied while the others ate, for she had little appetite.

Two servants entered from the kitchen, steaming dishes in hand. Rashers of bacon and a fragrant pot of cooked oats were added to the sideboard, joining a cold platter of sliced mutton and boiled hens' eggs. The twins stood to fill their plates, more subdued than Davina had seen them in many a morning.

She swallowed a bit of dry oatcake, then quietly sipped her tea, searching her mother's face for some clue of what the morning might hold. Was that a slight tremor in Leana's chin? a hint of moisture in her eyes?

All at once her father thrust aside his half-eaten plate of food and dabbed his mouth, signaling his intentions. "I have important news that cannot wait any longer."

Davina's breath caught. *Please, Father. Let it be good news.*

Her brothers turned to the head of the table, their expressions grim, as Davina found her sketchbook pencil. It seemed their questions were about to be answered.

Two

A mother's secret hope outlives them all.
OLIVER WENDELL HOLMES

Leana McKie did not close her eyes or bow her head, yet still she prayed in the deepest recesses of her heart. *Help my sons understand. Let my daughter not be dismayed.*

Watching Davina grip her pencil more tightly, Leana longed to smooth back the wisps of red hair from the young woman's brow to comfort her. To prepare her. Fearing the gesture might alarm Davina further, Leana folded her hands in her lap and gave Jamie her full regard. Her husband was not insensitive; he would deliver the news with care.

Though he did not stand, Jamie's straight back and lifted chin commanded respect. He was suitably dressed in a burgundy coat and buff breeches, his shirt collar pointed above his cravat, his sleek hair tied at the nape of his neck. Charles, his new valet, had performed his duties well; the laird of Glentrool looked the part.

Jamie drew a letter from his waistcoat with some ceremony. " 'Tis a post from a certain university, responding to my recent inquiry." He scanned the creased paper as if looking for a particular passage. "Principal Baird writes, 'Your twin sons are duly equipped for academic pursuits. Convey young William and Alexander to Edinburgh posthaste.' "

He could not have shocked their children more if he'd slapped their faces.

The twins stared at him, mouths agape. "Edinburgh?" Sandy managed to say, his voice taut as a rope.

When no one else spoke, Ian said, "Well done, lads."

"Aye," Leana said softly. "Well done." Except this was not their doing; it was Jamie's.

He waved the letter like a flag, capturing their attention once more.

"The principal goes on to say, 'The summer term commences on the tenth of May.'" Jamie laid the letter on the table, displaying the elegant script for all to see. "Come Tuesday next, Will and Sandy will be furthering their education in the capital."

Will shifted in his seat. "You sound eager to have us gone, sir." His even tone fooled no one; each word bore the weight of his anger. "I daresay we'll hardly be missed."

Oh, William. Leana looked away, undone by the pain in his eyes, in his voice, in his posture. The years of neglect had taken their toll. *Say something, Jamie.*

For a moment Will's challenge hung in the air, unanswered.

"On the contrary, you'll be greatly missed," Jamie finally said, "especially by the women of the household."

Leana touched her daughter's hand, offering what encouragement she could. *I am here, dearest. And always shall be.* She watched Davina's pencil scratch across the page of her sketchbook, her mouth pressed into a thin line and her eyes glistening with unshed tears.

Only Leana was close enough to read the words she'd written: *Must they go?*

"A fair question," Leana murmured, grateful for any discussion that might relieve the tension in the room. "Your father can explain why the lads are obliged to attend university." She nodded at Jamie, praying his answer might ease Davina's sorrow and the twins' as well. The lass adored her brothers and would not bid them farewell gladly.

"All four of you have been well tutored by Mr. McFadgen," Jamie reminded Davina, his manner toward her markedly kinder. "Now 'tis time your younger brothers sought their fortunes. In civil law perhaps. Or in the church."

Leana eyed the twins, with their unruly hair and untamed natures. William a barrister? Alexander a minister? Athletic as they were and prone to pugnacious behavior, they had little interest in legal or ecclesiastical matters. Military life held more appeal, though with British regiments battling Napoleon on the Continent, Leana had done her best to quash such aspirations.

Will turned to his sister, his features stony. "I'm sorry, Davina. We did not…expect this."

"We'll come home as often as we can," Sandy promised, though the doubt in his voice suggested otherwise. "Or perhaps you might visit us in Edinburgh."

"Your studies will keep you well occupied," Jamie said brusquely. "Do not extend invitations your sister cannot accept."

Davina quietly closed her book, the pencil tucked inside. Her heart was hidden from view as well, for she ducked her head and would not let them see her face.

The air felt charged, as if a storm were approaching. Something had to be done. "Gentlemen." Leana rose, prompting the men to their feet as well. "While you discuss your travel arrangements, Davina and I have plans of our own this morning."

Taking her cue, Davina stood and followed her into the hall.

Leana slowly closed the dining room door behind them, praying that whatever conversation followed would be redemptive. Jamie, anxious to have the matter out in the open, had been too abrupt. Will, as usual, had become sullen, defensive. As for their daughter, Davina's buoyant person-ality had been sorely tested with the unexpected news. Leana wished she might be in three places at once, smoothing all their ruffled feathers. Per-haps Ian would bring his calming influence to bear where she could not.

"Let us away, dearie." Leana clasped Davina's cool hand in hers and led her toward the stair, keeping her voice low. "Do not think ill of your father. He is acting in the twins' best interest, for their fine minds should be put to good use. Alas, that cannot happen here at Glentrool, and so to Edinburgh they must go."

Davina lifted her head at last, her eyes still wet with tears.

Oh my child. Without a word Leana drew her daughter into her arms, tucking her head beneath her chin. Seventeen, aye, but so small, this one. "They will come home, Davina. And they will never forget you, these brothers of yours. I can promise you that."

In the quiet entrance hall she heard voices rumbling behind the dining room door. Not raised, but not cordial. She would spare Davina imagining the worst.

" 'Tis May Day," Leana said softly, releasing her daughter from her embrace. "Whatever betides us, our neighbors will soon appear at our doorstep. And you've a fiddle that needs tuning, aye?" She started up the broad oak staircase, aiming her comments over her shoulder as Davina trailed after her. "Suppose we let Sarah dress your hair first, and then we'll see how Robert is managing in the garden."

The dark-haired lady's maid stood by Davina's dressing table, brush and comb at the ready. "I *ken* ye'll be wantin' *tae leuk* yer best *whan* ye play yer fiddle, miss."

Leana rested her hands on her daughter's slender shoulders and met her gaze in the glass. "Most ladies of your acquaintance wear their hair tightly gathered atop their heads. Might you prefer something else?"

Davina's expression brightened a little. She began weaving her long hair in a loose braid, then pointed to the dark green ribbons trailing beneath her bodice and to the pink gillyflowers in the china vase on her dresser. A thick braid plaited with flowers and ribbons was perfect for May Day, however unconventional the style. Parish folk had grown accustomed to Davina's eccentricities and had pronounced her "an original." When she brought Galloway's rural scenery to life with only charcoal lines on a page, her artistic nature was on full display. And when she tucked her fiddle beneath her chin and sent her bow flying across the strings, her surrogate voice rang out sweet and clear.

Someday a perceptive gentleman would not only see Davina, he would instinctively *hear* her, discerning her thoughts and identifying her deepest longings. Leana withdrew into the shadowy doorway, hiding her sadness. *Please, Lord, may that day not come too soon.* With the twins leaving home and Ian old enough to marry, Leana knew her mothering years were drawing to a close. No more drying their tears or polishing their manners. No more stories by the hearth or prayers by their bedsides.

Her *bairns* were grown now, her cradlesongs forgotten. "*Baloo, baloo,* my wee, wee thing," Leana sang softly, leaning her head on the doorpost.

Three

Time, like an ever-rolling stream,
Bears all its sons away.
ISAAC WATTS

"You might have told us privately, Father."

"Nae, you might have told us sooner."

Jamie McKie deliberately folded his hands and rested them on the dining table. "I received the letter from Principal Baird only *yestermorn*. Your mother deserved to know first." He fixed his gaze on Will and Sandy, lest they doubt his sincerity. "I chose to tell the four of you together so that Ian and Davina would not feel excluded."

Will shot back, "But *our* lives are the ones being disrupted, not theirs."

"That is not true," Jamie countered. "What happens to one member of this family affects us all."

After a moment's silence, Ian cleared his throat. "Would you prefer that I leave, Father?"

"I would prefer that you stay." Jamie rose, holding up his hand lest they consider pushing back their chairs as well. "Lads, I understand your frustration—"

"Nae, you do *not*!" Even while seated, Will stood up to him. "Sandy and I are being thrust out the door without any say in the matter."

"'Tis a fact, Father." Sandy, though less vocal, was no less antagonistic. "We chose neither the time nor the place—"

"They were not yours to choose." Jamie fought to keep his voice low, glancing toward the kitchen door. He would not fill his servants' ears with family gossip. "Since Walter McFadgen assured me you were ready, it seemed imprudent to delay your studies. No finer university exists in Scotland." He softened his tone by intent. "Even you must admit that."

"But to have no choice," Will protested. "You cannot imagine what it is like to be evicted from your own home."

I ken very well. Jamie looked down, lest his sons see the truth in his eyes. " 'Tis an accident of birth when an heir is born. Ian did not elect to be first, any more than you and Sandy chose to be second and third." He lifted his head, meeting their misery head-on. "I did what I believed to be best for everyone. As laird of Glentrool, I have the right to make decisions for my children, such as where the two of you will be educated and whom Davina will marry."

"Davina?" Will's eyes narrowed. "Have you plans for our sister as well?"

"Nae, not at present." He'd seen the look on Davina's face when Leana had ushered her from the room. " 'Tis my younger sons who concern me just now. I've arranged lodging in Edinburgh with Professor Russell and will escort you there personally. We leave at noon on Thursday."

"Hech!" Will stood, throwing his napkin on the table. "A blithe journey we'll have, the three of us."

"And a fine May Day in the meantime," Sandy fumed.

When the two stamped out of the room, Jamie did not demand an apology or insist they remain until dismissed. He'd challenged them enough. Later, when their tempers had cooled, he would mend whatever fences he could.

Still seated, Ian looked at him with a steady gaze, free of reproach. "I am sorry, Father. My brothers have not made this easy for you."

"Nor should they." Jamie began to pace in front of the hearth. "Ian, you cannot imagine how difficult life is for a second son. I asked you to stay so you might see for yourself what a vexing predicament your brothers face. Someday, Lord willing, you will have sons of your own." He stopped pacing long enough to catch Ian's eye. "And when the time comes, you will remember this hour."

"I'll not likely forget it, sir." Ian stood and offered a slight bow. "If I may…"

"By all means." Jamie bowed as well, sending the lad to his duties. Ian spent each morning at his desk, examining his ledgers and learning the intricacies of estate management. The Almighty had selected a fine heir in Ian McKie. "Aye, and left the others for me to manage," Jamie grumbled aloud. He had not handled things well. Though his gentle wife would never tell him so, he knew it to be true.

He quit the dining room, bound for the library. If Ian could bury himself in columns of numbers, he would do the same. Anything to clear his mind of a heartbroken daughter and angry sons. The muffled sounds of servants at work echoed through the cavernous house as he stepped into the entrance hall.

Leana's voice floated down the stair. "Aye, you look lovely, Davina. I'll watch for you and your fiddle in the garden at noon."

This was one fence he intended to repair immediately. Jamie waited as his wife descended the stair, his uplifted gaze searching hers.

"Where are the twins?" she asked softly.

He inclined his head toward the front door. "Off on their morning ride, I imagine. Pounding their anger into the bridle path round the loch." When she reached the last step, Jamie pulled her aside. "And what of your mood, Mrs. McKie?" He glowered at her in jest. "Are ye *fash wi'* me for sendin' yer *green* sons off tae Embrough?" His quaint use of Scots was meant to appease her. Few among the gentry still spoke the language, so thoroughly had King George's English plowed its way north.

"I am not unhappy with you, Jamie," she confessed, "though you might have been more genial toward the twins."

"Forgive me, my love." Jamie lightly kissed her cheek. "However poorly executed, my intentions were sound. I grew up as a second son in this house. I'll not see Will and Sandy coddled—"

"As your mother coddled you?" Leana did not say it unkindly.

"Just so," he agreed. "Her indulgence earned me a blessing from my father but a curse from my brother, and well deserved. 'Tis only by God's grace that Evan does not hate me still." Jamie sighed heavily. "I'll not send my sons into the world as I was sent: a *heidie* young man, ill prepared and irresponsible."

Leana laced her fingers through his. "As it happens, I fell in love with that young man and gladly gave him three sons and a fine daughter."

"They're fortunate indeed to have you for their mother." Jamie lifted her hand and kissed the back of it, her skin soft against his mouth and fragrant with soap. "I know this is distressing for you, Leana. How could it not be?" He glanced toward the second floor. "And hard for Davina as well. Is she prepared to live without the twins' company? For they'll not return soon."

"Will they not come home at Lammas?" A faint tightness crept into her voice.

"For a fortnight in early August, but no longer. Once they're settled in Edinburgh, visits to Glentrool will be rare. And when Ian marries—"

"Marries?" She did not hide her surprise. "Have you some lass in mind?"

"Nae, but Ian might." Jamie glanced toward the closed library door, ten steps away. "The last few Sabbaths he's tarried in the kirkyard with Margaret McMillan."

He'd noticed the two quietly conversing between services, Ian's dark head bent over Margaret's fair one. The McMillans of Glenhead were the McKies' nearest neighbors, and John McMillan one of his oldest friends. Though not people of great fortune, the family had earned the respect of the parish for their honest speech and good hearts. "A man's greatest wealth is contentment with little," Jamie often said of his friend.

"Will you approve the match?" Leana asked.

Jamie studied the library door, thinking of the young man within. "Our households share the same history, the same faith. And Margaret has a lively manner."

Leana smiled a little. "I remember her splashing in Buchan Burn last summer, her skirts kilted well above her ankles. Miss McMillan might be a good foil for your serious-minded heir."

He nodded, convincing himself. "Margaret has a keen mind, which bodes well for their future together. However comely a woman, 'tis her intellect that pleases a husband most."

"Truly?" Leana smoothed a loose strand of his hair into place, trailing her fingers across his brow. "My mind gives you pleasure, then?"

Jamie turned and drew her closer. "Aye, it does, dear wife."

Four

Music exalts each joy, allays each grief,
Expels diseases, softens every pain.

JOHN ARMSTRONG

Davina rested her cheek on the library door, listening for some movement within. Most of the household had already convened out of doors to welcome their guests. Her father and Ian were among them, it seemed; not a sound came from the library.

She pushed open the door and hastened across the spacious room, the sound of her footsteps lost in the thick carpet. Grandfather Alec had spent his last years in this room, sleeping in the ornate half-tester bed, bathing at the mahogany washstand, warming his fragile limbs at the hearth, listening as his grandson Ian read to him. Awash with tender memories, Davina stood before the bookshelves, her gaze trained on her grandfather's fiddle.

Might the familiar scent of the wood ease her distress or the taut strings hold her broken heart together? She'd assumed—naively, perhaps—that Will and Sandy would remain at Glentrool until they married many years hence. Instead they were departing for Edinburgh on Thursday, leaving her to fill the ensuing silence with her one true friend.

Davina carefully removed the worn fiddle from its hallowed perch between two bookcases, remembering the first time she'd held it. How enormous the instrument had seemed to her then. Now the curved wooden body fit snugly beneath her chin, and her left hand circled the ebony fingerboard with ease. She plucked each string, wincing until she'd adjusted the tuning pegs just so.

Alec McKie had bestowed the prized instrument on her, his only granddaughter, when she was seven—not long after her accident, not long before his death. "Take it, my wee *posy,*" he'd said, clutching the fiddle with gnarled hands as he'd held it out to her. "'Twill be your voice."

He'd spent his last days teaching her all he knew of gapped scales and bowing techniques, playing every fiddle tune in his repertoire—airs and pastorals, reels and *rants,* jigs and hornpipes, and his cherished strathspeys—until his willing young pupil had committed the many tunes to memory.

No one had mourned the death of Alec McKie more than Davina. Determined to honor his memory, she quit the room, headed for the garden. *Heartsome* voices beckoned from out of doors, lifting her spirits. She could neither speak nor sing, but she could make music. Aye, she could. And bless the One who gave her the gift: not her grandfather but her heavenly Father.

I love the LORD, *because he hath heard my voice.*

Familiar faces awaited her as Davina sallied forth, her fiddle held high like a standard. Hannah McCandlish, the weaver's daughter from Blackcraig, was the first to greet her, waving a branch covered with snow-white petals. "God *bliss* ye, Miss McKie! *Firsten* the *flooers,* then yer fine fiddle."

Davina dipped a curtsy, then stepped aside to watch their neighbors bring in the May. Young mothers with wriggling bairns, older children dressed in their Sabbath clothes, and lads and lasses of courting age—all came bearing fresh hawthorn. Robert Muir, gardener to the estate for many a season, grinned broadly as he collected their offerings, winking at each unmarried girl as if he were a lad of twenty. With her mother's guidance, Robert fastened the branches round the doorposts, assuring good fortune to the household. Though the petals would flutter to the ground long before the dancing ended, at the moment the massed tiny white flowers were newly blossomed, still wet with dew.

Waiting her turn, Davina breathed in the heady fragrance: strong, evocative, unmistakable. Some folk compared blooming hawthorn to the scent of a woman; others insisted the flowers smelled like death. "Decaying meat," Will once said, wrinkling his nose. "May's perfume," their mother had countered, and Davina agreed.

A sharp yank on her braid brought her whirling round.

"Beggin' yer pardon." Johnnie McWhae fell back a step and hung his copper-colored head. "I…I *howped* ye might…cry *oot*." The shoemaker's apprentice from Drannandow could not hide his embarrassment any better than he could hide the leather dye etching the creases of his hands. "I meant nae harm, Miss McKie."

Davina brushed her fiddle bow through the air, waving away his harmless trick. Johnnie was not the first lad in Galloway to attempt some canny ruse to make her speak. 'Twas fortunate that none of her brothers had seen Johnnie's foolish prank, or the lad might never have cobbled another shoe. Ian was merciful, but Will and Sandy preferred judgment, swift and terrible.

When a weaver's son from Creebridge had bedeviled her at market one Saturday morning, making choking noises and pointing at his throat, the twins had tied him up with his own yarn and left him badly bruised and shaking. They were no kinder to the blacksmith's son, who'd called Davina names—*stupit* and *dummie*—and so was treated to a severe beating with heated tongs from his own forge. Davina understood her brothers' need to protect her, to defend her, but she did not care for their methods. Most in the parish knew the twins' *wranglesome* reputation and therefore did nothing to merit the attention of their fists.

"Music! Music!" the crowd began to chant, clapping their hands as they ambled along the flagstone path toward the center of Glentrool's garden. A rowan tree covered with vivid green leaflets would serve as their Maypole—one not carved by man but grown by the Almighty. Planted years ago, the tree for which Grandmother Rowena was named had withstood many a wintry blast to bloom again each spring.

With Robert's assistance, Davina mounted a broad stone bench that served as her stage. She tested the fiddle with a light touch to the strings, then struck a more confident note, choosing a spirited reel meant to amuse Will and Sandy: "The Fairy Dance."

From her vantage point, she quickly picked out her three brothers, each with a *sonsie* lass in tow. However trying their breakfast hour, the twins appeared to have rallied. Agnes Paterson, with her softly curved figure, well suited Will, while raven-haired Bell Thomson stood eye to eye with Sandy. Ian, taller than his brothers by a handbreadth, had claimed Margaret McMillan, whose small face turned toward his like a daisy seeking the sun.

Davina blinked away tears. What a strange brew of emotions stirred inside her, seeing her brothers so paired. Was it simply because they each had a partner for the day and she did not? Or was it the sad realization that she would lose her place in their hearts whenever they married?

Och! Unhappy with herself, Davina repeated the opening measures of the reel with more fervor. She seldom gave in to self-pity and would not do so now. Let the lads choose whomever they pleased. With fiddle in hand and flowers in her hair, she alone was the May Queen. All would dance to her tune this day.

Hands clasped, folk circled the rowan three times *deasil,* or clockwise, rather than *widdershins,* the direction favored by witches. Dappled sunlight decorated their smiling faces as the sprightly tune carried them along. Callused, bare feet dinted the grass beside well-heeled leather boots. Woodcutter and landowner, dairymaid and gentlewoman—all moved as one, led by the laird of Glentrool and his fair-haired Leana.

Without missing a note, Davina launched into a second reel, livelier than the last, then a third, amazed at how easily the music poured forth. Was it the freshness of the air? the joyful occasion? seeing the twins in a better humor? Whatever the reason, her fingers were more nimble than usual. If only someone in the glen played the violoncello. She imagined hearing the accompanying bass notes of the larger instrument and tapped her foot to the duet that sang inside her, reel after whirling reel.

When the breathless revelers begged for mercy, she eased into "Miss Wharton Duff," a marching air with a pleasing lilt. She noticed her parents bowing out of the dance, bound in opposite directions—the hostess toward her kitchen, the laird toward his stables—both attending to the needs of their guests, who'd not depart for their homes until the four hours, when tea was served.

Taking advantage of the slower rhythm, the dancers formed two circles, one inside the other, and began weaving in and out, moving in opposite directions. Davina pretended not to see the couples who exchanged fleeting kisses whenever they met in passing. Tradition, to be sure, but had her father been present, he would not have approved— not for his unmarried sons and especially not for his only daughter, who had yet to be kissed.

The thought warmed her face. To have lived seventeen years and not felt the touch of a young man's lips on hers! She turned aside, concealing her pink cheeks behind her fiddle lest anyone spy her discomfort and question its source. While the gentlemen of the parish always treated her with the utmost kindness and respect, no one had sought her father's permission to court her, and for that, Davina felt nothing but relief. She'd been introduced to many a lad at kirk, yet none had made her breath catch or her heart dance. Not Andrew Galbraith, with his sandy hair and sizable inheritance, nor the handsome widower, Graham Webster, nor dark-eyed Peter Carmont in his lieutenant's uniform, nor any other gentleman of her acquaintance. Though perhaps tonight…

"*Hoot,* lass!"

Startled, she looked down to find young Jock Robertson, a laborer from Brigton farm, lurching toward her. She smelled the whisky on his breath and heard it in the slur of his words. The flask bulging from his pocket explained his condition; Mother seldom served anything stronger than ale. Pointing her gaze elsewhere, Davina started another tune.

But Jock would not be ignored. "Will ye nae speak tae me?" He planted one foot on her bench, listing to the side as he did. "*Losh,* but ye're a bonny wee thing!"

Flustered, she took a small step backward and nearly tumbled into her mother's rosebushes. Her music came to an abrupt halt, attracting the attention of the dancers, who craned their necks to see whatever was the matter.

She heard Will and Sandy before she saw them.

"Davina!"

The twins parted the crowd like a sharpened dirk separating bone from flesh. When the bleary-eyed lad at her feet tried to right himself by grabbing a fistful of her gown, her brothers came at him running.

"You're a dead man, Robertson." Will snatched the young man's broadcloth shirt by the neck and yanked hard, nearly choking him in the process, forcing Jock to release his grip on her clothing.

Davina recovered her balance, then watched in dismay as Sandy caught Jock behind the knees with his boot heel, pitching him forward with a sickening thud. Though the farm laborer was taller and broader than her brothers, he was no match for them both. They pummeled him with fists and lashed him with words until the ruddy-faced lad collapsed on the ground in an untidy heap.

Whispered comments traveled round the garden as Davina pressed her fiddle to her heart, waiting for its fierce beating to ease. Whatever were her brothers thinking, treating the man so roughly when he'd done little to deserve it? If her father had witnessed the ugly scene, he'd have purchased the twins' army commissions at once and sent them off to fight Napoleon instead of thrashing a poor, inebriated neighbor.

Oblivious to her distress, Will brushed the dirt from his sleeves, then stepped over Jock's body as one might a discarded roll of carpet. "Did he hurt you, Davina?" Will grasped her elbow and helped her step down, even as Sandy dragged the laborer to his feet and shoved him in the direction of the *byre*. "Worthless drunkard should know his place," Will grumbled, "and 'tis not next to my sister."

Davina acknowledged his words with a nod but did not look at him, ashamed of his behavior. When her brothers left for Edinburgh, she would miss them desperately. But she would not miss their cruelty or their love of vengeance. Sometimes it seemed her charming brothers had been stolen by fairies and changelings put in their place.

She consoled herself with one observation: Jock was not limping. Perhaps the contents of his flask had dulled his senses and spared him the worst of her brothers' blows. At least among the cows he could sleep off his whisky in peace.

With the brief spectacle ended, the company turned their attention to a row of tables draped in linens and covered with serving dishes. Davina presented her fiddle to a trusted servant, then surveyed the May Day feast. Her brothers stood beside her, piling their plates with smoked beef and pickled mutton, congratulating each other for their heroics.

A woman's voice carried through the air. "Are you quite all right, Davina?" Her mother hurried across the flagstones, a look of alarm on her pale features. "Jenny said there was a row with one of the neighbors..."

Will turned toward her, quick to vindicate their actions. "You did not see the look on Robertson's face, Mother." The set of her brother's jaw, the defensiveness in his voice said more than his words.

Violence, however, did not suit their mother's peaceful nature. "One should match the punishment to the crime, William. Though I do not approve of drunkenness, I was told Jock merely addressed your sister in too familiar a manner. And manhandled her gown quite by mistake." The mistress of Glentrool cast her gaze toward Agnes and Bell, who tarried near a plate of oatcakes, waiting for their dance partners to return. "I've noted the fond looks you've given Miss Paterson today and the many times you've touched her sleeve. Would her brother Ranald be justified in throwing you to the ground and beating you senseless?"

A dark stain colored Will's cheek. "Nae. Though *I* am a gentleman—"

"And Jock Robertson labors with his hands." Her soft voice did not diminish the power of her words. "He is a child of God, just as you are, William. And a guest of Glentrool as well." She rested a hand on each of them, her blue gray eyes shining with maternal affection. When Leana McKie disciplined her children, the strength of her love was even more apparent. "Later today," she told them, "when our neighbor has recovered, you will escort him home. On one of your own mounts."

Five

Hail, bounteous May, that doth inspire
Mirth, and youth, and warm desire.
JOHN MILTON

Davina lowered her gaze as Will and Sandy nodded in resignation rather than argue with their mother. Who could not respect so virtuous a woman? After a mumbled apology, her brothers joined Agnes and Bell, who surely would affirm the lads' brave efforts and thus affix a healing poultice to their wounded pride.

Her mother, meanwhile, was straightening the ribbons that Jock had unintentionally pulled askew. "Do forgive your brothers. They're young and brash and full of energy, with few opportunities to expend it. Like fine horses kept too long in the stables." She fell silent for a moment, smoothing Davina's hair. "Edinburgh will be good for the twins, though I know it will be difficult for you. At least your older brother won't be leaving." Her mother looked at Ian, standing not far from them, two dinner plates in hand, his attention fully engaged by Miss McMillan.

Nae, Ian would not depart from Glentrool. But it seemed someone else might be joining their family, perhaps by summer's end. Davina studied the couple, weighing the notion. Another woman in the house. A sister, by marriage.

Her mother's soft laugh brought her round. "I know what you're thinking. And I believe Margaret will fit in nicely." She presented Davina with a plate of her favorite foods, hard cheese and almond cakes among them. "I'll come check on you in a bit, aye?" She touched Davina's cheek, then made her way to the house.

Davina dutifully ate a few bites of mutton and a slice of cheese, intent on enjoying the beauty of the day and the companionship of her neighbors. The sky was sapphire blue, the clouds high and sparse, and a soft breeze fluttered the rowan leaves. Seated on the stone bench, she drank in the warm sun like a refreshing cup of tea, all the while looking about the garden for a friendly face.

Barbara Heron hurried to her side as if she'd been called by name. The miller's daughter, twenty-odd years of age and still unmarried, bore a cheerful enough countenance. Her ruffled gown of white sprigged muslin was two seasons old but no worse for the wearing. "How wonderfully you played today!" she began, perching next to her on the bench. Barbara did not pause as some did, waiting for Davina to respond, then remembering she could not. Instead Barbara related the day's news in a lively monologue, barely catching her breath between subjects. Imminent betrothals, new arrivals to the parish, proposed summer journeys—all were divulged in enthusiastic detail.

Davina almost didn't hear Janet Buchanan join them, so quietly did she light on the bench, like a wee meadow pipit. A sweet-natured lass from nearby Palgowan farm, Janet preferred to listen and did so with wide-eyed attentiveness, covering her mouth with her fingertips at each astonishing revelation. Several more young women were drawn into their circle before Barbara's store of gossip ran out.

"My, but 'tis warm." Barbara stood and curtsied, her performance at an end. "Will you entertain us again, Davina? I've yet to dance a strathspey with Peter Carmont." She looked round, then lowered her voice. "They say he's to sail for Portugal before Lammas." Even more quietly. "His regiment awaits orders." A mere whisper. "From Sir Wellesley." On that dramatic note Barbara quit their company and aimed herself like an arrow toward the unsuspecting lieutenant, who stood amid a knot of men on the far side of the garden.

When Davina rose, Janet did as well, lightly clasping her hand. "Might you play a slow air? For me?"

Davina squeezed her gloved fingers in response. She knew just the melody to please her soft-spoken friend. She waved to the manservant who'd kept her fiddle safely by his side for the dinner hour, then mounted the bench with his help, lifted her bow, and struck a vibrant chord. A chorus of gleeful shouts rang out. Enough of feasting; the assembled were eager to dance.

The ritual of May Day with its single circle was put aside for sets, with dancers choosing partners and forming lines. As the sun arced over the glen, Davina served up one tune after another, from Janet's gentle air, "The Nameless Lassie," to her brothers' favorite hornpipes.

She could not help noticing the tentative pairings the day's festivities had produced. Lads and lasses who'd marked each other from the first now shared a cup of punch or lingered after a reel, hands still touching. Sandy in particular seemed bent on wooing Bell Thomson, though she was as tall as he and had a fine temper of her own. As expected, Ian and Margaret were inseparable. Had she ever seen her taciturn brother so animated? Barbara Heron did partner with Peter Carmont for a strathspey, though he soon put her aside for a willowy brunette from the village.

A few folk inquired of Davina, "Is there no May King?" She only smiled, thinking of her evening plans. The day would end as it had begun—with a solo venture out of doors. Not to bathe in the dew nor to banish her freckles but to test an old Beltane tradition "from auld lang syne," as her father would say.

At the four hours, cups of fresh tea were brought out on trays before their guests were sent home, weary yet well sated. Most departed on foot, some on horseback; the narrow, rutted road into the glen did not accommodate wheeled conveyances. Will and Sandy did their duty by Jock, saddling the best horse in Glentrool's stables.

When the last rays of sunlight painted the horizon the color of orange marmalade, and the first quarter moon neared its zenith, the twins finally returned from Brigton farm. Davina flew to the front window at the sound of her brothers pounding up the drive, relieved to see them. Aubert Billaud, Glentrool's temperamental cook, served supper precisely at eight. Jamie insisted they all be seated on time without exception.

After handing over the horses to a stable lad, her brothers disappeared up the stair, then arrived at table with damp hair and loosely folded cravats. If any ill feelings remained between father and sons, they did not surface during the meal. Aubert's main courses—boiled salmon with fennel, kidney collops, and roasted plover—kept everyone's forks busy and their attention occupied. Ian and Mother carried much of the conversation and avoided any mention of Edinburgh.

As always the evening ended with family worship. In many Scottish homes, the practice had faded away with the last century, but not at Glentrool. Davina folded her hands in her lap, waiting as her father opened the wooden box by the hearth, lifted out the *Buik,* and placed it on the table with due reverence. A tattered ribbon marked the psalms. He opened the thick volume, smoothing his hands across its worn pages.

"For the LORD God is a sun and shield."

Her father could spend an entire evening's worship on a single verse. Davina did not mind the long hour, but the twins shifted in their seats, elbowing each other to stay awake. As for Leana, her gaze remained fixed on her husband, her face shining like the moon.

"The LORD will give grace and glory." Spoken like a promise, which her mother affirmed by lifting her hand to her heart. Her father had much to say about glory and more still about grace. "Mercy is a gift. Yet we are encouraged to ask for it, as David did. 'Have mercy upon me, O God.'"

Davina's brow wrinkled, considering his words. Was it seemly to request a gift? King David, for whom she was named, repeatedly cried out for mercy. Did the Almighty not grow weary of extending grace to his people over and over?

Her father didn't seem to think so. As the hour drew to a close, he finished the evening's verse. "No good thing will he withhold from them that walk uprightly." Davina missed most of his comments that followed, her mind circling round the last two words: *walk uprightly.*

The phrase nagged at her as she followed her family up the stair, knowing she would steal back down when their bedroom doors were closed and the entrance hall stood empty. Though her plans were innocent enough, custom required that she go alone, then return in utter silence. She dared not risk her boisterous brothers trailing after her, or this night would be lost to her for another twelvemonth.

Sarah undressed her with practiced ease, then slipped a fresh muslin nightgown over her head and brushed her hair until it fell round her shoulders like a soft cloud. "Sleep well," Sarah murmured before quitting her bedroom, bound for the servants' quarters behind the house.

The mantel clock in the drawing room chimed half past eleven when Davina pulled on a pair of cotton stockings and wrapped herself in a thin plaid. She tiptoed down the long staircase, holding the plaid with one hand and clutching a knife in the other. Pilfered from Aubert's knife drawer while he was distracted with supper preparations, the small utensil provided all that custom dictated: an ebony handle and a sharp blade.

Opening and closing the broad oak door without making a noise required a steady hand and infinite patience. Once the door was securely shut, Davina grabbed the iron lantern from its perch by the door and started down the front path, holding out the lantern with its windows of thinly scraped horn, twin candles lighting the way. The waxing moon was of little help, low in the sky as it was. As for the night air, it was chillier than she had expected. She tightened her grip on the plaid and peered along the edges of the path. No need to strike out for the hills if she could find what she needed closer to home. Yarrow— *milfoil,* her mother called it—grew everywhere.

By Lammas, the plant would reach her knees. Now it was not so tall, nor had it flowered. Surely she would recognize the angular stems covered with feathery leaves. Didn't her mother collect yarrow each harvest to make tea? She remembered the bitter leaves being broader than her thumb…

There.

Davina leaned down, placed her lantern on the walk, then pinched the hairy plant with her fingers. A familiar scent wafted up to greet her. Refreshing, like feverfew. And strong.

She gripped the knife in her right hand and pulled the yarrow taut with her left. The single cut sounded unnaturally loud in the stillness of approaching midnight. In her heart she whispered the lines of an old verse:

> Good-morrow, good-morrow, fair yarrow,
> And thrice good-morrow to thee;
> Come, tell me before tomorrow,
> Who my true love shall be.

Davina pressed the yarrow to her breast and imagined waking in the morning with a vision of her future husband. Since she had yet to meet such a man in Galloway, perhaps she would encounter him in her dreams, the one place her brothers could not possibly intrude.

According to the custom, she tucked the aromatic herb inside her right stocking. The leaves felt scratchy against her skin. She reclaimed the lantern, then held it aloft as she hurried toward the door. *Walk uprightly.* The words of her father—the words of the Almighty— resounded inside her.

Had she broken some rule? committed some sin?

Davina shook her head, refusing to believe it. A harmless weed, a simple rhyme, a girlish hope. Nothing more.

She entered the house as silently as she'd departed. After replacing Aubert's knife in the kitchen drawer, she climbed the stair, listening intently. Ian was sound asleep; she heard his shallow, even breathing. The twins, who shared a room, snored in a tuneless duet.

When she ducked inside her turret bedchamber, Davina took her first deep breath in several minutes. A successful outing with no one the wiser. She removed her cotton stocking and its precious contents, then tucked the yarrow beneath her pillow. After such an eventful day, sleep would not be long in coming.

She pulled her bedcovers to her chin and was soon lost in slumber.

Not until she'd dreamed many dreams did she rise with the sun and reach for her sketchbook, eager to commit to paper what the yarrow had shown her in the night.

Six

Guilt's a terrible thing.

BEN JONSON

Will McKie stuffed the last of his cambric shirts into a leather valise. A half-dozen *sarks* would suffice for the summer. Wouldn't Edinburgh harbor a bonny laundress or two?

"Will?" Sandy's voice, sharp and insistent, came from the stair. He strode into their bedroom a moment later, his expression troubled. "Have you seen Davina?"

He abandoned his packing, senses on alert. When he'd noticed their sister's place cleared at breakfast, Will had assumed she'd awakened early and taken to the hills for an hour of sketching. "Who saw her last and when?"

"Mother. *Yestreen* at bedtime." Sandy glanced sideways at the door and lowered his voice. "You know very well that Davina has been out of sorts since May Day."

Will grimaced, reliving the scene with Jock Robertson from two days past. He'd noted the displeasure in their sister's eyes, the gentle reproof in her demeanor.

"Better to risk Davina being unhappy with us," he told his twin, "than allow a laborer to sport with her and ruin her good name." *And ours.* Their innocent sister knew nothing of men—how their minds worked, what they were capable of. Davina needed Sandy, needed him. Yet here they were, leaving for Edinburgh within the hour.

Sandy gestured toward the window and the heath beyond. "The weather is foul. Rab has the dogs out on the hill, searching for her. Father and Ian are tramping round the orchard on foot."

"We're away to the loch, then. On horseback."

Striding across the lawn, the twins came face to face with May at its murky worst. A heavy gray mist, thick as goose down, had settled into the nooks and crevices of the landscape. The loch, the pines, and most of the buildings that comprised the farm steading—henhouse, *doocot,* granary, barn, stables, cart shed, and byre—were lost in a moist shroud.

Sandy mounted his gelding, the stable lad having already saddled the horses for the day's journey. "How do you intend to find her in the fog?"

"Loosen the reins and let the horses lead us," Will advised, fitting his feet into the stirrups. "She'll not have gone far."

He guided them in the direction of Trool, a long, sinuous loch that threaded through the steep glen. In better weather Davina often perched on the stone pier at the end of the front walk, absorbed in her drawings. Though a small boat was stored beneath the pier, she seldom took out the flat-bottomed skiff by herself. Will dismounted long enough to look round the moorings, glad to spot the oft-used craft bobbing on the water. A stout rope anchored it.

Sandy exhaled, visibly relieved. "She's not on the loch, then."

The brothers continued east, traveling single file on a narrow bridle path along the bank. They took turns shouting her name, then listened for a response—movement in the brush, the clatter of a rock, anything. Davina could not answer them verbally, of course, but surely she'd come to them. If she could.

Will's heart began to pound as the horses veered slightly north, leading them into the dense stand of evergreens that guarded an immense mausoleum. Other families in Monnigaff interred their loved ones in the parish kirkyard, but not the McKies. As the sharp scent of pine filled his nostrils, a sharper sense of dread flooded his soul. The deceased were not all that inhabited this burial ground.

Sandy called ahead to him. "Do you mean to do this, Brother?"

His twin knew him well; this was the last place he wanted to be. Their horses came to an abrupt stop as the square memorial rose out of the mist. Two generations had already been laid to rest behind its ornately carved facade, their names chiseled in stone: *Archibald and Clara McKie. Alec and Rowena McKie.*

"Faithful unto death," Sandy read aloud. They both knew which two names would likely be added next. *James and Leana McKie.* "Lord willing, countless years will pass before the stonemason returns to Glentrool."

"Aye." A shudder ran through Will's body. They'd tarried long enough. He tugged the reins, urging his horse to move on. But it was too late.

"Please, Will! Don't..." Davina's voice. High and sweet.

"Stop it, Sandy! You'll hurt someone..." The voice of their sister. The voice of a child.

Will leaned forward, pressing a gloved fist to his mouth, fearing he might be sick.

Sandy was already by his side. "She's not here, Will. Take some air into your lungs. Aye, that's it."

His head began to clear, and the roiling in his stomach eased. The memory, however, was sharper than ever. He and Sandy, all of six years old, had been standing there—right there, beside the mausoleum—wrestling with Grandfather's broadsword, stolen from beneath his half-tester bed.

While their parents were preoccupied with a visitor, the lads had dragged the heavy scabbard a good distance from the house, intending to take turns dueling with an imaginary enemy. Instead they'd fought each other. Argued over who would wield the sword first. Threatened bodily harm.

Davina had come looking for them. Had cried out in alarm when she saw the weapon. *"Sandy, let go of it! Please, Will!"*

Each twin had wrapped one hand round the hilt, their outstretched arms holding it above their heads as they struggled, the deadly blade pointed toward the April sky. Davina had drawn nearer, pleading with them to end their fighting.

That was when Will had yanked the broadsword free from Sandy's grasp. Or his brother had let go. To this day, the truth remained a mystery. Will had stumbled backward, the weapon in his right hand sweeping through the air in a wide arc.

The momentum had been too great. And the sword too heavy.

The flat of the blade had struck Davina squarely in the throat, knocking her to the ground with lethal force. She could not breathe. She could not speak.

Sandy had fled for the house, screaming for their father…

"Is that you, lads?" Jamie's voice sliced through the mist as neatly as steel.

Will straightened in the saddle, dragged into the present by an unseen hand. "Sir?" There stood his father and Ian next to him, fully grown, as if a decade had passed in an instant. Will shook his head, hoping to dislodge the painful memory and erase the dreadful diagnosis. *Trauma to the larynx. Nerve damage. Impaired vocal cords.*

The last word his sister had spoken was his own name.

Ian looked round the clearing with a wrinkled brow. "Did you think you'd find Davina…here?"

Will heard the tinge of judgment in his older brother's words. Or did he imagine it, richly deserved as it was? "The horses brought us," Will explained, then realized how ridiculous that sounded. He shrugged. "We thought perhaps they'd heard something."

Sandy spared him further embarrassment. "What news from Rab?"

" 'Tis what we came to tell you." Jamie put his hand to Will's bridle, turning his mount toward home. "Rab found your sister at Jeanie Wilson's cottage. Unbeknownst to us, Davina went for an early morning walk to the linns on the Minnoch. When the weather turned foul, she sought shelter with the midwife."

Will was relieved to hear it, though the tightness in his chest did not ease. "I'm grateful Davina is safe," he muttered, wishing he'd been the one to find her.

Two on horseback, two on foot, the McKie men slowly made their way back to the house. The mist was thick as ever, swirling round them as they walked. Nothing more was said of Davina, which Will found irksome. Had Father not marked her absence at breakfast? Why had he not looked for her sooner? Instead the man spoke of Edinburgh, outlining their plans to depart at noon with enough clothing and provisions for a few days. The twins were to visit a tailor once they arrived; their books and other effects had been sent ahead by mail coach.

"Your trunks are traveling the main carriage roads," his father continued. "We, however, will ride due east. Across the moors to Moniaive and Thornhill, through the Lowther Hills on the old Roman road to Elvanfoot, and on through Biggar." He'd often journeyed to Edinburgh on estate business and knew the shortest route. " 'Twill test your mettle," he warned them. "We'll not cross many gravel roads between here and College Wynd, where your future awaits."

"And what of Davina?" Will said bluntly, having heard all this before. "What sort of future awaits her?"

His father stopped to look up at him, incredulity stamped on his features. "Are you suggesting I will not provide for my own daughter?"

"She'll be provided for, aye." Will was glad he was mounted, glad he held the superior position. "But our sister must also be protected. Looking after Davina is—"

"*My* concern," Jamie countered. "Not yours."

Father and son locked gazes, along with wills, in a brief skirmish.

At last Ian spoke, the peacemaker among them. "Davina is loved by all Glentrool, my brothers. I promise she'll be well cared for when you leave."

"Which will be soon." Their father consulted his pocket watch, then snapped it shut, the discussion ended. "Once you bid farewell to the household, we'll meet at the stables."

Jamie strode away, shoulders squared, head held high, brooking no doubt who was laird. When he turned on his heel and marched back to face them, his formidable strength on full display, Will felt a strong urge to dismount and did so. Seconds later, Sandy followed his lead.

Their father stood before them, bristling with intensity. "I want this understood: No one loves Davina more than I do. I have seen my daughter well educated and will see her well wed." A brief pause, a slight softening. "Your desire to protect her is understandable, Will. Even commendable. But I will not keep her fine mind and bright spirit under lock and key. Davina cannot speak, but she can think, and very well."

Will swallowed hard. "Father, I…"

"Listen to me." Jamie clapped a hand on his shoulder, his grip like a carpenter's bench screw. "Your sister will come to no harm. Not this season, nor any season. Will you not trust me?" Releasing his shoulder with a firm squeeze, he added, "You ken what the Buik says: 'My son, be wise, and make my heart glad.'"

Will recognized the proverb, even as another came to mind: *A foolish son is a grief to his father.* He'd provoked the man enough this day and so held his tongue.

Aye, Father. I will trust you, if I must.

Seven

But fate ordains that dearest friends must part.

EDWARD YOUNG

Davina pressed her sketchbook against her lap. In the past she'd never cared who saw her drawings and scribbled notes. Now she cared very much. Even her mother would not be shown the entry from yestermorn, when Davina had lifted her head from her yarrow-scented pillow and captured her dreams in charcoal.

Candles burned in every corner of the drawing room, and a peat fire glowed in the grate, chasing away the gloomy forenoon weather. All the household staff and most of the shepherds and farmworkers—*herds* and *hinds,* Rab Murray called them—had assembled to see the twins on their way. The house servants wearing neatly pressed uniforms, the herds in faded blue bonnets and collarless linen shirts, the hinds ignoring the stains on their breeches—all seemed quite happy to while away an hour usually spent working.

After such a morning, Davina was glad to be counted among them. How daft she'd felt when Rab had knocked on Jeanie's door. She'd meant only to go for a brief walk to prepare herself for the sad parting to follow. Instead the head shepherd was forced to search the glen as if she were a lost lamb.

"Miss McKie, yer *brithers* are *hame.*" Eliza Murray, Glentrool's amiable housekeeper, swept open the front door, motioning the men withindoors. Neither tall nor short, neither slender nor round, Eliza had hair the color of sand, notably different than her husband's bright red thatch.

"We've found the twins." Ian was the first to enter the room, his face wet from the mist. He planted a kiss on Davina's brow, then glanced over his shoulder. "You see, Will? Our sister is well protected here."

Davina stared up at him, confused. She'd not been gone so very long. And from whom did she need protection?

Then Will appeared at the door, guilt etched along every line of his handsome face. *Whatever has happened?* She hastened to his side, her sketchbook forgotten. Clasping his hands in hers, she shook them lightly, forcing him to meet her gaze. *Tell me, Will. Please.*

"Sandy and I were…worried about you," he finally confessed, trying to pull away. "We searched along the loch…in the pines…and in the clearing."

The mausoleum. Now she understood. None of them ever went there.

She touched her heart, then opened her hand—a gesture he well knew. *I forgave you, Will. The very day it happened.* Would he read the truth in her gaze and remember?

When Sandy appeared, she reached for his hand, tears stinging her eyes. He, too, had suffered from that day until this. Blaming himself for an accident that was no one's fault.

Now that the hour had come to see them off to Edinburgh, Davina was loath to let them go. True, the twins hounded her incessantly and never gave her a minute's peace. But did she not love them all the more for it? They were too belligerent by half, too quick to come to her defense. Yet weren't they the bonniest lads in all Galloway with their strong chins and broad frames?

My dear Sandy. My beloved Will.

She bowed her head, embarrassed by her tears.

"Och, Davina! You'll unman us yet." Sandy pulled her into his arms, holding her close as he whispered in her ear, "Forgive us for leaving, lass." He smelled of heather and mist and felt as solid as the granite slopes of Mulldonach.

When it was Will's turn, she dared not look at his face; if she spied even a glint of tears, she'd be inconsolable. Wrapped inside his fierce embrace, she felt the tension in his body and heard the strain in his voice. "Don't cry, my wee fairy." However would she carry on without him?

Will released her at last, cupping her cheek before turning to shake hands with the servants, who'd formed a ragged line round the room. She watched her brothers nod to each one, offering their thanks, receiving their blessings. The maidservants dabbed at their noses with their aprons, while the laborers shuffled their feet and tried to appear stoical. Jamie waited at the door, arm in arm with Leana, her face shining with maternal pride. Davina knew there were times when the twins had frustrated or baffled or infuriated their father; surely this was not one of them.

As if aware of her appraisal, her father crossed the room, not stopping until they were toe to toe. "I am sorry, Davina." His voice was low and softened with benevolence. "I ken the loss of your brothers' company will cost you dearly."

She looked away, unwilling to let him see how great a price it was.

"They will miss you as well."

When he fell silent, curiosity soon got the better of her. She turned to find her father deep in thought, a pensive look on his face.

"Suppose…" He paused, then began again. "Suppose I find some diversion for you this summer."

Diversion? Whatever might that mean? A houseguest for the season? A midsummer ball at Glentrool? Or perhaps a horse of her own since she and Sandy shared the chestnut gelding shortly bound for Edinburgh?

Davina lifted her brows, seeking an answer. *What do you mean, Father?*

He did not elaborate. "Let me give it some thought, Davina. Astride a horse for several days, I can do little else but ponder."

The mantel clock chimed noon, signaling the hour of departure. Her father moved to the center of the room, then held up his hands to command the group's attention. "My sons and I must take our leave. 'Tis a good distance to Moniaive." He gestured to the twins to join him, then curled his hands round the backs of their muscular necks, squeezing so hard they both winced.

By tacit agreement, Davina and Ian stepped beside their mother, who wept openly, touching her lace handkerchief to her cheeks again and again.

In every corner of the drawing room, coughs were muffled and gazes pointed downward, anticipating the laird's benediction. "Almighty

God," Jamie began, "grant us mercy on our journey. Guard our paths and guide our steps. Travel with us night and day, and keep watch over the cherished ones we leave behind. According to thy mercy and lovingkindness, bless thou my sons…"

When his voice faltered, Davina opened her eyes long enough to see him bite his lip, fighting for control. *Dear Father.* He was not a perfect man. But he was a good man.

"Bless thou William and Alexander. Let them not depart from thine eyes. Keep them in the midst of thine heart. Lead them in the way everlasting."

Davina marked the unexpected tenderness in her father's words and sensed his conviction. Might he speak a blessing over her someday? Or were such words reserved for sons?

At last he finished. All present lifted their heads, many with a sheen in their eyes. Jamie led Leana toward the entrance hall, their heads touching, their exchange private. Will and Sandy followed a few steps behind, while Ian waited for Davina, a look of compassion on his face.

"Come, my sister." Rather than offering her the crook of his elbow, as any gentleman might, Ian slipped his arm round her shoulders and drew her to his side. A bird nestled beneath its mother's wing could not have felt more sheltered. "Let me watch over you, Davina, as my brothers did."

Eight

Hopes, what are they?—Beads of morning
Strung on slender blades of grass.
WILLIAM WORDSWORTH

Ian was as good as his word, serving as her watchman, like a *garitour* of old, whenever Davina left the safe confines of Glentrool.

On Friday he rowed her across Loch Trool for a proper view of Buchan Burn. The fast-moving waters cascaded down the rocky hillside from pool to pool, white and frothy one moment, blue as the May sky the next. Saturday afternoon he waited patiently while she sat among the pines round Glenhead and sketched a red squirrel perched on a tree stump, its busy tail twitching, its black eyes and tufted ears alert to the intruders' slightest movements.

Even this Sabbath morning, secure within the rubble walls of the parish kirk, Ian remained by her side. Many a sideways glance was cast in their direction, for the family pew was half-empty, the rough wooden surface bereft of its usual occupants. Her father had promised to return on Friday next, but Will and Sandy were gone until Lammas.

A full term. The whole of summer.

Davina's heart ached at the prospect. She missed her twin brothers at table, telling stories of their daily escapades. Missed them bounding over the hills with her, teaching her to climb as nimbly as they. Missed their hearty laughter, their bold speech, their palpable strength. Grateful as she was for Ian's quiet company, she knew his first responsibility was learning to manage Glentrool, not keeping up with his sister's whereabouts. An heir never knew when the mantle of leadership might fall on his shoulders. Ian needed to make the most of the long days—eighteen hours of daylight by midsummer.

A measured portion of that light penetrated the plain, rectangular interior of the kirk. Gray, unmortared walls rose from flagstone floors.

Dust motes hung in the air, as if suspended in place for generations, and the pews cried out for a fresh coat of green paint. At least the glazed windows invited the morning sun to stir the worshipers awake, though old Mr. Carmont, Peter's father, would not last long; his head already drooped over his chest.

The precentor's gathering psalm drew all eyes to the front of the kirk. While the Galbraiths found their pew and the McMillans made their way down the center aisle, black-haired Mr. McHarg began lining out the psalm, pausing for the congregation to echo each line back in unison. "O give thanks unto the LORD, for he is good."

On the other side of the narrow preaching house, Margaret McMillan took her seat with her parents. When she coyly glanced over at Ian, the corners of his mouth lifted ever so slightly. Ian would speak to her in the kirkyard between services, Davina imagined. She eyed the sketchbook at her feet. Had Margaret drawn a rendering of Ian as well or traced a silhouette of his handsome profile?

Mr. McHarg sang louder still, as if aware of Davina's wandering thoughts. She dutifully mouthed, "Let the redeemed of the LORD say so." The gathering psalm continued through forty more verses, enlivened by her mother's dulcet voice and Ian's baritone. As a young child Davina had recited portions of the Shorter Catechism and dozens of psalms by memory; even now, the words remained hidden in her heart. "Whoso is wise, and will observe these things, even they shall understand the lovingkindness of the LORD."

The last note faded into the morning air as Reverend Moodie, slight of build with thinning hair, stepped behind his pulpit. As usual he began by offering a nod of respect to the heritors present. His eyebrows arched when he turned to the McKie pew and realized the laird of Glentrool was not among them. More than one gentleman in the parish now rejected Sabbath rituals as out of fashion. Between services her mother would hasten to assure the minister that Jamie McKie was not of their ilk.

Two hours later the reverend's flock sat about the uneven kirkyard, enjoying cold victuals brought from home. The midday weather was pleasant yet chilly. More like April than May. The sky was a whitewashed blue and the ground damp beneath Davina's slippers. As she predicted, her mother sought the reverend's ear, while young Margaret McMillan plucked at Ian's sleeve, beckoning him to share her plate of sausages before the start of the afternoon service.

Her brother looked down at her with an earnest gaze. "Would you mind very much, Davina?" Ian was not one to shirk his duties, but Margaret's soft brown eyes had weakened his resolve. "We'll be seated beneath the yew…"

Davina waved the couple toward the centuries-old tree that towered over the kirkyard, content to have a moment to herself. Letting her feet direct her path, she meandered among the gravestones planted round the medieval kirk in haphazard rows, like an ancient stone garden. Absentmindedly reading the epitaphs, she noticed many a sad listing of children's names. If a child died in infancy, the next child was often given the same name. One family gravestone recorded three children named *John* and two named *Ann*; none had survived their first birthday.

"Miss McKie?"

She turned to find Graham Webster standing not far behind her. Dressed in somber colors with his black armband still in place, he tarried beside a newer gravestone. When he bowed to her, Davina curtsied in return and waited for the widower to speak.

"John McMillan tells me your twin brothers are away to Edinburgh." Compassion shone in his hazel eyes. "Glentrool must seem quiet indeed."

She nodded, thinking of his own home, Penningham Hall, with its many empty rooms. After ten childless years of marriage, his young wife, Susan, had died of consumption two summers ago.

"I know what it means to live in a house full of echoes." Mr. Webster stared at his late wife's grave. "Forgive me for not attending the May Day festivities at Glentrool. I am told your music was exceptional."

Though he did not look up, Davina offered a slight smile in thanks. She imagined he would not dance at Lammas Fair either or help build the bonfire on Hallowmas Eve or go first-footing on Hogmanay. His year of deep mourning had long since ended, yet folk in the parish said his heart was slow to heal.

Her artist's eye could not resist studying him for a moment. Prominent nose, like a Greek sculpture. Strong jaw and bearded chin. Thick auburn hair, fashionably cut. For a handsome man of barely thirty years, Graham Webster looked older. Careworn. Fine lines etched his brow and followed the contours of his features.

When he turned toward her once more, his eyes reflected both grief and longing. The first was almost too painful to bear; the second, rather unnerving. No gentleman had ever looked at her in such a way. Perhaps she was imagining things.

Nae. She was not.

Davina blushed and turned away, certain of his interest, yet not at all certain of her feelings. For years she'd thought of Graham Webster only as Susan's husband. And then as a widower in mourning. Never as a potential suitor. Would he continue their conversation? Should she open her sketchbook?

"I do hope you'll play your fiddle for me someday, Miss McKie."

The warmth in his voice only heated her cheeks further. Praying she did not offend the poor fellow, Davina offered him a parting curtsy and set out for Penkill Burn. The sound of rushing water, like music without notes, might be the very thing to calm her agitation.

She was poised above the steep banks, breathing in the freshly scented air, when the kirk bell rang in the belfry, recalling the parishioners of Monnigaff to worship. "At least the second service is shorter," Ian said, approaching her and offering his arm. "And don't I remember a basket of fresh treacle scones waiting in the carriage for our ride home?"

The thought of Aubert's rich scones carried her through the afternoon, putting to rest her concerns about Mr. Webster, who'd left for the day. On Sabbath mornings he worshiped in Monnigaff, his late wife's parish; for the afternoon service he visited his own parish, the Penningham church less than a mile south in Newton Stewart. She was sorry she'd deserted him so abruptly. He'd known her since she was a child. No doubt his gaze was one of neighborly affection, nothing more.

Later that afternoon, seated on her cushioned carriage seat, Davina discovered that Eliza had inadvertently packed enough scones for the whole family, even those not present.

"I'll eat Father's portion." Ian lifted the baked goods out of her hands before she could protest.

"You may also have mine," Mother said, raising her gloved hand to stifle a yawn. "For such a cool day, 'tis warm in the carriage." She soon drifted off to sleep, leaving the two of them to finish the scones and keep each other company until they reached the stables at House o' the Hill Inn, where the carriage would be stored and their horses saddled for the last three miles into the glen.

Ian, never far from a book, drew a slim volume from his pocket and held it close to the carriage window to read. "You'll not mind, Davina?"

He bested his younger brothers in this: Ian could be quiet for long stretches of time and require nothing of her. Communicating her thoughts by way of gestures often grew wearisome. With Ian, she could simply relax, knowing he was fully absorbed in his collection of essays.

From time to time he glanced through the glass, just as Davina did, and perhaps for the same reason: expecting to see the twins riding beside the coach on horseback, as was their custom. Her thoughts matched the rhythm of the horses' hooves. *Hurry home. Hurry home.* There was no cure for her rising melancholy except to open her sketchbook and day-dream about a certain gentleman.

Assuming an air of indifference so Ian would not ask to see what engaged her, Davina studied one drawing, then another, her charcoal pencil poised as if she might add to her artwork at any moment. Here were the linns on the Minnoch—badly rendered, she decided. Then the squirrel she'd drawn yestreen. When her gaze fell on the page she knew so well, she forgot to hide her smile.

How different this gentleman was from her dark-headed brothers and auburn-haired Mr. Webster and balding Reverend Moodie. In all her years she'd never seen such a man as this—not in any book or in any Lowland village. A golden prince with sunlit waves in his hair. Eyes as blue as the northern sky. Tall and strong as a mast on a ship. Bright and warm as summer itself.

Remembering how eagerly she had moved her pencil across the page, her heart quickened. Was it only four days ago? The charcoal was slightly smudged, yet Davina would recognize him when she saw him.

And see him she would.

Where or how, she did not know. But her dream had been too

Nine

It is a wise father that knows his own child.

WILLIAM SHAKESPEARE

You will see to Davina's welfare, Father? See that she's happy?" Jamie noted the sincerity in Will's voice, the genuine concern in his eyes, and forgave the irksome question, oft repeated during their journey east. "Depend upon it," he said, standing with care to avoid cracking his skull on the low beams of their lodging house. Professor Russell provided a good table and a sound mattress, but his bed-chambers were far from spacious, and mean in appearance. The carpet was worn thin, the small-paned windows admitted paltry light, and the porcelain washbowl was badly chipped.

Fortunately, young men paid scant attention to such things. The quadrangle and old library, the assembly rooms and public houses—those were the places where Will and Sandy would spend their time convening with fellow students. Hadn't he done the same?

Jamie leaned his forehead against the windowpane, staring down at the phaetons with their mud-splattered wheels and drenched bonnets. "I've stabled your mounts round the corner in Horse Wynd, though you'll find little use for them. Edinburgh is a town best seen on foot."

Sandy joined him at the window. "Even in the rain, sir?"

"Especially in the rain, when you're forced to seek shelter beneath the lowest of archways." Jamie scanned the familiar horizon. "Be advised, the skies are often bleak and the winds from the North Sea raw. When a cold sea fog rolls in from the east, the air is so thick you cannot see your horse's head, should you be unwise enough to mount the beast. Add the smoke from hundreds of chimneys, and you'll find they call the town 'Auld Reekie' for good reason."

He realized he was stalling, making idle conversation rather than saying what must be said and taking his leave. The ride to Edinburgh had been long and tedious; his sons had spoken with each other but not with him, except when necessary. Their resentment hung in the air, so thick it clung to his clothing, like dust kicked up from a hard gallop.

True, he had given them little notice of his plans to enroll them in university. But they had given him little choice. Ever since their tutor's departure, Will and Sandy had grown increasingly restless at Glentrool. "Children of wrath," one of the parish gossips called them. Pummeling neighbors with their fists, challenging his authority, chasing after the lasses rather than courting one woman properly as Ian did—ungentle-manly behavior all round.

Nae, he had not erred, not in this. Difficult as it was to entrust the twins to strangers, his sons' futures hinged upon their education.

When Will stepped to the window, flanking him on one side while Sandy remained on the other, Jamie slipped his arms round both their shoulders. " 'Tis time I started for home." He briefly pulled his sons closer—not a true embrace yet not lacking affection—then released them with a deepening sense of regret. Come Lammas, he would find Will and Sandy much altered. Not mere lads but men. Not sons of Glentrool but sons of Edinburgh.

"You've nae need to escort me down the stair," he told them, col-lecting his riding hat and gloves. "I ken my way to the front door."

The lads exchanged glances, then shook their dark heads in tandem.

"Nae, Father," Will insisted. "We are not so ill mannered as that. You've invested many guineas in our future. Our lodging, our school-ing, our allowance—"

"Aye, very generous," Sandy blurted out. "And we'll not soon forget this morning's visit to Mr. Chalmers, our new tailor."

Jamie held up a finger. "On Advocate's Close. You'll remember your way there?"

They assured him they'd find it with ease, to which Jamie merely nodded. In Scotland's capital, with its labyrinth of wynds and closes, locating a particular address was like searching for a shiny new coin in the town's filthy gutters—a vexing task with no assurance of success. Resting his hand on the doorknob, Jamie inquired, "And you ken the meaning of *gardyloo*?"

Will smiled, a rare sight of late. " 'Tis shouted from an upper story before a chamber pot is emptied into the street."

"Take cover," Jamie advised, "or your new clothes will be the worse for it."

The three of them descended the uncarpeted stair without speaking. For his part, Jamie had run out of words. Only trivialities remained, hardly worth the breath required to speak them.

Reaching the narrow entrance hall, where they were easily observed by the household, father and sons lingered in silence by the door. A sense of ending and of beginning flickered round them like candlelight.

"When your grandfather..." Jamie swallowed and began again. "When Alec McKie brought me to university in 1782, his parting words were, 'Virtue ne'er grows auld.' A wise saying, lads, which I trust you'll heed."

"We shall, sir." Spoken in unison, as if by prior agreement, with the dry-eyed confidence of youth. "Give our regards to Davina," Will added, "for I fear our sister will have a lonely summer without us."

"Aye, so she will." With some effort, Jamie held his voice steady. "Godspeed, lads."

The three bowed to one another like acquaintances passing in the street. Nothing else was required but to part.

When the door latched behind him, Jamie stared into the gray, misty rain, not quite seeing the brick facades across the narrow street, not truly hearing the shouts of pie sellers and fishwives, the whinnying of horses, the clamor of dozens of pedestrian conversations.

'Tis done.

He felt like a man adrift, without rudder or sail. Was he glad to see them gone from home, these headstrong sons whose carelessness had robbed their sister of her voice? Or did he mourn what might have been, the close relationship that his own pride and righteous anger had prevented?

Remember not the sins of my youth...

Alas, he remembered very well. Jamie hung his head, not caring if his hat should tumble into the mud.

according to thy mercy...

He stopped his thoughts, resisting the balance of the verse. How dared he ask Almighty God for mercy when he could not bring himself to forgive his own sons?

remember thou me…

Disconcerted, he lifted his chin and struck out for the High Street, ignoring the rain. Needing to walk, needing to think. He headed north across the Cowgate, his concentration so intent he nearly collided with a young couple huddled beneath a shared plaid.

Perhaps when the twins returned home at Lammas, the three of them could speak truthfully with one another. Address the past, however painful. Will and Sandy knew almost nothing of his own history. Might they benefit from knowing of his youthful failures, his struggles? After their summer at university—a humbling experience, to be sure— his sons might be better prepared to hear such things. And he might be better prepared to confess them.

Forgive, and ye shall be forgiven. In August, then.

His spirits somewhat restored, Jamie paid more attention to his surroundings. Not far ahead the medieval tower of Saint Giles thrust its crown spire into the wet skies, with the oft-rebuilt *mercat* cross just steps to the east. The slippery cobblestones beneath his feet slowed his progress as he turned onto the High Street, baffled by the changes that greeted him. Seventeenth-century masonry had given way to wooden faces. Refined properties that once belonged to gentry were now humbler abodes of tradesmen. The same town, yet not the same.

With a crack of lightning, the rain turned into a deluge, sending him running for the nearest merchant: a bookseller with "Manners and Miller" painted above the battered door. Four times as long as it was wide, the dimly lit shop was no less gloomy than the street. A single window provided the only natural light. Oil lamps were scattered throughout, candles posing too great a risk among papers and books. The smell of fresh ink and tanned leather permeated the air.

The proprietor, a stoop-shouldered man wearing spectacles, looked at him askance.

"Pardon me." Jamie stepped back from a display table with its neat stacks of books, newly printed and decidedly drier than he. "'Tis a *weatherful* day."

The older man slid a thick volume in place. "Aye." He shelved another book without further comment, though he cast a disparaging glance at Jamie's dripping attire.

Jamie touched the bag of coins hidden inside his waistcoat. Perhaps he could make a small purchase in appreciation for the dry roof over his head. "Do I have the pleasure of speaking with Mr. Manners or Mr. Miller?"

The bookseller answered to neither.

He tried a different approach. "Suppose I wanted to select a book for my wife. Something new…" Jamie looked about, at a loss as to where to begin. "A single volume might be best."

Without a moment's hesitation the man plucked a book from the nearest stack and held it out. "*The Cottagers o' Glenburnie* it is. *Verra* popular. The *scriever's* a woman." Whether his comment about the author was a recommendation or a caution was unclear. "Elizabeth Hamilton o' George Street," he said.

Jamie opened to the title page, then smiled when he read aloud, "'A Tale for the Farmer's Ingle-nook.' This will suit my wife very well."

When the bookseller grunted a price, Jamie reached for his silver. As he counted out the necessary shillings, his gaze alighted on another stack. "Is that also a novel?"

The man wagged his head, knocking his spectacles askew. "'Tis a *buik aboot* the Isle o' Arran. Aboot farmin' and fishin' and *sic* as that. The scriever's a minister."

Jamie was already flipping through the book. "Is he? I ken a minister on Arran. A relative of mine, Reverend Benjamin Stewart." If he was the author, how did the man find time to write a book on agriculture and antiquities when he had two daughters to raise and a parish to oversee? When Jamie turned to the title page, he found his answer. "Och, 'tis not my cousin but a Reverend James Headrick." He closed the book, his curiosity satisfied and his memory stirred. As a lad he'd visited the Isle of Arran, a short sail from the west coast of

Ayrshire. "Fine hill climbing in the summer," he murmured. "Goatfell in particular."

The bookseller shrugged before returning to his labors. "I dinna ken, sir, for I've *niver* been tae Arran."

Jamie thanked the man, then tucked Leana's book inside his coat pocket and reluctantly stepped into the street, only to discover the rain reduced to a fine drizzle. Low thunder still rumbled in the distance, yet a promising touch of blue appeared in the distant sky. Daylight, such as it was, would not fade until long past eight o'clock. By the gloaming he would reach his first night's lodging.

Retracing his route along the Fishmarket, he instinctively watched for Will and Sandy in the crowd. Were they still in their bedchambers getting settled or exploring the shadowy closes? Acquainting themselves with their landlord or determining the shortest route to a public house? Little time remained before their work at university began in earnest. The summer term commenced at daybreak.

When he caught a glimpse of the stables in Horse Wynd, Will's earlier request came to mind. *You will see to Davina's welfare?* Naturally, he would. *I fear our sister will have a lonely summer.* His daughter deserved every happiness he might provide. Jamie slowed his steps, again considering the possibilities. Could nothing be done to gladden the months ahead for her?

Of course. Jamie almost laughed aloud, so easily did the solution come to him. *Arran.*

Hadn't Reverend Stewart invited Davina to come visit his daughters whenever it suited? Now was the perfect time. What better place for a young woman to spend the long days of summer? With an island to explore and cousins to get to know, she'd not miss her brothers. And Leana would be delighted with the idea; Jamie was certain of it.

He strode toward the stables, full of purpose. A letter must be sent to Arran at once by way of a westbound mail coach through Glasgow— far more efficient than waiting to post a letter from Monnigaff. Should he inform Davina of the possibility when he arrived home? Or wait until an invitation came by return mail? That could take a fortnight or longer. The corners of his mouth twitched as he imagined Davina's expression. How his daughter would fuss at him for keeping secrets!

"Aren't ye the blithe one, sir?" The stable lad grinned at him from his perch at the arched entranceway. "I'll see tae yer mount. A black geldin', aye?" He disappeared for a bit, then returned with Jamie's horse, saddled for the journey. "D'ye *hae* a lang *raik,* sir?"

" 'Tis a few days' journey." Jamie took the reins in hand, eager to be on his way. "I've a letter to send first." He was already composing the lines in his mind as he mounted his horse, then fished out two coppers, the metallic sound muted by his gloves.

The lad accepted the coins with a bob of his scruffy cap. "Ye'll find the post office near the mercat cross, sir."

" 'Tis where I'm headed." Jamie aimed his gelding north, calling over his shoulder, "A fine summer to you, lad." *And to you, my darling daughter. And to you, my sons of Edinburgh.*

Ten

The silent countenance often speaks.

OVID

P romise not to tell your father, for the truth would surely wound him." Leana leaned across a freshly weeded corner of her garden and dropped her voice to a whisper. "But hasn't it been lovely having Glentrool all to ourselves?"

Davina nodded with enthusiasm.

"I'm so glad you agree." Leana laughed, then eased her hands back into the soil. She missed Jamie, of course, and longed for his return. But she'd enjoyed these quiet days with her daughter. Their summer together held great promise.

She worked the moist ground, tugging out weeds as she went. A broad-brimmed straw hat protected her sensitive eyes from the sun, and cotton gloves kept her hands pale and soft. Now and again she slipped off her gloves, indulging in the feel of the rich soil between her fingers. Jamie teased her about doing servants' work, yet few things pleased her more than her plants and flowers. Robert tended the large kitchen garden and many of the rose beds. The ornamental garden was her responsibility, as was the physic garden, which produced a host of medicinal herbs to keep her household in good health.

One rosy shrub was hers alone to care for: the Apothecary's Rose planted by the dining room window in memory of her sister, Rose. The deep pink blossoms did not appear until midsummer, releasing their sweet fragrance. From the moment the first bud bloomed each year, Leana kept a freshly cut rose in a small vase by her bedside until the last one faded to a purplish red. *Always remembered, dearie. Never forgotten.* With both their parents gone as well, her loved ones at Glentrool were all the more precious.

Leana tipped her head back, breathing in the rain-freshened air. " 'Tis good to see the sky so blue again." The afternoon sun warmed their shoulders, and a light breeze from the west stirred the air, fragrant with spring: a carpet of grass, newly scythed; fertile earth, turned with a garden fork; hawthorn, still in bloom. Though her daughter had pulled only a handful of weeds, her company was blessing enough.

"We truly do not have Glentrool to ourselves," Leana admitted, "since your brother Ian is here. Yet we've not seen much of him, have we?"

Davina pantomimed opening a book.

"You are quite right. Your brother is content to while away the hours reading."

Davina pointed east toward Glenhead, then touched her heart.

"Aye, and the charming Miss McMillan garners much of his time too." Leana relinquished her gardening for a moment, giving Davina her full attention, for her question was a vital one. "Will you mind very much when Ian marries? Nothing formal has been arranged, but a wedding seems inevitable, does it not?"

Again Davina nodded, with a bit less enthusiasm.

For a young woman unable to speak, her daughter said a great deal. Her facial expressions, her many gestures—all communicated her thoughts and feelings quite clearly. Even strangers soon grasped her unique language.

Leana noticed the sketchbook in Davina's apron pocket. "Why not try your hand at drawing one of my flowering herbs?" Her gaze roamed the physic garden, seeking a likely subject. " 'Til it blooms, bistort is too plain. The dandelions are quite colorful, if rather common. What of shepherd's-purse?"

Davina made a face.

"I agree, the flowers are too small to be of much artistic interest. And agrimony doesn't bloom until June. This is the month to harvest it, however." She snipped a few stems with her gardening scissors and tucked the herb in her roomy pocket. Scanning the rows of plants, some of them perennials she'd planted the autumn Davina was born, she found what she was looking for. "This one is not only bonny but also quite aromatic." Leana pinched off a hairy, egg-shaped leaf and rubbed the toothed edges between her fingers before holding it out for Davina to sniff.

Her deep blue eyes grew round.

"Strong, isn't it? One of the many speedwells." Leana brushed the bits of leaf from her fingers. "You may recall tasting it, boiled into a syrup and sweetened with honey." She plucked a flower to hold against Davina's cheek. "Just as I suspected, the petals are the exact color of your eyes. A deeper blue than mine and rimmed in a darker shade." She brushed her cheek with the soft petals. "No one else in the family has eyes like yours."

A tip of Davina's head signaled a question. She scribbled in the margin of her sketchbook, then held it out for Leana to read. *Aunt Rose?*

"Nae." Her throat tightened. "My sister had brown eyes. Quite dark, like her hair." Leana gently placed the flowers on Davina's open book. "She was very beautiful, your aunt Rose." *And so young. So very young.*

Davina did not press her further but instead began to draw.

Leana bowed her head as the sketch took shape. *May you never know such sorrow. May you never know such loss.* Wasn't that every mother's wish? To shelter her children from suffering and pain, to hold grief at bay for as long as possible? Yet here was Davina, separated from her twin brothers—both still alive but far from her side—with her older sibling destined to marry.

"I wonder when you will leave Glentrool," Leana murmured, "for the day will surely come. 'Twill not be your father who rides off with you but a handsome young man with love in his eyes and a melody in his heart."

Beneath her freckles, Davina's skin turned pink.

Leana peered at her more intently. Had some gentleman caught her daughter's eye? She'd noted Graham Webster's attentiveness on more than one Sabbath. Might the widower be to her daughter's liking? "You *are* seventeen," she reminded her, "and bonny as they come. Is there a man in the parish who hopes to court you?"

When Davina immediately shook her head, Leana wondered if she might simply be embarrassed and not know how to go about confessing such a thing. Intending only to draw her out, Leana reached for the sketchbook, which her daughter often shared with her. "Perhaps if I search these pages, I will find a gentleman's name—"

Davina snatched the book from her grasp.

"Oh! Pardon me, Davina. I only meant to help you."

She clasped the book to her breast, her face brighter still.

"Dearest, what is it?"

Davina was already on her feet and running toward the hills, the ribbons of her gown waving an unspoken good-bye.

Leana hastened after her, calling her name. "Davina, please! *Davina!*" Not until she ran out of breath did she realize someone was shouting her name as well.

She spun about at the sound of her husband's voice. Too winded to answer, Leana waved her handkerchief so he would realize she'd heard him, then started in his direction, unhappy with herself for agitating their daughter.

Jamie was running by the time he reached her. "Are you hurt, Leana? Whatever has happened?"

She sank into his arms, feeling a little faint. "Davina…ran off, and…"

"Shall I find her, then?"

"Nae, she's not gone far." Leana straightened, finally able to take a full breath. "I'm afraid I upset her." She turned to gaze across the hills and spotted her daughter amid the heather. "I pray she'll not be long."

"Having one of her moody spells, I'll wager. She'll come back when she's ready." Jamie tugged on Leana's sleeve, recapturing her attention and drawing her into his embrace. "As for me, Mrs. McKie, I am quite ready to be home."

Though his face was lined with dust from his travels, his smile was as potent as ever. When he kissed her, she blushed like a maid. "Jamie! 'Tis midday, and there are servants round the garden."

"*Our* servants," he reminded her. "In our garden. And you are my wife."

"I am and gladly so." Leana slipped her hand through the crook of his arm, grateful for his support. And for the Lord's provision. *He giveth power to the faint.* Leana drank in the remembered verse like cool water from the loch. *To them that have no might he increaseth strength.*

They continued toward the house, then stopped to greet Robert, hard at work among the coleworts.

"*Walcome* hame, sir." The lanky gardener straightened, then doffed his cap. "We've had rain *ilka* day syne ye left. Did ye have a *plumpshower* in Embrough as *weel?*"

"Several heavy rains, aye." Jamie nodded toward the tidy rows of plants. "I see your lettuces drank every drop."

"A *gairden* needs water," Robert agreed, wiping the sweat from his brow with his shirt sleeve. "What it doesna need are *mowdieworts,* which I'm plannin' tae catch come the *morn's morn.*"

Leana's gaze was drawn to a patch of bindweed that needed pulling, but Jamie tugged her away.

"I see that look in your eye," Jamie chided her. "No more gardening. We have important matters to discuss regarding our daughter."

"You're not worried because she's taken off for the hills? I feel certain she'll return—"

"Oh, within the hour," he quickly agreed, opening the door for her. "'Tis not Davina's present circumstances I wish to consider but her future."

Eleven

Imagination frames events unknown.

HANNAH MORE

H*er future?* Leana felt a strange fluttering inside her, like a small heath butterfly on the wing. Surely Jamie did not have plans for their daughter. Or was this why Davina blushed so, why she ran off, because something *was* afoot?

"As you wish," was all she said as she followed her husband inside, praying with each step.

He arranged two hard-backed chairs by the library's front windows, lit by the forenoon sun, then tugged on a slender rope that moments later brought a maidservant to their side. "Tea, Jenny. And have Charles meet me up the stair in an hour."

"Walcome hame, Mr. McKie." The maid dipped her curly head before hurrying to her duties.

Jamie rinsed his hands in the china washbowl next to the half-tester bed, then sat down by the window and crossed his booted legs, frowning at his dusty breeches. "Though I prefer that we speak before Davina returns, I beg your pardon for not seeing to my grooming first."

"We are both in need of soap and comb." Leana slipped off her apron, taking care not to crush the herbs in her pockets. She washed her hands, then took her place next to her husband. The tea could not arrive quickly enough, so parched was her tongue. "Please tell me, Jamie. Have you good news regarding Davina, or must I prepare myself for ill tidings?"

His mouth dropped open in astonishment. "Why, 'tis most welcome news!" He inched his chair closer and clasped both her hands in his. "Rather than have our daughter at loose ends all summer, missing her brothers' company, I thought of a place we might send her."

"*Send* her?" All thoughts of tea vanished. "Whatever are you suggesting?"

"The Isle of Arran." He punctuated the announcement by squeezing her hands, though she barely felt his touch. "I have a cousin there, you'll remember. On my mother's side, many times removed, but family nonetheless. Reverend Benjamin Stewart."

"Aye," she said faintly, "we've exchanged correspondence over the years."

"Exactly so." Jamie was warming up to his subject. "In those letters Benjamin and his wife, Elspeth, have repeatedly extended an invitation for Davina to come and meet their daughters, Catherine and Abigail. Would she not enjoy such an opportunity, this summer in particular?"

"She very well might." Leana sank back in her chair, overwhelmed. How could she lose her daughter for the summer, having just lost her sons to Edinburgh? Yet it was selfish to think of her own comfort when Davina might leap at the chance.

"What say you?" Jamie prompted her. "Though the road to Ayr is not coachworthy, Davina rides as well as her brothers. She is more than capable of a two-day journey on horseback."

Despite Jamie's assurances, an unnamed fear assailed Leana's heart, chilling her hands and tightening her throat. She jumped when a knock at the door announced tea, so distracted were her thoughts. Jenny carefully positioned the heavy tray, laden with Jamie's favorites: gingersnaps and buttermilk bread, caraway seedcake and currant loaf. As the maid filled their teacups, Leana bowed her head, ashamed of her lack of faith. Her daughter would not travel to Arran alone. Could her trust in God's provision not stretch beyond the boundaries of Glentrool?

Jenny politely curtsied and quit the room, leaving the McKies to their tea.

After lifting his cup, Jamie paused, waiting for his drink to cool. Or for his wife to respond. "You've not said aye or nae, Leana."

How could she explain what she herself did not understand? The queasiness in her stomach, the sense of foreboding. Nothing more than a mother's natural worrying, he would say, and rightly so. "That decision is yours, Jamie. And Davina's."

His teacup did not mask his frown. "You would permit your daughter to choose and yet have no choice of your own?"

Jamie, Jamie. Why did he make things so difficult? She looked down at her tightly clasped hands. "You know my heart. If 'twere possible, I would keep all my children beneath my roof 'til I breathed my last."

"But that is not possible, nor is it prudent. Bairns grow up and must make their own way in the world." He put down his cup, then laid his warm hands over hers. "I feel certain this is the right choice for our daughter. But I would never deliver her to Arran's shores without your approval."

She tried to smile, despite the dryness of her lips. "Very well, then. Allow me a few days to consider the idea before we mention it to Davina. Assuming she is amenable, I'll write to Elspeth Stewart and see what can be arranged."

The hands on hers stilled, then withdrew. "The letter has already been written, Leana. And posted."

Stunned, she could only manage one word. "When?"

His words poured out like tea from a full pot. "The notion struck me while I was still in Edinburgh. Will expressed concern about Davina having a lonely summer, and then I chanced upon a new volume on Arran at a bookseller's on the High Street." His hand went to his coat pocket as if he'd remembered something, though his words did not stop. "I naturally thought of the Stewarts at the manse on Arran and then of Davina visiting them. And since the post office was a short distance from the stables…"

He finally ran out of steam, exhaling the last of it. "In truth, it never occurred to me that you would be anything but overjoyed at the prospect."

Leana stared at him in disbelief. Overjoyed at sending her only daughter off to a distant isle? Surely Jamie knew her better than that. Yet there he sat, a look of repentance on his handsome face, waiting for her blessing on his plans.

Because she loved him, Leana longed to put him out of his misery. Yet she could not deny her disappointment, nor could she ignore the burden pressing on her heart. "Are you certain Davina will be safe?"

Repentance gave way to irritation, hardening his features. "Our daughter will be with me, Leana. And then with Reverend Stewart. Is that not assurance enough?" Jamie's tone made it clear: By not trusting him, she'd wounded him.

"Of course she will be safe with you and with our cousins. I only wish…" She hesitated, not wanting to hurt him again.

"You wish I had not proceeded without consulting you?"

"Aye," she admitted, embarrassed to hear it stated so bluntly. "We have usually discussed such things in the past."

"I am laird of Glentrool," he reminded her. "Whenever I can include you in decisions regarding our family, I certainly will. But time does not always permit me to seek your opinion."

And what of the Lord's opinion?

She dared not speak the words, though she feared what the answer might be. Since the hour of Davina's accident, she had watched her husband's dependence on God lessen in small yet measurable increments over the years. Such a shift did not diminish her love for Jamie; instead she cherished him more than ever, letting God's love pour through her. Praying it might heal her husband's grief, quench his anger. Aye, and assuage his guilt, for he blamed no one more than himself.

Leana pressed her back against the chair as if the wood itself might strengthen her resolve. "I trust you with our children's future, Jamie. Even as I trust you with mine."

She said the words and meant them. But there were other words that Jamie did not hear, whispered in her heart for another's benefit. *Cause me to know the way wherein I should walk; for I lift up my soul unto thee.*

Twelve

All but God is changing day by day.

CHARLES KINGSLEY

Leana felt the tension inside her ease, like a clock spring unwinding. Whatever the summer ahead might hold, she would not weather it alone.

"We've yet to discuss the twins," she said, keeping her voice even. "Are they well settled in Edinburgh?"

"They are, though I must confess, I do not covet their lodging." Jamie sounded less defensive now and more like her beloved husband. Between bites of currant loaf he described Professor Russell's residence in great detail. Then, using his hands, he mapped out Edinburgh for her. She remembered a few of the notable places—Saint Giles, the castle, Greyfriar's, Holyrood Palace, the *luckenbooths*—but had not visited the capital in a dozen years.

"I *do* picture it," she assured him when he stopped midsentence, his hands still busy lining out streets. "I only wish I might see Edinburgh in person again someday. But alas, I am too old to travel—"

"Too old?" Jamie thrust a teacup into her hands. "Drink this, madam, and let your strength be restored. No woman of forty years is too old to do anything."

She smiled and raised her cup. "To James McKie, who insists the women of his household be fearless."

"Indeed I do, and indeed they are." He lifted his cup as well and returned her toast. "Strength and honour are her clothing."

"And she shall rejoice in time to come." *May it be so, Lord.*

Jamie dug in his pocket and produced a clothbound book—new, by the look of it, and no larger than his hand. "A present for you, recommended by the bookseller in Edinburgh. *The Cottagers of Glenburnie.* Shall I read aloud while you enjoy your tea?"

He ate a prodigious number of gingersnaps—necessary sustenance before reading, she decided—drank a last gulp of tea, then stretched out his long legs, propping one boot atop the other. "Chapter One. An Arrival." Already he had shifted into his reading voice. Deeper, more formal sounding. The voice of a man who owned all that he surveyed and feared nothing. "In the fine summer of the year 1788—"

"Oh," she sighed, "the year you came to Auchengray." *And stole my heart without knowing it.*

"A very fortuitous year," he agreed before continuing to read. "As Mr. Stewart and his two daughters were one morning sitting down to breakfast—"

Leana interrupted him again. "Mr. *Stewart?* And two daughters?" Quite like his cousins on Arran. " 'Art imitates nature'? Or did you choose this novel on purpose?"

"I assure you, I did not," he said, feigning offense. "You well know that *Stewart* is a common name all over Scotland. And I believe you were one of two daughters, so 'tis not so unusual."

She swallowed a bite of seedcake, hiding her smile. "Pray, go on reading."

He held the book closer. "They were told by the servant that a gentlewoman was at the door who desired to speak with Mr. Stewart on business. 'She comes in good time,' said Mr. Stewart; 'but do you not know who she is?' " Jamie's voice trailed off, his face taking on a ruddy tint.

A family of Stewarts. Two daughters. A gentlewoman come to visit. The comparison was uncanny. Had it truly not been intentional?

Jamie read her mind. "Leana, my only goal was to entertain you, not to coerce you into sending Davina to visit the Stewarts."

"I quite believe you." She stood, hearing footsteps in the entrance hall. "Who is to say this book is not the Almighty's providential hand at work? But let us not mention anything to Davina 'til we've heard from the reverend."

"Agreed." Jamie stood as well, smoothing his rumpled waistcoat. "I'll not have our daughter anticipating a summer spent on Arran, only to be disappointed."

Two soft knocks—Davina's signature—sounded at the library door.

Leana found her daughter standing on the threshold, looking most contrite, her red hair tangled from running. "Bless you for coming home," she murmured, lightly touching her cheek.

Davina blushed and held out her sketchbook, opened to a particular page.

> Mother, I am sorry I ran off. The fault was entirely mine, not yours. Alas, there is no gentleman's name among these pages. I look forward to our summer together.
>
> Your loving daughter, Davina

"You are indeed loving." Leana read the words again, storing them in her heart, then clasped Davina by the hand and drew her into the room. "Come see who has returned to us, safe and sound."

Jamie held out his arms. "I believe we've both come home."

She flew into his embrace, like Davina of old, pressing her cheek into his chest.

Leana met her husband's warm gaze across a horizon of sunset-colored hair. Here was a man who adored his daughter, who wanted only what was advantageous for her, a man worthy of her trust. If the minister and his family made Davina welcome, Leana would put her groundless fears aside and rest in knowing her child's future was unfolding according to God's plan and not her own.

Davina stepped out of her father's arms, looking up at him as her hand moved to her mouth. *Speak to me.*

"You'll want to hear about Edinburgh, I suppose, and how your devilish brothers are faring. Might we save that long story for our supper table? I've an appointment just now with a basin of hot water and a sharp razor."

Davina smiled and touched her forehead. *I understand.*

"I hoped you might." He planted a light kiss on the same spot where her fingers had landed. "By suppertime—and by Charles—I'll be much improved."

No sooner had he taken his leave than Davina pounced on the remaining slices of buttermilk bread, barely sitting down before she had a plate and fork in hand.

"Hungry, I see." Leana smiled down at her. "The teapot has grown cold, and you'll need a clean cup. Suppose I brew some black currant for you." Davina's mouth was too full to smile, but Leana saw her eyes light up. "I'll not be long."

Before she left the library, she collected her soiled apron with its useful contents, intending to see to its preparation later. The agrimony would be hung to dry, then crushed and stored—stems, leaves, and flowers. Cool and drying, it had an astringent taste, well suited for sore throats and hoarse voices. Though it would not heal Davina, it also would not hurt her. And who knew when God might be merciful?

Leana returned to the library with a fresh pot of her daughter's favorite tea. "Enjoy your black currant while I tell you of a strange incident involving the herb we harvested today." If Davina was meant to visit the faraway isle, Leana was determined she know some of its traditions. "A century ago on Arran, a Mr. Ferquhar Ferguson was charged with using agrimony to cure people who were *elf-shot*."

Davina's eyes widened above the rim of her teacup.

Leana smiled, then leaned closer. "I've never known anyone shot through by wee folk, have you?" Lowering her voice, she added, "They say far more fairies live on Arran than in Galloway."

Davina hastily patted her mouth with a linen towel, then located her book, holding up her hand so Leana would know to wait. She turned away to write something, then whirled round and held out the page with its single, bold question: *Have you ever seen a fairy?*

Leana considered Davina's diminutive height, her fair complexion and luxuriant red hair, her gift for music, her playful nature, and her penchant for green dresses. Aye, and her utter silence. Fairy motion was said to be soundless.

"Have I ever seen a fairy?" Leana traced her daughter's freckled cheek with maternal affection. "Only when I look at you, lass."

Thirteen

Here is a promise
Of summer to be.
WILLIAM ERNEST HENLEY

'Tis a different sort of bow than you're accustomed to using, Davina, but you can master it just the same." A smile crept into Ian's voice. "It has but one string and never needs tuning."

Davina glowered at him, proud of herself for not sticking out her tongue or making a wretched face. Instead she would behave like a lady and pretend to be fascinated with archery, if only for her brother's sake.

Ian was determined to keep her occupied. Last week they had played hands of euchre and piquet while it rained incessantly. Then they made a tour of the local burns in spate—the Saugh, with its profusion of wildflowers, and the rock-strewn Gairland among them. Having read that gentlewomen in the English countryside were taking up archery, this morning Ian set about to teach Davina the sport, convinced she'd be the talk of the parish by Midsummer Eve.

"The ground is spongy," Ian warned, "so you'll want to place your feet just so." He'd located one of the few level places in the mountainous glen—near the loch yet free of evergreens. The target was neatly drawn by Rab with the scarlet paint he used to mark the sheep. At least no stray objects were in danger of being hit, hares being the exception. If any fell victim to her arrow, Aubert made a fine hare soup.

"You look quite graceful," Ian said. "Like Artemis, the huntress."

Davina tried not to smile, for it ruined her concentration. She took her stance, then pointed her left foot toward the bull's-eye.

"Hold the shaft in place with your forefinger," he instructed. "Then nock the arrow. Aye, where I've marked the string. Now look directly over your left shoulder and pull back with your right arm, straight as you can."

She remembered the rest: eye on the target; exhale before release; try to miss the loch. When the shaft flew from her hands, she missed the loch *and* the target. *Och!* Thrusting her bow into Ian's waiting hands, Davina stamped off to retrieve her lost arrow, glad the noontide meal would soon put an end to things.

The temperature had been mild all morning and the sky changeable. More white than gray, the clouds stretched across a pale blue background—the very color of her new gown. Not a fancy dress for Sabbath but a simple frock for days spent out of doors, like this one. "Because 'tis summer," her mother had said with an enigmatic smile when she finished her stitching, "and because you may have need of it."

Ian called out across the grassy meadow, "Might I be of assistance?"

Davina held up her hand without looking back. *I am fine, dear brother. Truly.*

How he hovered over her! She adored him for it but sometimes wished for a bit more freedom. Her parents seemed overly attentive too. Watching her, exchanging glances. Treating her like a young woman one minute, a naive child the next. There were times she felt weighed and measured like oats gone to market and other moments when she had no doubt of their affection for her.

Will and Sandy's absence was the only logical explanation.

Davina found the shaft at last, its goose-wing feathers easily detected against the verdant grass. Waving at Ian, she made her way back, relieved to see him packing up their belongings. She'd chased enough arrows for one morning.

He waited for her, target slung across his back, quiver and bow in hand. "An *ell* to the left, Davina, and you would have hit the mark."

Now she did make a face at him. Though her last shot was a vast improvement over her first one, which landed in the loch, she was still a far cry from Artemis.

As they started back, Davina was reminded again of how different Ian was from their younger brothers. Taller and leaner. Less muscular, more agile. Though his coloring was like the twins, his features were not.

Ian cast her a sideways glance. "You are thinking of Will and Sandy."

She looked up at him in amazement.

" 'Twas an easy guess." He shrugged off his clever appraisal. "You had a pensive look and then began to frown. I've observed the same expressions on our parents' faces, and invariably they had the twins in mind."

She touched her forehead, then reached up to brush his cheek. *I have you in mind too, Ian.* Did her brother understand how much she appreciated him?

Ian seemed to, for he kissed her hand before she had a chance to lower it. "I am glad you think of me, Davina."

Glentrool stood a quarter of an hour west. They walked on, keeping an eye on the heavens. More clouds had moved in, concealing the sun, hinting at rain. Davina hoped to spare her new gown a drenching.

Out of habit, the pair skirted the mausoleum, taking another route through the pinewoods. Ian held a low branch out of her way as he asked, "I wonder if you heard Mother speaking with Reverend Moodie in the kirkyard on the Sabbath last. She inquired if any letters addressed to the family had been delivered to the church." The mail coach from Carlisle to Stranraer made a daily stop at a coaching inn not far from Monnigaff kirk. Unclaimed letters often found their way into the parish minister's hands. "It weighs heavily on her, not hearing from our brothers."

Davina bore the same burden. Did Will and Sandy not realize how eager she was to hear from them? Or had the twins and Father not parted well? Resentment and disappointment, walking in tandem for a decade, seemed to have worn a footpath in Jamie's heart. Would he never forgive them?

A pair of curlews circled above, their cries echoing through the glen: *coor-lee,* the sound that gave them their name. Davina gathered her skirts in hand, if only to lengthen her stride. She missed the fuller gowns of her childhood. Modern dresses fell in straight lines, cinched high above the waist, with snug, narrow backs. Though fashionable, such gowns were not meant for walking. Or for breathing.

When Glentrool came into view, Ian turned toward the steading. "If you'll pardon my leaving you, I must deposit these in the barn." He hefted the archery target higher on his back, smiling at her as he did. "I enjoyed our morning together, Davina."

She pressed her hands together like a woman in prayer—her usual expression of thanks—then sent Ian off to the barn, watching him disappear round the corner of the house. Not far ahead stood Eliza. The moment she saw Davina, the housekeeper's features became even more animated than usual. Curious, Davina lifted her gown higher, propriety tossed to the winds as she hastened to Eliza's side.

"Leuk what Robert *jist* delivered by way o' the *toun*." Eliza held up her prize. "*Twa* letters by mail coach, *ane* from Embrough!" She pressed the correspondence into Davina's waiting hands. "Kindly *gie* these tae yer *mither*, for I ken she'll want tae see 'em. Ye'll find her in the drawin' room wi' her needle."

Davina hurried withindoors, glancing at the postal covers en route. One letter was stamped "Edinburgh," just as Eliza had said. Even without the postmark, Sandy's bold hand was easily recognized. The other, written in an unfamiliar hand, was stamped both "Arran" and "Ayr."

The moment Davina entered the room, Leana put down her sewing, the embroidered fabric in her lap forgotten. "What is it, dearie, that has you all *aflocht*?" When Davina presented the letters, her mother hesitated before she took them from her hands. "Ah, we've been waiting for these, haven't we?" She moved forward in her seat. "Your father will want to hear the contents as well."

"Indeed I will." Jamie's voice floated through the open doorway. "Eliza told me where I might find you both." He crossed the room and joined them, resting his hand on the small of Davina's back as he greeted her. "Your cheeks have a bit of color from the sun, I see. Very becoming."

She felt them grow warmer—and no doubt pinker—beneath his approving smile.

Jamie studied the letters for a bit, running his thumb across the postmarks. Some unnamed emotion flickered in his eyes. Guilt? Relief? Davina could not guess. Why did he not simply open the one from the twins? She very much wanted to stamp her foot but curled her toes instead and tried to be patient.

Her father turned to her at last. "I suspect both letters will mention you by name, Davina." He held out the two posts. "Which shall I read aloud first?"

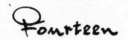

Fourteen

Letters, from absent friends, extinguish fear,
Unite division, and draw distance near.
AARON HILL

The choice of letters was a simple one. Merely seeing the lines of ink written in her brother's familiar hand made Davina's eyes water. She broke open the wax seal, her hands trembling with anticipation. Tempted as she was to scan the words, she relinquished the letter to her father.

He patted one of the straight-backed oak chairs, urging her to sit. "Let us see what the lads in Edinburgh have to tell us." After smoothing out the heavy creases, he began.

To James McKie of Glentrool
Thursday, 19 May 1808

Father,

Pardon the delay in writing to you, but our studies occupy us from dawn to the drum. We are daily afflicted with long-winded lectures and oral examinations. Saturdays are given to debates, and Sundays to the kirk.

Davina was not fooled. Though the letter was written in Sandy's hand, the bold words unquestionably belonged to Will. How natural they sounded in Jamie's voice. Perhaps father and sons were not so different after all.

"Such complaining would not surprise their old tutor." Jamie squinted at the letter. "Ah! 'Tis the word *fortunate*. Now then, to the rest."

> You were right, Father: We have yet to see the horses. The
> laundress has kept our shirts for a week, and we count our-
> selves fortunate to eat once a day. Please do not concern
> yourself, Mother. Our health remains strong, and our
> resolve, stronger.

He beamed at the letter, then at his wife. "There, you see? Univer-sity has proved to be the right decision. And here is the mention of you, Davina."

> As for our sister, we miss you very much and trust all is well.
> Not a lass in Edinburgh is the equal of our bonny wee fairy.
> I know Father will honor his pledge to watch over you since
> we cannot. You are ever in our thoughts.

Davina kept a handkerchief tucked in her sleeve for just such occa-sions and made use of it now.

Ian entered the drawing room, his shoulders dotted with the first of the raindrops. "I hear there's a letter from the twins."

"Aye." Father waved him toward a nearby chair. " 'Tis good that you arrived when you did, for you are mentioned as well."

> Tell our brother that he has been spared the terrible ordeal
> of a university education, an injustice that will not soon be
> forgotten. You may have been born first, Ian, but remember,
> there are two of us. Above all, do not fail to keep our sister
> safe from harm, or we shall be forced to take immediate
> action.

Jamie looked up as if to gauge Ian's reaction. The twins wrote in jest, of course; even on paper, their irony was apparent. But the words had an edge to them, and all in the room felt their sharpness.

Ian spoke first. "I trust I am fulfilling my duties as son and brother."

"You are indeed." Jamie folded the letter rather abruptly. "Let no one convince you otherwise." He handed Leana the missive, which would be read many times before finding a home in her dressing table.

"Now to our second letter. Posted from Ayr. I wonder what news this might contain." Her father's eyes bore a noticeable spark. "'Tis from a cousin on my mother's side: Reverend Benjamin Stewart."

Davina had difficulty placing the name. Father had so many distant relatives. Who could sort them all out?

"From the Isle of Arran," he added, as if to prompt her memory. "The Stewarts have two daughters, Catherine and Abigail. Not much younger than you, I'd say."

Davina offered a polite smile, hoping to appease him. But she could not lie and touch her forehead. She could not say *I know* if she did not.

Her father read silently for a moment, then looked up, smiling broadly. "This post addresses you almost exclusively, Davina. And your summer. Would you care to hear it?"

'Tis about…me? She was so astounded that she forgot to nod.

> To James McKie of Glentrool
> Tuesday, 17 May 1808
>
> Cousin James,
>
> We are in receipt of your letter dated the ninth of May and are delighted that, after many years, our offer of hospitality has been accepted. Davina is welcome to spend the summer with us at the manse in Kilbride on Arran.

Spend the summer? Davina fell back in her chair, mouth agape, staring at one parent and then the other. She would be permitted to travel so great a distance?

"An island!" Ian said with no trace of envy in his voice. "Won't that be grand?"

"I see the idea intrigues you, Davina," her father teased her. "There's more.

> "Escort her to Lamlash Bay at your earliest convenience. Perhaps the first of June would be to your liking. Be advised, Catherine and Abigail will not let her return to the mainland until Lammas. Even now they are formulating plans of how to entertain their cousin, and the list is quite long."

Her mind spun like a child's top on a polished floor. Now she remembered the Stewarts, if only from old letters. Catherine and Abigail were not much younger than she and lived in a manse overlooking a bay.

"Glentrool will be a desolate place without you," Ian confessed. "Still, you must go, my sister."

She blinked, as if it all might disappear: the letter, the invitation, the blessing of a lifetime. Nae, still there, along with her father, who was blithely describing an idyllic summer on Arran.

> My wife has inquired if Davina might inform us of certain
> foods she likes and dislikes and any other information of
> a similar nature. We have a mild climate here and few
> diseases. Have no concern for her health.

Davina clapped her hands at that. As if she cared one whit about climates or diseases! And she would happily consume every morsel on her plate. Not stewed eels, but all else.

"I believe we have our answer, Mrs. McKie." Her father smiled, and her mother tried to do so in return. "Ian, you will manage the estate for a few days while I see Davina safely to Kilbride parish."

"A privilege, sir."

Before Jamie could outline Ian's duties, Leana touched his arm. "Is there more to the letter?" she asked softly. "Does Reverend Stewart mention her...impediment?"

Davina looked away. *Impediment.* The word her mother used in polite company.

Until now, the thought had not occurred to her: She would not only be a stranger among them, but strange. *Tongue-tackit.* The mute lass from Galloway.

"He does make mention of it," her father admitted, "but only in the kindest of terms. I thought to spare you this, Davina, but perhaps 'tis best you hear it.

> "We are not frightened by your daughter's muteness. Did
> not Gabriel take away the voice of Zacharias? Did he not

say, 'Behold, thou shalt be dumb, and not able to speak'? God has not lifted his hand from Davina's life. She will be well cared for on Arran."

Whether unintentionally or by design, her father had read the balance of the letter using his shepherd's voice. Warm. Gentle. Soothing. In Aprils past, Davina had walked the hills with him as he examined the newborn lambs and crooned to them in just such a way. He'd often prayed for her in the same kind voice. And whenever he disciplined her, however severe the chastisement, the words did not hurt because of the manner in which they were spoken.

Dear Father. He had arranged this visit to Arran; she was sure of it.

Her mother placed her sketchbook in her hands, blue gray eyes shimmering like wet glass. "Have you decided to go, then? 'Tis a wonderful opportunity."

It *was* wonderful. Was there any reason not to go?

Davina turned the pages, considering her answer, when her gaze landed on a message she'd written earlier. For her mother. *I look forward to our summer together. Your loving daughter, Davina.*

Fifteen

Ah! there are no longer any children!

MOLIÈRE

Leana sat in the empty dining room with only the ticking mantel clock for company. A single candle flickered on the table. The light was not sufficient to dispel the shadows in the far corners but more than enough to illuminate the old Buik that lay open before her.

My children are gone forth of me, and they are not.

She had awakened with tears in her eyes, remembering the verse.

Up the stair Jamie still lay sleeping, for the hour was very late—or very early—not long past three o'clock. Soon the dark blue eastern skies over Lamachan Hill would take on a pearly sheen. The thirtieth of May would officially dawn. And Davina, the sweetest of daughters, would depart from Glentrool.

Only for two months. Leana comforted herself with that thought. But it did not relieve the pain of letting go. Did she mean to keep Davina dependent upon her? *May it not be so, Lord.* Yet she could not deny the possibility, for she delighted in having a daughter beneath her roof. Loved caring for her, loved mothering her.

Head bowed, eyes closed, she spread her hands across the pages of the Buik. *Strengthen thou me according unto thy word.* Her own strength would not be sufficient; had never been so. *Please, Lord. Give me the courage to say good-bye.*

Many minutes later she lifted her head. Nothing had changed. Yet she had changed, and that was enough.

Candle in hand, Leana adjusted the light plaid she'd thrown over her shoulders for modesty's sake and slipped up the broad stair to the second floor, where the twins' empty bedroom had been pressed into service. Laid out across the curtained bed were Davina's two traveling bags, carefully packed and waiting to be buckled shut.

Leana placed the candle where it would do the most good, then began running her hands over the folded contents of each valise to be sure nothing had been overlooked. She'd chosen Davina's clothing with care; the horses could be burdened with only so much. Fortunately, whaleboned bodices and hooped petticoats were no longer in style. Her daughter's slender summer dresses, stitched in lightweight fabrics, were easily packed. She tallied the remaining items: an extra pair of shoes, two cloth bonnets, a reticule, half a dozen gauzy muslin tuckers, and gloves in both cotton and lace.

"Here you are, my love." Jamie stood in the doorway, rubbing the sleep from his eyes. "When I found you missing from our bed, this seemed a likely place to look."

"Oh, Jamie." She drew him into the room, lest Davina hear them. "I did not mean to wake you."

"My troubled dreams are the culprit. Not you." He kissed her brow, then gazed over her shoulder at the valises. "Counting gloves and stockings again, I see. And have you tucked your heart among our daughter's gowns?"

Her throat tightened. "First the twins…and now Davina…"

Jamie wrapped her in his arms. "They will come back to us, Leana. Depend upon it."

The warmth of him, fresh from their bed, the musky scent of his skin, the solid feel of his chest—nothing on earth could offer her such solace. Though her children were leaving, her husband remained.

After a moment he leaned back, then lifted her chin until their eyes met. "You may trust the man who loves you, even as you trust the One who made you. 'Whoso putteth his trust in the LORD shall be safe,' aye?"

"Why, Mr. McKie." She smiled up at him. "When did you become such a *halie* man?"

Jamie returned her smile. "When I married such a *gracie* woman." Even with his breath thick from sleeping, even with the plaid chafing her bare skin, Leana welcomed his kiss.

Minutes later the sound of a door opening and muffled footsteps in the hall signaled the arrival of the servants, stirring the house to life as surely as Aubert would stir the breakfast porridge with a wooden *spurtle*.

"And so the day begins." Jamie slowly released her from his embrace. "We leave at six o'clock. Please see that Davina is dressed and at table by half past five, for I'll not have her ride off hungry." He stepped back, half turning toward the door, though his gaze still held hers. "I wish 'twere practical to bring you with us, Leana. But I'm afraid that Glentrool—"

"Needs a mistress," she finished for him. The possibility of her joining them had already been considered. "I am content to stay here with Ian, who'll have his hands full managing the estate. The maidservant we *fee'd* at Whitsuntide requires training, and my gardens would languish without me."

"Nae, you would languish without your gardens."

Much more so without my daughter. Leana kept her thoughts to herself and clung to the psalmist's words: *My heart shall not fear.*

"And when I return," Jamie added, "we will have a quiet house to ourselves."

"Too quiet," she confessed, "though 'twill not remain so. When will the shearing begin?"

"The sixth of June." Jamie yawned, then rolled his shoulders. "Rab has hired a goodly number of herds to handle things." He retrieved her candle, then led her into the hall, lowering his voice. "This morning there's only one wee lamb that requires your care."

While Jamie went off to tend to his ablutions, Leana lightly rapped on Davina's bedchamber door, then tiptoed inside the murky room, shielding the bright candle. Her precautions were unnecessary; Davina was already bathed and half-dressed, sitting on the edge of her bed.

"Did you sleep at all, dearie?"

An apologetic smile was answer enough. *Nae.*

"No wonder, with such a day ahead of you." Leana sat beside her daughter and took her hand, not surprised to find her skin cool. "Sarah will be along shortly to dress us both. In the meantime, I am glad we have a moment alone."

Davina nodded, then touched her heart. *I am glad too.*

Leana eyed the bedside table where she'd hidden Davina's parting gift: a linen handkerchief, delicately embroidered and scented with dried lavender from her garden. "I have a wee something for you." She reached inside the drawer and lifted out the fragrant present, breathing the sweet aroma once more before placing the handkerchief in her daughter's waiting hands. "To remind you of home."

Davina held the fabric to her nose, slowly closing her eyes. Her red lashes began to glisten.

"Nae, dearie," Leana pleaded, circling her arms round her. "Do not cry, or I shall do the same."

But it was too late.

"Davina, I..." The words would not come. *Help me, Father. Help me let go.* Leana pressed their wet cheeks together and tried again. "I will miss you...so very much."

Her daughter gave a small sob, more felt than heard.

"And I will pray for you." *Every day, lass. Every hour.*

Davina pulled away long enough to use her new handkerchief before wrapping her fingers round it and bowing her head, her meaning clear. *Pray. Now.*

Without hesitation, Leana rose, bringing her daughter with her. "Your father spoke a blessing over the twins," she whispered. "Now 'tis our turn." Her hand trembled as she rested it on Davina's head, having never done so bold a thing. "Almighty God, let my daughter dwell under thy shadow and take refuge beneath thy wings." With each word, her voice grew stronger. "Be with her in trouble, Lord. Deliver her and honor her. Give thy angels charge over her, to keep her in all thy ways."

Leana kissed her brow, as if to seal the words in place, then embraced her once more, only then aware of the room growing brighter and of Sarah tapping at the door.

Sixteen

Travel, in the younger sort, is a part of education;
in the elder, a part of experience.

FRANCIS BACON

Well seated on her mare and dressed in a light wool riding habit,
Davina already felt different. Not taller, alas, but older. Less like
Will and more like Ian.

Nae, more like Mother. Davina touched her gloved hand to her
bodice, where she'd tucked her new handkerchief for safekeeping.

"'Tis a perfect day for riding." Father swept his arm to take in their
surroundings. "We'll make good time if the weather holds."

Glentrool was an hour behind them. Crosshill, where they would
break their journey and seek lodging for the evening, was twenty miles
north across the mountain fastness. Few puddles remained from the
rainy Sabbath, and the air was clear and dry. Patches of blue appeared
above the towering pines, and a northerly breeze lifted the fine hair
round her face.

"There's a pied wagtail looking for a tasty morsel." Father pointed to
a black and white bird running across the stony path ahead. "Imagine the
shore birds you'll see on Arran. Ringed plovers and dunlins and red-
shanks." He turned to catch her eye. "You'll draw some for me?"

She patted the sketchbook tucked in her bag—almost left behind
until Ian discovered it in the library. "Fill the pages with memories," her
brother had told her that morning on the lawn. Bidding Ian good-bye
had been even harder than she'd expected. *Only 'til Lammas, dear
brother.*

"Take your time," Jamie cautioned as they approached their first
ford of the morning. "We've many more waters to navigate before we
reach the harbor at Ayr."

The pair eased down into the Water of Minnoch, a wide, meandering stream tumbling over a rocky bed. Her father's gelding found solid footing, as did her mare. When they reached the opposite bank without mishap, Davina smoothed her hand along the animal's sleek neck. *Well done, Biddy.* Her mother's dun-colored horse would return home to its mistress, leaving Davina to explore Arran on foot or borrow a mount from the Stewarts.

Another shiver of anticipation—beyond counting this morning—ran down her spine. Think what she would see! And whom she might meet. Only one book was packed in her bags: *The Lay of the Last Minstrel,* a yuletide gift from her father. Diverting enough for a rainy day, but reading poetry was hardly how she intended to spend her time on Arran.

No other travelers were in sight as they turned onto the main route, little more than an unpaved track. A farmer pulling a two-wheeled cart full of manure would block the way, it was so narrow. She'd traveled on this stretch of road before, but no more than a few miles. They rode side by side, the yellowish coat of her mare a stark contrast to her father's black gelding. Magnus, he'd named the beast—a large horse yet with a calm disposition.

"Listen, Davina." Her father held up his hand as the distinctive call of a cuckoo sounded among the trees. The bird was easier heard than seen, so swift was its flight. "How does the auld rhyme go? 'In May I sing all day.' Not much of a tune. Two notes." He imitated the bird, then chuckled when she patted the green baize bag strapped behind her. "I would much prefer to hear my daughter's music. Perhaps when we stop for our meal?"

Davina nodded absently. Food was the last thing on her mind. Had she even eaten breakfast?

Her father pointed to the broad, rushing river on their right. " 'Tis the same Minnoch we forded earlier this morning. We'll follow it to its source, Eldrick Hill." Two deep burns in succession momentarily slowed their progress, then a bit farther along they passed a neatly painted sign—Palgowan—posted where a dirt track veered toward the neighboring Buchanan farm.

At kirk on the Sabbath, Davina had promised Janet Buchanan a letter from Arran. "If you'll cross the letter and keep to a single piece of paper," Janet had said, "my father would be grateful." Davina had agreed, knowing a second page would double the postage the recipient was obliged to pay. Difficult as it was to manage, she would fill one page, then turn the paper at right angles and continue writing across it. Poor Janet, having to decipher such a thing.

They continued north for another hour, climbing past the Rig of Kirriereoch. "We're in Ayrshire now," her father announced. "Kirkcudbrightshire is behind us."

Davina looked round, as if the ground might change color or a line appear, as on a map, indicating the end of one county and the start of another. She'd not complain again about the remoteness of Glentrool, now that she'd seen the desolate Minnoch valley. Scarcely a house or tree adorned the wide, boggy landscape below, painted in a drab green.

When Biddy started breathing harder, Jamie slowed their steps. "In less than a mile we'll reach Rowantree Toll." He gave her a sideways glance. "And the Nick of the Balloch beyond it."

Davina shifted in her saddle and ignored the uneasiness stirring inside her. A nick was a narrow gap in a range of hills. Would the track be narrow as well? And steep?

"The pass offers a splendid view," her father promised as if to bolster her spirits. "Unlike anything you've seen in Galloway."

Perched on a rise, Rowantree Toll soon came into sight. Built without mortar and thatched with brown heather, the old stone tollhouse was the roughest sort of building. " 'Tis not much to look at," her father admitted, "but it nigh marks our halfway point this day." He dismounted with a gentlemanly grunt. "Come, let me help you, lass."

A brisk wind swept along the road that continued up Rowantree Hill, bending the tall grass across their footpath as they neared the tollkeeper's door. At her father's knock a voice bellowed from within, bidding them enter. The single-room dwelling was dark, the windows shuttered against the elements. A peat fire burned in the hearth, and two candles lit the table where the tollkeeper stood, a grimy ledger spread before him.

Davina tried not to stare, but the man appeared to be a giant. Taller than her father by a foot, broader than Will and Sandy put together, he looked quite capable of swallowing her whole.

The mammoth tollkeeper peered at her father through a haze of peat smoke. "Ye'll be headin' o'er the Nick, aye?"

"We will." Jamie slipped his hand inside his coat.

Knowing his purse and his pistol were both within easy reach, Davina prayed the weapon would not be necessary. When their brief transaction was completed, the man followed them out the door and lifted the stout toll bar that blocked the road. Davina was as grateful to be seated on her horse as she'd been happy to dismount minutes earlier. The horses seemed eager to be gone as well, setting off at a good trot.

"An *unco* place, even on a bright May morn," her father murmured as the toll bar dropped into place behind them. "Be glad we're not here on a *dreich* November eve with a cold north wind in our faces and the sky black with rain."

Davina had more present concerns on her mind. With each sharp turn round Rowantree Hill, she feared the road might disappear beneath her. All at once she was there, at the highest point, looking down into a valley that stretched so far below her she feared she might faint.

"Steady, lass." Her father gripped her elbow, holding her in place. "'Tis a slender track, to be sure, and a precipitous drop. Four hundred ells or more. Stay close to the hillside and away from the edge of the road." A half smile creased his face. "And try not to look down."

There was nowhere else to look *but* down.

Her father started down first, speaking softly to Magnus. She followed, keeping a tight rein on Biddy lest the wide-open vista unnerve the mare. To her right, narrow gorges dissected the hillside, the clefts as deep as a man was tall. To her left, the road was edged with thin air. Keeping an eye on the burn weaving its way along the valley floor, Davina held her breath until Biddy was at last walking along its banks and the hazardous descent was behind them.

Her father drew his horse next to hers. "You've earned a brief respite, and so have our mounts. The bridge o'er the River Stinchar lies just ahead. Suppose we break here for our dinner." They dismounted, spread their plaid across the grass, then sat down to enjoy Eliza's pickled herring and cheese. After giving the horses time to graze and drink their fill, Jamie stood and shook the crumbs from the wrinkled plaid.

"I'd hoped to hear a fiddle tune, but we've still eight miles of hilly country to cover. This evening, aye?" He fell silent as he helped her get settled on Biddy.

Davina sensed he was about to say something, then hesitated. She rested her hand on his shoulder, prompting him to look up at her, certain he would understand. *Tell me, Father.*

"How like your mother you are," he said at last. " 'Tis simply this, Davina: When I compare our day to the ones spent with your brothers en route to Edinburgh…" He rubbed his hand across his jaw, though he could not hide his disappointment. "I do not blame your brothers entirely, for I'd given them but two days' notice. Still…" He sighed heavily.

So the twins' journey had been trying. She'd suspected as much. *Poor lads.* As they crossed the bridge and left the Stinchar behind, Davina sorted through what she knew to be true: Her father still blamed Will and Sandy for her muteness. And her brothers would never forgive themselves if he did not show them mercy first.

Please, Father. Forgive them.

A startling notion began circling round inside her. If she could bring herself to write those words, could she show them to her father without trembling?

Aye. That very night when she sat across from him at table, her book and pencil in hand, she would plead on behalf of Will and Sandy. *'Twas an accident, Father, and long ago.* Her brothers had defended her for a decade. Could she not do one courageous thing in return? She prayed she would be strong when the time came, then set her mind on the hours ahead.

They traveled on through the afternoon, lifting their hands to greet farmworkers in the fields and shepherds on the hills. "Not much longer to Crosshill," her father informed her, eying his pocket watch as they neared a crossroad edged with yellow-centered *gowans.* "We'll be there by six. 'Tis a small settlement. Handloom weavers, mostly. I've in mind a particular cottager who might make us welcome."

Though she'd never traveled thus, Davina had heard the stories: *Kintra* folk were known for their hospitality. If supper and a bed were needed by a traveler, obliging farmers and villagers provided for their unexpected guests, even if it meant family members slept three to a mattress or a kettle of soup was thinned with water. Inns were the stuff of coaching routes; in the countryside, a knock on a cottage door was sufficient.

The hills were behind them now, the velvet green landscape gently rolling as they came upon a row of single-story cottages. Her father smiled at her, though the weariness lining his face was unmistakable. "Shall we see if Michael Kelly of Crosshill is receiving visitors?"

They dismounted at the unpainted door of a *bothy* no different than its neighbors: dry *stane* walls with straw fitted in the cracks rather than mortar; a thatched roof, held down with rocks on taut ropes of hemp; one small window without glazing, the shutter hanging open on a leather hinge; peat smoke curling out a bent chimney poking through the rooftop.

Her father knocked, then stood back. They did not have long to wait. The door was flung open by a spry, red-haired man of uncertain years, who blinked at them from the shadowy interior of his cottage.

Father nodded at the man. "Good day to you, Michael."

Davina hid her smile when she got a good look at him, for the weaver was as small as the tollkeeper was large. With an Irish name and wiry red hair, who was to say Michael Kelly wasn't a leprechaun?

"An' a *guid* day tae ye, sir." The man bowed politely. "Ye've stood on me *thrashel* afore, aye?" He stepped aside, waving them within. "Ye'll pardon me for not recallin' yer name, sir, but if 'tis *ludgin* ye're needin', ye've knocked on the *richt* door."

Davina followed the men inside, amused that the humble weaver did not remember the laird of Glentrool. Such a thing would never happen in Monnigaff parish. While the man saw to their horses, Davina studied their lodgings. Rough pine covered the dirt floor, and the plain, square hearth bore no mantelpiece. Two iron lanterns hung on either side of the loom, which took up a third of the one-room cottage, leaving space for a table with two benches and a single bed, low to the floor. Still, the bedcover was finely woven wool, and the iron stewpot gave forth the savory aroma of barley.

Michael lugged their saddles through the door and hung them near the hearth, then washed his hands with the pitcher and bowl beside the bed. "Ye'll be joinin' me for supper, aye?" He served their meal in simple crockery bowls with horn spoons. "Traded 'em from a tinkler," Michael explained, running his small thumb over the smooth contour of the spoon carved from ox horn, a specialty of the traveling Gypsies. "What aboot yerself, sir? What'll ye gie me for yer *nicht's* sleep? 'Twill not be yer *siller*, for I wouldna ask for it."

"I can tell a good tale," Jamie offered. "And I've all the *blether* from Monnigaff, if you care to hear it."

"Aye, that'll do," the small man agreed. "What aboot yer *dochter*?" He regarded Davina with a curious gaze. "She's too *quate* tae spin a yarn."

"Oh, she has much more to say than I do." Jamie nodded toward her saddle. "My daughter speaks by way of notes, rather than words."

"Hoot!" The man leaped to his feet. "The fiddle is yers, lass?" In an instant he had the green bag in his hands and held it out to her reverently. "Stay as lang as ye wish, miss, and eat *whatsomever* ye like."

She quickly tuned her instrument, then launched into a cheerful air. One melody led to another, from strathspey to reel to jig. While her father tapped out the rhythm on the tabletop, Michael danced round his cottage with unabashed exuberance. A passerby draped himself through the open window to listen, then the door was propped ajar for the whole neighborhood to hear. Unbidden, the cottagers of Crosshill soon came in to join the weaver in his revelry, dust rising from the wooden planks beneath their feet, their voices lifted in song.

> My heart was ance as blithe and free
> As simmer days were lang;
> But a bonny, westlin weaver lad
> Has gart me change my sang.

The throng begged for more, and she could not refuse them, having never entertained a more appreciative audience. Roses were plucked from nearby gardens and strewn at her feet, bairns were carried to the cottage for her blessing, and half a dozen starry-eyed lads seemed about to propose.

Jamie was the one who finally drew the curtain on her performance. "We've had a long day's journey, and another awaits us." He nodded at Davina to put her fiddle away, lest one more song be coaxed from her hands. An hour passed before the cottage was truly empty, for her father felt compelled to share a bit of gossip as promised. In rural areas, visitors were the only source of news, every crumb was a feast, and no one left until they'd had their fill.

When the door finally closed on the last visitor, Davina was given the bed, Jamie a pile of woolen blankets, and the weaver curled up on the floor near the hearth. The chaff-filled mattress was nothing like her heather bed at home, but tired as she was, sleep would not elude her long.

While her father arranged his bedding, Davina carefully wrote out her question by the faint lantern light. She'd show it to him tomorrow morning on horseback. Though he might look elsewhere while he weighed his answer, he could not ride off and leave her. She had to try, for her brothers' sake.

Davina closed the book, her pencil marking the page.

Seventeen

Good, to forgive;
Best to forget.

ROBERT BROWNING

Jamie sat up all at once, as if someone had tapped his shoulder while he slept.

A faint gray light filtered through the cracks in the shutter. Morning had broken, but only just. The shadowy loom with its tautly drawn warp, its shuttle and treadle, provided his bearings. Beyond the battered door a cock crowed, and the horses shuffled their feet. Whether he was well rested or not, his day had begun.

He bathed his face and hands in a washbowl, using tepid water and a sliver of lye soap. On the other side of the cottage Michael Kelly slept like an Irish setter, nose to knees in front of a hearth gone cold in the night. He would rise before long and attend to their breakfast. However mean his lodging, Michael was a generous host.

Jamie dried his face with his shirttail, gazing down at the narrow bed that cradled his sleeping Davina. With her hands pressed beneath her high cheekbones and her long red lashes fanned across her pale skin, she looked younger. Though not so young she might awaken and still be able to speak.

"Good morning, Father. Shall we visit the lambs today?"

He had never forgotten the sound of her voice. Like the sweetest notes on her fiddle.

My darling girl. Jamie reached down, longing to brush her soft cheek, yet not wanting to wake her. If love alone could heal his daughter, he would touch her throat and make her whole. But that task belonged to another. *Come and lay thy hands on her, that she may be healed.* How many times had he prayed those words, to no avail?

Davina, perhaps sensing his nearness, slowly opened her eyes. She mouthed the word, "Father," then took his hand to help her sit up, looking closely at him, as if she'd not seen him in days instead of mere hours.

Behind them a candle sparked to life. Michael was awake and busy at his labors. He added peat to the grate, then disappeared out the door with a pair of buckets. The Water of Girvan was not far to the north; its steep banks would require careful steps on so misty a morn.

"Less than a dozen miles to the harbor at Ayr." Jamie kept his voice low, as suited the hour. "We'll wait to see whether the fog lifts, though even if it does not, the road is easily followed."

He buttoned his waistcoat while Davina neatly plaited her hair, her hands as graceful as her mother's. Her red mane was soon beribboned and swept over her shoulder. So much for his concern about his daughter managing without her maid.

The weaver returned with a muted bang of the door, water sloshing in his bucket. "Yer horses are drinkin' from the *ither bowie*," he informed them. "I'll hae yer tea quick as I can. Will *parritch* do tae break yer fast?"

Jamie assured him porridge would suffice, then winked at Davina as he asked their host, "How is it that a man named Kelly sounds like a Scot?"

"Och!" He swung his teakettle over the heat. "Me *faither* was Irish, but me mither was from Ayrshire. 'Twas she *wha* raised me."

She'd also taught him how to make porridge, Jamie decided, sitting down half an hour later to a steaming bowl of cooked oats, lightly salted and topped with butter. Davina ate a spoonful now and again while he downed the contents of two bowls. His daughter was always quiet, but she was not always still; this morning she was practically motionless, her left hand resting on her sketchbook. He'd noticed her with pencil in hand yestreen. Had some worthy subject caught her eye in Michael's cottage and set her to drawing?

Putting aside his teacup, Jamie nodded toward the well-worn book. "Will you show me your latest entry?"

Her eyes widened.

"Perhaps later?"

Davina nodded briskly, then quit the table, clearly impatient to be going.

"'Twould seem we're away," Jamie told their host, who was already seated at his loom, raising and lowering the treadles with his feet, throwing the shuttle back and forth across the warp in a practiced rhythm. "You've not asked for silver, Michael, but I've left two shillings by your plate."

The weaver nodded his thanks in time with his pedaling. "I'm obliged tae ye, sir. May yer open hand *ayeways* be *fu'*."

Magnus and Biddy were brushed and saddled, waiting for their riders, when Jamie and Davina stepped out of doors. Dense, moist air swirled along the row of cottages, like the breath of a living creature.

"Rising from the river," Jamie guessed, helping his daughter get settled before mounting his own horse. "If the sun shines tomorrow, your mother would contend 'tis a rightful thing. 'Mist in May and heat in June bring all things into tune,' or so gardeners say." He guided their horses round to the north. "Walk on," he told them, and the second day of their journey commenced.

A stone bridge carried them out of the settlement and over the swollen Water of Girvan, where the moist air was at its thickest. The signpost for Dalduff farm appeared suddenly in the mist. Though they could not see the steading, the clucking of the brood hens signaled its location to the west. The road began to undulate—now rising, now falling, ever winding, one mile, then another. After one especially sharp bend, they left the mist behind. Jamie exhaled, glad to view the countryside again. The sun, still low on the eastern horizon, draped the land in a pale, clear light, with only a few wisps of fog remaining.

"Another fine day in the making." He turned to Davina, surprised to find her holding her sketchbook. "Surely you don't intend to draw while you ride?" He said it in jest, meaning only to make her smile, but she frowned instead and gripped the book more firmly. In one of her moods, perhaps? He'd not grown up with a sister; judging by his daughter, young women seemed prone to alternating fits of joy and despair.

"We can stop in Maybole, if you wish. A fair size village with several old ruins to tempt your artist's eye." He pointed out a few possibilities as they rode through the sleepy town, its residents only now beginning to stir. "Maybole castle?" Nae, she did not want to sketch its tower and turrets. "The Collegiate Church?" Nae, the arched stone doorways, however venerable, apparently held no appeal.

Davina had something on her mind; that was certain. He stole a glimpse at her profile—gaze straightforward, brow slightly furrowed, chin neither tipped up in defiance nor bowed down in dejection, mouth shaped in a pensive sort of pout. Was she worried about crossing the sea? The lass had never been in a boat larger than the skiff moored at their own dock. Might she be having second thoughts about so long a visit on Arran? Or some concern about her reception from the Stewarts?

His questions were not answered until they rode out of the village and started across the high ridge leading to Ayr. Davina touched his sleeve, then held out her sketchbook, opened to a page without any drawings, only words.

Jamie slowed his horse and took the book from her trembling hand. "Whatever is the matter, Davina?" Appalled to see tears in his daughter's eyes, he brought Magnus to a full stop. "Do you not feel well?"

Though she pointed to the open page, he could not look away from her face, so marked was her anguish. Instead he took her gloved hand in his. "I will read this, Davina, but only if you assure me that doing so will ease your distress."

She bobbed her head, which sent tears spilling down her cheeks.

"Oh my child." He released his hold on her and searched his waist-coat pockets in vain for a handkerchief.

But Davina had one of her own. After patting her cheeks dry, she held the dainty linen to her nose and drew in a long, shaky breath.

Jamie recognized the embroidery; Leana had finished stitching the handkerchief only days earlier. "A pleasant fragrance, lavender." He kept his voice even, waiting for Davina to compose herself. "Strong, like mint, but sweeter."

She lowered her handkerchief, then aimed her gaze at the page. Whatever was written there, the time had come to read it.

Jamie looked down, unprepared for what he found. *Please forgive my brothers.*

An ache rose inside him. The heaviness of grief and the sharpness of pain twined into one.

"William! What have you done to your sister?" His voice, roaring at a six-year-old boy.

"Oh Father! I did not...I did not mean to...hurt her..." Will, sobbing hysterically. Sandy, collapsed on the grass in shock. Davina, unmoving, pale and still as death.

Jamie shut his eyes, clutching the sketchbook in his hands, but the memory and the ache grew sharper.

He'd flung the broadsword into the pines as if it were made of straw, then gathered his small daughter in his arms and strode toward the house, his heart in his throat. *"Davina, Davina! Can you not speak to me?"*

Will and Sandy had circled round his heels like dogs, panting for air, trying to keep up with him. He'd ignored them, moving across the lawn toward Leana, who was running with arms outstretched, calling their daughter's name.

Davina did not answer. Would never answer...

A gloved hand rested on his.

Jamie lifted his head, bile stinging his throat. "I am sorry, Davina. You were very brave to ask this of me, but I..."

Eyes bright with tears, she touched her heart, then his, a gesture he knew well. *I love you.* No spoken words could have humbled him more. She slipped the book from his grasp and underlined the phrase with her finger, drawing a question mark at the end.

"Why can I not forgive your brothers? Is that what you are asking?" He saw the answer in her eyes. *Aye.*

The horses moved beneath them, restless. "Walk on," he said softly, praying the motion might dislodge the misery locked inside him. "Davina..." He swallowed again, despising the bitter taste in his mouth. "If your injury had been an accident. That is to say, truly an accident, with no one at fault..." He groaned, knowing how she would respond. *It* was *an accident, Father. The twins never intended this to happen.*

He started again. "I realize your brothers did not mean to injure you, Davina. But they stole Grandfather's broadsword, knowing they were wrong to do so." Hadn't he told them never to touch it? Hadn't they sworn they would not? "And they wrestled with it," Jamie said more emphatically, "ignoring the danger involved. Knowing they could hurt someone."

You, Davina. They hurt you.

He forced himself to continue. "Will said you warned them to be careful. In fact, begged them to stop. Is that not so?"

Davina shrugged, nodding slightly.

"But Will and Sandy ignored you, caring only who won the sword." His voice was strained from the telling, his heart from remembering. "Now do you see? How can I forgive your brothers when they alone are to blame? For that matter, how can *you* forgive them, Davina?"

He regretted his question the moment he asked it. When she looked away, he regretted it even more. Before he could apologize, a flock of bleating sheep wandered onto the road, trailed by a patient shepherd.

While they waited, Davina quietly reached over and reclaimed her sketchbook. She wrote in haste, then handed the book back to him just as the last sheep leaped out of their way.

Jamie glanced at the page, and his heart sank.

Mercy is a gift. His own words. Spoken at his own table.

Then Davina's words. *I gave my brothers that gift long ago, Father. Will you not do the same?*

Eighteen

Auld Ayr is just one lengthen'd, tumbling sea.
ROBERT BURNS

Her father's dark features were etched with pain.

Nae! Davina stared at him in dismay. This was not at all what she'd intended. In seeking to spare Will and Sandy further shame, she had merely redirected it.

Father, please. When she tugged at the sketchbook, he released it without comment. She then snagged his sleeve, forcing him to look at her as she briefly covered her eyes, the gesture she used to communicate embarrassment or shame. *I am sorry.*

"Nae, my daughter." He hid his own eyes for a moment, employing her language. "I am the one who is sorry." When he lowered his hand, naught but sincerity shone on his face. "Sorry that you, of all people, had to find the courage to ask this of me. And sorrier still for neglecting your brothers."

She pointed to the watch in his waistcoat pocket. Would he grasp her meaning? *It is not too late.*

"You are quite right, Davina. We still have time, your brothers and I, to make amends." He brushed the dust off his coat with deliberate strokes, as if considering something, then met her gaze. "When Will and Sandy return at Lammas, I shall speak with them at length. In truth, 'tis a decision I made while in Edinburgh."

She had not erred, then, in asking him so difficult a question. While her father's attention was drawn to a red-crowned linnet poking about the rough ground, she quietly put away her sketchbook; it had served its purpose well.

They rode in silence for a time, though not uncomfortably so. Their high vantage point gave them a fine view of distant blue hills and fertile farmland. As the morning progressed, she sensed her father's spirits beginning to lift. His brow was smooth once more and his posture straight. When he spoke, she heard no tension in his voice.

More travelers joined them as they neared Ayr. Farmers and gentlemen alike made their way to and from the royal burgh, tipping their hats as they walked by—strangers, all of them. She'd spent seventeen years in the same parish, surrounded by familiar faces, knowing everyone's station, gentry to servant. On Arran she would need her cousins to inform her, else she might address someone incorrectly or not give proper courtesy.

Her father eyed her green bag. "If the proprietor of the King's Arms requires music for our lodging, will you oblige him?"

She knew he spoke in jest—innkeepers wanted silver not song—but Davina gamely pantomimed sweeping a bow across her bent arm.

"You can be sure Michael Kelly will not forget *your* name. I believe you carried away his heart in your fiddle bag."

She shook her head, then hunched over her saddle, pretending to use a cane.

"Too old for you, eh? I presume a younger man would be to your liking. Dark haired, like your brothers? Or fair haired, like your mother?"

Golden like the sun. Davina had studied her cherished sketch yestreen. More Viking than Scot, she'd decided. And more braw every time she pictured him. She busied herself with the folds of her skirt, lest any color stain her cheeks and give away her thoughts.

"A gentleman with auburn hair, then," her father suggested. "Of sufficient property to merit my approval and sufficient intellect to earn yours."

Davina rolled her eyes. Property? Intellect? How very dull.

"I see you do not agree with my criteria for a suitor." His voice was stern and his visage more so. She was not fooled for a moment. "My complete list of qualifications is a good deal longer," he insisted, "and your mother's requires a second page."

Davina threw back her head in a soundless laugh, nearly losing her bonnet in the process. *A list?* The very idea.

Her father laughed as well, tugging her bonnet back in place. "However diverting you may find the subject, I can assure you of this:"—he paused, his expression more serious—"The gentleman who wins my Davina's hand will not do so easily."

She touched her forehead. *I understand, Father. And I am glad.*

The sun was nearing its zenith when they descended into a wooded valley and crossed the River Doon over an old sandstone bridge. Its single, high arch spanned the placid waters below and carried them into the village of Alloway.

"Ah, the auld kirk." Her father pointed to the roofless remains, an ancient bell still hanging in the belfry. Graves stood where pews once rested; the windows were naught but stone ribs. " 'Tis haunted, if Rabbie Burns is to be believed." He made an *ugsome* face, then whispered hoarsely, "When glimmering thro' the groaning trees, Kirk Alloway seem'd in a *bleeze.*"

Still holding the reins, she lifted her hands, wiggling her fingers like a blazing fire.

Her father laughed. "Aye, if only in the poet's vivid imagination."

The pair wound their way through the small farm village. Clay cottages, covered with lime and roofed with thatch, were set in haphazard fashion on both sides of the road. Each dwelling had its own garden of summer vegetables. Dairy cows were corralled by *dry stane dykes* and pigs confined to their sties, while geese and chickens had the run of the place, squawking and flapping about the congested roadway.

As they headed northwest, one-story cottages gave way to farmlands newly sown with barley. A stiff breeze, tasting of salt, bore down on them. "We'll arrive in Ayr in less than an hour. Keep an eye to the west." Jamie gestured in the general direction of the sea. "The blue outline of Arran should make an appearance shortly. Some say the island looks like a sleeping warrior."

She heard the anticipation in her father's voice and felt it in her spirit as she scanned the western horizon. The only shoreline she'd ever seen was Wigtown Bay at the mouth of the River Cree, a tidal, silt-laden estuary. Nothing like this wide-open view of deep ocean and endless sky.

And then she saw it: the Isle of Arran, a long, rugged silhouette of mountains rising from the sea. Bigger than she'd imagined. Remote and mysterious looking. As if the island were not part of Scotland at all but its own world. *My world.* Just the sight of it made her eyes water and her heart race.

"Come, lass." Her father tugged on her elbow. She'd brought Biddy to a stop without realizing it, her gaze fixed on the horizon. "Tuesday is market day in Ayr. We'll be trampled by cattle if we stand still."

Davina rode on, dodging the flow of people and livestock, trying not to lose sight of the majestic profile jutting from the water. The tallest peaks were hidden by a solitary bank of clouds, as if the island had its own weather. Might that be the case? The outskirts of Ayr closed in round them as they entered the town by way of the Carrick road. Though she craned her neck to catch a glimpse now and again, Arran was finally gone from view.

"You will have your fill when we sail in the morning," Jamie promised her. "For the moment, suppose we find the High Street, the King's Arms, and our dinner, in that order."

The air was thick with the smell of horses and laborers in the summer heat. Merchants and tradesmen lined both sides of the Carrick Vennel, their names boldly painted on crosspieces above the lintel. A carpenter named McClure had his door propped open, sweeping sawdust into the street. Two-wheeled gigs were available for hire from Thomas Brown, and an anvil rang out from Cuthill's blacksmith shop beside it. Coal merchants, ironmongers, and stonemasons added to the riotous din.

Eyes wide in wonder, Davina tried to absorb it all, half listening as her father described the bustling town. She'd visited other royal burghs but none like Ayr. Though Dumfries was larger, she'd been there just once, soon after her accident. Her parents had delivered her to the infirmary, hoping something might be done to restore her voice, only to return home despondent. Davina remembered nothing of Dumfries; she would not soon forget Ayr.

When they reached the High Street and turned west, the scene changed dramatically. The thoroughfare was much wider and the shops taller by another story, each one crowded next to its neighbor without a breath of air between them, save the occasional close. The aroma of freshly baked goods wafted out one open door, the scent of leather through another. Linen drapers filled their windows with bolts of fabric, and confectioners displayed trays of tempting sweets. Perfumers, chandlers, tailors, milliners—Davina's head was spinning.

Her father leaned toward her, raising his voice above the hubbub. "Will we need to stroll the High Street this afternoon?"

How unlike Father to ask a silly question! She nodded with enthusiasm. *Aye, please.*

Davina took note of each establishment before they reached the meal market and the town kirk. When they neared the fish cross, where the daily catch was sold, the smell of seaweed and rotting flounder was almost overpowering.

"Here's the King's Arms," Jamie said as she covered her nose with her new handkerchief. "I'll request a room that faces the River Ayr rather than the street." They could barely reach the entrance for all the carriages and horses milling about. " 'Tis not only an inn but also a posting house," he explained, eying the hectic stables.

When a bright-eyed lad appeared, offering to look after their horses, her father dismounted, then reached up to assist her, a broad smile on his face. "It seems you've arrived, Miss McKie."

Davina slipped her leg from round the pommel and leaned toward him, chagrined to discover she was trembling. So many strange and new experiences! Would she be able to eat a bite or sleep a wink?

Her father lowered her gently to the ground, then brushed the dust from her skirts. "You've no more need for your riding habit," he reminded her, offering his arm, "for the horses will lodge at the King's Arms for a day or two." He gazed at the sky, then started toward the entrance, keeping her close to his side. "With the Almighty's blessing, tomorrow we sail for Arran."

Nineteen

And thou majestic Arran! dearest far
Of all the isles on which the setting sun
In golden glory smiles: Queen of the West
And Daughter of the Waves!
DAVID LANDSBOROUGH

Jamie could not take his eyes off the sight before him: his beautiful daughter, standing on Ayr's north quay, the ribbons on her gown fluttering like a sail, her blue eyes fixed on Arran.

When had Davina grown up? The daughter he carried in his heart was an impish girl of twelve, hiding behind her freckles and her fiddle; this young woman, nigh to eighteen, was confident and poised, boldly taking on the world. Though he knew her apprehensions—employing her sketchbook, she'd inundated him with questions about Arran and the Stewarts through dinner, supper, *and* breakfast—none of those fears showed on her bonny face.

All at once Davina swiveled toward him, drew a circle round her eyes, then pointed at him rather sharply. *You're staring at me.*

"I am," he confessed, and they both smiled. "A father's prerogative. Especially when I'll not see you again 'til Lammas."

The sun had risen hours earlier, long before the citizens of Ayr had thrown back their bedsheets. Yestreen he'd visited with one of the skippers on the Sandgate. Aye, the man had said, Captain Guthrie could offer passage for two on a boat carrying woolen goods to Arran. No proper passenger vessels sailed the Firth of Clyde; Jamie had to make whatever arrangements he could. "O' course, we depend on the wind tae fill *oor* sails," the skipper had cautioned him. "Bring yer dochter tae the *nor* quay at nine, and be prepared tae wait." The man had filled Jamie's ear with stories of traveling parties abandoned on the quay or, worse, stranded for days on a calm sea with few provisions.

Jamie knew little about sailing but plenty about wind, as any man with five thousand sheep on the hills would; the strong gusts against his chest, blowing hard from the southeast, boded well.

Davina touched his arm, then looked inland. The *Clarinda,* a seaworthy vessel bearing a goodly quantity of crates, was headed their way. The bow was high, the stern rounded, and three masts pointed to the cloudless blue skies, the sails still furled to the yards. Half a dozen oarsmen brought the *Clarinda* beside the quay as an able-looking young captain hailed his passengers.

"Walcome aboard, Mr. McKie!" Sun-browned and smiling, Captain Guthrie extended his hand, guiding them onto the boat. The strength in his grip was reassuring; the salacious gaze he cast over Davina, bow to stern, was not.

Jamie slipped a protective arm round her shoulders. "My daughter and I are grateful for the passage."

"An' we're *thankrif* for yer siller." The skipper laughed, and so did his crew. "The wind *wull suin* fill oor sails." He gestured toward the crates. "Hae ye a sit."

Jamie chose the sturdiest crate amidships, where the motion of the boat would be less severe, and sat close to Davina, sending a clear signal to the sailors. He'd paid dearly for this passage—ten shillings apiece—and would not risk the journey costing him a goodly amount more.

Their baggage was brought on board, including Davina's fiddle, which she balanced across her knees. When the oarsmen had rowed clear of the harbor, the captain gave the order to unfurl the sails. Jamie resisted the temptation to ask how long the twenty-mile crossing might take. "Three or four hours," some had said. "A day," warned others.

If a strong wind was needed, that they had. The edges of the square sails shivered as a steady course of waves lashed the sides of the boat, sending a fine spray of seawater over their heads. Davina wore a stalwart countenance, but Jamie saw how tightly she gripped her fiddle. It was impossible to converse without raising his voice, so he rested his hand on hers and looked in the direction of Arran, hoping she would do the same.

The mainland was several miles behind them when one of the oarsmen burst into song in a whisky-soaked tenor, quickly overpowered by the others, each man singing in his own key. Their infectious music, blustery as the wind, brought a smile to Davina's face. Before long she was tapping her feet on the deck. Even Jamie had to restrain himself from singing the second verse.

> If I should sell my fiddle,
> The warld would think I was mad;
> For mony a rantin day
> My fiddle and I hae had.

Davina applauded on the final note, and the sailor who'd started the tune took a courtly bow. Whatever nervousness she'd felt seemed banished to the salty air. Her fiddle was out of its bag in an instant, greeted by the seamen with a roar of approval. Seated amidships, Davina plied her bow with sufficient energy to match theirs, even as the captain barked out orders time and again, directing the crew to trim the sails whenever the wind changed.

"In *anither* hour we'll be *thar*," Captain Guthrie announced, eying Davina. "Ye're walcome on me vessel *oniewise* ye like, miss. As lang as ye bring yer fiddle." He winked. "An' leave yer faither at hame."

"Not likely, Captain." Jamie squared his shoulders, his queasy stomach forgotten, his hackles raised. "My daughter is too young to travel alone."

The skipper stared at him with a quizzical expression. "I was told ye were plannin' tae leave the lass on Arran for twa months."

"Aye, but she'll not be on her own," Jamie argued. "My cousin is the minister of Kilbride parish." He clamped his mouth shut before he said more. Whatever was he doing, discussing private matters with a sailor? *Justifying your decision, Jamie.* Aye, that was the ugly truth of it. Convincing himself he'd not been mistaken in suggesting—nae, insisting upon—this summer excursion in the first place.

Are you certain Davina will be safe? Leana, voicing her concern. *Our sister must be protected.* Will, nagging at him. Jamie yanked his damp coat sleeves in place, trying to hide his irritation. Was he not laird of Glentrool? Did he not know what was best for his children? Davina would learn more on Arran than her lecture-burdened brothers would glean in Edinburgh.

"Lamlash Bay!" the captain hollered, and a general cry went up.

Davina lifted her head, her expression alert, her eyes wide with anticipation as they approached the southeastern coast of Arran, bypassing Whiting Bay for Lamlash with its sheltered harbor, shaped like a crescent moon and protected by an oblong island of its own. Davina gazed toward the dark mass of rock rising a thousand feet from the center of the bay, her face full of questions.

"Holy Isle," Jamie told her, "where Saint Molios once resided as a hermit." The smaller island, no more than five miles round, was ringed in vegetation and covered with heath, surrounded by calmer waters reflecting the gentian blue sky above. He pointed out the large, black-winged birds diving into the water. "Cormorants, looking for dinner."

They were in the bay proper now, the dying winds of little use. Sails were furled, and oars dipped into the water as the seamen pulled hard for the rocky shore. Lamlash Bay looked much as he'd remembered it thirty years earlier. Covered with coarse sand, the uneven coastline was dotted with an odd scattering of enormous boulders. Between them a dozen barelegged lads stood knee deep in the water, fishing poles in hand.

Other vessels were anchored a good distance from the shore, waiting for skiffs to ferry the goods and passengers to safety. Captain Guthrie had his crew row as close as they dared, then he dropped anchor. "We canna run the *Clarinda* aground. Ane o' the *cobles* wull *tak* ye in."

Jamie and Davina stood, helping each other find their balance as they scanned the coastal settlement, little more than a string of stone cottages with heather-thatched roofs. Behind the *kirktoun* the land sloped upward, a sweep of green hills and red sandstone, sheltering the inhabitants to the west as Holy Isle did to the east.

Jamie waited for his daughter's reaction. After the shop-lined High Street of Ayr, was she disappointed to find Arran so primitive and untamed?

Davina turned to him, eyes shimmering, one hand pressed to her heart.

A lump rose in Jamie's throat. "I'm glad you like what you see." He slipped his arm lightly round her waist as they turned toward an approaching skiff.

Jamie hailed the older man rowing steadily toward them. "I'd be much obliged, sir, if you'd deliver us to the manse. Reverend Stewart—"

"Aye, aye." He interrupted Jamie with a wave of his hand. "The minister said tae keep an *e'e* oot for ye. Said ye'd be comin' the first o' June. So it is, and here ye are." Despite his advanced years, the man handled their heavy valises with minimal effort, then assisted father and daughter into his craft. "Hugh McKinnon's the name. Walcome aboard, sir."

The crew of the *Clarinda* seemed reluctant to bid Davina and her fiddle good-bye. When the skiff pulled away, Captain Guthrie doffed his cap, and so did every seaman aboard. Davina waved to them with unbridled enthusiasm, a child again, if only for a brief moment.

Jamie laughed. "Have a care, Davina, or you'll tip our wee boat and have us swimming to shore." She lowered her arm at once, though her bright smile remained as she turned and faced Arran.

Whistling more air than tune, gray-haired Hugh pulled on his oars, drawing them closer to their destination with each stroke. Jamie had no need to look toward shore, for he saw the wonder of Davina's summer home shining in her deep blue eyes.

Twenty

O! Bonny little Arran,
Grand is thy mantle in summer.
TRADITIONAL GAELIC SONG

Davina breathed in the sea-scented air, cool and fresh. Had she dreamed of Arran and awakened to draw a sketch of it, this was precisely the picture her book would have contained: a score of humble cottages close to the shore; low whitecaps breaking on the pebbly coastline; seasoned fishing boats bobbing in the harbor. But only paint and brush could bring the scene to life, for Arran was awash with color: the bluest sky and water, the greenest trees and glens, limned in buttery sunlight and fringed with pink wildflowers.

Tears stung her eyes. Of joy, not sorrow. She heard Arran singing to her, like a suitor beneath her window. *Davina, Davina.* As if the island knew her name and had been holding its breath, waiting for her arrival.

In the *Clarinda,* her father's arm round her waist had felt like a rope tethering her to childhood. Now that the two were seated in the ferryboat, the separation had already begun; her gaze was aimed at Arran, even as he looked toward the mainland. Toward Glentrool. *Good-bye, Father.* She would practice saying it in her heart until she could bring herself to mouth the words and bid him farewell. Davina vowed to hold back her tears, if only to spare her father second thoughts. She had none. Her future was here.

Hugh plied the oars in a steady rhythm, straining as he pulled against the current. "Reverend Stewart an' the lasses wull be waitin' for ye at the manse a mile up the road. But the kirk is o'er thar if ye care tae leuk." He inclined his head toward a sizable building to the south, facing the bay. Without steeple, belfry, or vestry, it was as plain as the wooden box that held the family Bible.

" 'Twas new when I visited last," Jamie told him, glancing over his shoulder.

"Aye, whan Gershom Stewart was minister." Hugh grunted with another pull of the oars. "Back whan they still buried *fowk* on Halie Isle. Not lang after, a boat was ferryin' a funeral party o'er the water whan a squall o' wind turned o'er the boat." He shook his head. "God preserve us! Seven fowk *droondit* on their *wey* tae a burial."

The men's conversation faded to the low drone of a bagpipe, while Davina overheard a small knot of women speaking to one another on the shore. Her heart began to pound as their high-pitched voices carried across the water. Though she wrote fluently in French and had little trouble translating Latin, she knew nothing of Gaelic, the native language of the Scottish Highlands and islands. Over supper, Father had told her many folk would speak English as well, but all would speak Gaelic. "Do not fret, lass. Your cousins will interpret for you." He'd smiled at her across his plate of haddock. "I believe the parishioners of Kilbride will learn *your* language by summer's end."

She smiled now, remembering his words. The longer she listened, the more the women's blithe chatter simply became another chorus of the song that was Arran.

"Mrs. Stewart asked me tae bring ye *stracht* tae the manse," Hugh said, lifting his oars from the water. Unlike the harbor at Ayr, Lamlash Bay had no proper pier extending far into the water. Instead he eased their skiff into a rustic quay. "Mind yer step, for 'tis *slitterie*."

Davina appraised the narrow, sea-washed stair leading to the solid ground above, then gamely stepped out, clasping her father's hand as they slowly climbed the steps sideways.

Hugh followed her, steadying hands at the ready. "Ane *mair*, Miss McKie, an' ye'll be oot o' danger." When she had landed safely, he returned to the skiff, then handed up her fiddle and the two valises. Her father offered to carry one, but Hugh would not hear of it. "I'm at yer service, sir."

Davina admired Holy Isle from her new vantage point. A rounded peak in the center, with ledges on either side, the bay island looked quite different from shore. Closer, as if she might sprint across the water and touch land without soaking her hem.

"Miss McKie, may I escort you to your new home?" Jamie smiled, but she saw the sadness lingering in his eyes.

Good-bye, Father. Could she truly say the words without weeping? Two months was a very long time.

Davina took his arm and discreetly examined her gown as they began to walk. She'd chosen a moss green linen for the crossing, hoping any stains or wrinkles would not show, wanting to make a good impression on her cousins.

"Very distant relations," her father was saying to Hugh. "On my mother's side. Though it might take pen and paper to sort it all out."

The track ran parallel with the shore for a bit, then veered sharply left, turning its back on the sea. Hugh grunted as they started up a steep rise. "Ye'll find a warm walcome here. The lasses are aflocht tae think o' meetin' Miss McKie." After a bit Hugh swung her valise toward the right, leading them down a narrow lane. "The auld Saint Bride Chapel is here. Naught but ruins *noo.*"

They soon came upon a broad expanse of glebe on the slope of a hill, encompassing the decrepit remains of a once-proud sanctuary. In the old kirkyard scores of lichen-covered gravestones leaned this way and that, sunken with age. To the east stood a two-story house of stone and lime, oblong in shape and unadorned in design. A chimney rose from each end, curtainless windows faced the bay, and a path of crushed mussel shells led to the entrance.

The front door was propped open, beckoning visitors within, and the aroma of cooked beef greeted them. "Ye've come at the richt time." Hugh went ahead of them, quickening his steps. "Wull ye be wantin' me tae find yer passage back, Mr. McKie? I ken most o' the skippers an' can *mak* inquiries. After ye hae yer *denner,* o' course."

"The Lord bless you for handling those arrangements, Hugh." Jamie pressed some coins into the man's hand. "And I'm indeed ready for a hot meal. How many hours has it been since our porridge at the King's Arms, Davina?"

She patted the watch in his pocket, for she could not guess. Had they breakfasted in Ayr only that morning? It seemed days ago. Her heart was racing by the time Hugh knocked on the doorpost.

The minister was the first to appear in the shallow entrance hall, a smile on his brown-bearded face. Not as tall as her father, nor as fit, Benjamin Stewart was harmless looking, like a large, friendly dog. "They're here, Mrs. Stewart," he called, walking forward with his hand outstretched.

A black-haired maid suddenly ducked in front of him and curtsied, her cheeks the color of wild strawberries. "Beggin' yer pardon, Reverend. I didna hear them knock."

"Not to worry, Betty." His smile broadened. "Our guests are family members and may forgive our informality. Cousin Jamie, can it really be you?" The men shook hands warmly as Hugh ducked past them to deposit the baggage in the hall, then took his leave.

Reverend Stewart turned his attention to Davina. "So this is your daughter. Even more fair than her mother described her, I see." He bowed, then stepped back, making room for them to enter. "Welcome to the manse, Cousin Davina."

She curtsied, still holding her fiddle, then moved inside the house. An awkward moment followed when the minister stared at her as if waiting for a response, then said in a louder voice, "Well! Here you are, then." He looked round him, a ruddy tint above his beard. "Ah…Mrs. Stewart."

His wife scurried into the hall, a softly rounded woman with bright eyes and an eager manner. "Look what a wee thing she is!" She pulled Davina into the room with both hands. "A fairy from the glen come to the manse. Oh, and she brought her music with her. How glad we are to have you, lass."

Davina curtsied again, then entrusted her fiddle to Elspeth Stewart, who placed it on a sturdy table amid a stack of books. The parlor was small, made more so by the abundance of chairs and the scarcity of candles to brighten the dim corners. A dyed wool rug the color of port warmed the stone floor, and light gray paint covered the walls, where an indifferent still life was the only decorative piece. Still, the room was clean and well kept, the simple furnishings in good repair. Two glazed windows would afford her a glimpse of the sparkling blue sea and a taste of the salty air.

Elspeth took her arm and steered her to one of the upholstered chairs with exaggerated care, as if Davina were blind as well as mute. "Come and sit, for you must be weary. I always feel a bit unsteady after a sail." Dressed in a bleached muslin gown, her light brown hair pulled into a tight knot, the minister's wife had more color in her blue eyes than anywhere else on her person. She sent Betty to fetch their tea, then sat next to Davina, studying her so closely that Davina averted her gaze. Would her younger cousins be this curious?

When she heard the men entering the room, she glanced toward her father. Something must have shown on her face, for when his eyes met hers, one question was clear. *Will you be content here?*

On my bonny Arran? Davina made certain he saw her answer. *Aye, Father. More than content.*

Twenty-One

Farewell! a word that must be, and hath been—
A sound which makes us linger;—yet—farewell!
GEORGE GORDON, LORD BYRON

M ay we persuade you to tarry for a few days, Cousin Jamie?" Benjamin sat, then leaned forward in his wing chair, his expression as heartfelt as his words. "Or must you return to the mainland at once?"

Please stay, Father. Nae, go. Davina looked down at her hands lest he discern her thoughts. How strange to feel so torn, wanting her father's company yet longing to be on her own.

"If there's a fishing boat that will take me, I'd best claim it, for I'm told they are as unpredictable as the weather." He paused, as if waiting for her to look up, perhaps to assure him that he was free to depart. "I've left Glentrool in my son's capable hands, but when the sheep shearing begins—"

"Aye, say no more." The minister held up his hand, stemming Jamie's explanation. "I've a pastoral flock of my own that needs constant tending. Though at least not fleecing, eh, Cousin?"

Her father seemed relaxed as the two men swapped memories from the McKies' only visit to Arran. "I was a lad of ten," Benjamin reminded him, "and much impressed with my older cousins. We climbed Goatfell, the three of us. Was it you or Evan that reached the summit first?"

"Evan." Her father shifted in his chair. "But I was close on his heels and dragged him behind me to claim first place."

"Always rivals, the two of you," Benjamin said good-naturedly. "We last heard from Evan and Judith"—he looked to his wife—"at Eastertide, wasn't it?"

"Aye. She writes with a fine hand, Judith does."

Betty swept into the room with tea on a plain wooden tray, putting a temporary end to their conversation as each was served a steaming cup. "Denner wull be ready shortly, *mem*," the maidservant said before taking her leave.

"So, Davina," Elspeth began, "I pray you are as eager to meet my daughters as they are to meet you." When Davina nodded, her cousin continued, "I expect them any moment. They went to Clauchlands farm to fetch more eggs, for our hens are not laying well of late."

Davina envied her cousins' having neighbors so close. In the remote glen of Loch Trool, borrowing eggs would require a two-hour walk.

She'd taken her first tentative sip of tea when the door flew open and two girls burst into the room. "Och! We *did* miss greeting her."

"And after running all the way home," the younger one groaned, handing Betty a willow basket before both of them offered a tardy curtsy.

Jamie stood and their father as well. "Catherine, Abigail, come meet your cousins: Mr. James McKie, and his daughter, Miss Davina McKie."

As they found their seats, Davina quickly put aside her preconceived notions. The Stewart sisters were nothing like she'd imagined. Younger and less polished. Taller with ample figures like their mother's. And full of energy.

"I prefer the name Cate," her cousin insisted, her light brown curls escaping their pins to dangle about her round cheeks. "Catherine suits a queen, not a minister's daughter. Though Davina quite fits you," she added with an endearing smile, "for aren't you bonny enough to sit on a throne?"

"Aye," her sister said with a giggle, "you are that. And I am Abigail only to my papa. My friends call me Abbie."

Davina smiled and nodded across her teacup. Who could find fault with such affable, unpretentious girls? If they were concerned about her lack of speech, the sisters did not show it. They launched into an entertaining account of their errand to Clauchlands farm while their mother poured their tea, then excused herself and hurried off to the kitchen.

"Tell me about your summer plans for my daughter," Jamie asked, sharing a smile with Davina. "She will see some of the island, I hope."

"Oh, as much of Arran as she wishes!" Cate said, her color rising with her enthusiasm. "We'll begin this afternoon, for the weather is quite fine. And we've friends in every cottage in Kilbride parish who'll be pleased to make her acquaintance."

An older woman wearing a cap and apron appeared at the door.

Reverend Stewart greeted her with a nod. "Thank you, Mrs. McCurdy. Dinner is served."

With the housekeeper leading the way, they crossed the hall and were soon seated in the informal dining room, as small and dark as the parlor. Two windows illuminated the room, along with a cluster of candles in the center of the rectangular dining table, which was draped in a printed cloth. The table easily accommodated the six of them, with the men in chairs at either end and the women perched on benches. A hearty meal of nettle soup and veal collops was blessed and served. Davina was too nervous to eat, but her father practically picked up his soup dish and drank, so swiftly did he drain his portion. Mrs. McCurdy also served the household as cook, keeping them well supplied with dishes of roasted potatoes and onions.

The Stewarts were a lively family at table, the minister regaling his guests with Arran lore, his daughters prompting him whenever he omitted important details. He told of an *etin* named Scorri, who was chased by the men of neighboring Kilmory parish; when the giant fell, he created Glen Scorradale, where the Sliddery Water flows. Then he described the night a smack was crossing to Ireland from the western shore, sinking low in the water from the weight of its unusual passengers: All the fairies of Arran were departing, the island having become too holy for them to remain.

"I believe one of them came back," Abbie said, grinning at Davina.

The moment Mrs. McCurdy presented the gathering with a baked almond tart, Betty ushered Hugh McKinnon through the door, his hat in his hands.

"Beg pardon for interruptin' yer denner, Reverend." His contrite expression was apology enough. "I've jist come from the quay. Thar's a fishin' boat wi' room for Mr. McKie aboot tae sail for Ayr. I fear thar wull not be anither for a day or twa."

Davina's breath caught. *So soon, Father?*

"Forgive me." Jamie dabbed his mouth with his linen. "How impolite of me to quit the table when pudding has just been served."

"Nae, you must go when you can." Reverend Stewart stood first, making it easier for Jamie to take his leave. "Let me see you to the door. Perhaps Davina would like to send you off as well?"

She rose on trembling legs, wishing she had her sketchbook in hand so she might write all that was on her heart. *I love you, Father. I will miss you very much.* An hour ago she had been prepared to bid him goodbye. Now she could not even think the word, let alone write it. *Must you go? And leave me behind?*

Hugh was waiting on the lawn, his hat back in place. "Ye dinna hae flat feet, d'ye, Mr. McKie? Fishermen canna abide a *sclaff-fittit* passenger. 'Tis *unchancie*, ye ken."

"Not to worry," Jamie assured him, doing little to hide his smile. "My arches are sufficiently high. I'll not bring the men ill luck."

The male cousins shook hands once more. "Godspeed." Benjamin seemed genuinely sorry to see Jamie leave. "When you return at Lammas, bide a wee while, aye?"

Lammas. She pressed her hands to her stomach, glad she'd not eaten much veal. *Such a long time away.*

"I shall look forward to my return," Jamie promised. As the minister stepped back, her father turned toward her, holding out his arms, a tender expression on his face. "Davina?"

She fell into his embrace. *Oh, Father.* Though she squeezed her eyes shut, she could not stop her tears. *Who will ever care for me as you do?*

Jamie held her against his chest, smoothing his hand over her hair. "Two months, my darling daughter." His voice was low, edged with emotion. "Then I will come for you. And make things right with your brothers. Depend upon it."

Twenty-Two

And life is thorny, and youth is vain;
And to be wroth with one we love
Doth work like madness in the brain.
SAMUEL T. COLERIDGE

They'll soon be banging the ten o'clock drum, lad."
Will lifted his pewter tappit-hen, eying Sandy across the tavern table. "And when they do, I'll be drinking John Dowie's ale, and so will you." Above him tallow candles sputtered in a wooden chandelier, the yellow light reflected in the polished drinking vessels lining the shelves and hanging from wall hooks. Plates scraped clean of toasted cheese and beef tripe waited to be collected from their table.

Parliamentarians and antiquaries, lawyers and booksellers alike convened nightly at the tavern by West Saint Giles. Will's gaze circled the small room, noting the patrons fishing out their watches and wiping the last drop of ale from their mouths. Let the rest of the town toddle home to bed at the sound of the drum. His night had only begun.

"O Dowie's ale! thou art the thing," Will sang to himself before swallowing another mouthful. Some said Edinburgh ale was so potent it could glue a drinker's lips together. Will insisted if he could still sing, he could still drink. He slapped his waistcoat to be certain his purse was where it belonged. *Aye.* Plenty of silver for a serious debauch.

Sandy wagged his head, half smiling. "Auld Reekie's sons blithe faces wear."

"Aye, don't they just?" Will downed another long swallow, the folded letter from home still clutched in his left hand. He'd almost thrust it into the candle flame twice, then stopped when his gaze fell on the address written in their mother's elegant hand. *William and Alexander McKie, College Wynd, Edinburgh.*

He could not fault her for the letter's *hatesome* contents. The blame rested squarely on Jamie McKie's broad shoulders. *Your father has arranged for Davina to spend the summer with our cousins, the Stewarts, on the Isle of Arran.*

"Arranged," Will muttered, taking a final swig before banging the empty tappit-hen on the table with a noisy clink of its ornamented lid. "The same way Father arranged for us to move to Edinburgh, I suppose. Does the man never tire of playing God?"

Sandy rose, weaving only slightly as he reached for the pewter tankards. "Perhaps Davina wanted to go to Arran. Have you thought of that?" He went off in search of fresh ale, leaving Will to stare at the dying coal fire and contemplate a response.

Did you want this, lass? The news would be easier to bear if she'd chosen to go. Yet, even if she did relish a visit to the island, Davina was not the issue. 'Twas Father's broken promise that rankled. "How can you watch over our sister," Will growled under his breath, "when she's on an island days away from Glentrool?"

He unfolded the letter again, punishing himself with yet another reading. *I trust you are finding your place in Edinburgh.* Will scanned the smoky, windowless room—one of several in the busy tavern—certain this was not the place his mother meant. He read on. *Glentrool is woefully empty without my twin sons.* At least Mother missed them. No mention of Father or Ian in that regard. *Your older brother continues to court Miss McMillan.* Will snorted at that. Once Ian married and produced an heir, there would be no hope of *heirship* for him or for Sandy. *Now that June is here, the gardens are lovely.* That comment eased his ire a bit, picturing his mother with an apron full of colorful blooms.

But then came the fateful line that ruined everything, *Your father has arranged for Davina to spend the summer...* Two long months without one of the McKie men to guard the lass, to escort her safely about, to keep her from harm. Who were these Stewarts of Arran? Will could not recall hearing much spoken of them. Was there a strong enough man among them, one worthy of the task?

Nae. He alone knew what was best for his sister.

Will creased the folds with a rough hand, nearly tearing the stationery in the process. His mother's words were still emblazoned on his mind. *Your father has arranged...*

The letter had arrived in the afternoon post. After a single reading, he and Sandy had marched up the Cowgate, bound for John Dowie's in Libberton's Wynd, intending to feed their hostility with black pudding and drown their anger in ale. Sandy had been marginally successful, growing more philosophical by the hour. *Perhaps Davina wanted to go.*

"Hech!" Will dragged a hand across his jaw, rough with beard stubble, trying to remember if he'd shaved that morning. After a month without a valet, the two of them had become lax in their grooming. The professors did not notice, and the lasses did not care.

I fear our sister will have a lonely summer without us.

Will abruptly sat up, banging his head on the wall behind him. He rubbed the back of his scalp, cursing himself for his carelessness.

"'Tis my fault," he told Sandy when his brother returned, tappithens in hand. "*I* am the fool who mentioned to Father that our sister would be miserable this summer." Will slumped in his chair, stung by the realization. "He never would have packed Davina off to Arran if I hadn't made so daft a statement."

"You don't know that, Will."

"Aye, but I do!" he roared, eliciting a stern glance from a gentleman whose head poked out from behind a brown paper screen meant to offer a measure of privacy. Lowering his voice slightly, Will said through clenched teeth, "The laird of Glentrool takes pleasure in ordering his offspring about."

Sandy toyed with the lid of his tankard. "He also was pleased to pay for our tuition and fill our wardrobe with new clothes and line our pockets with silver."

Will swore. "You're on his side now, is that it?"

"You know better," Sandy said evenly. "Father was purchasing our forgiveness, nothing more."

"An odd turn of events when 'tis he who has yet to forgive us. Ten years, Sandy. *Ten years.*"

His brother shrugged as if weary of the subject. "Drink your ale. If we tarry much longer, we'll find naught on the dark streets but thieves picking our pockets or *limmers* raising their skirts."

Will downed the balance of his drink, half standing as he did. "We must write to her, you know." The tappit-hen landed hard, another outlet for his frustration. "A long letter. Tomorrow after Professor Gregory's lecture."

Sandy frowned at him. "Write to Mother, do you mean? Or to Davina?"

"Both," Will shot back, then curbed his anger. Sandy was not to blame, not for a moment. "We'll write Mother to thank her for her letter. Without it, we'd have no knowledge of Father's negligence. And then we'll write Davina to pledge our devotion to her, even from so great a distance."

"Should we not write to Father?"

"*Oo aye,*" Will growled. "As soon as ever he writes us."

Twenty-Three

Up the airy mountain,
Down the rushy glen,
We daren't go a-hunting,
For fear of little men.

WILLIAM ALLINGHAM

en days, Davina!" With an artless sigh, Abbie dropped beside her
on the low stone monument. "Ten days and you've almost filled
the pages of your sketchbook."

Davina smiled as she retied the broad silk ribbons of her straw bonnet, grateful for the elongated front brim that protected her complexion
from the sun. The morning had been delightfully dry, though each day
on Arran offered a variety of weather: rain, clouds, sun, wind, and always
a hopeful patch of blue.

Abbie burst into rhyme, "'Barnaby bright! Barnaby bright! The
longest day and the shortest night.' Though this *is* Saint Barnabas's Day,
'tis not the longest day of the year anymore. Not since they added twelve
days to the calendar all at once." She groaned dramatically. "What a
nuisance that must have been for our grandfathers!"

Davina simply listened, more aware than ever of the difference in
their ages. Was she this childlike at fourteen, skipping across lawns,
throwing herself about? *Aye, and sometimes still.* She blushed at the
thought, for indeed the Stewart sisters brought out an aspect of her
nature she'd thought relegated to the nursery. Under their playful influence, Davina had clapped her hands, spun round on her toes, and
danced over the Clauchland hills with joyous abandon. No wonder they
thought she was a fairy come back to Arran.

She flipped through her sketchbook until she located a drawing finished earlier that week, then held it out for Abbie's approval.

"Sakes me!" The younger sister peered at the page, her brown curls bouncing as she shook her head in disbelief. "Wherever did you see the wee folk?"

Davina winked and pointed to her head. *Only in here, lass.* Her fanciful drawing showed a mischievous creature poised on a rock, her rose-petal gown outlining a lithe body, her gossamer wings unfurled. A daft notion, nothing more.

Abbie looked over her shoulder toward the manse, then whispered, "Betty thinks you truly *are* a fairy. She says you glide rather than walk. And that all fairies play musical instruments, though none perhaps as well as you, Cousin."

Once they'd heard Davina play, the Stewarts did not let an evening end without an hour of tunes round the hearth. And if guests appeared at the door, they were presented with Davina and her fiddle more quickly than they were served tea.

Abbie eyed the house again. "Have you noticed the tiny bells Betty carries in her apron pocket? They're meant for protection."

From me? Davina looked at her in astonishment.

"You see, those who've lived on Arran for generations respect—aye, even fear—the *sith.*" When Davina wrinkled her brow at the word, Abbie explained, " 'Tis Gaelic for 'fairy.' The sith dance on a *sithean,* a fairy hill, which is why the farmers in our parish plow with care, so they won't disturb them."

Davina had already been introduced to numerous examples on their daily walks. Helen Murchie showed her a moss-covered mound in her garden. Ivy Sillar pointed to a flat-topped stone rising from the burn behind her cottage. A perfect circle of bluebells grew on Sarah McCook's lawn. And on the hill above Peg Pettigrew's farm stood a sheltering hawthorn tree, bent by the wind.

Davina had responded to each neighbor's proud discovery with a look of interest; now she wondered if they expected her to return at midnight for a round of dancing.

Abbie averted her gaze. "You'll forgive me for saying so, but most fairies have a physical…well, a deformity that makes them…different."

Ah. Davina touched Abbie's hand, hoping to put the girl at ease.

Though her parents had shared a few details in advance, the topic of her muteness had not been broached since her arrival.

"I'm sorry." Abbie still could not look in her direction. "I should not have…"

Davina quickly wrote across a blank page. *Please do not apologize. I lost my voice when I was seven. An accident.* To temper the harsh truth, she added, *No fairies were present.*

When Abbie read the words, a sad smile crossed her lips. "Cate and I have grown exceedingly fond of you." Her eyes shimmered in the morning sunlight. "We are certain you had a sweet voice."

Touched, Davina wrote, *My father insists I sounded like my fiddle.*

"Oh, your *father!*" As if glad for a change in subject, Abbie sat up, hands clasped beneath her chin like a red squirrel with a newfound acorn. "What a fine-looking man. Though quite old, of course. Are your brothers half so braw?"

Davina pictured the three of them and answered with a broad smile. *Aye.*

Abbie said, "Too bad *they* won't be coming to take you home," then she blushed to her light brown roots. "Well…ah…show me what you are drawing now."

Nodding toward the crumbling east wall of the auld stone kirk, Davina turned to a fresh page and began to sketch the square carving before her. Within the raised edge was an old crown, the year 1618, and in large letters a stern admonishment: FIR GOD.

Abbie rolled her eyes. "Surely they meant to write '*Fear* God.'" She hopped to her feet a moment later. "I'll leave you to your sketching. Cate should be home from the Kelsos' soon, and Mrs. McCurdy has promised salmon fritters for dinner." Abbie set off for the house, humming a lilting air Davina had played yestreen.

A capricious breeze fluttered her pages whenever she lifted her pencil, making it difficult to sketch. When another gust nearly closed the book on her fingers, Davina gave up drawing and thumbed through some of her artwork from two months past. Her mother's cherished roses. Grandmother's rowan. The corner of the garden where she'd weeded with her mother, waiting for Father to return from Edinburgh, and the words she'd written that afternoon. *I look forward to our summer together.* Instead they were spending the summer far apart, all of them.

Davina quickly turned the page before a wave of homesickness washed over her.

Ah. The perfect antidote. She looked down at the page with the thumb-worn corners and smiled at the thickness of his wavy hair, the generous shape of his mouth, the firm jut of his chin. Dreaming of him was no longer necessary, not when he lived in her thoughts and in her sketchbook, ever close at hand.

"There you are, Davina!" Cate came flying across the lawn, her eyes shining with excitement.

Startled, Davina closed her sketchbook in haste and stood, trying not to look guilty.

Cate clasped her free hand and squeezed it tight, so out of breath she had to gasp between words. "I have the most…wonderful news! Guess who'll arrive…on Arran…Tuesday next?"

Twenty-Four

O, what are you waiting for here? young man!
JAMES THOMSON

"Y ou did say Tuesday at noon, Mr. McKie?"

"Indeed I did." Jamie stood, greeting the younger gentleman with a bow, while the mantel clock in the drawing room struck the hour.

Graham Webster bowed as well, his smile wreathed in a closely trimmed auburn beard. Before Jamie could offer him a seat, Graham drew a letter from his waistcoat pocket. "I traveled by way of Monnigaff this morning, and among the mail waiting at the inn was this post for Glentrool. I took the liberty of paying the postage. I trust you'll forgive me for handling your letter."

"Nothing to forgive when you did me a kind service." He reached for his coin purse. "May I reimburse you?"

"Think nothing of it, sir."

"Much obliged." Jamie noticed three things as he placed the letter on the tea tray: The postmark was *Edinburgh,* the writing was Will's, and the address was *Mrs.* James McKie. "How was the weather for your ride, Mr. Webster?"

Quiet and unassuming, Graham Webster had not exchanged a dozen words with Jamie in the last year, yet his reputation spoke for him. Honest in his dealings, well mannered and well traveled, he was a fine shot and a good horseman. And handsome, according to the women of the household. Jamie paid no attention to such things, though he did notice the man was no longer wearing the black armband of a grieving widower.

"A stiff westerly breeze escorted me through the glen," Graham said as Jamie offered him an upholstered chair, the most comfortable in the room.

"I know the value of a brisk wind, having sailed from Arran a fortnight ago." They both sat, a small table positioned between them in anticipation of tea. "If not for a hard wind blowing from the west, we might still be paddling our way to Ayr."

Graham's expression, always sincere, grew more so. "Miss McKie is enjoying her stay on the island, I trust?"

Jamie had been asked the same question—on the Sabbath, at market, in the village—countless times since returning home. "She is keeping quite busy," he began, then motioned Jenny forward with her tea tray. "We received a letter last week describing her adventures on Arran. Frequent visiting of parish cottages and farms, apparently, and rambles over the hills and glens."

The moment his tea was poured and milk added, Graham took a lengthy sip, no doubt parched after the eight-mile ride from his estate in neighboring Penningham parish. "Your daughter is expected home at Lammas?"

"Aye." Jamie sensed something lurking behind the young widower's question. Was he making polite conversation or a pointed inquiry? To his knowledge, Graham Webster had courted no one since his wife's passing, not even after his year of mourning had ended. Surely the proprietor of Penningham Hall had no interest in Davina. The lass was but seventeen.

Jamie studied him more closely. "You've come to discuss a purchase of sheep, I believe."

"Aye, sir. Sheep." Graham cleared his throat. "As my property rests on the banks of the Cree with woods to the south, hills to the west, and moss to the north, I've not much grazing land, but I'm keen to have a healthy flock of blackface." His smile was genuine, if a bit strained. "I saw no need to look further than Glentrool, renowned for its fine breeding."

Jamie acknowledged his compliment with a nod. "I'll tell Rab you said so." Mr. Webster had more than sheep on his mind; no gentleman fiddled with his shirt cuffs over livestock. "We had particularly fine lambs born three springs ago. The flocks are freshly sheared and will be ready for market in another few weeks. I'd be pleased to have my herds deliver twentyscore to Penningham."

"Begging your pardon, Mr. McKie, but fivescore was what I had in mind." Graham spread out his hands in apology. " 'Tis not the expense, mind you, but the limitations of my property. Until I have more land cleared…"

"Fivescore it is, then. Shall we say…sixty pounds?" Though an honest price, Jamie waited for a lesser offer, which any canny Scotsman would extend. Unless the buyer, however competent, was interested in the seller's daughter.

Graham agreed to the full price at once. "Sixty pounds sterling it is. My factor will arrange things."

" 'Tis done, then, Mr. Webster." Jamie had to drink his tea to keep from grimacing. Would Davina be his next order of business?

"Sir, I do wish you'd call me Graham."

"Fine." Jamie uncrossed his legs. "Now, if we're quite finished—"

"How nice to see you, Mr. Webster." Leana stepped into the drawing room, curtsying as both men stood. "I hope you will join us for dinner. Though our noontide meals are less elaborate, Aubert assures me you'll not taste better veal flory on the Continent."

"It's been a decade since I visited Florence, Mrs. McKie. I will no doubt find your cook's veal pie far superior."

Jamie followed his guest into the dining room, more convinced than ever of Graham's intentions: Visitors were expected to refuse a meal at least once, if not twice, until pressed into staying by their host; this young man had not hesitated for a second.

A genial guest, Graham consumed proper quantities of every offering, praised their hospitality after each course, and extended an invitation for dinner at Penningham Hall at the McKies' earliest convenience.

"Is it your wish that our daughter be included?" Jamie asked, gauging his reaction. "And our son Ian?"

Graham remained cooler than he expected. "By all means, sir."

As they reclaimed their chairs in the drawing room for sherry and biscuits, Leana said, "Mr. Webster, I believe you have just celebrated a birthday."

Graham accepted a glass of sherry. "Aye, my thirtieth. On Thursday last."

"My housekeeper and yours spoke in the kirkyard on the Sabbath," Leana explained. "I hope you'll forgive the mention of something so personal, but thirty years is significant. A time when one evaluates what has been and considers what will be."

"I quite agree, Mrs. McKie." Graham watched the maidservant curtsy and close the drawing room door, then positioned himself so he faced them both. "In the process of evaluating my future, I have come to realize that I will most honor my wife's memory by marrying again."

"How wise you are," Leana said softly. "Do you have a young lady in mind, sir?"

"I do," he confessed, putting his glass aside. "Your daughter."

Twenty-Five

Guilt is present in the very hesitation,
even though the deed be not committed.

CICERO

Jamie swallowed the myriad objections that threatened to choke him, except one. "Davina is too young."

Graham held up his hands, a gesture of surrender. "I am in no hurry and will gladly court her for however long you deem appropriate. Your daughter's youthful innocence—her purity, if you will—is part of her charm."

"You do know…" Leana wet her lips. "You do understand…"

"Aye." Graham spared her the rest. "I remember when the accident happened. My wife and I were newly wed. Davina…ah, Miss McKie… had strewn rose petals from your garden across the kirk step on our wedding day. A few weeks later…" Sympathy shone in his eyes. "I cannot imagine your suffering."

Jamie started to say, *'Twas the worst day of our lives,* then held his tongue. *Thou shalt not tempt the Lord thy God.*

"I know what the physicians have said," Graham continued, "but your *loosome* daughter is whole in every way that matters. You can be certain her many gifts and talents would be appreciated at Penningham Hall. I do not…" His strong voice faltered at last. "I do not fool myself that she bears any affection for me, yet I can assure you that I would love and cherish her completely."

Jamie stared at Graham's hands, larger than his own. Felt his stomach clench at the thought of those hands on his daughter. He listened to the man recount Davina's many fine attributes—all the praiseworthy comments a father might want to hear—yet he could not bring himself to smile and nod and affirm and agree when everything inside him wanted to scream in protest. *Nae! Not yet. Not ever.*

Ashamed of his reaction, Jamie forced himself to ask in as civil a tongue as he could, "Is Davina aware of your interest?"

"Not to my knowledge, Mr. McKie. I wanted your permission before even approaching her."

Jamie shot to his feet, irritated by Graham's thoughtfulness. The man had no faults whatsoever. Except his desire to woo Davina.

"We will discuss the matter with our daughter," Jamie said, looking down at him more sternly than necessary. "Nothing is agreed upon until we are certain of her willingness to be courted. And even then, sir, you will proceed slowly."

Graham stood, and their eyes met. "I will respect whatever decision you and your family reach. Kindly inform me when that time comes." He stepped back and bowed. "Mrs. McKie, Mr. McKie, thank you for your indulgence."

Leana, ever the gracious hostess, saw him to the door, leaving Jamie to pace the carpet, more annoyed with himself than he was with Graham. He had known this day would come. Why did it unnerve him so?

When Leana returned, she hastened to his side. "Jamie, whatever is the matter?" She landed on the embroidered settee, then gently pulled him down beside her. " 'Tis not like you to be so short with a neighbor. Graham Webster is a trustworthy gentleman of good repute. He is perhaps more reserved than Davina might choose, yet he is in all ways honorable, considerate, dependable, a man of means—"

"She is too young," Jamie said again. Did he have no other rightful complaint? "I will not make any promises on her behalf when she is not here to offer an opinion."

"Exactly what a good father should do." Leana's voice was as soothing as his was strident. "Shall I at least write Davina? Tell her of Mr. Webster's interest?"

"Nae," Jamie said, then searched for a valid reason. "Such things are best discussed in person." He met her gaze, wanting to be sure she understood him. "Graham said he is in no hurry. I prefer that we not be either."

Leana sighed more heavily than usual. "Very well. Though I believe Davina would want to know. Now, while she is on Arran."

To what end? Jamie swallowed the words, refusing to let his irritation get the upper hand. "Davina can do nothing with the information except to fret over it." He took Leana's hands in his, thinking his touch might assuage her. "I have asked Graham to wait, Leana. I'm asking you to do the same. When Davina comes home, we will consider his offer. Together."

She nodded absently, then looked off to the side. "When did a letter arrive?"

Och! He'd forgotten the post from Will. "Graham brought it from Monnigaff." He stood long enough to slide the letter from the tea table, then sat again and placed it in her hands. " 'Tis addressed to you."

"In Will's hand, I see." Her fingers shook as she opened it. "I wrote to the twins when Davina left for Arran—"

"And told them what?"

"That you'd arranged for Davina to spend the summer with the Stewarts. That I missed them. That Ian was still courting Margaret." With the letter unfolded, she gave him a puzzled look. "Jamie, what is it? Should I not have written to our sons?"

"Nae, nae." He brushed his hand through the air as if frustration were candle smoke, easily dissipated. "Naturally you should write to them. Now then, what does Will have to say?" He leaned back, trying to relax, trying to ignore the fact that the letter was not addressed to him.

She scanned the page in silence, her skin growing paler, and her eyes filling with tears. "Will is unhappy with me."

"Unhappy with *you?*" Jamie tugged the letter from her grasp. There were only a few lines. Will's bold handwriting quickly covered the paper, and he'd wasted no time on pleasantries.

> Mother, we are deeply grieved to learn that Davina is visiting
> Arran without a chaperon and are surprised that you allowed it.

"A *chaperon?*" Jamie huffed. "Benjamin Stewart is the parish minister. Our daughter could not have a better escort."

> We will not rest until we have heard from Davina herself
> and are assured of her well-being. Father should never have

suggested so perilous a journey. We pray he will not live to regret it.

Jamie folded the letter, understanding what his sensitive wife did not. "Will and Sandy are unhappy with *me*, Leana. Not you." He kissed her brow, hoping to ease the furrows there. "I alone am responsible for Davina's summer on Arran."

"Then I, too, pray you'll not regret your decision, Jamie."

Her words, though spoken softly, pierced him to the core. Was there some way to convince her that he cared about their children's welfare just as she did?

Jamie placed his hand beneath her chin, lifting it until their eyes met. "Leana, you need to know that Davina and I had a…conversation, of sorts. About the twins."

She listened, hope rising in her eyes like the sun, as he described his plans to speak with Will and Sandy when they returned at Lammas. "We have snarled at one another like ill-tempered dogs long enough. 'Tis time we spoke as men."

Leana smiled at him through her tears. "Nothing could make me happier, Jamie."

"You have no doubt been praying for this for years."

"Ten years, to be precise." She eyed the letter in his hands. "But must you wait until Lammas? Why not ride to Edinburgh now? Put to rest their fears about Davina and settle your own differences as well. Please, Jamie, will you consider it? I do not wish to lose your company for a week, but think what your efforts might mean to the twins."

He looked away, feeling trapped for the second time that day—first by Graham, now by Leana. Could he not handle his children according to his own schedule?

"Surely their tempers have cooled since they wrote you," Jamie said, convincing himself, if not his wife. "And Davina has no doubt written them as well, easing their concerns." He smiled at her, deliberately at first, then with increasing sincerity as she slowly returned his smile. "That's better," he said, relieved to have Leana's support. "Now suppose we let summer take its course."

Twenty-Six

I have heard say that in Arrane
In a strong castle made of stane
An Englishman with a strong hand
Holds the lordship of that land.
SIR JAMES DOUGLAS

He visits the castle every summer," Abbie said, "for a fortnight or more."

"We can never be sure when," Cate cautioned, "though the news travels quickly. His guests include the finest families in Scotland."

Davina turned first to one cousin, then the other, as arm in arm the trio made its way north toward Brodick Bay. Their intent was to reconnoiter the castle, like British soldiers crossing the French border, seeking information.

Word first came on Saturday from a family of Gypsy tinklers making their way round the island, peddling horn spoons and the latest blether: The Duke of Hamilton would arrive from the mainland on Tuesday, perhaps this very hour. "There'll be no better time for you to see the grounds of Brodick castle," Cate had insisted yestreen when the three concocted their plan. "With servants running about, we'll hardly be noticed."

Davina had seen old castles before—Galloway was thick with them—but she'd never clapped eyes on so noble a member of the aristocracy. A *duke*! Even if he was older than her father by a score of years, the ninth Duke of Hamilton was also a marquis, an earl, a lord, and a baron. She could not fathom one gentleman holding so many titles.

The mild temperature and westerly breeze were both welcome, but the skies were less favorable. Hanging low over their heads, the clouds were the color of rock doves and full of secrets. Would they unload their watery burden until the burns ran in torrents or drift toward the Ayrshire coast and usher in a sunny afternoon?

As the trio crested the first small hill, Abbie slowed so they might catch their breath. "I'll warn you, Davina. It's not the sort of castle one could live in year round, for it's centuries old and barely furnished. The duke and his family reside on the mainland at Hamilton Palace in Lanarkshire. Brodick castle is little more than a hunting lodge."

"Sometimes His Grace comes in June," Cate said, "when the salmon fishing is fine, or in August for grouse shooting." She looked about the rough moorlands, her cheeks flushed from walking. "He used to come in the autumn, but Father says after years of lawless hunting, there aren't a dozen stags left for deer stalking, and the wild boars have vanished."

Near the summit of the hill separating Lamlash Bay from Brodick Bay, Abbie swept her plump arm in the direction of the sea. "If we continued eastward to the cliffs, we'd come to Dun Fionn, where the ancients lit their beacon fires to signal the alarm." She laughed as they continued walking. "No need to light a beacon today. The gentry are coming, not the enemy."

At the summit Davina drank in the peerless view. Goatfell, rising from the dark blue waters and green foothills, thrust its peak into the low clouds like a broad iron spear. Had Father and Uncle Evan truly scaled so fearsome a giant?

They picked their way across frothy burns lined with pink thimbles of fairy foxglove and leafy bracken, dipping their fronds in the moving waters. Some of the burns were deep enough to require wooden bridges. Davina crossed the primitive structures with due haste, made nervous by the creaking of the boards beneath her feet.

In her fortnight on the island, Davina had seen no more than a handful of carts, drawn by little Arran ponies. Folk were fortunate if they owned a single horse, as the Stewarts did. A healthy beast sixteen hands high, Grian accompanied the minister on his parish visits, while the girls walked everywhere. Didn't she do the same at home except when a gravel track allowed a carriage? There were precious few paved roads in her corner of Galloway and none whatsoever on Arran.

When they reached the coastline, the threesome continued round Brodick Bay, similar in shape to Lamlash but without sharp points of land protruding into the sea or an island nestled in the center. The fresh breeze off the water was salty and a bit brisker, fluttering the sails of the fishing boats in the harbor. South of the bay, the low green hills were gently sloped and rounded, like the Lowlands; to the north rose a jagged range of mountains and moors, like the Highlands, as if the whole of Scotland had been squeezed onto one small island.

Cate glanced at the darkening clouds overhead and groaned. "We'll see rain before we see home. But *not* before we see His Grace."

On level ground it was easier to quicken their steps along the coast road. They hurried past a scattering of stone cottages, nodding politely at a knot of fishermen whose chapped faces were as weathered as their boats. At water's edge a pair of noisy oystercatchers piped at each other and stabbed their bright orange beaks into the seaweed, looking for food.

Davina sympathized with their search. Even without a visible sun to help gauge the time, she knew the four hours were near, for her stomach growled incessantly.

"Glen Cloy," Abbie called out, turning inland down the narrow lane. "We'll not go far, just to the smithy's. Not all the way to Kilmichael House or the Fairy Hills beyond. But isn't it a bonny spot?"

Despite the beauty of the glen she called home, Davina could not deny this one was lovely too. A dark avenue of trees drew her eye toward an estate house of white-painted stone, barely visible through the trees, with a valley of purple hills beyond it.

"The Fullartons own Kilmichael," Cate said, lowering her voice as if someone belonging to the family might be hiding behind a hedgerow, thick with bramble. "I mean truly *own* it. The whole of Arran belongs to the Duke of Hamilton. But not Kilmichael."

"Fullartons have lived here for five centuries," Abbie said proudly, as if she were describing her own ancestors. "Of course the house is not so old as that, but 'tis quite grand. John Fullarton is a dashing naval officer, not much more than thirty. He's commander of the *Wickham*." She added airily, "Cate and I have been to Kilmichael on a few occasions."

"*Very* few," Cate reminded her sister as they walked on.

They crossed a meadow of melancholy thistle, the purple heads still waiting to bloom. In a week the meadow would be alive with color.

Reaching the track leading north, they were greeted by a standing stone poking out of the ground like an ancient signpost. "There's one of our monuments," Abbie said casually as if every village in Scotland had vertical stones planted along the main roads.

They were much closer to the mountains now, rising straight up from the meadows to their left, where a cluster of thatched cottages stood. "They call the settlement Cladach because 'tis by the shore." Cate tugged on her sleeve, drawing her attention to the sea. "And that's where His Grace's boat will land." She nodded toward the stone quay, empty for the moment.

The solid square of stones sat well above the high-tide mark for larger vessels, with a broad curve of stone steps leading down to the water for skiffs. Davina did not find the small harbor especially ducal, but she pretended to be impressed for her cousins' sake.

Then she turned and saw the castle. And she *was* impressed.

High above the bay rose four stories of red sandstone, an oblong fortress built in sections of differing heights, chimneys marking each addition. Windows marched from one end to the other in a random pattern—some rectangular, others square, a few with arches like regal eyebrows. A rounded tower near the door looked older than the rest, but all bore the stamp of history.

"Cromwell built the battery on the east end soon after he beheaded the first Duke of Hamilton. But then Good Duchess Anne came." Abbie smiled, as if she'd just beheld the woman walking out the castle door. "There are none on Arran who do not think well of her, even now."

As they climbed the steep hill, Cate was describing what they might find inside should they have the chance to peek in a lower window. "The kitchen is very large, with flagstone floors and broad pine dressing tables. The brick bread oven has the longest paddles I've ever seen, and there are fancy copper pots—"

"*Wheesht!*" Abbie yanked them to a stop, her eyes widening as she pointed toward the battery. "Someone's coming."

Twenty-Seven

Perhaps it may turn out a sang,
Perhaps, turn out a sermon.

ROBERT BURNS

Davina held her breath as round the eastern side of the castle came a bowlegged man, head down, his tall, black hat aimed at them like an accusing finger.

"He manages the property," Cate murmured. Then she called out in a cheery voice, "Good day to you, Mr. Nichol!" The three of them stood, shoulders touching, as the man advanced.

When he finally looked up, his scowl faded, and he slowed to a stop a few feet from them. "Miss Stewart, why didna ye tell me wha ye were?" He bobbed his head toward each of the sisters, giving Davina a curious glance. "Yer faither had a fine sermon on the Sabbath."

"He'll be glad to hear it, Mr. Nichol." Cate, looking vastly relieved at not being chastised for trespassing, turned to Davina. "Do meet our guest for the summer, Miss McKie of Glentrool."

He bobbed his head once more. "Pleased tae mak yer acquaintance, miss."

Davina simply curtsied, certain he knew of her condition. She'd met none on the island who were surprised when she did not speak.

"I ken why ye've come, lasses, but thar's naught but servant fowk here tae ready the castle." He cast a wary gaze at the skies. "The *wather* isna guid for sailin'. I leuk for His Grace tae come in the morn." Turning his attention back to them, he wagged his finger. "But dinna be comin' round, thinkin' ye'll see the duke, for he'll hae his guardsmen as weel."

"Will the..." Cate swallowed and started again. "Will His Grace have many guests coming this year?"

"Oo aye!" He nodded so hard he almost unseated his hat. "*Gentrice* from Argyll and Stirlingshire and Fife. Not a woman *amang* them, *sae* 'twill not be proper for ye tae be seen on the castle grounds. *Awa* wi' ye noo, Miss Stewart, and gie yer faither me best."

Cate murmured their thanks, and the three took their leave, hurrying back down the hill as the ominous clouds made good on their threat—first in fat drops, then in a steady downpour.

"Och!" Abbie took shelter beneath a leafy oak, pulling the others with her. Water dripped off their noses and ran down their necks, and their bonnets were already sagging. "We'll be as good as drowned by the time we get to the manse."

"Aye, but we cannot tarry, or Mother will wonder why we're not home for supper."

They had no choice but to link arms and brave the rain together, heads bent against the onslaught, their shoes quickly soaked through. Expecting to see a nobleman, Davina had worn her favorite gown. Now the fabric was dark and colorless, clinging to her legs as she walked, the embroidered hem streaked with mud. Would she never learn to dress with Arran's changeable skies in mind?

The harbor, the glens, the hills, and the mountains—all were lost in a gray wash of rain. To keep their spirits up, Cate and Abbie sang beneath their bonnets.

> There's news, lasses, news,
> Guid news I've to tell!
> There's a boatfu' o' lads
> Come to our town to sell!

"How true," Cate cried. "Even if we cannot watch them sail into our harbor."

"If they're all as old as the duke, we'll not miss much," Abbie teased her.

"Old or young, handsome or no, we cannot go back to the castle, or Mr. Nichol will mention it to Father on the Sabbath." Cate looked over at Davina. "Many apologies, fair Cousin, for we'd hoped to send you home to Glentrool with a story to tell."

They started up the long hill, their enthusiasm beginning to flag, for the ruts in the road were rain filled and treacherous. After struggling to reach the summit, they discovered that going down toward Lamlash was no improvement. The slippery mud made their footing unsure, so they hung on to each other and inched their way down, unable to move out of the way when a horse galloped past, splattering their costumes. All three were close to tears by the time they stumbled through the door of the manse, holding up their dripping hems and shivering uncontrollably.

"Mrs. McCurdy, towels if ye please!" A wide-eyed Betty ushered them into the kitchen, where Elspeth and her housekeeper quickly disposed of the girl's hats, then dried their hair and gowns as best they could before sending the bedraggled girls off to their second-floor bedroom to change.

"Haste ye back tae the hearth," Mrs. McCurdy urged them, "for I'll hae *het* tea waitin' and a het supper not lang after."

The girls did not have a lady's maid—a luxury seldom needed on Arran—and so helped one another dress in the gray afternoon light. Neither the flickering candles nor the small hearth in their bedroom dispelled the chilly gloom as rain continued to lash the windowpanes.

"What a dreich day," Abbie murmured, tying the bow on Davina's gown. "We'll be lucky not to catch cold."

Pulling on her white cotton stockings, Cate was still humming the tune they'd sung in the rain. "There's a boatfu' o' lads, all right. But who'll be on that boat? That's what I'm keen to find out." She did not wait for her sister to answer but spun out the possibilities. "From Fife, it's certain to be a MacDuff, and from Argyll, either a MacDonald or a Campbell. Not both, of course. The Borders might mean an Armstrong. 'Tis hard to say," Cate finished with a shrug, "but blithe to contemplate."

Davina's teeth finally stopped chattering when she had on dry clothes and was seated by the hearth, combing her fingers through her hair. Had she ever been so wet in all her life?

"Drink this," Elspeth said, placing a hot cup of tea in her hands.

Davina considered pouring it over her hair, simply for the warmth, but sipped it instead, breathing in the fragrant steam. She exchanged glances with the sisters, glad their mother had asked so few questions. Not because what they did was wrong, but because they were daft, thinking they could waltz up to the castle and see His Grace. The three of them were soon grinning at one another over their teacups.

Reverend Stewart emerged from his study, blinking at the brightness of the kitchen. "Happy to see you safely home on this weatherful day." He took his place at the head of the table and invited the household to join him, blessing the meal before they took their seats.

Plates of muslin kale were served, rich with barley, and *tattie* scones fresh from the griddle. Davina consumed her supper with relish. Whatever fine meals the ducal kitchen might produce, they could taste no better than this.

The minister dabbed at his mouth as their soup plates were removed. "We had a visitor not half an hour before you arrived home. A messenger on horseback. Did he pass you on the road?"

Abbie sighed. "He passed us, all right, with his muddy hooves flying."

"What news did he bring?" Cate asked.

Davina's curiosity was piqued as well. The rider had seemed most intent on his mission.

"He brought an invitation." The minister held up a crisp card written in a fine hand. "From John Fullarton of Kilmichael."

Davina's gaze met Abbie's across the table. *The dashing young officer.*

"On Thursday the twenty-third of June," the minister read, "Captain and Mrs. Fullarton will host a dinner party for His Grace, the Duke of Hamilton, and his guests."

"A dinner! Surely…" Cate stared at the card. "Surely we are not… invited?"

"Indeed we are, for our names are listed quite clearly. 'The Reverend Benjamin Stewart, Mrs. Stewart, Miss Stewart, and Miss Abigail Stewart.'"

Davina felt a twinge of jealousy but dared not let it show.

As if she'd read her mind, Cate took up for her. "Father, we *cannot* leave Davina at home."

"No, we cannot." Even his full beard could not hide his smile. "Our cousin will most certainly be included."

Davina gaped at him. Was such a thing permitted if her name was not on the invitation?

His smile broadened. "Look at the card, Catherine."

Cate took it from his hands. "Oh!" She read aloud in a breathless voice, "And Miss McKie of Glentrool, with her fiddle."

My fiddle? Davina stared at the card in disbelief. She would be entertaining a duke?

Reverend Stewart smiled at her warmly. " 'Twould seem news of your exceptional talent has found its way to Kilmichael." He reclaimed the invitation and tucked it inside his waistcoat. "I daresay His Grace's company will be quite taken with you."

Twenty-Eight

Far off
his coming shone.
JOHN MILTON

S ir, I've polished yer brass buttons 'til they *glent* like stars in the nicht
sky."

Somerled MacDonald turned, already smiling. "Well done, Mina."

The shy maidservant held up his dark blue coat. "Is thar *oniething*
else ye'll be needin', sir?" Mina blushed as she said it.

An invitation, lass? Somerled took the garment, then captured her
hand and drew her closer. "My father is expected any moment. But in
an hour, when the candles are snuffed—"

A sharp knock and a sharper voice put an end to things. "Somerled!"

Mina stepped away, averting her eyes. "I canna, sir," she whispered,
then hastened to open the door to the laird, curtsying before she fled the
room.

Sir Harry MacDonald filled the doorway, the crown of his silver
head not far below the oak lintel, his shoulders blocking the light from
the hall candles. He did not bother with a greeting. "Beguiling the lasses
as usual, I see."

Somerled shrugged, tossing his freshly ironed coat onto the tester
bed, where it landed in a heap. "'Tis not my fault you've decorated
Brenfield House with bonny maids."

"And a valet who will press your coats whenever needed." His father
swaggered into the room, then frowned at the yawning leather trunk,
empty except for a few cambric shirts. "Dougal has not finished packing for you?"

"I asked him to wait until you and I spoke." Somerled pitched his
tone just so, neither overconfident nor desperate. After twenty-two years
beneath the man's roof, he'd learned how to handle Sir Harry. "Father,

is it necessary that I accompany you tomorrow? Loch Fyne has salmon and trout enough for my taste." Somerled did not state what his father already knew: He cared little for sporting ventures in drafty castles, preferring a private rendezvous with a wee dram, a good book, and a willing female.

His father's silver brows gathered like storm clouds. "Your name is mentioned in the letter of invitation. I'll not offend His Grace by sailing to Arran without you."

"But more than a fortnight of angling—"

"Aye, with the *Duke of Hamilton*!" Sir Harry thundered. "Have you no sense, lad? However ancient our name, we own naught but grazing moors filled with blackface sheep. Hamilton has titles, power, and wealth beyond counting. If such a man bids us join him—"

"Fine." Somerled cut him off. "I will go." He needed no reminder that others had attained far greater rank. Hadn't he heard that complaint all his life? Though his father claimed the title of baronet and extensive MacDonald holdings, including the mansion in which they would lay their heads this night, his riches and honors were never enough to satisfy the man.

"See to your packing." Sir Harry headed for the bedchamber door. "We take our leave at dawn."

Somerled grimaced; only six hours hence. "Do we sail from Tarbert?"

His father paused in the doorway long enough to answer him. "Nae, from Claonaig. I'll not waste more silver than necessary on a vessel."

Sir Harry was already halfway down the hall when Somerled laughed aloud, not caring if the man heard him. The expense had nothing to do with his father's choosing the shorter sail to Arran's northern harbor: Sir Harry suffered terribly from *mal de mer* and was too proud to admit it. His only son and heir, on the other hand, sailed the high seas like their Viking ancestors, his stomach calm, his legs steady on the deck.

Now who is proud? Somerled ignored his nagging conscience and yanked on the braided pulley bell beside his bed, summoning Dougal. The sooner his trunks were packed, the sooner he might climb into bed. Alone, unless dark-eyed Mina changed her mind.

Beyond his chamber, the last traces of evening sunlight gilded the smooth surface of Loch Fyne. His south-facing window afforded a fine view of the undulating blue hills along both shores and the distant waters of the Sound of Bute. On the clearest days he could see the Cock of Arran, the jutting northern curve of the island that protected Lochranza harbor, where they'd be met by the duke's man and escorted to Brodick castle. Endless rounds of fishing would begin, with fresh trout and salmon on the table far too often and even less variety among the guests. Depressing, really, to watch grown men currying favor with the duke, like terriers licking their master's hand, begging to be petted.

A soft rapping at the door announced Dougal. "Do I pack, sir?" the valet asked, his English improving each season.

Somerled would happily converse with the man in his native Gaelic, but his father wouldn't hear of it. "The gentry of Edinburgh and London do not speak *Erse*," he insisted. "Neither will it be spoken in my household."

When Sir Harry was not in the room, Somerled ignored his dictum. "*Paisg*," he told his elderly valet, who quietly went to work folding Somerled's garments: coarser fabrics for climbing the hills and fishing during the day; and for evening at table, tail coats from Paris, snug breeches, and ornate waistcoats. Even in the bleak rooms of old Brodick castle, one did not appear at His Grace's table improperly dressed.

Somerled remained at the window, watching Dougal out of the corner of his eye. The balding man with his stooped posture and gnarled hands was an ideal valet, discreet in his manner and efficient in his duties. Had Dougal not tied his cravat to perfection before dinner? Tamed the waves in his hair? Pressed his coat lapels and shirt collar into smooth, neat points? A brief glance in the mirror confirmed his valet's skills. Dougal would travel with them, of course. It was not done to arrive and expect the host to provide a manservant.

Dougal looked up from the trunk, half-filled with clothing. "*Inneal ciùil?*" he asked, then stammered, "Ah...musical...instrument?"

Somerled eyed the remaining space. "The wooden flute," he decided, the other instruments in his collection being either too large or too fragile to transport safely. He would forgo certain pleasures for a few weeks; music would not be one of them.

He claimed the long flute from the top of his dresser and fitted the instrument to his mouth, the light brown boxwood warm beneath his fingers. With little effort on his part, a plaintive melody floated through the air. Clear and round, low and masculine, the legato notes seemed to rise from the depths of his chest. Nae, from his very heart, though no one was the wiser.

Dougal paused in his labors, closing his eyes. *"Tàlantach,"* he said softly.

Gifted. Dipping his flute in acknowledgment, Somerled finished the melody, then placed the instrument in Dougal's waiting hands, ready to be carefully packed among his clothing. He would manage without his flute during the journey itself, since he always took with him the most portable instrument of all: his voice.

"Sing for me, lad."

Sir Harry did not look well, hanging on to the mast of the small vessel that had transported them halfway across the Sound of Kilbrannan. The man's face was the color of seaweed discarded by an ebbing wave, his mouth clamped shut in a thin line, his gray eyes fixed on the choppy water.

Somerled obliged his father at once, his tenor lifting above the salty breeze and the splash of the oars.

> The simmer is gane when the leaves they were green,
> And the days are awa that we hae seen;
> But far better days I trust will come again,
> For my bonny laddie's young, but he's growin' yet.

When the older man nodded, Somerled sang another verse of his mother's favorite ballad, hearing her parting words as she bade them farewell. "Come home to Brenfield as soon as you can, for you know I'll not sleep well 'til you return."

"Don't be daft, woman," Sir Harry had chided her as they stood in the front hall. "Do you fear you'll not clap eyes on us again?"

"Aye." Lady MacDonald, accustomed to her husband's gruff demeanor, had lovingly placed her hand on his arm. "That is always my fear when you cross the water. And so I shall pray until you are safely home." They were not idle words; she would do exactly that—pray to Saint Brendan, the protector of sailors and travelers at sea.

Somerled kept an eye on his father, even as Lochranza harbor came into view. "Almost there, sir." Rising from the south shore of the bay, the gray ruins of a fourteenth-century tower house stood their ground. Recently abandoned, Lochranza castle still proved useful to approaching boats, offering them a point of reference. Gulls soared over the surface of the waters redolent of fish and shimmering in the afternoon sun.

The skipper of their craft took up where Somerled's ballad ended, filling the air with cheerful discourse meant to distract his sickly passenger. When the boat finally was rowed into the shallow harbor by the crew of able oarsmen, Sir Harry deposited his last meal over the bow, then leaned heavily on the wooden frame, gathering his strength.

"Hoot! Ye'll be feelin' better afore lang, sir." The skipper tipped his cap to Somerled when he paid for their passage, then helped father, son, and valet disembark without incident. "A guid visit tae ye," he said cordially. "Howp ye'll find time for a wee bit o' climbin'. The peaks o' Arran are *ferlie*."

"Aye." Somerled gazed inland, beyond the marshy shore. Though he cared little for fishing and even less for climbing hills, the savage beauty of the mountains was undeniable.

"Sir Harry? Mr. MacDonald?" A man with the look of a gamekeeper marched toward them, his tweeds stained with mud. "Welcome tae Arran." He introduced himself, then loaded their trunks and helped Dougal into a two-wheeled cart. "I've horses for the raik tae Brodick. Yer *kists* an' yer man wull follow *ahint*."

"Fine, fine." Sir Harry waited impatiently by the offered horse until the man helped him mount. Then he said, "I imagine His Grace has a busy visit arranged for us."

"Aye, he does, sir." With the gamekeeper leading the way, the men headed south on a slender track skirting the rushy water, bound for the steep glens ahead. "Captain Fullarton o' Kilmichael Hoose has an evenin' o' entertainment planned for ye gentlemen as weel. On Midsummer Eve."

Somerled shifted in his saddle. "Entertainment?" Far more civil sounding than fishing poles and salmon nets. "Might that include music?"

"A bonny fiddler, I'm told, though I dinna ken the lassie's name."

For the first time that long and tiring day, Somerled smiled. A lass who played the fiddle. What saint might he thank for that generous provision on so festive a night? He mentally crossed the days off his calendar. "'Tis but one week away."

Twenty-Nine

How still the morning of the hallow'd day!
JAMES GRAHAME

Davina awakened with the sun, rising when the first tendril of light slipped through the crack in the bedroom's shuttered window. On the longest day of the year she resolved to embrace every minute, until the last rays of the sun disappeared over the summits toward Beinn Bhreac.

Would this evening's dinner party convene beneath the Midsummer Eve sky in all its painted glory? Or would the distinguished guests gather withindoors, seated round a crescent of chairs, waiting to hear Davina McKie of Glentrool play her fiddle? The thought sent a chill skipping along her bare arms. Tonight, of all nights, she needed the notes to pour forth with ease. She could not fathom all the talented violinists His Grace had enjoyed over the last sixty years—musicians from London and Paris and Vienna who had come to Hamilton Palace at his invitation. She was naught but a Lowland lass who treasured her grandfather's generous gift. *Please, heavenly Father. Let it be enough.*

Davina sat motionless on the edge of her narrow cot, not wanting to disturb the sisters, asleep in their shared bed. Three gowns hung from the clothes press, airing until Betty could iron them later that morning. Cate's was a pretty silk in salmon pink with a matching fringed shawl, and Abbie's a pale yellow satin with a fine chiffon yoke and ruffled sleeves. The smallest costume was hers, a red and green silk brocade jacket made of fabric her father had purchased in Edinburgh on Martinmas last, worn over a damask gown embroidered with an array of swirls in matching ivory silk. Her mother had knotted the last thread the day before Davina had left home.

Mother. Davina's throat ached as she pictured Leana humming while she stitched. *'Tis a loosome gown.* Davina had tried it on to be certain the short jacket buttoned snugly beneath her bodice. Frothy lace circled the elbow-length sleeves, and a broad band of gold brocade edged the stand-up collar. *Fit for a duke.*

Restless, Davina stood and made her way to the window, then peered through the gap between the shutters. Already the pale blue sky was growing brighter, the first rays of the sun having chased away the last of the twinkling stars.

"We will leave for Kilmichael immediately following the four hours," Reverend Stewart had announced yestreen, insisting they not depart without first having tea and scones. Bless the man, he'd arranged two pony-drawn carts with drivers for the women, meaning to spare their hems and shoes from the muddy roads. Arran seemed to weather a brief shower every afternoon, often with the sun still shining. Davina had never seen so many rainbows—watery pastels arching across the sky for an instant, then fading from view.

But rainbows meant rain, and rain meant drooping curls and soggy gowns. *Please, Lord, not today.*

She turned toward the door, longing to slip down the stair. Locating one of her cotton gowns in the crowded clothes press would surely wake her cousins, yet she could not leave the room wearing her nightgown. In any case, it was far too early to venture out of doors and pluck violets from the lawn—one of her morning tasks—and Mrs. McCurdy would not serve breakfast on the sideboard for another two hours.

Resigned to tarrying in their bedroom, Davina eyed the small packet of letters tied with one of her satin hair ribbons. She never wearied of reading them, hearing the writers' voices as she scanned their words. On the top were a half-dozen letters from Mother. The most recent hinted at some news involving a neighbor; perhaps her next post would be more forthcoming. Will and Sandy's two letters were filled with much gnashing of teeth over their lives in Edinburgh, as well as pointed inquiries about her welfare on Arran. They were furious with Father; that much was obvious. Davina had written the lads, assuring them she was well situated at the manse and not to worry. Rather like telling lions not to roar or bulls not to charge.

Ian had written her on one occasion, the lines as neat and evenly spaced as a ledger sheet. She smiled at his careful script telling her all about Margaret McMillan. Her brother was truly smitten. Janet Buchanan's letters were her favorites, brimming with parish gossip. Barbara Heron had a tooth extracted, poor girl. Andrew Galbraith was courting Agnes Paterson—Davina wouldn't dare mention that to Will. Someone actually heard Graham Webster chuckling at market on Saturday last. And Jeanie Wilson delivered Mrs. McCandlish of another son.

Reading it all again, Davina shook her head. Had she been gone only a few weeks?

"Can you not sleep, Cousin?" Cate propped herself up on one elbow, blinking at her across the rumpled bedsheet. Keeping her voice low, she offered to help Davina dress. "Though 'tis an early start to a long day."

Davina was already pulling one of her plainer gowns from the clothes press, shaking out the wrinkles as she did. Without another word Cate was by her side, guiding Davina's arms through the sleeves. They would dress in their best clothes after the noontide meal; the blue cotton would do for now.

Cate crawled back into bed with a sleepy yawn. "Gather ye violets while ye may," she said blithely, knowing Davina's plans. "You'll find the *Flora Scotica* in Father's study."

Davina hastened down the dimly lit wooden stair. The ground floor was brighter, though the interior shutters remained closed. She tiptoed along the short hall, listening intently for any sounds of life. The minister's cramped study had but one window. Even with the shutter cracked open, she had a difficult time finding what she needed, squinting her way along the musty bookshelf. At least she knew what the spines looked like; her mother owned the two-volume set as well.

Ah. She pulled out one of the thick books with care. *Flora Scotica.* The passages she needed were easily located. Unlike most wildflowers, the scientific name for violet—*Viola tricolor*—sounded like the English one. *Or like a stringed instrument.* She smiled, picturing the yellow, purple, and white flowers with their heart-shaped leaves.

Davina ran her finger along the sentence in question, wishing the author had been more specific in his instructions. *Anoint thy face with goat's milk in which violets have been infused.* The manse kept one goat, milked daily for curds and whey. She'd asked kindhearted Rosie, the dairymaid, to save a bowl of fresh milk for her. But how many violets and infused in what quantity of milk? Her mother would know; Davina could only guess. Since the mixture would eventually be strained, perhaps it did not matter.

The text did offer one assurance: *There is not a young prince on earth who would not be charmed with thy beauty.*

She grinned at so bold a promise. His Grace was far from young and merely a duke; she had no intention of charming so elderly a man or his unmarried son. Alexander, the duke's heir apparent, had chosen to remain in London rather than join his father for three weeks of sport. 'Twas just as well: Alexander was forty, nearly as old as her father.

According to the local blether, there were younger men to be found at Brodick castle. Names and descriptions were hard to come by. A broad-shouldered Macleod from Skye. A red-haired Keith from the Borders. A long-legged MacDonald from Argyll. The duke's guestlist was smaller than usual this summer; some said no more than a dozen. Who knew if the men would even notice her, however soft her complexion? Still, she had little to lose and a whole day to spend wisely.

After replacing the minister's book, Davina headed for the front lawn, lifting a garden apron from a hook in the entrance hall as she passed. The salty breeze from Lamlash Bay felt cool against her skin. On the eastern horizon the sun was inching upward, hinting at fine weather.

Clustered along the front path grew all the violets she might need. Davina knelt to pick the delicate flowers, taking care not to crush them as she pinched each slender stem. Her apron was soon filled with the colorful blooms favored by fairies. "Heartsease," her mother called them. Davina stood, losing only a few blooms in the process, then carried the wildflowers into the kitchen, relieved to find the room vacant. Betty, who was already convinced Davina was one of the wee folk, would drop in a faint if she saw her with violets.

She emptied the contents of her apron into a plain, round teapot, then added hot water just off the boil and dropped the lid in place. Her mother's voice whispered to her while she worked. "Not too hot, dearie, or you'll lose the precious oils in the steam." Ten minutes for the herbs to infuse the water—that much she remembered.

Davina was busy straining the cooled liquid when the dairymaid appeared at the back door, a small pail of goat's milk in hand.

"Here ye go, Miss McKie." Rosie held it out, wrinkling her nose as she did. "Whatsomever tea is that ye're brewin'?"

Davina pointed first to the goat's milk, then to a stray violet caught in her apron strings, and mimicked washing her face.

"Oo aye!" Rosie's expression brightened. "I heard tell o' sic a thing."

Davina thanked her by smiling and nodding her head, to which the dairymaid dropped a curtsy and went whistling out the door. Rosie had the Stewarts' cow to milk before moving on to the Pettigrews' farm and the rest of her morning rounds.

After pouring equal parts goat's milk and violet infusion into a shallow bowl, Davina lowered her cupped hands into the lukewarm mixture and splashed it on her face. She felt a bit daft, hanging over the bowl, milk dripping off her nose, yet she washed her cheeks again, then her neck, pulling her gown loose, lest she miss a spot. "In for a penny, in for a pound," her father often said.

"May I try some?" Cate stood in the kitchen doorway, rubbing her eyes.

Minutes later Cate was bathing her face in a fresh bowlful, sputtering as she did. "Och! You didn't swallow any of this, I hope."

The two were still drying their faces when Mrs. McCurdy found them. "Awa wi' ye, lassies. I've parritch tae mak." Her tone was not unkind, and in her eye shone a knowing gleam. "I *maun* say, ye leuk bonny. This evenin' the gentrice wull be wooin' the *baith* o' ye."

Davina blushed as they quit the kitchen in search of a looking glass. Had the goat's milk accomplished what the May dew had not?

When they reached the bedroom with its small dressing-table mirror, Cate said, "You look first."

Chagrined at what she saw, Davina did not linger in front of the glass. Her skin was still sprinkled with color, her ferntickles darker than ever from a month of Arran sunshine.

"But feel how smooth it is." Cate touched her own cheek, then

Davina's. "As silken as your damask gown." She nodded toward her sister, curled up in their bed. "Abbie cannot wait to see you wearing it with that wonderfully tailored jacket. Isn't that so?"

When Abbie sat up and stretched, Davina's sketchbook protruded from beneath her bedsheet.

"Abbie!" Cate scolded her. "Whatever are you doing with our cousin's property?"

"I'm sorry, Davina." Her face bright as red campion, Abbie pulled the borrowed sketchbook from its hiding place. "I only meant to look at your fine drawings. This one is my favorite." She opened the book to a particular page, then held it up to her. "Is he someone you know?"

Davina looked down at her golden prince. *Not yet, young Abbie.*

"Hoot!" Cate's eyebrows shot up at the sight of him. "If our cousin knew such a braw lad, would she be spending her summer with us?" She nudged Davina with her elbow. "Nae, she'd be getting fitted for her wedding gown and hiring a piper." Laughing, Cate pulled her sister out of bed. "Come, Abbie, we've much to do. Your hair needs a good brushing, and Davina and I intend to wash ours in egg whites and rose water." She clasped both their hands and squeezed tight. " 'Tis not every day we're joined at table by a duke."

Thirty

Where doubt
there truth is—'tis her shadow.

PHILIP JAMES BAILEY

L eana knew that spending time in her daughter's bedroom would not ease the pain of her absence. Even so she found herself sitting there, lightly fanning away the afternoon heat as she gazed into an empty oak cradle. She well remembered nestling each of her children inside its wooden confines, lined with linen and decorated with a sprig of dill.

First came Ian, born in the Newabbey manse on a dark October eve with Auchengray's dear housekeeper, Neda Hastings, in attendance. Then Davina, delivered in their own bedroom at Glentrool, with Jamie grasping her hand, straining with her to bring their daughter into the world. And lastly the twins, who shared the cradle for only a month before they outgrew it. Jeanie Wilson had nearly crowed, she was so proud of herself for delivering two sonsie bairns minutes apart.

Now all four were grown and scattered to the winds: William and Alexander in Edinburgh, Davina on Arran, and Ian with his father at Keltonhill Fair away to the south.

Jamie had promised to visit her Aunt Meg in Twyneholm before returning home from the annual horse fair with all its diversions. Margaret Halliday, her only living aunt, was nearing eighty. When Leana had seen her last, Aunt Meg's hair and eyes had faded to a pale gray, yet her spirits were bright as ever. *May that still be so, dear Aunt.*

Leana was grateful the men would break their journey with Meg at Burnside Cottage, though it meant she would not see them again until Saturday. On this, the longest day of the year, Glentrool felt as empty as the cradle at her feet.

Refusing to give in to melancholy, Leana stood and took a turn round the turret bedroom, pausing at the clothes press bearing Davina's older dresses and a new gown, finished that morning. Leana pulled the buttery yellow silk from its resting place and shook it out, admiring the rich fabric once more. How perfectly the soft color would complement Davina's hair and skin. A pair of slippers from the same silk had been fashioned by the shoemaker from Drannandow.

Welcome home, Leana would say when she showed Davina her new costume. *How I've missed you.* She'd asked Jamie to bring home a bolt of fabric from Keltonhill so she might sew yet another gown for her daughter before Lammas. What else could she do with her home so empty? At least her hands would be filled and her mind occupied with stitches rather than fretful thoughts.

With a lengthy sigh she turned her attention to the narrow window that looked down on her gardens, a sight that never failed to comfort her. After a month of mild days and gentle rains, her roses and perennials were at their peak. The musk roses in particular, with their delicate white blooms, spilled over their corner of the garden in fragrant profusion.

Leana was still admiring them when she heard Eliza's steps in the upper hall, then her voice from the doorway.

"Are yer flooers callin' ye, mem?"

She glanced over her shoulder and smiled. "Aye, they are." Even from this distance, Leana could imagine the rich scent of her roses and feel their silky petals.

"I *jalouse* ye hear Davina callin' ye even mair." Eliza held out the sealed letter in her hands. "She's a guid dochter tae write ye sae *aften.*"

"So she is." Leana had broken the wax seal before her housekeeper finished speaking. "Bless you, Eliza."

She bobbed her head. "Rab carried the post from toun. And a new silver thimble for me as weel."

Leana heard the affection in Eliza's voice and took secret delight in it. Like Eliza, Rab had once lived in Newabbey parish and had accompanied the McKies from Auchengray to Glentrool. Eliza had stayed with her mistress, but Rab had returned home. Two years later, when Glentrool had lost its head shepherd, Jamie inquired after Rab at Leana's request. The affable, red-haired shepherd had come at once. And Eliza and Rab had married a twelvemonth later, just as Leana had prayed they might.

Grateful for Eliza's faithful service, Leana touched her hand in thanks, then smoothed out the folds in Davina's post.

"I'll leave ye tae yer letter," Eliza said with a parting curtsy.

By the time the door softly closed, Leana had already begun to read.

> To Mrs. James McKie of Glentrool
> Tuesday, 14 June 1808
>
> Dearest Mother,
>
> Please forgive the brevity of this letter, but I have thrilling news that cannot wait. Reverend Stewart is bound for the harbor within the hour, and I do not want my post to miss the packet boat sailing from Lamlash.

Her heart quickened at Davina's breathless prose. Whatever had excited her daughter so?

> We have just learned that the Duke of Hamilton and his guests will be entertained at Kilmichael House on Midsummer Eve, and we are invited to join them.

The Duke of Hamilton? Leana stared at the words, incredulous. Davina had never been in the presence of so exalted a member of society. Jamie occasionally traveled in such circles, but not their inexperienced daughter. Leana mentally reviewed all that would be expected of Davina in the way of deportment. Could she count on Elspeth Stewart to instruct her, or should she pen a letter at once?

Then she noticed the date. *Midsummer Eve.* In a matter of hours Davina would be dining with a gentleman eclipsed in power only by King George himself.

Leana looked toward the window, gauging the late afternoon light. Six o'clock or so. Perhaps Davina had already arrived at Kilmichael.

The invitation names me specifically and requests that I bring my fiddle. If my letter reaches you in time, pray that I may please the duke and the gentlemen in his party. I must go, Mother, for our cousin is anxious to leave with the mail. Do pray!

Your loving daughter

Oh lass. She did not need to ask; Leana prayed for her children without ceasing. *Even now, Lord, watch over my Davina.*

She studied the letter closely. *The gentlemen in his party.* Who might that include? Something about the phrase troubled her. *Gentlemen.* A sporting party, she imagined. Men of high social standing yet without wives on hand to ensure their behavior matched their titles.

Another gentleman came to mind, one worthy of the description: Graham Webster of Penningham Hall. How she wished Jamie had allowed her to inform Davina of Mr. Webster's interest. It seemed dishonest not to do so. As if they were hiding something from their daughter. Which, in fact, they were.

Try as she might, Leana did not understand why Jamie was so averse to the man's suit. Aye, he was a dozen years older than Davina but hardly old. He was a kind man, a devout man, who would love and cherish their sweet daughter. Did he not find her youthful innocence— her "purity," as he'd delicately put it—charming?

Distraught, Leana tossed the letter onto Davina's neatly made bed. What would Mr. Webster think of Davina plying her bow for a roomful of his peers? 'Twas not like being presented in court, a formal affair replete with rules. Davina would be simply introduced as…what? A performer?

Nae! Leana pressed her hand against her knotted stomach. Manners among the gentry were not always what they seemed. What if—

Och! Now she sounded like the twins, always imagining the worst. In truth, the lads could not protect their sister this night, nor could Jamie.

But thou, O LORD, art a shield for me.

Leana closed her eyes and prayed in earnest, standing in the center of the room where she'd taught her four children to fear God. *I know that thou canst do everything.* Her hands were clasped so tightly, her fingers began to ache. *Please, heavenly Father. Please.* What else could a mother pray? *Protect her. Defend her.* Her throat tightened. *Keep her, O Lord, from the hands of the wicked.*

And then she made a vow, for she could not seek God's favor and offer him nothing in return. *What time I am afraid, I will trust in thee.*

Head bowed in the weighty silence, Leana heard a faint tapping at the door.

"Mrs. McKie?" Jenny's voice.

Leana slowly opened her eyes. "Come in, lass."

The young woman, no older than Davina, stepped into the room and curtsied. "Mr. Billaud sent me. He *thocht* ye might want yer meal noo rather than waitin' 'til eight." A hint of color stole into her fair cheeks. "Syne ye're dinin' alone and *a'*."

"How thoughtful of Aubert," Leana murmured. For a man who insisted on serving supper at the same hour night after night, the offer was a generous one.

Leana's gaze was drawn to the window and the abundance of roses below. "Kindly set up a small table for me in the garden. 'Tis too fair an evening to spend inside."

Thirty-One

The hill, the vale, the tree, the tower
Glowed with the tints of evening hour,
The beech was silver sheen,
Such the enchanting scene.
SIR WALTER SCOTT

With each passing moment, Davina found it harder to catch her breath.

On either side of her stood majestic firs and tall, silvery beeches, flanking the private lane. To the north unfurled a vast lawn, groomed by unseen gardeners and bordered by a high-spirited burn. Stone benches placed here and there afforded an impressive view of Goatfell, watching over the property like a dour benefactor. Beyond the avenue of trees loomed the white rubble walls of Kilmichael, an estate house of imposing proportions.

Nature had also done her part: The sun was beginning its slow descent, staining the western sky a vibrant orange and casting Glen Cloy in dark blue shadows.

"The stables are directly behind the house," Cate announced, sounding eager to climb out of their uncomfortable conveyance. The sisters had traveled side by side in a small, two-wheeled cart, as had Davina and Mrs. Stewart, while the reverend rode astride Grian. Poor Abbie in her satin gown had slithered about every time they hit a bump, which was often; Cate had not fared much better in her silk, despite the clean woolen blankets her mother had used to line the rustic carts.

"Almost there," Elspeth called out to her daughters. Turning to Davina, she said in a softer voice, "No need to be *timorsome*, Cousin. Play as if you were in our parlor, and you'll win their hearts with a single tune."

Davina nodded, though she knew the grand drawing room of Kilmichael would be nothing like the crowded parlor of the manse. And it was one thing to please a neighbor but quite another to impress a duke. She clasped her fiddle to her waist, hoping her letter had reached Glentrool so she might depend upon her mother's prayers.

The house faced northeast toward the bay, its only ornamentation mounted above the slender double doors. "Three otters," Reverend Stewart explained as they drew to a stop before the gilded Fullarton crest. "And the clan motto: *Lux in tenebris*. Light in darkness."

Despite her nervousness, Davina managed a smile. Leana McKie would heartily approve. *My God will enlighten my darkness.*

A liveried footman stood at the doorway, waiting to escort the ladies inside. He handled them with aplomb, as if helping gentlewomen climb out of farm carts was a daily occurrence at Kilmichael. Since the front door was at ground level, there were no steps to climb; he simply escorted them through the double doors and into the spacious entrance hall, richly tiled with marble and ablaze with candles.

Though sparsely furnished, allowing room for guests to congregate, the square hall was not without adornment. A tall-case clock stood below the stair, the even swing of the brass pendulum visible through the glass-fronted case. Several fine landscapes hung on the walls, and a spray of artfully arranged garden flowers in pinks and blues had been placed before a long mirror, enhancing the colorful display. Convivial voices—mostly male—floated down the curved stair from the second-floor drawing room.

"Captain and Mrs. Fullarton will greet you shortly," the footman said, then politely bowed before disappearing through a doorway to his right. Presumably he would return to announce the new arrivals after they'd had a few moments to make themselves presentable.

"Quickly, everyone!" Mrs. Stewart adjusted the shawl round Cate's shoulders, then helped Abbie shake out the ruffles on her sleeves. Skirts were smoothed, dust brushed away, stray hairs patted in place, gloves straightened.

Davina peeked in the ornate mirror, relieved to find her dress had weathered the jostling ride. With Cate's help, she had swept up her hair into a knot of curls, secured with a comb on top of her head. The style exposed her long neck and accentuated the gown's low neckline; Davina blushed at the sight of so much pale skin.

Reverend Stewart held up her fiddle in its green case. "I'll see this well cared for until after dinner, Cousin. Then 'tis all yours."

The footman reappeared so quietly that they didn't notice him standing at the foot of the stair until he caught the minister's eye and bowed. "Whenever you are ready, sir."

Davina moistened her dry lips and tried to smile as she followed her cousins up the carpeted steps, taking care not to brush her gown against the marble statuary set into the wall where the stair began to curve.

The footman preceded the Stewarts into the high-ceilinged drawing room, bowed to the small gathering, and formally announced them. "The Reverend Benjamin Stewart, Mrs. Stewart, Miss Stewart, Miss Abigail Stewart, and Miss McKie of Glentrool."

The five of them offered their courtesy in unison, taking their time in deference to those of higher social rank. Davina was the last to look up, wanting to be very sure not to offend. A dozen or so well-dressed men of varying ages stood about—some smiling politely, others staring at the party, their curiosity manifest. To a man, they all wore their hair fashionably cut, rather than pulled into a pigtail like her father's. Their tail coats were dark, their waistcoats and trousers white. At a quick glance, none of the gentlemen appeared old enough to be the duke.

A number of familiar-looking young women were scattered throughout the room as well. Confronted by so many faces, Davina could not decide where to land her gaze.

"You've met some of the ladies at kirk," Cate whispered. "The daughters of Arran's best families. Grace McNaughton. Lily Stoddart. Jane Maxwell."

Davina understood why they'd been included. Since a hostess preferred having men and women seated alternately up and down her dinner table, all the young ladies present equaled the number of men in the duke's party; they would be paired off by status and rank before going down to dinner. Compared with managing the long hour at table, where the man seated to her left was expected to engage her in witty repartee, playing her fiddle might be the least daunting task of the evening.

John Fullarton—easily identified in his Royal Navy uniform—stepped forward and offered a smart bow, living up to Abbie's description of "dashing" with his fringed epaulets and bold manner. "Welcome to Kilmichael, Reverend Stewart." The captain's dark eyes shone as he greeted each of the women in turn. "We anticipate His Grace's arrival momentarily. I trust you had a pleasant journey from Lamlash Bay?"

The men continued speaking as round the drawing room conversations resumed, giving Davina a chance to explore her surroundings, if only with her eyes. Early evening sunlight poured through the windows, with their painted shutters and foot-deep sills. The carved mantelpiece and screened hearth claimed the inside wall; approaching the house she'd counted two long rows of chimneys in the peak of the roof. One could only guess how many rooms Kilmichael contained.

Cate moved next to her. "You look very calm," she murmured.

Ever so slightly Davina rolled her eyes, and they both smiled.

"Have you decided which tunes you'll play?"

Davina nodded, easing her jacket collar away from her neck. Despite the room's generous dimensions, the crowded space was growing stuffy. Her sketchbook remained in the bag with her fiddle, so she could not write out the titles for Cate, but, aye, she had chosen her first few tunes. Whether or not there would be more depended entirely on the duke.

Without warning, a deep male voice was heard on the stair. The drawing room fell silent as glances and nods were exchanged. A single phrase crept round the room, like a stockinged child on tiptoe. *His Grace.*

The footman seemed taller when he stepped into the room, his chin thrust forward and his neck stretched to its limit. "May I present His Grace, the Duke of Hamilton and Brandon, the Marquess of Douglas and Clydesdale, the Earl of Arran, Lanark, and Cambridge."

Despite how much she wanted to gape at the gentleman, Davina dropped into a deep curtsy, waiting until everyone round her straightened before she slowly did the same. It seemed His Grace had met most of those in attendance on previous visits, including the Stewarts; only the few strangers were being introduced. While she waited her turn, Davina studied him through her lashes. He had wiry hair, white with age and worn swept back from his high forehead, revealing thick brows and piercing eyes. His long nose came to a decided point, as did his chin. For a man nearing seventy, the duke was surprisingly erect, patiently standing for each formal presentation by Captain Fullarton.

When he announced her, Davina curtsied again, only to have the captain reach down and gently bring her to her feet. "Your Grace, Miss McKie is a gifted fiddler from the mainland. You will hear more from her later this evening."

"Why can I not hear from her now?" The duke's smile did not lessen the note of authority in his voice. "What shall you play for me this evening, Miss McKie? Will it be a lament? A strathspey?" His dark eyes bored into hers. "Come, miss, speak up. One does not keep a duke waiting."

Thirty-Two

Now heard far off, so far as but to seem
Like the faint, exquisite music of a dream.
THOMAS MOORE

Forgive me, sir. I cannot speak.
Beneath the duke's scrutiny, Davina felt her trembling knees start to weaken as the silence in the room pressed down on her. *Please, Lord. Please.*

"Your Grace." A strong, masculine hand cupped Davina's elbow, lifting her up, then holding her steady. "I believe you've frightened the lady speechless."

Stunned, she simply stood there for a moment. Her rescuer was directly behind her, too near to be fully seen. Davina sensed the warmth of him through her damask gown and caught a brief glimpse of him over her shoulder. He was quite tall. A young man. Fair-haired. A Highlander, by the sound of him.

He spoke again, his melodic voice shaping each word like a note. "I am certain she will play 'The Fairy Dance.' Every Scottish fiddler worthy of the title has mastered it." He paused, as if waiting for her to acknowledge him. When she nodded once, he continued. "And if a slow air is more to your liking, then Miss—ah, McKie, is it?—aye, Miss McKie undoubtedly knows 'The Nameless Lassie.' Though for her sake, we'll dub the song 'The Speechless Lassie.'"

He meant it only in jest, Davina realized. The gentleman was a visitor to Arran; he couldn't know of her impediment, or he would not have spoken so freely.

When the duke laughed at his quip, the assembly heartily joined in as if only too happy to fill the room with sound again.

Davina smiled too. The clever man had unwittingly done her a kindness, sparing her trying to explain herself with gestures. Though her knees were now strong enough to support her, his gloved hand remained at her elbow. Might she find some way to thank him, this stranger who appreciated music? She took a breath, preparing to turn and greet him properly, when Reverend Stewart appeared at her side.

The gentleman behind her slowly withdrew his hand.

"You speak more truth than you know, sir," Reverend Stewart told him, before bowing to the duke. "Your Grace, I beg your indulgence. Miss McKie is mute and cannot answer you."

Davina heard a collective gasp circle the room and wished she might crawl beneath an upholstered chair. *Oh, Cousin.* He meant well, of course. But she'd hoped to perform as a simple fiddler, nothing more. Now she feared they would applaud for the wrong reason, misjudging her as a poor wee lass with no voice. And what must the kind gentleman behind her be thinking after his *blithesome* comments?

The duke broke the silence. "You are wise to let your music speak for you, Miss McKie. I shall enjoy hearing you play."

She dropped into a curtsy, never more thankful for the common language of social graces. When she rose, Captain Fullarton was bringing forward another young woman to meet the duke as the rest of the guests began talking among themselves. Davina stepped back to make room for the lass and firmly planted her heel on a gentleman's instep.

To his credit, he did not cry out, though she heard a low groan. If it was the same man who'd come to her aid, he deserved an apology and more.

Davina turned round, then had to look up to meet his gaze.

" 'Tis only fair that you trampled my foot, Miss McKie, since I injured you far more grievously." The young man gave a courtly bow. "Please pardon my error. I did not know your…situation."

Eyes as blue as the northern sky. That was the first thing she noticed. Not dark blue, like hers. Bright blue. *Sunlit waves in his hair.* Against the dark collar of his coat, each wayward curl looked like spun gold.

He smiled down at her. "If that's forgiveness in your eyes, Miss McKie, I accept."

Tall and strong as a mast on a ship. Had this gentleman been on board the *Clarinda,* Captain Guthrie would have insisted on hanging a sail from the man's broad shoulders. *Bright and warm as summer itself.* It seemed the golden prince of her sketchbook had come to life.

"Davina!" Abbie tugged on the sleeve of her brocade jacket. "Mrs. Fullarton is sorting out couples for dinner." Her cousin frowned at the gentleman, barely giving him a second glance, then guided Davina toward the other young women waiting to be paired with their escorts. "Whoever might that be? Did Captain Fullarton introduce you?" Growing up in the manse, Abbie well understood the rules of etiquette: Without a proper introduction, men and women of quality were not allowed to converse socially.

Davina allayed her guilt as best she could: She'd already met the man in a dream on a fortuitous May morning, and tonight he'd learned her name.

Though her feet dutifully carried her across the room, her thoughts remained fixed on the golden-haired stranger. Why had she not seen him earlier? The crowded room, perhaps. The opulent décor distracting her. From a distance he was an even closer match for her pencil drawing, though mere paper could never capture his strength. Or his warmth. Or his voice.

"Miss McKie?" Elizabeth Fullarton approached her, ivory hands folded at the waist of her green silk gown. As slender as Davina was, yet taller, the mistress of Kilmichael demonstrated a confidence beyond her twenty-odd years. "If you will kindly stand behind Miss McNaughton, the captain will bring your escort to you."

Davina took her place, consoling herself when Grace McNaughton did not turn and greet her, as was customary. People were seldom rude by intent; they simply did not know how to engage a mute person. She was still the chosen topic of discussion; furtive glances were aimed in her direction, followed by whispered words behind fans and gloves.

Captain Fullarton's countenance, on the other hand, was open and kind. "Miss McKie, may I present Mr. Somerled MacDonald. Your dinner companion, at his request."

She didn't bother to hide her smile. *My golden prince.* This time she noted his high forehead, his patrician nose, his generous mouth. And his name. *Somerled.*

"We meet again, Miss McKie." He was still smiling, as he had been a moment earlier. Was he always so amiable? Aiming his gaze toward the front of the line, he added, "And that is my father, Sir Harry Mac-Donald." He lowered his voice. "A toady to the duke, though he'd never confess it."

This smile she did hide, pinching her lips together. What a *gallus* lad he was! A rascal since birth, Davina suspected. She'd not imagined him so when she had sketched her dream; perhaps his mischievous ways were part of his charm.

When he proffered his arm, she took it, despite the fluttering in her stomach. He was nearly a foot taller than she and broad shouldered, like his father. Odd that she didn't feel more secure, the way she did standing next to Ian.

The line of couples began moving forward in a genteel shuffle as the duke led the procession down the stair. Somerled—his Christian name suited him far better than "Mr. MacDonald"—inclined his head down to hers as they walked. Though he did so because of their difference in size, it felt vaguely intimate. As if they'd known each other for ages rather than for minutes.

They'd not yet reached the upper hall when he asked, "Miss McKie, I imagine you've developed some method of communicating with others. Might you be willing to show me?"

The request took her by surprise; he was not only gallus but sensitive as well. She touched the corner of her eye, then waited.

"Would that be 'I see'?"

She continued by touching her ear, then her forehead, then her heart, nodding as he guessed each one correctly. *I hear. I understand. I feel.*

He laughed, pointing to the approaching steps, then to his eyes and hers.

A quick study, this one. *We must watch where we're going.*

As they started down the stair, she rested a gloved hand on the polished hardwood railing, if only to steady her knees, which were feeling shaky again. Half an hour ago Somerled was confined to the pages of her sketchbook. Now he was flesh and blood, utterly male and inescapably real.

At the turn in the stair she looked back to find Reverend and Mrs. Stewart walking a few steps behind. Davina smiled, hoping to assure them all was well. Her cousins followed, paired with agreeable-looking young men. Were they enjoying themselves too?

"Miss McKie, 'tis ill-advised to gaze over one's shoulder while walking down the stair," her escort teased.

Davina quickly straightened, taking more care with her steps. She did not have a free hand to convey her thoughts and hoped her apologetic expression would suffice. Somerled seemed unconcerned, relaxed enough for both of them.

A few turns and they reached the dining room. The longest table she had ever seen was draped with a damask cloth as finely woven as her gown. Sterling silver candlesticks and freshly cut white roses alternated down the table, even as windows and mirrors by turns illuminated one long wall. Immaculate servants in stiff white aprons stood against the opposite wall, waiting for the butler's signal. Reflected in the mirrors, the staff doubled in size. The china gleamed, the crystal shone, and the last rays of the midsummer sun streamed through the long windows facing west.

The effect was dazzling.

"Lux in tenebris," their host said, taking his place at table. "Light in darkness."

Davina held her breath, committing to memory the splendid display. However would she describe it to her mother? *Like the sun and the moon, captured in a room.*

Once the duke was seated, they all followed suit—Somerled to her left, an older gentleman introduced as Mr. Alastair MacDuff of Fife on her right. Protocol dictated that couples exchange remarks with each other and refrain from turning elsewhere for conversation. Rather like a roomful of private dining for two, Davina decided, instead of one lively party, which was how things were done at Glentrool. Up and down the table white gloves were quietly removed and the bills of fare beside their plates consulted. Davina marveled at the extensive menu, carefully written out by hand. From pheasant consommé to Caledonian cream, she counted ten courses. The usual round of coffee and walnuts was not even mentioned.

Somerled must have seen the glazed look in her eyes. "No one is expected to finish what is on their plates. Eat only what pleases you." With a faint lift of his brows, he added, "I shall be interested to see what that might entail."

She tasted everything and ate almost nothing, far more engaged by Somerled's running commentary on the duke's summer guests. He was not at all like her twin brothers, for whom trout fishing and hill climbing were favorite pursuits. Nor was he like Ian, quiet and even tempered. Somerled MacDonald resembled the varied courses that swept into the dining room upon silver-domed *ashets*—one sweet, one savory, now cold, now hot, yet each with something to commend it.

Davina soon learned the meaning of his name—*summer traveler*— and the glory of his ancestors, the MacDonald Lords of the Isles.

"I am not the first Somerled to land on Arran's shores," he told her between swallows of braised lamb with red-currant jelly. "The ancient *seanchaidh* described Somerled the Great as a well-tempered man of quick discernment with a shapely body and a fair, piercing eye." He gave her a sidelong glance, as if curious how the modern version compared to Somerled of old.

Quite well, sir. Did he see the answer in her eyes?

"Somerled still remains on Arran," he said finally, "buried on Holy Isle."

When the tablecloth was removed and a fluted glass of Caledonian cream was placed before her, Davina gave it the attention it richly deserved. Her first spoonful of the fresh cream, whisked with marmalade and brandy, tasted divine. So did the second. And the third.

Then Somerled leaned forward and whispered in her ear. Davina slowly put down her spoon, realizing what came next on the bill of fare.

Thirty-Three

Backward, turn backward,
O Time, in your flight!
ELIZABETH AKERS ALLEN

In the entrance hall the tall-case clock measured the waning hours of Midsummer Eve. The flickering candles now provided more light than the sky, draped in navy and rimmed in gold along the far reaches of the western horizon.

Soon the gloaming would give way to the moonless night.

Davina stared at the ambrosial dessert, her appetite gone, for there was no turning back: Her performance was the final course. The women would repair to the drawing room for coffee while the men remained at table for half an hour, drinking port and discussing the political outrage that was Bonaparte, before rejoining the ladies for an hour's entertainment.

"Miss McKie." Somerled leaned back in his chair like a well-sated man and dabbed the last drop of cream from his lips. "They'd never have invited you to play if you were not a very talented musician indeed."

A comforting notion. Davina acknowledged his words with a grateful nod, then folded her hands in her lap, gathering courage round her like a cloak. Countless times over the last ten years she'd played her fiddle for audiences large and small. Could she not tell herself this drawing room was Glentrool's garden? Or Michael Kelly's humble cottage? Or the *Clarinda's* sea-washed deck?

"I, for one, am eager to see you perform." Somerled leaned closer, a half smile on his face. "I feel certain I will not be disappointed."

She'd covertly studied his features throughout dinner. Thick, expressive brows, the same golden color as his hair. A strongly drawn jaw and high cheekbones not unlike hers. Only now did she notice that one blue eye was slightly smaller than the other, which explained why Somerled always seemed to be winking at her.

Davina smiled back at him, hoping he might see the confidence growing in her eyes. *I am ready to play for the duke—or will be soon. 'Tis what I do best and what I love most.*

When Captain Fullarton invited the women to take their leave, they rose with their escorts' assistance, then collected their gloves and discreetly brushed any stray crumbs from their skirts. Davina locked gazes with Cate at the far end of the table, longing to have a moment with her. *Has the evening gone smoothly for you? Was your escort cordial?* Abbie caught her eye as well. The three cousins would have endless things to discuss once they returned home. She only prayed Somerled MacDonald would not see them climb into a farm cart. He'd traveled the Continent, and his family owned an estate in Argyll even larger than Glentrool; Davina was certain most women of his acquaintance did not resort to riding in carts.

He moved toward the other men taking empty chairs round His Grace, who was sampling the port. "Until later, Miss McKie," Somerled said with a parting bow and an enigmatic smile.

Davina sensed him watching her as she skirted the table, flattered and a little disconcerted at his attentiveness. Perhaps dinner couples commonly indulged in a flirtation at table, only to part at dessert and never cross paths again. If so, best to concentrate on entertaining the Duke of Hamilton rather than pleasing a braw Highlander.

Mrs. Fullarton stood in the entrance hall, directing the young women away from the stair and toward an inviting doorway on the ground floor. "Coffee will be served in the music room, ladies."

Davina's brows arched. A room devoted to music? Very promising.

"Miss McKie." The hostess motioned Davina closer. "Your instrument is waiting for you on the pianoforte. I've taken the liberty of removing it from the bag. If there is anything else you might need…"

Davina bobbed her head in thanks and started across the candlelit hall, anxious to tune her fiddle before the room grew too crowded. Then she'd be free to seek out Cate and Abbie for a few minutes at least. The doors leading to the front lawn were open, ushering in the warm evening air, fragrant with honeysuckle. She paused to breathe in the heady scent, letting it calm her nerves, then swept into the music room, bound for her fiddle.

The charming room with its silk-covered walls and gilt chairs was aptly named: A grand pianoforte, a cittern, a violoncello, a harpsichord, and an old treble viol were displayed among the furnishings. Young ladies with feathers in their hair sat perched on chairs, like colorful plumed birds, and vases brimming with yellow roses covered every available surface. A manservant moved through the room, silently pouring tea and offering candied walnuts, while a maidservant lit more candles, then drew the curtains.

Intent on her mission, Davina clasped her fiddle, played the G below middle C on the pianoforte, and then began tuning in fifths, inclining her ear to the strings so she could hear above the hum of conversation. Since she'd practiced earlier in the day, her fiddle was easily tuned. One concern was quickly dispatched: Her jacket was not as confining as she'd feared, nor would the broad ruffle of lace at her elbow interfere with her playing. She drew the bow across the strings, listening for the sweetness of the tone.

Aye. Her fiddle was ready, and so was she.

Carefully replacing her instrument and bow on the pianoforte's polished top, closed for the evening, Davina watched for her young cousins and their mother to appear, which they soon did, looking for her as well. By tacit agreement, she joined the Stewarts in a corner of the room not yet spoken for, all of them hastily taking their seats.

"Davina!" Cate paid little attention to the coffee placed in her hands, though her eyes were as round as the saucer. "You must tell us everything about your handsome dinner companion. Shall I fetch your sketchbook and pencil?"

Not certain of its location at the moment, Davina held out her empty hands, then touched her lips, inviting Abbie to continue.

"So I shall," she agreed, "for I've learned several things about Mr. MacDonald."

"Guard your tongue, Abigail," Mrs. Stewart cautioned. "Gossip is never appropriate."

"But it's not gossip when it's *true*," she said petulantly, and Cate laughed behind her gloves. Abbie wasted no time divulging her store of knowledge. "Somerled MacDonald is twenty-two years of age, the only son of Sir Harry and Lady MacDonald, and heir to Brenfield House and his father's title."

Davina was impressed. Somerled had told her much of the same but rather nonchalantly, as if none of it mattered to him. She'd no sooner affirmed Abbie's words with a nod than Cate chimed in.

"He also has a bit of a reputation…" Her cheeks took on the same pink hue as her silk gown. "That is to say, the young gentleman who escorted me said that Mr. MacDonald—"

"That's quite enough." Elspeth frowned at her elder daughter. "Rumors and accusations honor no one, Catherine. Neither the one speaking nor the one spoken about. The fact is, Mr. MacDonald comes from a good Highland family, has impeccable manners, and came to our cousin's aid this evening when she was asked to address His Grace."

Elspeth turned to Davina, a look of regret on her soft features. "Do forgive my husband. I fear he stepped in where he wasn't needed and said more than you might have wished."

Davina gently shook her head. In such a small gathering her secret would not have remained so for long.

The door to the hall swung open, and Captain Fullarton entered, his eyes bright from the port. "May we join you, ladies?" He stepped aside for His Grace to enter and be seated in the place of honor, closest to the pianoforte. The other gentlemen followed, Sir Harry MacDonald included, finding vacant chairs wherever possible while coffee was poured.

Somerled stood inside the doorway for a moment, eying the room. His gaze flickered over Davina, pausing long enough for her to note his regard before moving on. He spoke to his father briefly, then chose a straight-backed chair next to the violoncello.

Despite her nervousness, Davina smiled. Did the man always prefer a silent companion by his side? She moved to the chair by the pianoforte and awaited her turn.

In a matter of minutes the audience was settled, ready for the evening's program to begin. Though her heart still raced and her hands were icy, Davina was not alarmed; such apprehension always ceased with the first note. She settled her gaze on the duke and took a long breath. *Please, sir. Just let me begin.*

Captain Fullarton extended his hand and brought her to her feet. "Your Grace, Miss McKie will perform several selections for us on a fine Italian instrument that once belonged to her grandfather, Alec McKie of Glentrool." He released her with a gallant sweep of his arm. "Come, Miss McKie, and fill Kilmichael with music."

Bathed in the light of a chandelier, Davina tucked her fiddle beneath her chin as lovingly as a mother nestling her bairn in a cradle. *Safe. Home.* She lifted her bow with a flourish, then struck the opening chord of "Highland Laddie," a spirited dance tune in cut time.

Tapping her toe as she played—it was impossible not to, so infectious was the rhythm—Davina spied the duke's well-shod foot soon keeping time with hers. Round the room, ladies bobbed their heads, and gentlemen drummed their fingers. Though propriety would not let them leap to their feet, Davina watched the gentry dance in their hearts.

No one was more engaged than Somerled MacDonald. He'd put his coffee aside and was leaning forward, as if he were steel and she a magnet. Or perhaps the music drew him, lighting his face and warming his gaze.

Surrendering to the moment, Davina threw herself into the tune with merry abandon, the notes streaming from her hands, the words singing through her heart. *The bonniest lad that e'er I saw—Bonny laddie, Highland laddie!*

Thirty-Four

Bring therefore all the forces that ye may,
And lay incessant battery to her heart.

EDMUND SPENSER

S omerled saw the truth in her eyes.
Bonny Highland laddie. Davina McKie meant this song for him.

He knew the next verse too. *Bonny lassie,* Lawland *lassie.* Aye, she
was bonny, this wee thing from Galloway. And talented far beyond her
years. Look how she controlled the bow, bending it to her will. Had he
a jealous nature, he'd resent her musical skills; instead they made the
young woman even more desirable, if that were possible.

A second tune now. "Miss Hope's Strathspey." Was this one chosen
by intent as well? Somerled grinned, certain she would notice. *What is
it you hope for, Davina? For I have hopes of my own.* He leaned back in
his chair, studying her technique as she lifted the bow smartly off the
strings, snapping her wrist just so. Each note was distinct and precise,
the melody never lost in the complex rhythm. In truth, he'd not heard
her equal; neither had His Grace, judging by the man's alert expression.

Somerled scanned the audience, not surprised to find their mouths
open in wonder. They were accustomed to a gentlewoman sitting before
a pianoforte or embracing a pear-shaped cittern, not standing before a
crowd and driving a bow across her fiddle strings as if her life depended
upon it. Davina, both spirited and gifted, already had the entire assembly at her feet. *Was that your intent, lass? To win every heart?* He would
not give his heart so easily, but she was welcome to the rest of him.

"Garthlands" now, in the same key and written by a MacDonald.
Another of your ploys, eh, Davina? Clever girl, letting her songs make
subtle overtures on her behalf. Though she was small, her confidence
suggested she was not as young as she appeared. Twenty years of age, he
guessed. Old enough.

From the moment he learned their dinner party would include a lady fiddler, he'd been curious to meet her, never guessing she would be so accomplished a musician or so delectable a creature. Her red hair was positively scandalous. Her deep blue eyes communicated everything her voice could not. And a silent woman? Every man's fancy. Not to mention her prominent cheekbones, which drew a lovely line straight to her pout of a mouth. He had plans for those lips and those small, lithe hands as well.

Oh, she might be called *Miss* McKie, but Davina did not fool him for an instant. No virginal maid played so passionately or chose her songs with such *braisant* intent. When he'd touched her lace-covered elbow in the drawing room, she'd not resisted. Nae, she'd backed into him on purpose so they might have a chance to meet, tossing convention to the dogs.

Not an innocent, this one. He knew the signs. If Davina had given herself to some other man, she could give herself to him.

When she ended the third tune with a flourish, Somerled joined the audience in sustained applause, humming a ribald Burns song for his own amusement.

His Grace, meanwhile, was effusive with praise for his fiddler. "Excellent, I say! And what of jigs, Miss McKie? Might you know any?"

Apparently she knew several. "Hamilton House" had the duke practically dancing in his upholstered chair, and "Dumfries House" was a tip of the hat to Miss McKie's corner of the mainland. "Admiral Nelson" delighted the captain in particular, the hornpipe requiring a shift in both key and meter, which Davina handled with ease.

Somerled was enchanted with her performance and more determined than ever to have her in his arms. Tonight, if it might be arranged. Or would she return home shortly to the manse in Lamlash Bay? Nae, that would never do.

Even more enthusiastic applause greeted the final note of the hornpipe. He could only guess what tune might come next. Too soon for a lament. An air, perhaps? Or might she recall his earlier suggestion of a certain reel…

She looked directly at him when she launched into "The Fairy

Dance," starting at a tempo that would leave her breathless by the last measure. Was that a challenge he saw in her blue eyes? *Watch me, sir.*

Nae, he would do more than that. The busy melody, with its continuous string of eighth notes, called for a steady bass line beneath it. Somerled reached for the violoncello at his side and maneuvered it in place before she reached the fourth measure. He'd tuned the instrument when he first arrived; now he would put it through its paces. Davina did not blink an eye or miss a note, plying her bow with even more fervor as he provided the distinct rhythm a reel demanded.

The crowd stared at them in amazement, yet Somerled was vexed. He'd not said a word about his musical abilities. Could the lass not at least *pretend* to be shocked? But he soon overlooked her impudence for the sheer delight of accompanying her. Each time they repeated a bar, she added more embellishments until the rose-scented air of the music room was filled with grace notes.

Tradition required they slow the tempo at the end, then strike four accented chords at precisely the same instant—forte. Even rehearsed, such things were not easily managed. Somerled watched her closely, prepared to follow her lead.

One. Two. Three. And four.

Perfect.

His Grace was applauding before Davina lowered her bow. "Well done, miss. Well done!"

Somerled rested the violoncello against his knee, hardly noticing if they were clapping for him, so taken was he by his "Speechless Lassie." What a fool he'd been to make so careless a jest. Davina had forgiven him, it seemed, for which he was elated. He could think of no better way to spend his last days on Arran than sporting with a willing gentlewoman.

Davina already had her fiddle back in position, a faraway look in her eyes. She'd not so much as glanced at him. Did she mean for him to accompany her, or should he put his instrument aside? The evening was hers in every sense; he would wait to see if she made her desires known.

When she drew her bow across the strings, he realized she had something gentler in mind. The room fell silent. No idle words were whispered; no spoons rattled in china saucers; no throats were cleared. She had saturated the air with notes; now she was spinning a thread of music so singular, so finely wound, they'd soon find themselves wrapped in it, unable to breathe.

Familiar as the tune was, Somerled almost did not recognize "Niel Gow's Lament," for she'd made the plaintive melody her own. The expressiveness of her phrasing—slower here, a bit more movement there—was masterful. As if she were the grief-stricken composer himself, mourning the loss of his second wife.

Davina would not grieve alone. Without making a sound, Somerled positioned his instrument firmly between his legs, horsehair bow poised. When she reached the refrain, he would be waiting for her.

Thirty-Five

The light of love, the purity of grace,
The mind, the Music breathing from her face.
GEORGE GORDON, LORD BYRON

E yes closed, Davina let the music take her where it would. As often
as she'd played Gow's lament, each time the sorrowful beauty of
the piece washed over her anew. Yet in the midst of the elegy she sensed
a note of hope, and so she played toward that end, wanting to leave her
audience not tearful but joyful.

When Davina began the refrain, slightly increasing the tempo, the
low, warm notes of the violoncello rose to greet her once more. *Somerled.*
Why had he not mentioned his musical abilities at dinner? She sensed
him fitting his notes between hers, like fingers sliding inside a silk glove.
When she altered the tempo, so did he; when she paused, his instrument fell silent.

Not only was Somerled an exceptional talent, he was also unselfish,
anticipating what she might need, yet never providing more than she
wanted. How did he know? Did he hear in the music what she heard?
When they played in perfect harmony through a tender passage, did his
heart soar too?

Davina slowly opened her eyes and found her answer. Somerled's
golden head was bowed over his instrument, his expression intent, as if
he were listening, waiting for her, as lost in the music as she was. They
played on, their gazes never quite meeting, speaking only in notes rather
than in words. *Follow me here. Aye, just that. Longer still. Now 'tis right.*

At the duke's bidding, more tunes followed until the hall clock
chimed eleven, and the duo closed with a lilting Gaelic air, "Mary,
Young and Fair." As Davina had hoped, the Highlander knew the tune
well, infusing every measure with heartfelt expression. Their last note,

played in unison, hung in the air for a breathless moment before a final ovation overpowered it.

Davina and Somerled bowed as one. She still could not bring herself to look at him, nor did he turn toward her, as if some spell might be broken, some invisible thread torn.

The audience urged them to play another, but Captain Fullarton stood and held up his hands in protest. "The hour is late, and our performers have given their all. Young ladies, you will find your fathers in the hall, prepared to escort you home."

Davina placed her fiddle and bow on the pianoforte with care, her hands trembling as she watched Somerled return his borrowed instrument. No one had ever listened to her more carefully nor spoken to her more deeply. She, in turn, had withheld nothing. How did one proceed from here? For there was no hope of going back, of pretending she was unchanged.

Davina remained by the pianoforte, one hand resting on it for support, as the audience collected their shawls and wraps, offering words of praise in passing, which she acknowledged as best she could. Somerled, standing an arm's length from her, murmured his thanks as well, while Captain Fullarton bade his guests good night.

Between duties, their host confessed, "I was not apprised of your talents, Mr. MacDonald. Do forgive me for not introducing you properly at the start."

"Ah, but you introduced me to Miss McKie," Somerled reminded him, not quite looking her in the eye. "For that, I will ever be in your debt, sir."

" 'Tis hard to believe you've not performed with this lady before." The captain smiled at them both. "I do hope this will not be the last evening you spend together."

"That is my hope as well," Somerled murmured before their host was called away. The music room was emptying quickly as horses were brought round for the duke and his party. "Some of the younger men have left for Brodick castle on foot," Somerled commented offhandedly, glancing toward the door. "Less than half an hour's walk." He stepped aside to make room for an exiting couple, then moved closer to her.

Lifting her face toward his, Davina hoped he might look at her at last. Might speak to her with words the same way he spoke to her with music.

Somerled gazed down at her. "After such an evening, Miss McKie, I find it difficult to bid you farewell."

And I, the same. She was certain he saw the truth in her eyes. When he touched the small of her back with his ungloved hand, she felt unsteady on her feet.

He started to say something, then caught sight of the duke preparing to leave. "Pardon me, but I must speak with His Grace on a matter of some urgency. I shall not be long." Somerled adopted a stern expression, so exaggerated as to be comical. "In the meantime, see that you do not leave this house, Miss McKie, or I shall be forced to hunt for you."

They both smiled; he loathed hunting even more than fishing.

After offering her a courtly bow, Somerled strode toward the door, the tails of his dark blue coat flapping.

"Cousin Davina?"

Still a bit dazed, she turned to find the Stewarts standing not far behind her.

"You were wonderful!" Cate breathed, and Abbie echoed the same, her eyes bright.

Oddly, Elspeth said nothing, though her features were drawn. Had she not enjoyed the evening? Perhaps the rich food did not suit her.

Reverend Stewart was more forthright. "Cousin, you know how very proud we are of your musical talents. But tonight I fear your playing was rather…unrestrained." A ruddy tint crawled up the minister's neck as he hastened to add, "The blame rests entirely on Mr. MacDonald, of course, and his wanton manner of accompaniment."

Wanton? Now it was Davina's turn to blush. Had they played so passionately as that?

"Please." Elspeth nervously plucked at the reverend's sleeve as her gaze darted about. "Do not embarrass our cousin on so special an occasion. Perhaps you might address this matter at home."

"Aye, and so I shall." He straightened his hat as if prepared to leave at once. "I assured Jamie McKie I would protect his daughter. I'll not have some *slaoightear*—"

"Reverend!" she said in dismay, then bowed her head. "Kindly arrange for our ponies and carts."

Davina had never seen the couple so upset. Was her music the only reason? She did not recognize the Gaelic word her cousin had spoken.

Cate watched her father make his way to the front door as she fidgeted with her shawl. "I'm sorry, Davina. Father seldom gets this agitated. Truly, you played beautifully."

What of Somerled? Davina waited, but his name was not mentioned.

"Oh, Miss McKie, *there* you are!" Elizabeth Fullarton sailed toward them, skirts in hand. "I was afraid you'd already slipped out the door." She smiled at the Stewarts, and a few pleasantries were exchanged before Mrs. Fullarton took Davina's hands in hers. "His Grace has requested that you remain here in Glen Cloy for a fortnight while his guests are in residence at the castle. He very much wants to hear your music each evening after dinner."

Davina felt her hands grow cool in the woman's clasp. Mrs. Fullarton delivered the news with obvious delight, anticipating a favorable response. And Davina was honored. But...

"'Tis a great privilege, as you know. In the days of Duchess Anne, her husband kept a permanent piper at Brodick castle. Now you shall be the duke's summer fiddler." Her hostess laughed a little. "Of course, the décor at Brodick is less...ah, refined. But you needn't appear there until just before dinner. The rest of the time you'll be our guest here at Kilmichael." She turned to Mrs. Stewart, as if she'd only now remembered her. "Assuming that arrangement suits your family."

Elspeth tried to smile. "I shall...speak with the reverend."

Davina knew the Stewarts would have little say in the matter. As sole patron of Kilbride parish, the Duke of Hamilton appointed its minister; Reverend Stewart would be hard pressed to oppose the man who ensured his salary. If His Grace wanted a fiddler to entertain his visitors, a fiddler he would have.

Mrs. Fullarton arched her brow with an aristocratic air. "Surely your husband would agree 'tis imprudent for a young lady to travel the coast road five miles each afternoon and again late at night, even with an escort."

"Aye, well…" Elspeth eyed the door. "I suppose he might agree with that."

"All is settled then." Mrs. Fullarton squeezed Davina's hands. "What a pleasure it will be to have your company. No need to send for your dresses from the manse. I have several summer gowns we can easily hem to fit you."

Davina nodded, wanting to appear grateful; the woman's offer was more than generous. But could she truly be comfortable in an unfamiliar house, spending her days with people she did not know?

Her hostess leaned forward and said in a softer voice, "I think you'll find the ground-floor guest room to your liking. It faces the garden and is quite my favorite bedchamber in the house. When you're ready, one of the maidservants will escort you there and serve as your chaperon whenever required. You have only to ask." She released Davina at last, glancing toward the hall. "Do forgive me, but I must speak with my housekeeper. After a large dinner party there is much to be done. And undone." She smiled, stepping back. "Our home is yours, Miss McKie."

The instant Elizabeth Fullarton was gone, Davina's cousins gathered round her.

"Does this arrangement suit *you?*" Elspeth asked, her blue eyes filled with concern. "I hate to think of leaving you with strangers."

"Mother, these are the Fullartons." Cate aimed a pointed gaze at their surroundings. "They're the only landed gentry on Arran and far from strangers. Davina will be well cared for here." Cate gave her jacket sleeve a playful tug. "In truth, I am jealous. What a fine visit you'll have, Cousin!"

"The manse won't be the same without you," Abbie said, pouting. "Promise us you'll be all right? And you won't forget us?"

Touched by her youthful concern, Davina held up her hand. *I promise, dear girl.*

Reverend Stewart appeared at the music room door, a look of resignation on his face. "I've just spoken with the duke." Though the family had the room to themselves now, the minister kept his voice low. "His Grace has informed me of his plans. Tell me, Davina. Are you willing to do his bidding?"

She saw the conflict in his eyes. Wanting to take her home. Needing her to stay. If she refused, the Fullartons might take offense and the duke even more so, making things difficult for the reverend. Could she not do this for him?

Aye. She nodded firmly so the Stewarts would not leave with any misgivings. *I am willing.*

Reverend Stewart clasped her hand. "We shall see you at kirk on the Sabbath. 'Til then, you may depend upon our prayers."

So I shall, Cousin.

Thirty-Six

Hope! thou nurse of young desire.

ISAAC BICKERSTAFF

Davina stood on the flagstones outside the front door, flanked by tall iron torches that held the darkness at bay, waving farewell until her cousins rolled out of view. On the lawn all was quiet. The Stewarts were the final guests to leave, and the servants of Kilmichael House had tasks to attend elsewhere. Even the footman had deserted his post.

Taking advantage of the solitude, Davina remained out of doors, drinking in the refreshing night air, letting the events of the last few hours find a resting place in her mind and heart.

You shall be the duke's summer fiddler. 'Tis a great privilege.

Davina took a few steps along the graveled walk, hoping to calm her nerves. She had hours of entertainment to provide. However might she fill them all? Fiddle tunes were short and often grouped together in sets of three and four. Her repertoire would quickly be depleted, particularly without anyone dancing; when lines of blithe dancers were involved, a repeated reel was hardly noticed.

If the Fullartons did not object, she would spend her days at Kilmichael working on a dozen tunes she'd yet to master and practicing some of her grandfather's old strathspeys she'd neglected of late. One was "Monemusk" and "Tullochgorum" another. Davina smiled, hearing the frolicsome notes in her head, and imagined the duke's foot keeping time with her bow. Aye, she would have sufficient music to keep His Grace entertained and his company as well—one guest in particular.

See that you do not leave this house, Miss McKie. Davina glanced toward the empty entrance hall, her smile fading. Somerled MacDonald had not come looking for her as he'd promised. She sighed, remembering his words. *I find it difficult to bid you farewell.* Perhaps he'd found it altogether too difficult and left without saying good-bye.

She chastised herself at once for thinking ill of him. The duke's other guests might have insisted Somerled return with them. And she would see him tomorrow evening, would she not? Considering how deeply the man and his music had affected her, that might be soon enough. His gaze, his smile, his voice, his words spun round inside her, thrilling and confusing her all at once. Dared she hope for more than one night of music?

Shivering at the prospect, Davina continued in the direction of the garden, stopping when she reached the outermost light cast by the torches. The June night was seasonably mild, without a hint of rain. With the new moon gone from sight, a faint blanket of stars covered the velvety sky. The sun, not long set, would soon rise again on this shortest of nights, then skirt the treetops throughout the long Midsummer Day. Even now, at almost midnight, she could discern shapes in the garden, bathed in a dark blue sort of twilight.

Davina tipped her head back, picking out the northern constellations: Lyra, high in the southern sky; Ursa Major, growling down at her from the north; and to the east, Cassiopeia, shining in a distinct W.

She heard footsteps. Then a voice behind her softly said, "Light in darkness."

You remembered.

Davina gazed over her shoulder into Somerled's star-bright eyes. She turned round to face him, then stepped back for propriety's sake, and curtsied.

After a low chuckle, Somerled bowed. "How very formal, Miss McKie."

At least the darkness hid the color in her cheeks.

"Perhaps you've forgotten what transpired in the music room this evening." With one step he closed the gap between them. "You can be sure I have not."

When his fingers touched hers, she jumped slightly.

"Pardon me, for I did not mean to startle you." He lifted her hand and kissed the back of it, an innocent gesture common to every gentleman of the realm.

Then why did it feel so intimate? And why could she not stop blushing?

A diversion was called for. Davina pulled her hand free as gracefully as she could, then turned and swept her arm in an arc above her, inviting him to gaze at the night sky—safe, cool, distant—while she sorted through her scattered thoughts. She was attracted to Somerled; she was frightened of him as well. They should return to the house at once or procure a chaperon, yet she was loath to do either, having never stood beneath the stars with so handsome and charming a man as this one.

"Draco," Somerled murmured over her shoulder, pointing straight up. "The Dragon. 'Tis that spindly constellation with three stars forming its head. And below it, toward the horizon, is Boötes, the Herdsman. Four stars in a diamond pattern, like a kite with a bright tail. A favorite of your sheep-breeding father's, I'll wager."

She nodded, though she was not quite listening. Would her father approve of Somerled? Her dear mother?

"Low in the sky is Perseus," Somerled explained, moving closer. "Shaped like a bent T. Do you see?"

Nae, she did not see, for she was too aware of the nearness of him, the summery scent of him, like heather and sun and ocean.

"One constellation in particular reminds me of you, Miss McKie. Can you guess?"

She pretended to play a harp, plucking unseen strings while the lace on her sleeves fluttered.

"Lyra is a fine choice," he agreed, "for you are a musician without peer. No wonder the duke desires your company at table each evening."

But do you desire my company? She bowed her head, ashamed of her feelings—unfamiliar yet undeniable.

"You'll not find your stars down there." She heard the smile in his voice and a note of something else. He reached round and gently lifted her chin, pulling her closer.

Her breath, her heart seemed to stop in place.

"Do not be afraid, Miss McKie." His hand lingered on her chin,

Thirty-Seven

He sees only night,
and hears only silence.

JACQUES DELILLE

He stilled, waiting for Davina to soften beneath his touch. To yield to him, if only a little. No gentlewoman gave herself easily. What pleasure was there in that?

If Davina required wooing, he would woo her. Gladly.

"Let me show you the constellation I had in mind." Somerled tipped her chin toward the southern sky, leaning over her shoulder as he did. He positioned his rough cheek next to her smooth one, almost touching but not quite. "There it is, like a cross in the heavens. Cygnus. Do you know what the name means?"

When she nodded, her cheek brushed against his. *On purpose, lass?*

" 'Tis a mute swan," he told her, "the sort that glides across your Lowland lochs. Beautiful and silent. Very much like you, Miss McKie, in your fine damask gown." He lightly stroked her neck, marveling at the silken texture of her skin. "How did Milton phrase it?" he murmured. "The swan with arched neck between her white wings."

When Davina tried to move again, he gently released her, determined not to rush things. Time was not a hindrance; the night was young and the weather cooperative. He'd warned Sir Harry not to expect him at the castle until breakfast, hinting of a dairymaid who'd promised to share her narrow bed. Fathers paid little attention to trysts with servants.

As for Davina, Somerled felt certain no one would bother her until morning. He'd learned the location of the guest room from a loquacious maid, then locked the bedchamber door from the inside and slipped through the open sash into the garden. When the time came—much later, if all went well—he would escort Davina home by way of that same window without raising the alarm at Kilmichael.

She suddenly turned, as if considering a return to the house.

"Please, Miss McKie. Tarry with me a minute longer?" Somerled captured her small hand and tucked it round his arm, playing the part of a trustworthy gentleman. When she didn't resist, he knew he'd chosen wisely; they were on comfortable footing again.

"Might we follow the gravel path to the burn? There's a torch staked along the bank for guests who want to enjoy the water without tumbling in. The footman apparently forgot to extinguish it." As well the man should have: Somerled had paid him to forget.

Davina frowned at the darkened walkway, then shook her head.

"We needn't spend long there," he assured her. "And we'll be doing the Fullartons a service if we put out the fire for them."

However reticently, Davina let him lead her toward the burn. His boots were noisy on the gravel-strewn path, yet he could not ask her to walk in the grass and risk staining her ivory gown, much as he preferred they not be seen or heard. Though he cared nothing for his own reputation, he cared very much for hers. *Miss* would never become *Mrs.* if the respectable gentlemen of Galloway learned of Davina's indiscretions. He was a rake, aye, but not a scoundrel.

They passed a rose shrub in one grassy curve, a Grecian urn in another, though Davina's attention remained fixed on him. Was she signaling her interest? Trying to discern his? Surely he'd made his intentions clear. Keeping their conversation light, he pointed out the cotoneaster in the nearby garden, a dozen branches thrusting up from the ground, each one thick as a fist. Even on a moonless night, the newly bloomed white flowers were visible.

" 'Tis a night for fairies," he said softly. "Could be we'll discover some dancing on a flat stone in the burn, aye?" She smiled a little, which pleased him. "On Midsummer Eve the auld wives used to collect the brown spots on the fronds to protect themselves from the wee folk." He winked at her. "There are some especially large ferns along the water, Miss McKie. Shall I pluck one to keep me safe from you? After all, fairies have been known to play fiddles."

She blushed most becomingly in the meager torchlight.

"And here's the burn," he said, guiding her to a curved stone bench secluded beneath the trees. Silvery gray willows crowded along the banks of the stream, edged in moss and damp earth. The torch beside them was reduced to a flicker. A passing breeze would have extinguished it, but he made a show of putting the fire out for safety's sake, dousing the coals with water from the burn.

"Are you thirsty, Miss McKie?" When she nodded, he produced a small pewter flask, only to watch her eyes widen. "But not for the water of life, eh?" If she would not join him, he'd restrict himself to one drink. Some ladies did not care for the taste of whisky on a man's lips; he suspected Davina might be one of them.

After swallowing a bracing gulp, he capped the flask and slipped it back in place. "'Tis sufficient for me," he said, hoping to ease her mind on that score. "On a perfect night like this, I do not wish to disappoint you. In any way."

Davina looked at him with an expression of such innocence, she nearly unmanned him.

Och, lass. Somerled gazed down at her, haunted by those guileless eyes of hers. Had he misjudged her? Despite the considerable passion in her playing, was she, in fact, an untried maid? If so, he would not be the one to ruin her. A gentleman who valued his neck and his purse did not trifle with virgin daughters of landed gentry, lest he find himself at kirk, standing before the bride stool. Somerled had no such plans, not for a very long time.

Was Davina so naive as to think that he...

Nae. She was smiling up at him now, her mouth slightly open, as if she might welcome a kiss. Somerled settled down next to her on the stone bench. "Miss McKie, when we played together this evening, I sensed something...ah, developing between us. Did you as well?"

She nodded and touched her heart.

Easily understood, that one. "I'm glad to know I am not alone in my feelings." Somerled inched closer. "In truth, since we first met in the drawing room, I have imagined this moment."

Though Davina looked away, she could not conceal what he'd seen in her eyes: She'd imagined their tryst too.

He needed no further permission, no clearer invitation. He would follow her lead, just as he had when she'd played her fiddle. And because Davina could not speak, he would remain silent as well.

When he slowly began to caress her hands, rubbing his thumbs across her satiny skin, she did not pull away. *Good, lass.* He lifted her hands to his mouth and kissed the back of each one, tenderly but with purpose. Again, she did not flinch. *Ah, better.* And when he turned over her hands and took his time kissing first her palms and then her fingers, she trembled, but she did not resist him. *Much better.*

The two of them were so close now, breathing the same night air, that shifting his mouth from Davina's fingers to her lips was almost effortless.

Thirty-Eight

The silent soule doth most abound in care.

WILLIAM ALEXANDER, EARL OF STIRLING

Davina's heart quickened as the heat of uncertainty rose to her cheeks. Should she open her eyes and gaze into his? Open her mouth at his gentle insistence?

Nae. Suddenly shy, Davina turned away, breaking their kiss.

Somerled responded at once, cradling her face in his hands. "Please, my bonny wee girl." He kissed her again, so tenderly she could not resist him. "We have shared much already, have we not?"

Aye. She nodded slightly, letting him kiss her cheeks, drowning in a pool of sensations. To be so desired, so cherished...was this not what she'd always hoped for?

When he kissed her lips again, weaving his long fingers into her hair, freeing her toppling crown, Davina opened her eyes and opened her mouth and opened her heart.

Somerled took them all.

"Davina..." Breathless. Muffled against the curve of her neck.

No longer *Miss McKie* but *Davina.* Scandalous as it was, she liked hearing him speak her name.

"Come with me, lass." His voice was low, almost dangerously so. When he lifted his head, his eyes were like the night sky: the dark, round centers impossibly wide.

He looked older now. Stronger. Taller. When he stood and pulled her to her feet, she suddenly felt very small.

"We must not make a sound." He clasped her hand and started across the grass toward the house.

Why was he so eager to see her delivered to Kilmichael's door? Though the hour was nearing midnight, she was far from sleepy. Ah, but they were bound for the garden instead. How strange, when it was so very dark. Nae, not the garden; the stables behind the house. She tugged on his arm, confused. Did he think to send her home to the manse at this hour? Or ride off with her to the castle? *Wait, please!*

When he did not slow his steps, she dug her heels into the grass, desperate to get his attention.

Somerled turned to her at once. "What is it, Davina?" He wrapped her in his embrace, enveloped her with his voice. "Is something wrong?"

She had too many questions and no means of asking them.

"Relax, milady." He kissed her, dispelling her unspoken fears. " 'Twill be so much better when we are withindoors. Alone."

He started out again, this time with his arm round her shoulders, yet with just as much haste. Davina did not understand why. The night was pleasantly warm, and they were already alone. Could they not simply sit by the burn? She heard the horses whinnying, even as she felt her heart pounding inside her stays. Might she faint before they reached the stable door?

Somerled guided her down a long row of stalls. Red sandstone buildings formed a three-sided square, the open end facing the rear of the house. Outside the stables, everything lay dark and still; inside the house, candles remained lit in Kilmichael's ground-floor rooms.

She found herself wishing someone might look out the window and see them, question them, stop them. Tears sprang to her eyes, but she quickly brushed them away. What would Somerled think of her? That she was childish, that she was foolish. Once he kissed her again, all would be well.

"Now then." He slowed his steps, perhaps not wanting to disturb the horses, leading her past one stall, then another, until they reached the corner farthest from the house. Somerled claimed a small lantern hanging beside the stable door, then held it aloft. "Ladies first."

Davina entered with hesitant steps, letting her eyes adjust to the darkened interior. The vacant stall smelled of leather and oats. Straw covered the floor, tin pails hung from pegs on the wall, and woolen blankets were piled in the corner.

Somerled closed the wooden door behind them and slid the iron bar in place. "Won't this be better, lass?"

Better than what? She shivered, though she was not cold.

"Better than a hard stone bench," Somerled answered as if he'd heard her thoughts. He hung the lantern on a peg, then shook out one of the blankets and spread it across the straw. "Better than you spending the night alone in your guest bed and me sleeping in a drafty old castle with a dozen snoring men."

She tried not to stare as he unbuttoned his tail coat and hung it on one of the pegs. Did he intend to sleep here? And expect her to join him?

"So, Davina." He loosened his neckcloth, smiling at her all the while. "What might we do to make you comfortable as well?"

She had never been more uncomfortable in her life. When she started to back away from him, Somerled swiftly pulled her into his arms.

"What's this now?" He must have felt the stiffness in her body. "A case of nerves, when you've traveled this road before? But perhaps not in a stable, is that it?" He leaned down and nuzzled her neck. "Many apologies, lass. I'll see we have better arrangements for the rest of my stay on Arran."

Davina could not fathom what he meant. *Better arrangements?*

He straightened, then lightly kissed her brow, her cheeks, her chin. "You caught me by surprise, don't you see? I came to a dinner party and found the woman of my dreams."

And I thought I'd found the man of mine.

She wriggled from his embrace, but he laughed and captured her once more, then kissed her again, so hard she could not breathe. Or think, or reason, or sort out her feelings. *Aye. Nae. Aye.*

"What a *jillet* you are." Somerled pressed his body against hers. "I confess, I cannot wait much longer, lass." His hands were quick. Already her brocade jacket was on the floor.

Now she was certain. *Nae.* When she pushed against his chest, his hands stilled on her shoulders.

"Am I being too rough with you, Davina?" His eyes probed hers, searching for answers. "Pardon me, but some women...well..." He smoothed his hands down her back. "I should have known better, watching you perform. Legato, not staccato." The arm that had bowed across four strings now encircled her waist, giving her little room to move.

She shook her head, hoping he understood. *Somerled, please. Don't.*

But then he filled her ear with whispered endearments and ardent professions, and she relaxed in his arms once more, convinced that he cared for her. The man in her dream, the man in her drawing, the man who'd bared his soul to her through his music—that man would never hurt her.

In one smooth motion he picked her up and cradled her across his chest, as if she weighed nothing. "Let me hold you." He gently lowered her to the blanket, then stretched out beside her. "My darling Davina." His voice was rough, his breathing ragged as he pulled her arms round his shoulders, then rolled on top of her, pinning her to the ground.

Fear rose inside her, stronger this time. She tried to move but could not.

"Please, Davina. I want to feel your heart against mine." The woolen blankets chafed her neck as his kisses grew deeper, his hands more insistent, inching her skirts toward her waist.

When the evening air chilled her legs, her senses snapped to attention. *Nae. Not here. Not this.*

But she did not know what *this* was. She did not understand all the words that he said. Did not understand why he touched her as he did. If he meant his actions to be pleasurable, they were not.

Nae more. She shifted beneath him, tears stinging her eyes. *Please stop.* The harder she struggled to escape his embrace, the more firmly he held her down. Frantic, she pushed against his chest, but he was far too heavy for her. Far too strong.

Never in all of her life had she needed her voice as she needed it now. *Please, please don't. Don't!*

But he could not hear her. And he did not heed her.

Thirty-Nine

O man! man! hard-hearted cruel man!
what mischiefs art thou not capable of!

SAMUEL RICHARDSON

Davina, why did you not tell me?"
Somerled stared at the faint streak of blood on her pale thighs. No wonder she'd resisted him, embarrassed by her monthly courses. "Had I known, I would have…" *Waited?* Nae, that was a lie. He could not have tarried another minute before taking her. "Pardon me, lass, for not understanding."

He quickly found a cupful of water in one of the hanging pails, then dabbed her delicate skin with the wet tail of his shirt. She watched him, unmoving, almost unseeing, as if her thoughts were altogether elsewhere. "Is that better now? Do you have what you need to…ah…" He supposed she must.

Somerled dressed in haste, giving her a moment to gather her wits and find her shoes amid the straw. Though he was reluctant to tell her so, they could not remain in the stables much longer. The midsummer sun was not far from the horizon.

Davina was standing by the time he finished buttoning his tail coat. How vulnerable she looked with her soiled white stockings pooling round her ankles. The ruined damask gown was his fault entirely. He should have slipped off her dress and hung it on one of the pegs. But he'd been too intent on seducing her to remember such practicalities. Despite her dishabille, she was still fetching. A red curtain of hair hung down her back, the curls reduced to twisted strands.

"You've need of your maid this morning," he said lightly, plucking bits of straw from her hair and gown. He knelt long enough to tug up her stockings, then slipped on her shoes, intrigued once again by the smallness of her hands and feet. He'd not asked her age. Was she younger than twenty after all? "Such a fine gown," he murmured, trying to smooth the many wrinkles. "You have a talented dressmaker at Glentrool."

All at once Davina began shaking from head to toe. Chilled, no doubt. Her gown was too narrow to allow a chemise, though at least she'd not adopted the vulgar new fashion of wearing drawers. "Come, let me warm you." He drew her into his arms, fitting her head well below his chin.

Then he realized she was not simply shaking. She was weeping.

"Davina?"

She grasped the lapels of his coat, her slender fingers disappearing beneath the folds of fabric, her head buried in his chest. The faint sound she made was like nothing he'd ever heard before. A silent keening that was naught but air. And anguish.

"Dear woman, what is it?" He tried to lift her chin and could not. "Are you…in pain?"

He felt her head move but could not tell whether 'twas *aye* or *nae*. Was all this distress because of her courses? "Truly, the wee bit of… blood…matters not."

This time he was certain she nodded. *Aye, it does matter.*

"Davina, you've no need to be ashamed…"

When she lifted her head and looked into his eyes, the despair he saw there shocked him. "Please, Davina. Can you not tell me what's wrong?"

Her lips trembled as she tried to form words, her grip on his coat tightening each time she had to start over. Finally she mouthed a single syllable, difficult to make out in the murky interior of the stall.

But he tried. *"First?* Is that what you're saying?"

Nodding, she collapsed against him, soaking his waistcoat with her tears.

First? Somerled's mind was reeling, trying to make sense of it. *First. Her first…*

Nae. His mouth dried to dust. "Davina, you do not mean that…I was your first…that you were chaste…before tonight?"

Please, Davina. Please don't nod.

But she did.

Stunned, he fell back against the wall, taking her with him. "Oh, lass…I thought…I was so certain…"

He could not hear her sobs, but he could feel them.

"Surely you must have realized when I kissed you…when I led you to the stables…"

She shook her bowed head. *Nae.*

He ran his hand through his hair in frustration and disbelief. Could any woman be so naive? "How old are you, Davina?" Though he dreaded the answer, he had to know.

She wrote the number in the air with her finger.

Seventeen. He turned his head, sickened by the news. *My bonny wee girl.* He'd called her that when they sat by the burn, never imagining the truth, never dreaming the young woman who'd kissed him so willingly was an innocent maid.

Yet hadn't she pulled away from him more than once? Tried to break free from his embrace? He'd thought she was toying with him, challenging him, urging him to be more aggressive. Instead she'd been trying to stop him, silently pleading for help.

He'd misread her completely. And misused her abominably.

"Davina…" He looked at her sweet face, forcing himself to see the pain there, knowing he was the cause of it. "I have wronged you in the worst imaginable way. I took what you did not offer." He swallowed hard. "I took what was not mine to take."

She stepped back, beyond his reach, as tears spilled down her cheeks.

"And what have I given you in return? One night of pleasure?" His heart sank when she looked away. *Nae, not even that.*

A cock crow echoed through the stables.

Och! He'd forgotten the time. If he did not deliver her unseen to her bedchamber, Davina's reputation would be in tatters by breakfast. And he would have far more explaining to do than he wished. One did not rob a gentlewoman of her virtue without consequence.

"Come, lass." Somerled eased the stall door open. The hour was still early; the last of the stars had not blinked out, and none of the stable lads were in sight. "I left the window to your room ajar," he whispered, motioning her closer. "Let me help you…"

But she was gone, running past him, her unbound hair streaming behind her.

Forty

For there are deeds
Which have no form, sufferings which have no tongue.
PERCY BYSSHE SHELLEY

D avina stared at the bruise.
'Twas the size of his thumb. Pressed into the soft flesh of her shoulder. *There.* She ran a wet cloth over it, then winced. Another tear slipped down her cheek.

I took what was not mine to take. Aye, he had. Though she had given him her heart—foolishly yet willingly—she had not given him her body. He had claimed that without asking.

Please don't. Please stop.

But Somerled had not stopped. He'd ignored her when she struggled against him and laughed when she'd tried to evade his embrace. "My darling Davina," he'd said before pinning her to the floor. How could anyone be so cruel?

Davina scrubbed at her skin, washing every trace of him from her body, cringing at each tender spot. At least he'd not followed her to the house. She'd climbed over the windowsill, her limbs trembling, her heart in her throat. In the shadowy guest chamber a fourposter bed loomed behind her, thrusting its sharp spears toward the ceiling. She had yet to light a candle at the hearth or to look in the mirror, dreading what the glass might reveal.

Please, God. She mouthed the words, wishing she might cry out. *Help me. I did not want this. I did not know...*

At her feet lay her damask gown, stained and reeking of dung. She saw her mother's pale hands clasping the fine fabric. Pictured her silver needle threading its way through the silk-embroidered linen. Remembered how proudly she'd held the dress to her shoulders and kissed her cheek. *'Tis for a special occasion, dearie.*

Davina sank to the floor, clutching the gown to her heart. *Mother.* If she were here, Leana would hold her in her arms and stroke her hair and whisper words of comfort and sing softly in her ear. *Baloo, baloo, my wee, wee thing.* But her mother was not here. Davina was alone in a house full of strangers, holding her mother's gift, ruined beyond any hope of redemption.

She dragged her gown into the washbowl and soaked it with her tears. *Forgive me.* She scrubbed the stains with soap, then rubbed the fabric together, harder than was prudent, trying in vain to get it clean. *Please.* She rinsed the dress over and over, using the last of the water, then rolled it inside a linen towel and hid it in the bottom of the wardrobe.

Later she would find a place to let the fabric dry. Later, when she could reason.

For now her mind could grasp but one thing: *I am no longer a maid.* Davina clutched the carved edges of the washstand, imagining her father learning of her disgrace. The news would break his heart, and the scandal would destroy his good name.

No one must ever know. *No one.* Not on the mainland and not on Arran. She could hide the truth forever. Unless…

Nae. Davina stared at the carpet, fighting to keep her balance. *Please, Lord. Not a child. Not his child.*

Guilt tightened round her heart as firmly as Somerled's arm had wrapped round her waist. Had she not welcomed his kisses? Had she not followed him to the stables?

Forgive me, Lord. Please, please forgive me.

Dared she ask for mercy? She had to; she must. *Withhold not thou thy tender mercies from me.*

Even if the Lord might forgive her sins, no one else would. Instead the world would soon come knocking at her door, expecting to find a young woman who'd spent the night alone, sleeping. She slipped on the white cotton nightgown waiting by the clothes press. Brushed the tangles from her hair. Hid her filthy stockings in a drawer. Unlocked the door, lest it rouse suspicion. Turned down the bedcovers.

A wave of exhaustion rolled over her, like standing on the *Clarinda* and feeling the slap of the choppy surf. Beyond the curtains dawn had broken. The sky was slowly growing lighter, yet the house remained silent. Sleep would be hard to come by, though she needed rest, desperately so.

Davina slid beneath the covers, her body still tense, her heart still pounding. She would sleep if she could. And pray that no gentleman came looking for her in her dreams.

A persistent tapping at the door woke Davina from her fitful sleep. She struggled to sit up as a brown-haired maid poked her head round the door.

"Guid mornin' tae ye, Miss McKie. Me name's Nan Shaw." The servant, perhaps thirty years of age, swept into the room with a pitcher of steaming water in hand. "I thocht ye'd be wantin' yer breakfast by noo. 'Tis ten o'clock."

Davina rubbed her eyes, trying to get her bearings. The guest room at Kilmichael House. Midsummer Day.

"I see ye've bathed yerself." The maid gathered the wet towels draped over the washstand.

Davina prayed Nan would not count them and notice one was missing.

"If ye're ready for me tae dress ye, thar's a *goun* o' Mrs. Fullarton's hangin' in yer wardrobe."

Davina held her breath as Nan reached into the wardrobe to retrieve the borrowed gown.

The maid held the dress out to her. "I'll raise the hem for ye, if need be." Though the pale gray did not suit Davina's coloring, it well matched her mood.

She slipped down from the high bedstead, grateful that the curtains were still drawn; no wonder she'd slept well into the morning. Unless Nan insisted on lighting more candles, Davina might be able to conceal her bruises long enough to dress. She stood as far away from the candle and mirror as she could, then turned her back toward Nan and loosened her nightgown, letting it drop to the floor, hoping her hair would cover any marks on her back. Davina lifted her arms while Nan wrapped her cotton stays round her middle. Though Nan's movements were efficient, she was not very gentle, tugging hard on the laces, putting pressure on Davina's bruises, bringing tears to her eyes.

Because of you, Somerled. Because of what you did to me.

"Och, I forgot. I've a message for ye." From her apron pocket Nan produced a folded paper, sealed in wax. "Here ye are, miss. Delivered last hour by ane o' the servants from the castle."

While Nan brushed her hair, Davina rubbed her thumb across the address. *For Miss McKie, a Guest at Kilmichael House.* She did not know his hand but feared the bold script belonged to Somerled. She laid the letter aside long enough to don her gown and have her hair dressed, though her eyes remained fixed upon it and her thoughts more so. *There is nothing to be said, sir. Nothing to be done.*

"Ye'll find breakfast on the sideboard, miss." Nan tied back the curtains, bobbed a curtsy, and was gone, leaving Davina to draw the candle near and read her note at last.

She broke the seal and unfolded the paper, her gaze going directly to the bottom of the page. *Aye.* Above his signature appeared a handful of words.

> Miss McKie,
>
> I am more sorry than pen and paper could ever express.
> If you are willing, meet me at two o'clock at our bench by
> the burn.
>
> Somerled MacDonald

Davina thrust the note into the candle flame, though she took no delight in seeing it burn. When it became too dangerous to hold, she tossed the letter into the fireplace, watching the paper grow black and charred until it was naught but ashes.

Forty-One

Trust me, 'tis something to be cast
Face to face with one's Self at last.
JAMES RUSSELL LOWELL

Somerled did not need to consult his pocket watch. The hour was well past two. Davina was not coming.

He abandoned the stone bench, striding along the path toward the house, then abruptly turned on his heel. Knocking on the Fullartons' door was out of the question. Who knew what sort of tearful confession Davina might have made to her hostess? As it was, he'd evaded the gardener for an hour lest the man discover him lurking by the burn and inquire about his business there.

"I wanted to view Goatfell from this vantage point" would hardly serve. But an honest answer would be worse. "I wanted to apologize to Miss McKie. To make amends…"

Disgusted with himself, Somerled stamped the mud off his boots, then started down Kilmichael's long road through the glen, headed for the bay. Late morning rain showers had left the ground soggy and the lane full of puddles. The avenue of trees dripped great, splattering drops of water on his face as he walked; Somerled wiped them off, grumbling under his breath.

The duke was expecting his lady fiddler at seven o'clock; surely Davina would not disappoint His Grace in the manner she'd just disappointed him. When a quiet moment presented itself after dinner, Somerled would say what must be said in order to spare their reputations.

Aye, and clear your conscience.

He strode along the edge of the lane, kicking the heads off every oxeye daisy that crossed his path. He'd never felt so misunderstood in his life. Had he known Davina was chaste, he never would have escorted her to the stables.

Escorted? Or did you drag her there?

Stung, he tramped through a puddle on purpose, soaking his boots.

What if the packet boat sailing for the mainland carried a letter from Davina to her father, naming Somerled MacDonald as her molester? He could not deny he'd been too forceful. Too determined to have her. Too intoxicated by the heady scent of her and the sweet taste of her and...

Och! Another daisy lost its petals.

But hadn't Davina welcomed his kisses? Hardly the behavior of a virtuous maid. True, he'd been most persuasive, but she'd also been responsive. Hadn't she? Somerled fumed at a red-breasted robin hopping about, as if the bird were intentionally in his way. He lengthened his stride, his anger rising. If the lass so valued her maidenhood, why didn't she wrestle free of him when he laid her on the floor of that deuced stall?

Because you're a foot taller and six stone heavier than she.

The argument raged inside him as he turned north onto the coast road, where fishermen trudged by, hauling creels brimming with the day's catch. He glowered at the local folk who stared at him and ignored those who offered a polite greeting, whether in English, Scots, or Gaelic. Could they not see he was in no mood to be cordial?

When he passed the standing stone, he was still fuming. By the time he reached Cladach and started uphill toward the castle, his defense was weakening. The facts were irrefutable and not in his favor. He was a rogue; she was an innocent. She could not speak; he would not listen. He was a gentleman of both title and fortune; she was a gentlewoman from whom a priceless gift had been stolen.

By you.

"Somerled!" Sir Harry's voice bellowed across the castle grounds.

Groaning, Somerled acknowledged his father with a lifted hand, then veered in his direction. Sir Harry knew nothing of his reckless act yestreen. Would anything be gained by telling him?

"You missed a fine morning of fishing and a tasty meal of potted trout." Sir Harry fell in step with him as they walked along the castle wall. "Dougal heard you shuffling about our bedchamber at some ungodly hour yestreen while I was well asleep, then could not rouse you for breakfast. I take it you bedded that dairymaid. Is she at Kilmichael House?"

Dairymaid? Somerled had forgotten his ploy. "Aye, she's…at Kilmichael."

"Be mindful of your seed planting, lad," Sir Harry cautioned. "I'll not spend your inheritance feeding and clothing your *bystarts*."

Somerled only nodded, speechless at the very suggestion that Davina might be carrying his child. All the more reason he must speak with her, and quickly. Aye, and make a confession to his father, much as it pained him to do so. If his conquest had indeed been a willing servant, no more need be said. If she were a highborn strumpet who'd brought others to her bed, she'd not likely make trouble for him. But a lady of quality—even a silent one—would not keep her ruined state a secret for long.

"Sir…" Somerled waited for the Fraser brothers from Inverness to stroll by, then lowered his voice. "The woman was not a dairymaid."

Sir Harry gave him a sharp-eyed look. "Who then? And do not say that fiddler from Glentrool—"

"Aye." Somerled looked down at his boots as he walked. " 'Twas she."

His father uttered a mild oath. "What *hizzies* these Lowland gentlewomen are! Did I not hear that Miss McKie was but seventeen? Perhaps 'tis why her father sent her to Arran." He rolled his broad shoulders, then sniffed the rain-washed air. "Ashamed of her, no doubt."

"On the contrary." Somerled stopped, forcing himself to address his father face to face. "Miss McKie was utterly chaste. But I assumed—"

"Assumed?" Sir Harry's countenance grew livid. "You did not ask the lass?"

"Perhaps you've forgotten, sir, but Miss McKie is mute."

"Aye," he growled, "but she is not deaf. Did you or did you not ask that young woman if—"

"Nae." Somerled swallowed, suddenly feeling ill. "I did not."

Sir Harry's silvery eyebrows drew into a single thick line across his brooding face. "Why would a Lowland daughter with beauty, talent, and a good name give up her virtue for a Highlander she'd ne'er laid eyes on before?" When Somerled did not have a ready answer, his father plowed on. "Might it be that wee lass had no say in the matter?"

His face heated with shame. "Very little, sir."

"Och!" Sir Harry cuffed his son's head, hard. "What am I to do with you, lad? You've a fine mind and talents of your own. Could you not put them to better use?"

Somerled fell back a step. His father had never upbraided him so severely. "I am…sorry to disappoint you, sir."

"Disappoint?" His father snorted. "'Tis far more serious than that. What you've done is not only an affront to society; 'tis also against the law. McKie is a landowner of some renown. Did you think to steal his daughter's honor and escape unscathed?"

"Father, I did not think—"

"Nae, you did *not!*" Sir Harry stamped about, his anger barely contained. "What of my good reputation? And yours?"

Somerled could no longer look at him. "Forgive me, sir—"

"Och! Forgiveness is not the issue." Sir Harry grabbed both his shoulders and shook him. "Listen to me: I have no wish to see my heir imprisoned for his profligate ways. Do your duty by her, lad, and act quickly. Before the damage cannot be undone."

Somerled did not need to consult his pocket watch.

The hour was well past seven. The first course had been served at the duke's table, and still Davina McKie had not arrived.

Somerled glanced down at his creamy plate of partan *bree*. Even the aroma of fresh crabmeat held no appeal. He wanted Davina by his side, though not at all for the reasons he'd desired her yestreen. And not only because his father had made his expectations clear.

We must speak, lass.

Up and down the table, spoons clattered against china as men boasted of their prowess with bow and arrow, archery being the next morning's activity. "You're quiet this evening, MacDonald." A fellow named Armstrong, son of a baronet from the Scottish Borders, regarded him with an amused expression. "Or would you rather be plying your bow with a certain fiddler?"

"Miss McKie will be along shortly," Somerled told him, glancing at the doorway. "As to my accompanying her again, that remains to be seen."

Thoughts of Davina consumed him. Nae, tormented him. Guilt, an unfamiliar emotion, hounded him, while anger, his old friend, had lost its teeth. He had no one to blame but himself for what had happened on Midsummer Eve. No one.

He would tell Davina that and a great deal more. But first he had to see her.

Far down the turnpike stair the old castle door creaked open, then banged shut. He listened to the footfalls on the stone steps. *A man's boots.* Not Davina, then.

When the footman from Kilmichael appeared in the doorway bearing a note, Somerled's spirits sank. Davina was not coming. He had pushed back his chair, preparing to rise, when the footman—Clark, he was called—came forward and presented the note to the duke.

Somerled frowned at the servant, the very one he'd paid to leave the torch burning. Was there no note for him? Apparently not, for the man took his leave without glancing in Somerled's direction.

The duke pursed his lips as he read, then tossed the paper aside. "Gentlemen, I regret to say Miss McKie will not be entertaining us this evening. Our Midsummer feast at Kilmichael House did not sit well with her, poor lady." He trained his gaze on Somerled. "It falls to you, MacDonald, to provide tonight's music."

"With pleasure, Your Grace." Somerled pulled his chair closer to the table, resigned to honor the duke's request. He'd brought his wooden flute and could easily sing unaccompanied. But it was Davina he would miss, not her fiddle.

The soup course was whisked away and plates of *cabbieclaw* placed before the guests. Somerled picked at his salted cod, his thoughts elsewhere. Was Davina truly ill? That would explain her absence earlier and this evening as well.

Except she'd eaten very little at dinner yestreen, And he'd spent hours with her after their meal, observing no sign of illness.

At least, not from the food.

Somerled pushed aside his dinner, his appetite vanished. *Please, Davina, do not hide from me.* There was one possibility, one remedy he wished to offer her.

'Twas the best solution. Nae, the only solution, as his father well knew.

But would she want him for a husband after all he'd done? Or would she wed him to avoid disgrace, then detest him the whole of their marriage?

Somerled rose from the table, composing a letter in his head. Not so brief a note as the one he'd sent that morning. Rather, an honest entreaty that would coax Davina from the safe confines of Kilmichael and give her a reason to trust him again.

Forty-Two

I wish, I wish, I wish in vain;
I wish I were a maid again.
<small>TRADITIONAL FOLK SONG</small>

Davina retrieved the still-damp towel from her wardrobe, then unrolled the thick bundle across her bed. Could it be that her ivory damask was not ruined after all? She held a candle over the dress even as she held her breath.

Nae. Several dark stains remained. The silk embroidery was roughened where she'd scrubbed it, and a faintly pungent aroma from the stables lingered in the folds of the fabric.

It seemed her gown could not be restored. Nor could she.

Ruined. A terrible word for a young woman who was no longer chaste. Like a once-grand castle reduced to rubble or a lovely dress beyond repair.

Forgive me, Lord. Not for how the night ended. But for how it began. She should never have kissed him. Never have followed him. Never have trusted him.

With a soundless sigh Davina put aside the candle, then shook out her gown before hanging it from a peg in the wardrobe beneath a long cotton wrap. It would take days to dry there. If she were a country laundress, she'd spread her linens out on the heath or drape them across the shrubbery.

She scrutinized her open window, then pushed aside the curtains and examined the clipped yew just beyond the sash. A tempting proposition. But if the gardener happened by, there'd be gossip in the servants' quarters. *Wasna that the dress she wore the nicht o' the fancy denner? How d'ye suppose it got a' the ugsome stains on it? Did ye hear her playin' her fiddle wi' that* Hieland *laddie?* Nae, she could not display her shame for any passerby to see.

"Miss McKie?" Mrs. Fullarton tapped on the door. "Are you feeling better this morning? I thought we might take a turn in the garden."

Davina quickly placed a potpourri of dried rose petals in the wardrobe to sweeten the air, then rearranged her tucker at the mirror before opening the door to her hostess.

Mrs. Fullarton's personality was as warm as her russet-colored hair and brown eyes. "I declare, that eyelet gown is far more becoming on you than it ever was on me." Her thin lips curled in a smile. "You must take it with you, Miss McKie."

Embarrassed, Davina curtsied her thanks. Would her young hostess be so affable if she knew what had transpired in her stables? Davina had considered telling the Fullartons, eliciting their sympathy and their help. But then she imagined the scandal. The suspicions raised and the accusations made. *Nae.* She knew what had happened on Midsummer Eve, and so did Somerled. That was enough.

Her hostess cupped Davina's elbow and guided her through the house and into the garden. The morning was dry, and the color of the sky matched the tall bank of delphiniums, brilliantly blue against the lush grass. As the two women walked, Mrs. Fullarton kept up a steady stream of lighthearted comments, punctuated with an airy laugh.

"I never touch the soil myself, of course, but I do enjoy choosing what is planted. This red ornamental along the border is a French honeysuckle." When her hostess paused, Davina dutifully studied the tall plant with its long cluster of flowers and oval leaves. " 'Tis a biennial. I'm glad you are visiting this year, Miss McKie, for you'll not find it blooming here next summer."

Davina's gaze wandered toward the burn. Though she could not spy the bench from where they were standing, the unlit torch could be seen through the trees. Yesterday afternoon, a book of poetry in hand, she'd observed the curved bench quite clearly from the second-floor drawing room window. Somerled had tarried there for almost an hour—sometimes sitting, sometimes standing—waiting for her.

She did not regret avoiding him; the man was not trustworthy. But she did wish—oh, how she wished!—things between them had taken a different turn. If they had simply parted ways at Kilmichael's door with a proper farewell, they might have enjoyed many evenings of pleasant exchanges at the castle. He might have sought her father's permission to court her…

Nae. However charming and intelligent, Somerled MacDonald was not the courting sort.

"Did you wish to walk by the burn?" Mrs. Fullarton stood beside her, gazing in the same direction.

Davina promptly shook her head, casting aside any thoughts of a certain Highlander as she turned toward the rose garden.

"Ah." Her hostess beamed. "The queen of flowers." Mrs. Fullarton swept along the pebbly beds, introducing them as one might present friends. The moss rose with its hairy stems. The musk rose, a fragrant climber. The double velvet rose and its scarlet petals. "And here's our lovely maiden's blush." She touched the pale pink blooms affectionately. "A rose as fair as ever saw the North." Taking Davina's arm, she drew her closer as they walked. "No bloom in my garden is a finer complement to your complexion, my dear. I'll have Nan prepare a vase for your chamber."

Davina tried to smile. *Maiden's blush.* Aye, the color suited her but not the name.

At the sound of someone walking through the grass, Davina glanced over her shoulder in time to see Clark approach.

"Mrs. Fullarton?" The footman held out a sealed letter. " 'Tis for your guest, madam. Delivered by a messenger from Brodick castle."

Davina received it with a nod of thanks, though her hands were less than steady. She recognized the handwriting this time, though her hostess did not.

"An entreaty from the duke, I'll warrant. Pleading with you to join him this evening." Mrs. Fullarton pointed them toward the door. "Suppose we have a light meal and see how you're feeling. Then you can judge if you are well enough to play."

Davina knew she could not keep the duke waiting indefinitely. Nor was it her nature to hide behind a falsehood. Aye, she would play her fiddle for His Grace that evening. But first she would read Somerled's letter and learn what she might find when she arrived.

Davina held up the folded paper, hoping Mrs. Fullarton would grasp her meaning.

"Naturally you'll want to read that before we dine." She smiled as the footman held open the front door for them. "Nothing piques my curiosity more than an unopened letter."

As they walked through the entrance hall, Mrs. Fullarton said, "Since the captain is aboard the *Wickham* today, I'll have them set up a small luncheon table for us in the music room. Won't that be cozier?" She stopped when they reached the guest room. "Here you are, then. Come join me whenever you finish your letter."

Davina had barely closed the door before she'd broken the wax seal and unfolded the paper.

> Miss McKie,
>
> I trust that you are in good health and simply do not wish to see me. I understand completely and do not blame you in the least. Yet I long to speak with you and make whatever amends I may.

His humility, however genuine, provided little comfort. *Unless you can make me a maid again, sir, I cannot imagine what remedy you might offer.*

> My conduct Thursday night was reprehensible. You have every right to despise me.

Davina stared at the word in his bold hand. *Despise.* Was that what she felt toward Somerled now? Hatred? Loathing? Nae, what she felt was distrust. And fear.

> I dare not ask for mercy. But I would beg for an opportunity to speak with you.

Mercy? For the man who had stolen her innocence? Only the Almighty could manage such a feat.

> And so I will ask you again, Miss McKie, with all my heart. If you are willing, kindly meet me at two o'clock this after-

noon. I will be waiting at our bench by the burn, just as I waited yesterday.

Aye, you did. She saw him again in her mind's eye, standing there, looking forlorn.

A final remark appeared above his signature.

There is one possibility I would like to discuss with you.

The paper nearly slipped from her hands. *He cannot mean... He cannot think that I would...* Tears made the phrase swim before her eyes. *One possibility.* She was not too young or too innocent to know what that might be.

You are wrong, sir. 'Tis not possible.

He was standing near the stone bench by the burn at the stroke of two.

Davina forced herself to take small steps, lest she appear eager without meaning to. Lifting the hem of her borrowed gown, she continued down the narrow path, not quite looking at him. She'd never again need to pinch her cheeks for color; the mere thought of Somerled Mac-Donald was enough to stain them red as poppies.

Her sketchbook and pencil were by her side, for she was determined to be fully understood this afternoon and not swayed by his handsome face. She'd already written a list of questions that begged for answers.

Somerled waited until she was an arm's length away before he spoke. "I was afraid you might not come." His eyes were as blue as ever, but the faint shadows beneath them were new; perhaps he'd not been sleeping well either. "I feared you might flee to the manse," he confessed, "or, worse, to Glentrool before we had a chance to speak."

Davina heard no playfulness in his tone, saw no mischievous twinkle in his gaze. She was grateful, yet wary, for she'd never met a man more disarming than this one. A warm breeze ruffled the waves in his hair as he looked down at her, apparently choosing his words with great care.

"May I tell you first how truly sorry I am." There was no doubting the sheen of tears in his tired eyes.

I am sorry as well. Davina looked away, grieved by the reminder of what she had lost. *Sorry that I was so trusting. Sorry that you were so forceful.*

"Perhaps you might be more comfortable if we were seated." Somerled escorted her to the curved bench, then joined her, sitting a proper distance away. "I have given our predicament much thought." He paused, but for only a moment. Not long enough for her to respond. "The wisest course—truly, the only course—is for us to marry as soon as the banns can be read."

One possibility. Davina stared at her hands, willing away her tears. *The only course.* Was that true? Did she have no other choice but to marry a heartless stranger?

"I cannot think of your reputation being compromised because of me. Nor your future marriage prospects. I have already spoken with my father on the matter—"

Davina lifted her head. *Your father knows?*

"We discussed no particulars," he hastened to assure her, his neck taking on a ruddy tint. "But Sir Harry understands the situation and is in agreement. You are a lady of gentle birth. And though I seldom behave like one, I am a gentleman. For me to abscond with your virtue and not offer you the protection of my name and fortune would be…" He sighed. "*Unconscionable* was the word I chose. My father listed several others."

Davina sighed and turned away. *The protection of his name.* A legal arrangement, a means of avoiding scandal. Not a genuine marriage.

"I realize this suggestion may be…abhorrent to you. I confess, I did not come to Arran in search of a wife. But then I saw your beautiful face…and heard your exquisite music…"

Davina's throat tightened. Why must he say such things?

"And then I held you in my arms…"

Nae! She did not want or need to remember.

"And then I kissed you."

When he touched her sleeve, she jumped, startled first by his warmth and then by the earnestness of his gaze.

"In truth, Miss McKie, I've thought of nothing else but you since we parted."

She wanted to glare at him but could not for the tears pooling in her eyes. *How dare you be so tender!*

"Still her silent looks loudly reproached me," he murmured. "Ovid's words, not mine, though I see 'tis true." With the tip of his gloved finger, he caught the teardrop that started down her cheek. "You've yet to say a word to me with your graceful hands. What am I to think? Though I've never proposed to a woman before, I always imagined there being a response, aye or nae."

Aye, because I must. Undone, she bowed her head, brushing away his hand. *Nae, because I cannot.*

He sighed heavily. "I would have you for my wife, Miss McKie. But only if you truly are willing. For I'll not make that mistake again."

Forty-Three

Mistake, error, is the discipline
through which we advance.
WILLIAM ELLERY CHANNING

Somerled eyed Davina's knot of curls and tried to forget the silky feel of her hair between his fingers. "Please, miss. If you do not look at me, I cannot guess your thoughts."

Davina lifted her head at last, dabbing her nose with a handkerchief pulled from the sleeve of her gown. How could he not have marked her youth on Midsummer Eve? The firm line of her chin, the soft curve of her cheek, the smooth, lightly freckled brow.

He moved farther down the stone bench, giving her room. Giving her time to consider his offer of marriage. "You've brought a sketchbook, I see. Are you an artist as well as a musician, or do you write out words in conversation?"

When she began turning pages, he had his answer. *Both.* Finely rendered drawings of Arran's peaks and glens flew past, with words and phrases scribbled in margins, and the occasional longer note by itself. Finally she stopped at a page covered with single lines in an angular script. Questions, by the look of them. She presented the sketchbook with some hesitancy and pointed to the first one on the list.

Why did you come to my rescue when His Grace asked me to speak?

An easy question, to begin. "You seemed flustered," he said, hoping not to offend her. "I thought I might be of service. Though I do beg your pardon for the 'Speechless Lassie' remark. I did not realize—"

She turned her head, as if dismissing his apology.

"I can tell you this, Miss McKie. 'Twas not calculated, my intervening on your behalf."

That seemed to placate her. She looked at him once more, then pointed to the next question. *Why did you ask to be my dinner escort?*

"Ah. That *was* calculated." He'd seldom been so honest with a woman. "From the moment I saw you, I wanted you." When she blushed, he knew she understood. "Aye…just that." He exhaled, wishing she did not need to hear the worst of it. But a lady deserved to know whom she was considering marrying. "I've made rather a career of seducing women."

When her countenance fell, he was sorry he'd spoken so bluntly.

" 'Tis my history, Miss McKie. Not my future, I promise you." His conscience jabbed at him. *Truly? No other woman but this one?* Somerled jerked his chin, as if his opponent were there in the flesh. *A man can change his ways, can he not?*

Davina interrupted his mental argument with a light tap on her sketchbook.

He glanced down and was taken aback at her question.

Why did you choose me rather than someone else?

"Do you truly not know?" The openness of her expression—still innocent, despite his savage behavior—touched him deeply. Had no man ever courted her? complimented her? Her mirror alone should have offered encouragement enough. But not all women believed what they saw in the glass.

"Miss McKie, you are a rare beauty. Yet 'tis not your appearance alone that makes you desirable. Your musical abilities are extraordinary. And now that I've had a glimpse of your drawings, I suspect there are more hidden talents I've yet to discover." He paused, studying her for a moment. "You are more than worthy of a gentleman's admiration. This one's in particular."

She was softening toward him. In her posture, in her expression, she was a bit less guarded. He'd not have blamed her if she'd appeared that afternoon wearing a suit of armor and bearing a steel mace, though her white eyelet gown was far more becoming.

"More questions, I see." As he read the next one, his chest tightened.

Why did you not stop when I asked you to?

Davina had not protested with words but with actions. He knew that now. Had known it then but had pretended not to. Could he speak the truth even if it hurt them both? "I did not stop, Miss McKie, because I did not want to."

She sighed, then slowly touched her brow. *I know.*

His selfishness overwhelmed him, disgusted him. Somerled gripped the sketchbook, staring down at her list. Davina had already asked more of him than he cared to confess. But he was not prepared for this.

Did you intend to hurt me?

He felt the blood drain from his face. "I had no...that is, I did not..."

She slowly pulled aside the neckline of her gown and turned her head, giving him a clear view of her shoulder. Of a dark purplish bruise. The size of a man's thumb.

Mine.

"Oh, lass..." His stomach twisted at the sight of it. "By no means did I intend..." Even after she eased her gown back in place, he pictured the bruise and remembered pressing her against the stable floor. "Please...tell me there are no others."

When she did not look at him, he knew the answer. *Others.*

God help me. No wonder she didn't leap at his offer of marriage and respectability. He had forced himself on her in every sense of the word. Knowing that fact was one thing and confessing it aloud another. But seeing her bruised body made his crime abundantly clear: He had raped her and could never plead otherwise.

He stared at the mossy ground, struggling to find the right words. "I dare not presume to ask your forgiveness, but...I truly am sorry, Miss McKie."

Neither of them moved for a moment, the cheerful birdsong and brilliant sunshine a strange counterpoint to their discussion. There was no hiding the truth from such a woman. Or, any longer, from himself.

He turned back to her sketchbook with a heavy heart. The lines of script had grown uneven; such questions must have been very hard for her to write.

Why should I ever trust you again?

Why, indeed? As he looked up from the page, searching inside himself for an honest reply, he met her gaze. And saw in her eyes a tiny flicker of hope. She wanted to trust him. And he wanted, more than anything he'd ever wanted, to be worthy of her trust.

"Miss McKie, 'tis a great deal to ask after all that I've done, but…might we begin again?" He held her gaze, wanting her to see that he meant every word. "I'll not touch your hand without your permission nor kiss your cheek unless you offer it. Is that…acceptable to you?"

She nodded almost imperceptibly, then turned the page of her sketchbook. A single question remained, the most heartrending one of all. *What is to become of me now that I am ruined?*

For this one, he had an answer.

Somerled closed her sketchbook and laid it on the bench, marshaling the strength to say what he must. "Miss McKie, please let me redeem what you have lost. Nae, what I have taken from you." He knelt beside her, then held out his hands, letting her choose to rest hers there or not. "You need not answer me now. Only let me know of your willingness to think upon it."

She examined his hands for some time, as if counting the stitches in his gloves, though he knew better; 'twas not his gloves that gave her pause. *Please, Davina.*

After a long, quiet moment, she sighed and placed her hands in his.

"Bless you." Tears clouded his eyes as he held on tight. "I want you for my wife. You alone are meant to be Lady MacDonald." Saying the name, he was even more convinced. *Aye. Only her.* "Please consider my offer of marriage. Not because 'tis the proper thing, the needful thing to be done, but because you would choose me for your husband."

When he looked into her eyes, hoping to find his answer, he did not see *aye* or *nae* in their dark blue depths. But he did see a small measure of grace. The faint possibility of forgiveness. And hope for the future, which was far more than he deserved.

Forty-Four

I know not what inexplicable and fated power
that brought on this union.

MICHEL EYQUEM DE MONTAIGNE

As yet, she has not consented to marry me, Father, but—"
"Consented?" Sir Harry spat out the word. "Son, have you not explained the gravity of her predicament? And the extent of our property?" He stamped about the flagstone floor, ignoring Dougal, who held out his coat, waiting to finish dressing him for dinner.

"I have made her aware of both those things, sir." Somerled was relieved the other guests were well out of earshot, for he would not have them thinking ill of Davina. Nor of him, if he could manage it. "In the meantime, perhaps you could approach her father. At breakfast I spoke with Randall Keith, a Lowlander who knows something of her family. By his description, I'd say James McKie of Glentrool is a reasonable man."

"Aye, with three sons," his father said with a grunt. "Brothers do not take kindly to a sister being ravished."

Ravished. Somerled loathed the word. Hated that it was true. "For her sake, I thought 'twould be best not to tell the McKies that—"

"What?" His father whirled round, his face turning purple. "And pay the full bride price for used goods?"

"Used by me, sir." Somerled fought to keep his temper in check. "The family must be compensated for their loss."

"Och!" Sir Harry shoved his arms into his coat, nearly knocking Dougal over in the process. " 'Tis no way to negotiate a marriage, lad. You have the position of strength. In a plight such as this, society punishes the woman far more than the man."

Somerled bit his tongue rather than engage his father in a lengthy debate. "I wish to marry her," he said in a low voice, "not punish her. I will not have her reputation ruined for the sake of silver."

"You sound like a besotted suitor," Sir Harry said gruffly, standing still long enough for Dougal to tie his neckcloth. "Who's to say whether the tongue-tackit lass was willing or unwilling?"

"Miss McKie was decidedly *not* willing," Somerled shot back. "Which is why I shall spend the balance of my days on Arran trying to regain her trust. And why you shall pay whatever amount is necessary to meet her family's expectations." He pulled a sealed letter from his waistcoat pocket and forced himself to sound polite. "Sir Harry, if you would, kindly write a letter to Mr. McKie at once and express our intentions. I've already written one for you to include—"

"Aye, aye." He cut him off, snatching the letter from his hand and tossing it onto the bed. "And since you insist, I'll mention nothing of the sordid situation. Only that my son met his daughter on Arran and cannot abide the thought of living without her by his side at Brenfield House. Will that suit you?"

More than you know, Father. Somerled could not explain his growing feelings for Davina McKie any more than he could deny them. *Besotted? Quite.*

He followed Sir Harry to the dining room, anticipation coursing through his veins. Davina was expected at seven o'clock. They had parted well, he thought. The wariness in her demeanor had eased slightly by the time he'd taken his leave. Still, she was far from won, and he had less than a fortnight left.

Somerled looked about his surroundings with new eyes, wondering what Davina would think of Brodick castle. Commodious, aye, but not lavish. Cromwell had housed his army here in the seventeenth century; the place still bore the look of a fortress. The rough walls were constructed of red sandstone, cut but not dressed, and the floors made of the same rose-colored stone in large, uneven squares, mortared together. The furniture was sparse, the carpets few, the ceiling beams exposed, yet the windows commanded an impressive view—from the lapping waters of Brodick Bay to the bank of firs leading up to the castle, perched on its high plateau. The walled garden was well tended, the meals more than adequate, and His Grace had gone to great lengths to make his visitors comfortable.

Somerled took his place at the massive table, watching for one visitor in particular. The door on the ground floor closed with a muffled bang. Women's footsteps moved up the turnpike stair. Two maidservants were chattering. And then Davina appeared, fiddle in hand, wearing the same eyelet gown and the same winsome expression.

For a fleeting moment her gaze sought his. A good sign.

"Miss McKie!" The duke welcomed her with obvious pleasure, seating her on his right, the place of honor. "Glad to see you are in good health. We shall feed you well and then hear you play for us, aye?"

Somerled sat with his father on the opposite side of the table, several places down from His Grace and too far away from Davina. A brown-haired servant from Kilmichael was on hand as her chaperon. An *ill-faured* woman, but she could not help the sharpness of her nose or her thin-lipped frown. If Davina was to be his wife—and she was—no one must be given a reason to blether about improprieties.

Dinner commenced with *souchet* of trout, a flavorful fish soup, followed by haricot of lamb and roast ptarmigan. With a lady at his table, His Grace had significantly improved the menu. The other gentlemen were also aware of Davina's presence, guarding their tongues and keeping their stories seemly, even as they regarded their bonny guest with blatant interest.

Somerled soon found himself grinding his teeth between courses. *She's mine, lads. Look at her no more.* He would find some way to make his suit clear without compromising her reputation in the process. The sooner Sir Harry sent their letters, the better.

"Are you gentlemen staying through the sixth of July?" Alastair MacDuff inquired.

"Aye," Sir Harry answered for them both, then downed the last of his claret. " 'Tis when the duke sails for home, and so shall we."

MacDuff, a middle-aged landowner from Fife, rubbed his hand across his beard, dislodging any loose crumbs. "Alas, I have business in Edinburgh that requires I take my leave at the end of June. With any luck, I'll have a good day of fishing before I go." He nodded down the table toward Davina, then lowered his voice. "What of this lassie with the bright red hair? She's a rose waiting to be plucked, aye?"

Somerled bridled, but his father shot him a warning look. "Rumor has it that a lad at this table has already written her father, seeking permission to court the lady."

"Is that so?" Alastair shrugged. "Just as well, for she's too green for this old widower. Not a day over eighteen, I'd say."

"Seventeen." Somerled was on his feet as Davina stood, the dinner hour ended. When he caught Dougal's eye, the elderly manservant nodded and slipped from the room, off to retrieve an instrument from his master's leather trunk.

"Come, gentlemen," the duke announced. " 'Tis time for the music to begin."

Forty-Five

There when the sound of flute and fiddle
Gave signal sweet in that old hall.

WINTHROP MACKWORTH PRAED

Davina lifted her fiddle from its green baize bag, fearful the instrument might slip through her trembling hands. However would she manage an hourlong performance, knowing Somerled was in her audience? *The LORD is my strength and song.* She would remind herself of that truth, measure by measure, until she could bundle up her fiddle and flee for Kilmichael.

His words had echoed in her heart all through dinner. *The only course is for us to marry.* But how could she marry a man she barely knew and did not trust, for good reason?

A semicircle of chairs faced the hearth, its glowing embers warming the chilly dining hall. Davina positioned herself in the center while the duke and his guests took their seats. One gentleman in particular sat on Davina's far left, his head framed by the window like a silhouette, his features hidden from view.

You are a rare beauty. You are more than worthy of a gentleman's admiration. I want you for my wife.

Somerled MacDonald was as clever at weaving words as Michael Kelly was at weaving wool. The Highlander well knew those were sentiments most women longed to hear. To be seen as pretty, to be considered worthy, to be wanted. Davina was not immune to such flattery, but she wished for more. To be treated with respect. And to be truly loved.

This much she would concede: He'd answered her questions more frankly than she'd expected and had left the question of marriage in her hands. *Only if you truly are willing.* Each hour brought her no closer to a decision. Her head said *aye,* her body said *nae,* and her heart was too wounded to consider such a brash proposal.

Davina tucked her fiddle in place, wincing as the curve of wood pressed into her bruised shoulder. *Strengthen thou me.* Releasing a deep breath to steady her nerves, she plucked the strings once more to be sure they were in tune, then launched into a set of strathspeys and reels meant to stir her audience awake after their richly seasoned meal. His Grace was most responsive, so the others followed suit, marking the spirited rhythm with heads, hands, and feet. Though she could not see Somerled's face, she sensed him watching her and heard his vigorous applause.

At hour's end she shifted from the breathless pace of the duke's favorite jigs to the cadence of slower tunes. When the setting sun cast the room in bronze, she began the last song of the evening, a Highland air, "Well May My True Love Arrive." No sooner had she drawn her bow across the strings, than the unexpected notes of a wooden flute, sweet and low, floated across the room, each phrase perfectly timed with hers. *Somerled.*

Her throat tightened at the tenderness of his playing. If he intended to woo her with music, he could not have chosen a more fitting instrument. The long, hollow woodwind sounded like the human voice. Like his voice. Warm, compelling, persuasive. *Might we begin again?*

He walked toward her as he played, not stopping until his arm brushed against hers. She recognized his scent, like freshly pressed linens sprayed with heather water, and heard every breath he took just before the notes poured forth.

The tune was slow and expressive, brimming with emotion. Why, oh why, had she not chosen something else? Her heart was in every phrase, and so was Somerled's. As they played, his words circled round inside her head. *I've thought of nothing else but you.* Turning her back to him did not help; his notes embraced her, caressed her. *Nae!* Tears clouded her vision as she plied her bow, trying to ignore him but failing.

On the last note he took the lead, easing into "Hard Is My Fate," another plaintive Highland melody. The series of high sixteenth notes in the refrain let her fiddle take center stage while he spun a languid harmony with his flute. His thoughtful accompaniment undid her. How could a man be so considerate in one instance and so ruthless in another? They held the last chord until her bow and his breath reached their limits, then they bowed to enthusiastic applause and more than a few cheers.

"You two are meant to play together," Alastair MacDuff said loudly, having sipped too many drams of whisky. "I hear there's a man in this room who intends to court you, Miss McKie, provided your father will allow it. If 'tis not you, MacDonald, you've sorely missed your chance."

The others laughed or nodded in agreement, slapping Somerled on the back as they stood and began moving about. Aghast at the gentleman's careless words, Davina tried to put her fiddle back in its traveling bag. But this time her hands would not obey her. Even less so when Somerled came up behind her.

"We've my father to thank for that outburst, I'm afraid." He pitched his voice beneath the murmur of the room. "MacDuff's a widower, so Sir Harry meant to spare you his advances. Instead the drunkard from Fife seems to have given us away."

Davina turned round, wishing she had paper and pencil, hoping Somerled would see the concern on her face and deduce its source.

"MacDuff spoke out of turn, lass, but he did not lie." His gaze grew more intense, his voice lower still. "I've asked Sir Harry to write your father and to send my letter with it." When her mouth fell open, he hastened to explain. "You may still refuse me, Miss McKie, though I pray you will not. But with mail from the island being so slow, I thought we should put things in motion."

He looked over her shoulder at the room full of garrulous men. "'Tis better that your father hears the news from us than to hear gossip from a stranger. If even one person suspects what happened on Midsummer Eve…"

Somerled said no more, but she heard the rest and shuddered.

Davina awakened late on the Sabbath morning, dismayed to find a downpour pelting Kilmichael's windows. Ill weather for traveling to Lamlash Bay for kirk.

Nan Shaw stood by Davina's open bedchamber door. "I didna

wauken ye earlier, thinkin' ye'd not want tae mak a lang raik a' by yerself on sae dreich a day." The maidservant deposited a pitcher of steaming water and fresh towels on the washstand. "The captain is off tae the mainland and not expected hame 'til Friday, and me mistress is abed wi' a worrisome cough. The ithers left for kirk lang syne." Her point was well made: If the kirk in Lamlash had a bell, it would have already rung. "I'll fetch a goun for ye," she said, then closed the door behind her.

Davina sank back on the pillows, miserable with herself. Mother never missed a service on the Sabbath due to bad weather, let alone from oversleeping. And what would the Stewarts think of her not appearing at kirk? There was no afternoon service in light of the distance churchgoers were required to travel; Kilbride parish included the entire eastern half of Arran, fourteen miles from Lochranza to Dippin. On the first dry day she would visit the manse and make amends. And come next Sunday she would be sure Nan roused her early.

At least her Sabbath duties did not include providing entertainment for the duke's guests. Or playing unexpected musical duets with Somerled. Or avoiding his relentless gaze.

Two days away from him would give her time to think.

Please consider my offer of marriage.

Was a hurried wedding her only option? If the truth of her unchaste state remained hidden, might she not return to Glentrool at Lammas and resume her life? Should a suitor come calling, she'd need some reason to refuse him; no gentleman wanted a sullied bride. But it might be managed.

Except then she would have no husband at all and no children to call her own.

You may still refuse me, Miss McKie. That remained to be seen.

Davina eased back her bedcovers, determined to honor the Lord's day as best she could. The drawing room shelves were lined with devout books, waiting to be read. And she'd write to her parents, for if they received letters from the MacDonalds, they'd expect to hear from her as well.

Whatever would she tell them? Only the truth, and precious little of that; a very short letter indeed. *I have met a gentleman from Argyll. A guest of His Grace. A talented musician. He has shown me favor.* Of the worst kind and in the worst manner, though that truth would not find its way into her letter. Nor would the words she longed to write: *Help me. Save me.* It was too late for that.

Davina bathed her hands and face in haste, knowing Nan would return shortly. The less time the woman had to see her bruises, the better. The ones Davina could spot were no longer quite so purple but remained painfully visible. She was prepared to mimic a fall from a horse if an explanation was demanded of her.

"Here ye go, miss." Nan swept through the door with a fresh gown for her to wear—a pink one this time. It seemed the mistress of Kilmichael had an endless store, for which Davina was grateful. Though the dresses were two summers old, they were in good repair and hemmed to suit her shorter frame.

Half an hour later, her growling stomach appeased with porridge and tea, Davina climbed the stair, wondering if she might spend a moment with Mrs. Fullarton, inquiring after her health. But Nan was standing outside her mistress's door, a stern look on her face. "She's restin' noo and doesna need tae be disturbed. I'll tell her whan she waukens that ye asked aboot her."

Davina nodded, though the news disappointed her. Was she to spend the entire day alone and perhaps Monday as well? Though she was in no hurry to face Somerled, the lively company at the castle held some appeal on so gloomy a day.

She visited the drawing room next, where the guilt of missing Reverend Stewart's sermon prodded her toward the Buik displayed on a wooden bookstand and opened to the psalms. Davina let her gaze fall on the page, then wished she had not. *The wicked borroweth, and payeth not again: but the righteous showeth mercy, and giveth.*

Surely Somerled MacDonald would be counted among the wicked, among the borrowers who did not repay their debts. *I took what you did not offer.* But if she was to be counted among the righteous, did that mean she was expected to show him mercy? A man who had ravished her, body and soul?

Nae. She stared at the words through a stubborn sheen of tears. *'Tis not possible.*

Though she quickly turned the page, the truth was not so easily put aside. Hadn't the Lord forgiven her for the sins she'd committed that night? Most would say her transgressions were small in comparison to his, but Davina could not deny her need for mercy. Nor could she pretend she did not know what was expected of her.

Please, Lord. She pressed her hands to her waist, sickened at the thought. *I cannot forgive him. I cannot...*

Forty-Six

Sometimes from her eyes
I did receive fair speechless messages.

WILLIAM SHAKESPEARE

Somerled focused on the well-trod path that led south from the castle, as if by sheer will he might hasten Davina's appearance.

Two days, lass. 'Tis long enough.

A dreary, wet Sabbath spent with a book by the hearth was one thing, but a second day of drenching rain had tried his patience mightily. How could he woo the woman if she was not by his side?

Ah, there. His heart quickened at the sight of her emerging from the pine woods. A light shawl covered her head and shoulders, no doubt to protect her fiddle more than her hair. She held the instrument close as she walked, eyes lowered. Watching for puddles, perhaps. Or avoiding his gaze.

"Welcome, Miss McKie." He walked toward her, wiping the water from his face with the back of his hand. "I am sorry the weather is so inhospitable."

When she looked up, her blue eyes gave away nothing. Was she the slightest bit glad to see him?

Somerled offered his arm, though she did not take it, patting her fiddle instead.

"Aye, we cannot have you dropping that." He glanced at the sullen maid trailing behind her—Nan, as he recalled—dragging her skirt hem through the mud. "Let us get you withindoors where 'tis dry."

He led the women up the turnpike stair, addressing Davina over his shoulder. "Miss McKie, might I have a word with you before dinner?" Watching her maid's eyes narrow, he added, "The music you've planned for this evening is what interests me." *Aye, and other things as well, which Nan had no business knowing.*

When they reached the top of the stair, Somerled motioned to one of the duke's maidservants, then lifted the dripping shawl from Davina's shoulders and deposited it in the maid's waiting arms. "Miss McKie requires several dry towels and a cup of tea. Nan will be glad to assist you." The Kilmichael servant turned on her heel and followed the younger maid toward the ground-floor kitchen as Somerled regarded Davina, shivering by his side, and fought a strong urge to take her hand or touch her cheek.

"Come sit by the hearth. Even in midsummer Brodick feels dank as a tomb." The dining room remained vacant except for the occasional servant; the duke's footman would not ring the dinner bell for another hour. Somerled drew her chair near the fire, eying her all the while.

"Here ye are, miss." Nan reappeared with linen towels draped over her arm and a small tea tray in hand. The one instance when she might have dallied elsewhere, the maid was irritatingly prompt.

"I must see to my own grooming," Somerled admitted. "Will you pardon me for a few moments? Upon my return, we shall have our discussion, aye?"

When Davina dipped her chin in response, he bowed and strode through the empty hall, bound for his bedchamber and Dougal's assistance. He found Sir Harry there instead, pacing about the room, shirtless and smoking a cheroot.

"Where do things stand with Miss McKie?" his father demanded, his silver head wreathed in smoke. "Surely you have her answer by now."

Somerled frowned at the man's obstinacy. "She's not had but two days to weigh my proposal."

"Och!" Sir Harry flicked a bit of tobacco from his lip. "In so precarious a situation, the only decision to be made is *when*. Not *if*."

"Father, I would have a willing bride."

" 'Tis too late to speak of willingness." His words dissolved into a cough. "Be firm with her, lad. Explain what happens to a respected family—ours, for instance—when society's doors are shut against them. I daresay, young as she is, Miss McKie has ne'er given the matter of public disgrace a minute's thought."

Somerled grimaced, having seen how cruel the peerage could be.

Even a baronet's family would be barred from the best circles. Hearing footsteps in the hall, Somerled lowered his voice. "To my knowledge, no one is aware—"

"Bah!" Sir Harry coughed again. "Midnight trysts seldom remain a secret. How can you be certain one of Fullarton's servants did not spy the two of you? You heard the men Saturday evening, congratulating you on your supposed conquest of Miss McKie's heart. How long will it take them to deduce the rest?"

Somerled knew the answer. *Not long.* "I'll do what I can to convince her."

When Dougal slipped into the room, a freshly ironed shirt in hand, Sir Harry thrust out his arms. "Finally."

Dougal saw to the elder MacDonald first, then dressed Somerled in a clean shirt and cravat. *"Nighean,"* he murmured, glancing toward the door. *"Teinntean."*

Somerled nodded, understanding: Davina was waiting for him by the hearth. He ran his hand through his hair, still damp to the touch, then quit the bedchamber, preparing his speech. *Miss McKie, I am afraid we have little choice in the matter.* That would hardly win her hand, however truthful. If only he'd not been so single minded on Midsummer Eve, he might have courted Davina properly, at his leisure.

Oh, is that so? His conscience taunted him as he walked down the narrow corridor. *When was courtship ever your aim?* Indeed, his change in attitude toward marriage was astonishing. The only explanation was Davina herself: a clever, talented, beautiful young woman who deserved more than bruises and shattered dreams.

Please, lass. Let me right what is wrong.

He found her seated as before, by the mantelpiece, her hair patted dry and her gloves draped near the fire. Her maid stepped back as he approached. "I'll not be far awa," Nan said—more warning than consolation—then curtsied and moved to a corner of the room where the other servants had congregated.

Somerled pulled a chair next to Davina, grateful the rest of the dinner guests had yet to arrive at table. "You've not brought your sketchbook?"

She shook her head, imitating the falling rain with her fingers, then produced a sealed note.

"Ah." Somerled broke the wax with some reluctance, fearing its contents. *I cannot marry you. Will not marry you.* He unfolded the paper, surprised to find only a few lines. Already her penmanship looked familiar: small, neat letters with a decided forward slant. No salutation, he noted. Perhaps she feared the letter might fall into someone else's hands.

> I wonder if you realize what you are asking of me.

Somerled closed his eyes, struck afresh by her honesty. And her pain. *I do, lass. I am asking the unthinkable.*

When he looked up, he found her mouth pressed into a tremulous line and her eyes wet with tears. "Miss McKie, I…" What could he say when there were no words? He reached for her, then withdrew his hand, frustration and shame heating his face. "I am asking you to marry me."

She shook her head, then began moving her hands apart in small increments, as if measuring something.

"More?" He searched her face, wanting to comprehend. "I realize you bear no affection for me…"

She shook her head, then pointed to the letter, her expression resolute.

> You are asking me to marry you. You are asking me to spend
> my life with you. But those are nothing compared to the
> most difficult thing required of me.

Somerled stared at her letter in confusion. "I know not what you mean."

Averting her gaze, she touched her heart, then opened her hand, as if offering him a gift.

He'd not seen this tender gesture of hers before. What did it signify? "Your heart? Your…love? Truly, Miss McKie, I have no such expectations." Hopes, perhaps, though he might never voice them. When she did not respond, he knew he'd missed the mark. He also knew why she'd not written down this most difficult thing: Davina was testing him. He did not intend to fail.

She hesitated for a moment, then pantomimed a large, thick volume being opened. Slowly, reverently. Only the Buik matched her silent description.

Like many Highlanders, he was Episcopalian. Did their religious differences trouble her? "I do not wish to alter your beliefs," he told her gently. "Though our families do not worship in the same manner, we worship the same God."

When she sighed, he realized he'd still not discovered what she was trying to say. After a lengthy pause, she drew an unmistakable sign across the pages of her imaginary Buik: two lines, first top to bottom, then side to side.

The cross? He sat back in his chair, more bewildered than ever. "This difficult thing you must do…is it a sacrifice? A penance?"

"MacDonald!" Alastair MacDuff's voice carried across the room, abruptly ending their private conversation. "Will we have the pleasure of hearing you play after dinner?"

Och. They had yet to speak of the evening's program. Would Davina welcome his accompaniment? Somerled looked into her eyes and found one answer at least.

"Aye, MacDuff. We shall both fill the air with music." He leaned toward Davina to whisper, "And while we dine, I shall give your note much consideration."

All through the meal Somerled sifted through the clues she'd presented him. What was he asking of her? Naught but her hand in marriage. *And her body in your bed,* his conscience prodded him. Aye, but what else? Not her love or her trust, though he hoped he might earn both in time. *The most difficult thing required of me.* She'd indicated it came from her heart. And from the Buik. And from the cross.

His fork nearly clattered to his plate. *Mercy.* That was what she felt compelled to offer him. *Difficult? Nae, impossible.* Especially when he'd not had the decency to beg her forgiveness. Aye, he'd admitted how sorry he was, but that was not at all the same. *Forgive me, Miss McKie.* Had he ever said those words aloud and meant them?

Somerled turned toward the opposite end of the table where she sat taking bites of salmon as she listened to His Grace. The rain had framed her face with wisps of hair, like a halo. Like an angel. She pursed her lips, tilted her head, acknowledged the duke's words, yet Somerled sensed she was also aware of his gaze fixed on her, despite the table full of men between them.

Look at me, lass. And she did, as if he'd spoken the words aloud. *Please forgive me. For hurting you. Forcing you. Dishonoring you.*

Davina's gaze was riveted to his. Could she read his expression? Discern his thoughts? Even if she had such powers, he would not take the coward's way out, merely hoping she understood him. Nae, he would plead for her forgiveness that very night.

When the duke's table was cleared and his guests assembled, Somerled accompanied Davina on his flute with particular care, letting her shine on every tune, counting the minutes until she finally lowered her bow.

As soon as the applause ended, he stepped in front of her, lest she bolt for the door. "A last word, if I may, Miss McKie." He saw Nan walking toward them, her gaze sharp with suspicion, and held out his hand to halt her progress. "Wait by the door for your mistress." The note of authority in his voice was intentional; he would not be rushed by an impertinent maid.

He looked down at Davina, with her fiddle in one hand and her bow in the other, wishing he might divest her of both and take her hands in his. But he had promised not to touch her; now of all times he would not break that vow. "Will you join me by the window?" Though hardly more private, the rain might muffle his words. Not for his sake, but for hers.

They crossed the room as the other guests started for their bedchambers or milled about with whisky glasses in hand. Standing by the open shutters, as close to her as propriety allowed, he lowered his head and his voice so she alone might hear his confession. "Miss McKie, your efforts to explain yourself earlier were not in vain."

The sorrow in her gaze assured him, convicted him.

"I do realize what I am asking of you." He swallowed what remained of his pride. "I am asking you to forgive me, Miss McKie."

With servants shuffling about, he dared not enumerate his sins, vile as they were. But he did not need to name them; no one knew better than Davina how grievously he'd erred. "Please, Miss McKie. If there is any mercy for me hidden in your heart, may I see it in your eyes?"

What he found there was only what he deserved: a fresh pool of tears.

Forty-Seven

Without your knowledge,
the eyes and ears of many will see and watch you,
as they have done already.

CICERO

M iss McKie, I believe you are keeping something from me."
Davina stood at the foot of Mrs. Fullarton's fourposter, hands
clasped behind her back. *Nae, madam. I am concealing nothing except a
bruised body and a heavy heart.*

Her hostess was seated upright, supported by silk-covered bolsters.
After several days of recuperating in bed, she was pale and her features
drawn, yet her brown eyes still bore a warm glow. "Nan tells me that
Mr. MacDonald has been particularly attentive during your evening visits to Brodick. Is that so?"

She nodded slightly, hoping that would suffice.

"He certainly caught you by surprise on Midsummer Eve…"

Davina's body stiffened.

"…playing the violoncello with such skill."

Oh. She relaxed enough to pantomime a flutist.

"Indeed, I've heard that he is a master of that instrument as well."
Mrs. Fullarton coughed, then dabbed at her mouth with her handkerchief. "However, I do not believe music is Mr. MacDonald's sole passion. If Nan's assessment is correct, he is quite taken with you, Miss
McKie."

Davina's cheeks bloomed like the roses in Kilmichael's garden.

"I see that I am right." Mrs. Fullarton's tone grew more serious. "As
your hostess, I cannot offer my blessing on any sort of courtship, no
matter how informal, without your parents' consent. Have you written
to them?"

Here was a question Davina could answer. *Aye.* She pretended to write on her palm, then waved her hand toward Brodick Bay since her letter had sailed with Tuesday's packet boat.

"And has Mr. MacDonald done his duty and sent them a post as well?" When Davina nodded, Mrs. Fullarton released a troubled sigh. "As you two are thrown together every evening, I shall ask Nan to be especially diligent in her duties."

Davina had never known a more watchful maid.

"You are fortunate to see him so often. I miss my husband terribly whenever he's on the mainland or at sea." She coughed again, deeper this time. "Might you keep me company today while practicing your music?"

Since the rain had finally ceased, Davina had hoped to ride to Lamlash Bay and visit her cousins. But she could not abandon Kilmichael's mistress to a lonely afternoon in her bedchamber. She curtsied in response, then hurried off to fetch her fiddle.

Approaching the curved stair, Davina raised her skirts rather than let an uneven hem send her tumbling headlong down the steps. She'd pretended not to notice Nan's slipshod alteration work—what houseguest would be so ungrateful as to mention it?—and chose to overlook the careless manner in which Nan had thrust pins into her hair that morning. The maid had been kinder to her the first day or two. Had she done something to offend the woman? Or did her muteness make Nan increasingly uneasy? If so, Davina would not add to the maid's discomfort by pointing out her shortcomings.

Fiddle in hand, she returned to Mrs. Fullarton's second-floor chamber and began rehearsing a slow air. She'd hesitated to play this one at the castle, fearing that "My Heart Is Broken Since Thy Departure" might communicate more to Somerled than she intended. Would her hostess recognize the Highland melody?

"Oh, Miss McKie," she protested a dozen measures later, "'tis too sad by half, whatever the title."

She did not repeat the chorus but eased into a more cheerful tune, "The Bonny Banks of Ayr." Her audience of one rested against her bed pillows with a wistful smile. "That one I do know."

Davina's repertoire was thinning. Six more performances and her role as the duke's summer fiddler would end. Perhaps Somerled might be willing to include a few more solos. Yestreen he'd surprised her with yet another talent: singing. His tenor voice, strong and true, had echoed off the stone walls, sending a chill down her spine. When he'd come to the end of the second verse, rather than using the name Eliza, as the composer had intended, Somerled had sung his entreaty to a different lass.

> I know thou doom'st me to despair,
> Nor wilt, nor canst relieve me;
> But, O Davina, hear one prayer—
> For pity's sake forgive me!

Though the men had chuckled at his canny substitution, Somerled had not winked at her when he'd sung her name nor smiled after the last note. Instead he'd implored her with an expression so sincere, she'd begun another fiddle tune at once, hiding her dismay behind her fast-moving bow. *For pity's sake?* She felt many things toward Somerled, but pity was not one of them. *Forgive me?* That was a request she had yet to honor.

"What a shame," Mrs. Fullarton was saying, "that you and Mr. MacDonald must part one week hence. Given time, he might have become a proper suitor."

There were times, albeit few, when Davina was grateful she could not speak.

At the four hours Nan Shaw appeared at the bedchamber door. "Tea, mem." She placed a round silver tray by her mistress's bedside. Slices of caraway seedcake were arranged on a china plate beside a steaming pot of tea and a single cup and saucer.

"Nan, have you forgotten Miss McKie?"

The maidservant made a slight face, which only Davina could see. "I'll fetch her a cup, mem." She gave a halfhearted curtsy before slipping out the door.

"I beg your pardon," Mrs. Fullarton murmured. "Nan is seldom so forgetful."

Davina laid her fiddle and bow on the dresser, then started to cross the room when she tripped on her hem, tearing the fabric loose at the seam.

"Careful, lass!"

Davina recovered her footing at once but was embarrassed to find a gaping hole beneath her bodice.

"Do not fret, Miss McKie. 'Tis easily fixed." Her hostess sat up straighter, assessing Davina's lettuce green gown with a critical eye. "Kindly come closer." She reached over and tugged at the fabric. "No wonder you stumbled, for your hem droops on the right. Whatever can Nan have been thinking when she stitched this?"

Davina's gaze followed hers, surveying the damaged gown. By the time Davina lifted her head, Mrs. Fullarton was frowning at her crown of curls and gently pushing hairpins in place. "Here I am, languishing in bed, while my household goes to wrack and ruin. I cannot apologize enough, Miss McKie."

Davina touched her hand, meaning to assuage her, as the hapless maid returned with another teacup.

"Nan?" Mrs. Fullarton pinned her with a sharp gaze. "Press another gown for Miss McKie at once. The pink one she wore on Sunday will do. When she is dressed to my satisfaction and hers, I would speak with you alone."

"Aye, mem." Nan offered her mistress a contrite curtsy, then quit the room.

"Please do not take offense, Miss McKie." Mrs. Fullarton's voice was growing raspy. "For some reason Nan is not herself lately. After I've spoken with her, I trow you'll find her manners much improved."

Nan Shaw did not walk; she marched two steps ahead of Davina, swinging her baize bag with such careless disregard that Davina feared the maid might drop her fiddle in the mud. At least their late afternoon walk to the castle would be shorter than usual and quiet, for Nan had not spoken two words since they'd departed Kilmichael House. Whatever Mrs. Fullarton had said to Nan had only made things worse.

Davina did her best to keep up with the long-legged maid, eying the blacksmith hammering away at his anvil as they walked past, then nodding at the gentleman who rode by on a chestnut mare. When they turned onto the shore road—wider than the lane to Kilmichael but no smoother underfoot—Nan turned and thrust a letter into her hands. "This came yestermorn. Carried by a neighbor who'd been tae see the Stewarts."

Yestermorn? Davina frowned as she broke the seal. Had the letter remained in Nan's pocket all this time? In another week she would gladly return to the manse and leave her disagreeable maid behind.

Her cousin Cate's penmanship—as artless and blithe as the lass herself—looped across the paper. Merely seeing her familiar hand made Davina long for Lamlash Bay. She read as she walked, slowing her pace, requiring Nan to do the same.

> To Davina McKie
> Monday, 27 June 1808
>
> Dearest Cousin,
>
> We missed you at service yestermorn and pray this letter
> finds you in good health.

A wave of guilt washed over Davina. *I'll not disappoint you on the Sabbath next, dear Cate.*

> How dreary our lives are without you! Mother is transplanting
> coleworts and beets, Abbie and I weed between plumpshowers,
> and Father is minding the bees. Mrs. McCook at Kingscross
> suffers from the ague. We are to visit her before long.

Cate's letter was filled with domestic details, written with a carefree innocence that weighed on Davina's heart. Their lives could not be more different now. While her cousins tended the garden, she contemplated a marriage proposal from a rake.

Davina scanned the closing paragraph twice, trying to read between the lines. Was Reverend Stewart genuinely unhappy with her?

> Father is still fretting over your performance on Midsummer
> Eve. Can you imagine anything so daft? Abbie and I thought
> you two played beautifully together. Does Mr. MacDonald
> accompany you at Brodick castle each evening?

Aye, lass. He does.

She folded the letter and slipped it into her reticule as she and Nan started their climb from Cladach to the castle grounds. Assuming the dry weather held, Davina would borrow one of the Fullartons' mounts and ride to the manse tomorrow, if only for a short visit. To put her cousins' minds at ease. And to remind herself of simpler days.

Somerled was waiting for her when she reached the dining room. "I'm glad to see you've arrived early." He claimed her baize bag, then sent Nan to join the other servants. "Rest assured," he told her. "Miss McKie and I will not stray from your sight." Davina heard the note of sarcasm behind his words; Somerled had wearied of their chaperon.

He'd arranged two chairs by a window overlooking the bay. The faint cry of gulls wafted through the open sash as he seated her, then pulled his chair closer. "At least we'll have a few moments to ourselves," he said, then tapped her bag. "Have you brought your sketchbook?"

Davina pulled it from her bag, avoiding his warm gaze, knowing he had more in mind than idle conversation. *I am asking you to forgive me. I am asking you to marry me.* He was asking far more than she was ready to give him. But at least he was asking rather than taking.

Searching for an empty page, she came upon her drawing of one of the wee folk.

Somerled eyed the sketch with a raised brow. "The maids say a fairy has been seen above ground in Brodick Bay, raiding houses in broad daylight and poking round the kitchen, investigating all the dishes being prepared for dinner."

Davina promptly wrote across the page. *Fairies only do so on Fridays. This is Wednesday.*

He sobered at that. "And on what day do fairies marry mortals? For we must plan accordingly."

Somerled had not veered from his stated course: He wanted her for his wife. "We cannot delay much longer," he'd told her yestreen. "The eyes of many are upon us, making what they will of our duets. The sooner we are betrothed, the sooner Arran's gossips will look elsewhere."

Only one pair of eyes remained fixed on her now. "Pink is quite becoming on you," he said, though his gaze did not linger on her gown.

"I have a blithe song in mind to end the evening. You are welcome to accompany me on your fiddle if you like, but do pay particular attention to the last verse."

Once they were seated at table, Davina watched him as they dined on venison soaked in claret, his fork no busier than her own. If she might be certain that his remorse was sincere, that his apparent affection for her was genuine, that his wish to marry her stemmed from desire and not duty...

But she could be sure of none of those things.

As promised, Somerled closed with a heartsome song, to which she added sparse accompaniment; his fine tenor voice needed no help from her strings. When he reached the final verse, he turned and sang the words directly to her, as if no one else were present.

> She has my heart, she has my hand,
> By secret troth and honour's band!
> Till the mortal stroke shall lay me low,
> I'm thine, my Lowland lassie, O!

Davina blushed at his altered lyric. The song was "*Highland* Lassie, O," as everyone in the room well knew.

Somerled bowed low before her while their small audience generously applauded. Except for Nan Shaw, who stood to the side, a smug expression on her face.

Forty-Eight

Gossip is mischievous, light and easy to raise,
but grievous to bear and hard to get rid of.

HESIOD

Thursday dawned gray and cool. Sitting alone at the breakfast table, Davina sensed someone tarrying outside the door leading to the hall: two maids speaking Gaelic in hushed voices. Then she heard her name, stark amid the unfamiliar words. *McKie.* Nan was not the only servant at Kilmichael who behaved oddly round her; other maids frowned when Davina entered a room or whispered when she passed them in the hall. Maybe, like Betty at the manse, they assumed their silent houseguest was a fairy.

Her breakfast finished, she rose from the table, intent on riding to the Kilbride manse and paying her cousins a long-overdue visit. No one was in the hall by the time she opened the door. Nor did she find Nan straightening her room as the maid often did, even though all was in order.

Davina searched through the wardrobe, hoping she might locate a pair of shoes better suited to riding. Though she came up empty handed, she discovered that her damask gown was fully dry. Come Lammas she'd take her dress home and see it properly washed and ironed, with the hope of sparing it from the rag bin. At least her lace-trimmed jacket had survived.

Her heart thudded to a stop. *My brocade jacket.* In the painful aftermath, she'd not given it a moment's thought.

But she remembered the jacket now. Remembered where she'd left it. *Nae!* How could she have been so careless?

Fighting to catch her breath, she opened her bedchamber door, praying no servants were in sight, then hastened down the hall, through the front door, and round the house. One small grace: With the master of Kilmichael away, the stables were deserted.

A gray mantle of clouds hung overhead as images flooded her mind: Somerled unfastening the buttons beneath her bodice. Sliding the jacket over her shoulders. Tossing it onto the straw-covered floor. *I cannot wait much longer, lass.*

Tears stung her eyes afresh. *But I could have.*

When she neared the far corner of the stables, she slowed her steps, overcome with a sense of dread. Still, she had to look now while she had the chance. She'd not be long finding one small jacket.

Davina pulled open the stable door and nearly fainted.

The stall was empty. Swept clean. Even the tin pails were gone from the pegs.

She stumbled along the perimeter, staring at the wooden pegs, willing her jacket to appear. But it was not there. Had never been there. She'd left it on the floor, neglected, forgotten. A jacket stitched by her mother's loving hands.

Davina collapsed against the rough wall, her heart aching, her thoughts disjointed. The jacket was lost. Nae, it was found. Discovered by someone. A stranger? A servant? Did that person know it was hers and guess how it had landed here?

Each possibility she envisioned was worse than the last. What if someone was watching the stables, waiting to see who came looking for it? What if one of the lasses in the neighborhood began wearing the jacket, telling folk where she'd found it?

Nae, nae! Davina could not fathom the consequences any further.

Unless…unless the jacket had been raked up by a stable lad unnoticed, then burned with the straw. *Please, let that be the truth of it!* Though she hated to lose her beautiful jacket, it would be a thousand times worse to lose her reputation.

She fled from the stables, haunted by memories, hounded by remorse. If only she'd had her wits about her that night and claimed her jacket. If only she'd stopped Somerled from removing it in the first place. If only they'd never kissed by the burn. *If only. If only. If only.*

Davina had just turned the front corner of the house, drying her tears with her sleeve, when a familiar male voice brought her to an abrupt stop. *Reverend Stewart?* Aye, there he was. Standing at the front door with his back to her. Talking to Clark and handing him a valise.

Had her cousin come for a visit? When the minister disappeared through the front door, she shook out her skirts and pinned her hair back in place, then hurried after him, praying her fears were not written across her features.

Reverend Stewart was waiting in the entrance hall, his clothes rumpled and dusty from the ride. He greeted Davina with a nervous smile. "The footman just went looking for you. But I've found you first. Or you've found me. Have you been in the garden?" The flurry of words was unusual, as if her presence discomfited him. "Come, let me have a look at you, Cousin."

When he clasped her hands, she noticed his were clammy, and his forehead was covered with a sheen of perspiration. Was he ill? Was there trouble at the manse? Had he come to take her home?

Clark reappeared, then seated them in the music room. Tea would follow within minutes. Despite Mrs. Fullarton's concerns, Kilmichael was an efficient household even with its mistress confined to her bedchamber.

The moment they had the room to themselves, Reverend Stewart said, "I was sorry to hear that your hostess is nursing a persistent cough. And Clark indicated that Captain Fullarton is on the mainland."

She nodded, though she could tell the news upset him.

"Davina, I confess I'm grieved to find you here…unprotected. Had I known, I would have come sooner." He lowered his voice, though no one else was in the room. "I had hoped the captain might offer some explanation of why you were not at kirk on Sunday."

Of course. The instant she saw Reverend Stewart she should have realized why he'd come. No wonder he was perspiring, having to question his own cousin's devotion to God. Had she called on her cousins yesterday, she could have put their worries to rest.

Davina retrieved her sketchbook from her baize bag on the pianoforte and wrote a brief explanation: *I'm sorry to say the maid did not awaken me, and so I overslept.* Though every word was true, it looked inadequate on paper.

"In your weeks at the manse you were usually up at dawn." Reverend Stewart mopped his brow with a linen handkerchief. "Did you retire late on Saturday evening?"

She wrote again, determined to remain honest. *It was eleven o'clock before I returned to Kilmichael from the castle. His Grace has been most appreciative of my music.* By the look on his face, her comments were not improving matters.

He cleared his throat. "Perhaps on the mainland parishioners do not find it necessary to attend church weekly, as they once were obliged to do. I can assure you we are not so lax on Arran."

She wrote out a heartfelt apology, assuring him she would be in the Kilbride kirk on the Sabbath next. Though he nodded as he read it, he did not look appeased.

"The girls miss you very much," he finally admitted. "The sixth of July cannot come soon enough for them."

Davina nodded, touching her heart. *I miss them too. And you, Cousin. And Elspeth.*

"I've brought some of your dresses, your riding habit, and so forth. I believe the valise has been delivered to your room."

Davina offered her thanks, then put aside her sketchbook as tea was served. Though her precious jacket was lost to her, she would have several dresses made by her mother to console her. A tender reminder of home.

Reverend Stewart lifted his teacup, then said, almost as an afterthought, "I wrote to your father last Friday, letting him know you're here at Kilmichael."

The notion made her uneasy. What had Reverend Stewart told her parents? That the duke had honored her by requesting she entertain his guests? Or that Somerled had dishonored her with his "wanton" accompaniment?

Her one solace was this: The minister knew nothing of what had happened in the stables.

"I realize the house is brimming with servants, Cousin, and you are hardly alone. But I'll be happier when you are safely at the manse and the duke's guests have returned to Argyll…or, ah…to Fife or…well, Stirlingshire or whence they hail."

Somerled. Davina was glad the reverend couldn't read her thoughts. *You were not entirely wrong about him, Cousin.*

He placed his tea saucer on the table, no longer meeting her gaze. "People can be cruel, Davina. They see things…or hear things…and make judgments that are not fair." He stood, as if he'd run out of words or could no longer bring himself to say them. "Resist the devil, lass, and he will flee from you."

She did not need to be told the devil's name.

"Now I must discharge my ministerial duties," he said, attempting in vain to smooth the wrinkles from his coat, "assuming Mrs. Fullarton is awake and will not object to a brief visit. My physic books are in my saddlebag, should her symptoms warrant."

Davina followed him up the stair, then stood in the corner of the room as he listened intently to his patient's cough, touched her brow, then prayed for her health. On Arran, ministers and midwives usually sufficed as medical practitioners.

"How good of you to call." Mrs. Fullarton sounded weak, but her spirits remained strong. "Miss McKie, kindly see your cousin to the door since I cannot."

Davina watched him depart, saddened by the slump of his shoulders as he threw himself onto his horse. He had traveled all these miles to admonish her. And to warn her. Perhaps he'd sensed it was too late.

She sighed as she walked through the quiet house, feeling very alone. There was no one she might confide in, no one she could trust with her secrets, which were mounting. If her mother were here, could she even tell her what had happened? The thought of writing her experiences on paper made Davina blush. *Nae.* Some things could never be discussed.

At least she had the gowns her mother had made, waiting in the guest room. After luncheon she'd spend the afternoon airing them and choose one to wear that evening for the duke. Which ones had Elspeth packed, she wondered. Undoubtedly Cate and Abbie had slipped notes in her valise.

Anticipation quickened her heart as she swept open the guest room door. But what she found was not at all what she'd expected.

Her brocade jacket lay on the bed. Cleaned and pressed.

She fell back against the door, grasping the cold brass knob for support. *God, help me!* One of Kilmichael's servants had found her jacket. There could be no other explanation.

If one servant knew, they all knew. If one household knew, the whole parish would know come the Sabbath. The captain would be informed upon his return. Reverend Stewart would be told on the road before he reached home. The truth would travel faster than any newspaper headline on the mainland: *Davina McKie disrobed in the stables of Kilmichael on Midsummer Eve.* A woman would only do such a disgraceful thing in the company of a gentleman.

She sank to her knees on the carpeted floor. *Somerled.* He alone could save her.

Even if she could not trust him…even if she did not love him… even if her father did not approve of him, marrying Somerled was her only hope.

Forty-Nine

A lost good name is ne'er retriev'd.

JOHN GAY

Jamie McKie eased his oars into the loch, watching Leana's eyes drift shut, a faint smile on her face. The fine lines in her skin were beginning to show. Her hair was threaded with silver, like her Aunt Meg's, and lately Leana needed her spectacles more often than not.

She had never looked more beautiful to him.

He guided their skiff across Loch Trool with slow, even pulls, not wanting to disturb her. Leana had not slept well of late, worrying about their children, longing for their homecoming at Lammas. Neither Davina nor the twins had written her in a week, which only heightened her concerns. If a forenoon outing on the glassy surface of Trool afforded his wife the rest she needed, he would let her nap. Ian was visiting the McMillans that morning; the house was as peaceful as the loch.

High above them the sky resembled a watercolor painting in pale blues and soft grays, without sun or rain in the offing. The air was cool for the last day of June, and a light breeze moved across the water. He leaned forward and draped a thin, woolen plaid across Leana. She stirred, but her eyelids did not flutter open. *Sleep, dear wife.* He had loved her for nearly twenty years. Lord willing, he would have her with him for twoscore more.

"I can feel you watching me." She gradually opened her eyes, and her smile grew. "How lovely to catch a wee nap." She sat up slowly, taking care not to tip the bow of the skiff toward the water, then winced as she rolled her shoulders. "I spent too long in the garden this morning."

"Easily done when the sky is light by four o'clock."

She nodded, adjusting the plaid across her gown. "After that soaking rain on Sunday, everything's blooming. I've never seen the field poppies so bright. And the fairy foxgloves nearly reach my chin."

Jamie thought of another fairy that nearly reached his chin, though he wouldn't mention her name and risk dampening Leana's spirits. He never should have taken Davina to Arran, never should have suggested it. Not because he'd infuriated the twins, but because he'd disappointed his wife, who missed their daughter more each day.

"We have company." Leana was staring over his shoulder. "Galloping hard on the glen road."

He started rowing toward the pier, listening for the hoofbeats. "A single rider?"

"Aye. Reverend Moodie has a roan gelding, does he not?"

Jamie nodded, grunting as he dragged the oars through the water. In summer the minister often made monthly rounds of the parish. But not at a full gallop.

By the time they reached the stone pier, Reverend Moodie had already dismounted and sent his horse off to the stables. He stood waiting for them, his face flushed. "May I give you a hand, Mrs. McKie?" he asked with a tip of his hat, revealing his balding pate. "Good day to you as well, sir." The minister offered him a slight bow, then started up the walk. "Pardon me if I've interrupted your boating."

It was then Jamie noticed the strain in the man's voice, the reserve in his demeanor, and was convinced this was no monthly visit.

Leana tried to smile. "Reverend Moodie, will you honor us with your company at our noontide meal? Or would you prefer tea?"

"Tea," he said quickly, walking ahead of them through the front door. "I'm afraid I've not much time. Nor much appetite."

Once the three of them were seated in the drawing room and tea was served, Jamie dispensed with any small talk. "Reverend Moodie, 'tis obvious you've come to Glentrool on some matter of import."

"So I have." He pulled two letters from his waistcoat. "These arrived by mail coach this morning." The letters appeared to be identical, written in the same masculine hand on the same stationery, except for the colors of the wax. One was sealed in red—a business letter, already opened—and the other, sealed in amber beeswax, was personal. "They're both from Kilbride parish."

Arran. Jamie's heart quickened as Leana's hand sought his.

"Is Davina…" Her voice was barely audible. "Is she ill? Has she been harmed?"

"Not to my knowledge, Mrs. McKie. I believe your daughter is in good health."

"Thanks be to God." Leana let out an airy sigh. "Pardon me, Reverend, for being anxious."

Though neither letter was sealed in black, the color of mourning, Jamie felt no such relief. *To my knowledge… I believe…* The man was hedging. *Whatever has happened?*

"You have every reason to be anxious," the minister assured her, "when your children are not under your roof." With compassion in his brown eyes, he handed Jamie the sealed letter. "This is from Reverend Benjamin Stewart. Your cousin, I believe." He held up the other. "As you can see, he wrote to me as well."

"But…" Leana stared at him. "Why would our cousin…"

"My letter is of a ministerial nature," he explained, "requesting that I deliver your post at once. Reverend Stewart writes, 'As a fellow minister, you will appreciate my desire to impart this urgent news to the McKies. Kindly place it in their hands at the earliest possible hour.' Your cousin must have feared your letter would languish at a coaching inn, unclaimed for days."

Leana apologized profusely. "He could not have known what a burden he placed on you, Reverend, asking you to ride so far."

"I have other business in the glen," he insisted. "And the postscript was enough to persuade me to saddle my horse." He glanced down to read the closing words. "As Davina McKie is a member of your parish, I would urge you to pray for her moral fortitude, lest she be tempted beyond what she is able to resist."

Jamie heard the words, but they barely registered, so outrageous was the notion. *Her moral fortitude? Davina?*

"You must forgive me, but I was not the first to read this letter. As it bore a business seal, the session clerk opened it first." Reverend Moodie glanced at their sealed post as he stood. "Knowing your dear Davina, I feel certain your own letter will not bear further tidings of that nature."

"I pray you are right," Leana said faintly as the minister took his leave.

The moment they had the drawing room to themselves, Jamie slid his thumb under the seal, the snap of the wax unnaturally loud in the silent room, his heart thudding.

"Hurry," Leana pleaded, "for I cannot think what has happened."

Jamie scanned the opening lines. " 'Tis dated almost a week ago. Friday, the twenty-forth of June. Midsummer Day. He extends the usual greetings…ah, here.

> "Last evening our family attended a Midsummer Eve dinner party at Kilmichael…"

"Davina wrote me about that dinner." Leana twisted a lace handkerchief round her fingers. "She was to play for the Duke of Hamilton."

"It seems she did. And does still.

> "At His Grace's bidding, Davina has remained behind at Kilmichael House with Captain and Mrs. Fullarton for a fortnight. She is to play for the duke and his visitors each evening at Brodick castle."

Leana stared at the letter. "Is your cousin unhappy with the Fullartons?"

"Nae." Jamie grimaced, reading ahead. "With one of the duke's guests.

> "Davina was accompanied last evening on the violoncello by Somerled MacDonald, heir of Sir Harry MacDonald of Argyll.

"A Highlander," Jamie muttered. His grandfather, Archibald McKie, had fathered an illegitimate son, born to a Highland woman and raised near Inverness. Hamish had supported the Jacobite rebellion; his own father, Alec, had supported the Crown. For more than a century, the two families had stood on opposite sides of every battle—political, religious, or social. Though Hamish and Alec were both gone, their descendants remained hostile, Jamie among them.

Leana touched his hand, calming him. "What does your cousin say about this young man?"

> Though Mr. MacDonald is a talented musician, he played his instrument with a sense of wanton abandon and so induced your daughter to do the same.

"Oh, Jamie." Leana sank onto his shoulder. "Our innocent Davina. Is it possible?"

The paper shook in his hands. *I made it possible. By taking her there.*

> It grieves me to write this, and yet I would be remiss as your cousin and Davina's minister this summer if I did not express my deep concern for her reputation. I overheard several of the ladies present commenting on the unseemliness of her playing and the familiarity of her manner toward Mr. MacDonald.

Enraged, Jamie threw the letter to the carpet. "How *dare* they speak ill of our daughter!"

Leana leaned down and retrieved it, her hands shaking. "I cannot believe 'tis true. Davina would never do anything that might harm your good name."

" 'Tis already harmed." He was on his feet, pacing the floor. "Though I trust Reverend Moodie will keep our cousin's postscript to himself, I have no such hopes for the session clerk."

"But what is there to tell? Benjamin's letter said almost nothing—"

"Och! 'Moral fortitude'?" Jamie threw his hands in the air in frustration. " 'Tis enough to set tongues wagging 'til Martinmas."

She looked stricken for a moment. "Still, we do not know what happened—"

"Well, *something* happened on Arran, just as the twins said it would." The truth pierced his soul like a sword thrust between his ribs. "Just as you said it would, Leana."

Color stained her pale cheeks. "I could not be certain if I was right—"

"But you were," he fumed, not willing to be appeased. Not when he was to blame. "You asked me if Davina would be safe. You told me of your concerns. I should have listened to you."

Leana looked up, her eyes filling with tears. "Please do not think ill of our daughter."

"Och, Leana." His fury died down as quickly as it had risen. "Whatever has happened, Davina is not at fault. I am."

"Do not chastise yourself, dear husband." She pressed the letter into his hands. "Perhaps it is not too late."

But it was too late. The final words made that painfully clear. He read them aloud, nearly choking on each phrase.

> By the time you read this letter it is difficult to say what else may have transpired. Suffice to say that last evening does not bode well for the future. Should you choose to collect Davina before Lammas, I would be greatly relieved—for her sake and for yours. If she were my daughter, I would come without delay.

"Please, Jamie." Leana threw herself into his arms, crushing the letter between them. "Bring her home to me. The sky is light until nine o'clock—"

"I shall leave at once." He tightened his embrace, pressing a fervent kiss to her lips. He'd not fail her again. "Forgive me, Leana. Forgive me."

Fifty

Whispering tongues can poison truth.

Somerled had to be told. Tonight. The moment Davina saw him. *I accept your offer of marriage and the protection of your name.*

She had no choice in the matter. The appearance of her brocade jacket that morning meant someone at Kilmichael knew of her disgrace. A stable lad, the laundress, a dairymaid—she could not guess who'd found it. Or how many others had been told.

Praying with each step, she climbed the turnpike stair of the castle, with no appetite for dinner and little joy at the prospect of playing music. *Let not mine enemies triumph over me.* Davina could not name her enemies, but she sensed them all round her. Whispering, accusing, condemning. How she longed to write out the truth for anyone to read: *Somerled MacDonald robbed me of my virtue.* But what purpose would her confession serve, except to salve her wounded pride and injure her future husband? *Nae.* She would use the silence of her tongue to advantage this time.

Nan was two steps ahead of her, lifting the hem of her drugget gown as she climbed. Unlike the barefoot farmworkers they'd passed that afternoon, Nan wore shoes and stockings, as any proper lady's maid would. But her manners were better suited to a shearer in a barley field. Nan seldom knocked on her bedchamber door before entering and no longer addressed her as "Miss." Davina was not in a position to complain—she was a guest at Kilmichael and not Nan's employer—but each hour the maid's attitude toward her grew more insolent.

Perhaps when the captain returned tomorrow, Nan would mend her ways.

The two women reached the main hall of the castle and were given a cool reception by the duke's staff. Cooked trout was the dominant aroma once again. Though few gentlemen had gathered as yet, servants darted about making final preparations. Nan traipsed off to join them, having deposited the fiddle in her mistress's waiting hands without comment.

Davina was glad to have a moment alone to prepare her thoughts. *Let me not be ashamed of my hope.* Praying where she stood, Davina scanned the room for the gentleman who would be her husband.

"I trust I am the one you are looking for."

She spun round to find Somerled dressed in a blue coat that matched his eyes. Smiling, as if he already knew what she'd come to tell him.

"We've half an hour before dinner. Shall we tally the music you have in mind for tonight?"

Davina took his arm, pulling him gently aside.

"A more intimate discussion, I see." He steered her toward a quiet corner where they might sit unobserved—except by Nan, who kept an eye on them from across the room. Even from this distance, the maid's smirk was apparent.

"What an impudent woman," Somerled grumbled, turning his chair round to afford the couple a small measure of privacy.

The gray afternoon made the hour feel later than it was and cast the room in a gloomy light, dispelled only by the bright array of candles. Dinner would begin soon; Davina could delay no longer. She pulled out her sketchbook, watching his expression as she did.

"More questions?"

She shook her head. *Answers.*

Turning to the page she'd written just before leaving Kilmichael, Davina then placed in Somerled's hands both her sketchbook and her future.

After reading the first entry, his face was ashen. "Your jacket… I am so sorry… I did not remember…"

Nae. She pointed firmly to herself. *'Twas my fault.* Somerled could be blamed for many things but not for this.

"I fear there may be consequences, Miss McKie. Beginning with the Fullartons." Somerled studied the page, his concern mirroring hers. "Do you have any idea who might have found it?"

Nan strolled up as if she'd been invited to join them. "I ken verra weel wha found her bonny red *jaicket* on Sunday last."

Somerled glared at her. "I beg your pardon."

"Ye should be beggin' Miss McKie's pardon, should ye not?" Nan had the audacity to wink at him when she said it, then turned to Davina. "Can ye not jalouse wha cleaned and *preesed* yer jaicket whan the *washerwife* wasna leukin'? And wha placed it on yer bed *wi'oot* bein' seen?"

Davina's mouth fell open in dismay. Her own maid?

Somerled stood, no doubt to put the woman in her place, for he towered over her. "What do you think you've found? A fancy jacket, nothing more."

The maid rolled her eyes. "Oo aye, 'tis *meikle* mair than that. 'Tis proof that a *leddy* shucked her *cloots* in the stables, like a limmer."

Davina shrank back in her chair when she saw the look on Somerled's face.

"Do not use that word again in her presence." Had he not been a gentleman, Davina feared he might have struck the woman. Instead he spoke to her through gritted teeth. "Who have you told about finding Miss McKie's jacket?"

"I've yet tae tell a soul," Nan bragged, enjoying the power such illicit knowledge gave her. "But I wull. I'll tell *onie* person I please. *Onless* ye pay me what 'tis worth tae *haud* me tongue."

Somerled's blue eyes almost disappeared, so narrow was his gaze. "Are you blackmailing us, woman? I cannot think Captain Fullarton would retain so pernicious a maid in his employ."

"Whan I tell him what I ken, 'tis Miss McKie wha'll be shown the door. He's a gracie man, the captain, and so's his wife. They willna stand for *hochmagandy* at Kilmichael."

"That is a very serious charge." Somerled stepped closer to her, his tone menacing. "You merely found a jacket where it did not belong."

"Fowk dinna need mair than that tae get their jaws flappin'." Nan did not put her hands on her hips, but the defiance in her voice was unmistakable. "I can tell 'em mair, if ye like." She lowered her voice to a harsh whisper. "I can tell 'em aboot the bruises I saw whan I bathed her."

Davina looked away in shame. First the forgotten jacket. Then the forgotten bruises.

Somerled withdrew from his waistcoat a calfskin purse, the coins muffled by his grip. "Truth or lies, I'll not have you speak ill of Miss McKie. How much silver will it take to hold your vicious tongue?"

Nan stated a bold sum, then quickly pocketed the coins. "Ye have a bargain, Mr. MacDonald." She composed her face to suit her station, then walked off, cool as lemon punch.

Still reeling from their exchange, Davina scribbled across the page. *How do we know she has not already confessed this to others?*

Somerled sat in the chair opposite her, his features hard as stone. "Perhaps she has. But if we'd refused her, she would have been certain to tell every lad, lass, and bairn on Arran." He released a heavy sigh, staring at the carpet for a moment before finally meeting her gaze. "This means we must wed. Surely you see that now."

There was no going back, no time for second thoughts. She showed him the bottom of her sketchbook page. *I accept your offer of marriage.*

A faint sheen appeared in his eyes and was gone. "Thank you, Miss McKie. I shall endeavor to make you happy—"

She stemmed his words with her gloved fingertips, then turned the page so he understood the rest. *We cannot marry without my father's permission.*

"But you are seventeen. By Scottish law…"

Davina tapped the page. *Please.*

"Very well," he agreed at last. "My father's letter and mine were posted the first of the week. Come Monday your family should know our intentions. You can be sure our letters were most persuasive. If they respond at once, and I'm certain they will, we will be free to read the banns."

Davina wanted to nod, to mouth the words he'd said a moment earlier—*thank you*—to show her gratitude for his willingness to redeem her reputation. But she would not begin their marriage with a lie. She was willing; but it was hard to be grateful when she'd had so little choice. He'd vowed to make her happy. Could she learn to trust him in return?

"To dinner," he said, standing and offering his arm. "And when the first toast of the night is offered, know that my glass will be lifted to the lady at the far end of the table who will soon be my bride."

Fifty-One

Contentions fierce,
Ardent, and dire, spring from no petty cause.
SIR WALTER SCOTT

H ere's one truth I'll ne'er dispute." Will elbowed his brother as they stumbled down Libberton's Wynd, the uneven stones under their feet covered with muck. "John Dowie pours the finest bottle of ale in Edinburgh. Is that not the man himself, standing at his *couthie* tavern door?"

A relic of the last century, still wearing knee breeches and shoe buckles, John Dowie was nonetheless neatly groomed and well mannered. When Sandy called out a greeting, the ale seller tipped his tricorn hat. He'd seen enough of the McKies this summer to know their names and welcome their silver. "Table in the Coffin, lads?"

The smallest room in the tavern, the oblong Coffin seated only half a dozen patrons. Sandy usually protested, but Will favored the privacy. " 'Tis just the place for us," he told John as they entered from the narrow wynd. "We're here to toast the month of July."

" 'Tis as good a reason as any," John said cordially, lifting three clean glasses from the bar. He opened a fresh bottle of ale while they took their seats, then joined them in a small drink, as was his custom. "To your health, lads. And to the month ahead."

Sandy held up his glass. "And may July be drier than June." He took a generous swallow. "Though 'twill likely rain half this month as well. So says our father."

"A wise man," John observed, leaving them to their drink.

Will licked the ale from his lips. "Aye, Jamie McKie is wise, all right. And wealthy. And weak." He cared not if he sounded bitter; his brother had heard it before.

Sandy rubbed the scratchy beard on his unshaved cheek. "Suppose we blether about something more interesting. The lasses, perhaps."

"You mean that maid from Dickson's Close?" Will yawned and leaned back in his chair. Friday had been long in coming. "The one with eyes the color of *glessie*?"

Sandy grinned at him and lifted his ale. "The very one."

Will had just begun describing her *flindrikin* ways when two older gentlemen were ushered into the Coffin. Gentry, by the look of them. Fife men, by the sound of them. They nodded at Will and Sandy in greeting before they sat down at their table behind a privacy screen. The brown paper blocked the view but did nothing to muffle the sound.

Sandy prompted him, "You were telling me about Meg, the toffee-eyed *tairt*."

They kept their conversation low, in deference to the other patrons, but the gentlemen from Fife did not return the favor. The longer they drank, the louder they grew, until Sandy stamped off to order their supper, leaving Will to nurse the last of his drink and a mounting temper.

"Och, she was a bonny wee thing," the older of the two men was recounting. "Seventeen and sweet as a plum."

"A Lowlander? And a redhead, you say?"

"You've ne'er seen hair this color. Like a sunset. And such a *douce* face! She could've had her pick of any man in that room."

"Including you, Alastair?"

"Oo aye." The bearded man chuckled, then banged down his glass. "Especially me."

Will turned his back on the men, disgusted. Whoever the poor lass might be, she'd found an admirer in old Alastair.

Sandy returned with John Dowie on his heels. In one hand John bore a fresh bottle of ale and in the other a plate of whitings in cream, smelling of onions and chives.

"Two more months, lads, and we'll have oysters," John promised. "And then you'll see how many folk we can fit into this Coffin." He served them their supper, then disappeared into one of the nearby rooms, propping their empty ale bottle on the shelf above their heads before he left. When the reckoning came, the tavern owner would tally their empty bottles and charge the lads threepence apiece.

Will sank his teeth into a tender whiting, still hot from the pan, while the men on the other side of the screen continued their discourse on the loosome redhead.

"Who ever heard of a wee lass playing the fiddle?"

Will froze. *Davina?* Nae, 'twas impossible. She was on Arran, far from Fife.

Sandy looked up from his plate. His thoughts were running along similar paths, judging by his guarded expression.

"She's especially good with strathspeys," the Alastair fellow said. "The Duke of Hamilton invited her to entertain his guests 'til Wednesday next."

Will relaxed and swallowed another forkful. Hamilton Palace was in Lanarkshire. Not on Arran.

"Any other musicians with her?" his companion wanted to know.

"Aye, a Highlander by the name of Somerled MacDonald. Sir Harry's son, if you ken the family. He joined her on violoncello one night and wooden flute another. They performed many a fine tune for His Grace." Alastair chuckled. "And played another sort of duet for the horses in the stables, if you ken my meaning. At least that was the blether making the rounds before I sailed from Arran."

Will choked on his fish, struggling to spit it out.

"Is everything all right, lads?" Alastair stood and looked over the screen, his complexion ruddy from his ale. "Should we order the ham instead?"

Sandy pushed away his plate. "I beg your pardon, for 'tis a private conversation you gentlemen are having, but…"

The older man tapped on the flimsy screen. "Not much use, these. You heard my gossip from Brodick castle on Arran, I'll warrant. About the fiddler lass and her braw Highlander."

"Aye." Will wiped his mouth and took a long gulp of ale; the fish did not go well with bile.

"Make no mistake, she's a beauty." Alastair stepped out from behind the screen, yanking at his waistcoat. "And small as they come."

Will rose on unsteady feet. "Like a fairy?"

"Aye." The man's gray eyebrows arched as he smiled. "Just that."

It cannot be Davina. Cannot possibly be our sister.

But Will had to know. Had to be sure. "Do you happen to recall the lass's name?"

"Well…" Alastair studied the ceiling as if her name might be written there. "I cannot remember her Christian name. I might recognize her family name if I heard it. Och, but where are my manners?" He bobbed a clumsy bow. "I am Alastair MacDuff, and this is Roy Dalrymple of Fife. You two young gentlemen attend university, I'll wager. And are brothers, unless my bleary eyes deceive me."

"Correct on both counts, sir." Sandy stood, and they both offered shallow bows. "William and Alexander McKie of Glentrool."

"McKie?" Alastair looked pleased with himself. "Why, that's it! That's the lassie's name. She is not a"—his brassy voice lost its luster— "not a relative of yours, I…ah, presume."

Will and Sandy stared at each other. If by any chance, any small chance, the woman was not Davina, they would never sully her name by mentioning it here. But if the unfortunate lass was indeed their sister…

Sandy's nod was almost imperceptible. *Aye. Tell him.*

Will tried to wet his lips, longing for a sip of ale. "As it happens, the young woman you are discussing so freely may be our sister. Davina McKie."

"*Davina,* you say?" The florid cheeks of Alastair MacDuff turned pale. "Aye…aye, that was the young lady's Christian name." In the close quarters of the Coffin, his swallow was audible. "N-not a c-common name, Davina."

'Tis not your fault, lass. Will stared at the floor as heat rose through his body, sparking his anger, fueling his vengeance. *'Tis the Highlander's fault. And Father's fault. And mine.*

"Gentlemen…" Alastair had sobered considerably. "I must beg your forgiveness for speaking as I did." He spread out his hands, a silent plea. "I did not ken…nae, I *could* not ken that you…that she…"

"Well, now you do, MacDuff." Will ground out the words. "See that you do not drag our family name through every tavern in Edinburgh."

"Aye, to be sure." Alastair wiped his brow, sweating profusely. "Though the Highlander's the one who deserves your wrath." He lowered his voice, casting a glance at the door. "'Twas a rough wooing, I'm told. Her maid said the young lady was bruised—"

"Hech!" Will grabbed his wooden chair and flung it across the room, splintering the legs in pieces, roaring at the top of his lungs, "How *dare* he!" Their table went tumbling after it, fish and ale crashing to the floor. Then Sandy's chair sailed from his own hand, followed by a string of curses, as the men from Fife cowered at the far end of the Coffin.

"Gentlemen!" John Dowie was at the door, his scowl fierce. "I'll not have such behavior in my establishment. Must I summon the Town Guard—"

"Nae." Will yanked out his purse. "'Twill not be necessary." Breathing hard, his head ready to burst, Will emptied his store of coins into the ale seller's hands.

"You'll not be welcomed here again," John warned.

"'Tis of no consequence." Will brushed past him, his face set like flint. "My brother and I depart for Arran within the hour."

Fifty-Two

And when once the young heart of a maiden is stolen,
The maiden herself will steal after it soon.

THOMAS MOORE

Davina moved the charcoal pencil across the page of her sketch-book with short, firm strokes. Drawing a building, however grand, held little appeal for her. Too many straight lines, almost no color, and the stones were lifeless. A stand of sweet cicely waving in the breeze, smelling of anise, or a long-legged sandpiper with its brown wings and white belly, bobbing its head and wagging its tail, were far more interesting subjects for an artist. Buildings remained the same. Living things were ever changing—captured for a moment, then gone forever.

But Somerled wanted a sketch of Brodick castle. "To remember the place," he said.

What Davina remembered was climbing up to the castle last month with her cousins on a rainy Tuesday afternoon. And Cate singing, "There's a boatfu' o' lads come to our town." One boat especially, sailing from Claonaig, had changed Davina's life. She dearly missed Cate and Abbie, both of them bright as a pair of copper buttons. Missed eating Mrs. McCurdy's simple meals and playing the fiddle for a handful of undemanding neighbors. Missed sleeping in a cozy bedroom with two sisters who cared about her.

Davina sighed, pausing to look up at the stony parapet that marched along the roofline, and caught a glimpse of the Highlander strolling down the sloping path to the walled garden, his golden hair rivaling the bright July sun. Nan was scurrying to keep up with him. The maid had been sent up to the castle to inform Somerled of Davina's early arrival, well before the start of Saturday evening's meal and the music that would follow.

Somerled and Davina had much to discuss. If they hoped to hold back the swift-moving tide of rumors for another few days, it was safest to meet out of doors, in plain view, and well chaperoned.

"What fair flower is this, growing in the duke's garden?" Somerled smiled, but she saw a deeper question in his eyes. Had there been further trouble?

"I'll be sittin' o'er thar," Nan said with a halfhearted curtsy, then flounced off to take a seat on one of the broad sandstone benches in the garden. She landed far enough away to let them converse privately, yet close enough to notice if their hands touched.

Somerled joined Davina, giving the woman his back. "What a *glib-gabbit* creature!" he muttered. "Spreading lies like a Lowland farmer spreads manure."

His silver had stopped Nan's tongue, but the damage had already been done. Wherever Davina went she sensed people staring at her and felt the daggers of their pointed looks. Nan had not told anyone about the jacket, perhaps, but she'd told them enough.

"We'll not let her spoil our afternoon," Somerled insisted, leaning over Davina's shoulder to study her drawing. "You've been working on my castle, aye?"

Davina waited for his reaction. Unlike playing the fiddle, when she experienced the audience's joy and her own at the same moment, sketching was a solitary pleasure. Months might go by before anyone saw her work, and who knew how they would respond?

"You've rendered it perfectly," Somerled said at last. "Will you sign it?"

She was about to write *Davina McKie* across the bottom when he stayed her hand.

"Why not try your new name?" He was winking at her again, or so it appeared in the slanted afternoon sunlight. "See how it looks on the page."

Davina would never confess it, but she'd written it several times that morning. *Davina MacDonald.* How strange and frightening a prospect, to be married so young in life. To be married to a Highlander.

Honoring Somerled's request, she signed the sketch with her married name, even though it felt unchancie. The banns had to be cried in the kirk three Sabbaths in a row, meaning the earliest they could wed was Lammastide. Was it wise to write a name that was not yet hers?

Somerled seemed to think so. "I like the look of it, don't you?" He withdrew a slender dirk from his boot, then pressed the sharp point into the gutter of the book, preparing to cut the page free. "Do you mind?"

She did, a little. His presumptuous habit of simply taking what he wanted remained vexing.

"I see that you do mind." Somerled tucked the knife back into his boot, his even gaze locked with hers. "Do not be afraid to say nae to me, Miss McKie."

It was difficult to resist a man so determined to please her.

Then his smile returned, his greatest weapon; surely he knew that. "There is one exception. You may not change your mind about marrying me. Once your father has blessed our union, we shall sail for the mainland and leave all this unfortunate gossip in our wake."

My bonny Arran. She'd come to the island with such high hopes. Would she leave nothing behind except unkind whispers and a lingering sense of shame? Her only consolation was knowing the slander would remain on Arran. She'd be a married woman and off to Argyll before the folk of Monnigaff parish even expected her home.

Home. Her throat began to tighten. *Glentrool. Mother.* How could she bid farewell to the world she knew and the people she loved, knowing she might not see them for months, even years at a time? What husband, however wealthy or handsome, could appease so great a loss?

Distracted by her thoughts, she didn't realize Somerled had taken the sketchbook from her lap and was scanning the pages with great interest. When she gave a silent gasp and tried to reclaim it, he held her book out of reach. "I believe I saw a familiar face. One crowned with wavy hair."

Mortified, she looked away as he turned to the page. He would find it a poor likeness. And think her a silly schoolgirl for drawing it.

He gazed at the sketch longer than she liked, holding it this way and that. "An uncanny resemblance," he finally said. "Though I see you omitted the pale birthmark on my neck. A kindness, that. How clever of you to draw this while I was not paying attention."

Davina shook her head and tapped her pencil on the date she'd scribbled in the corner. *May Day 1808.* When he started to protest that they'd not met until June, what else could she do but write out the truth? *I dreamed of you that night in May.*

"Dreamed of me?"

Pencil and paper were not enough. She picked a stray gowan that had escaped the gardener's scythe, pretended to slide it beneath an imaginary pillow on which she laid her head, then opened her eyes and reached for the sketchbook as she sat back down.

He shook his head, incredulous. "Does every unmarried lass in Scotland put wildflowers under her pillow on May Day?"

She began pulling off the daisy petals, one by one.

"And the man she dreams about…is he meant to be her husband?"

Davina shrugged, but she didn't fool him. *Aye.*

"Then 'tis no accident." His voice had a note of awe. "The two of us, visiting Arran this summer, crossing paths as we did. My love, we were betrothed before we met."

My love. The torn petals slipped through her fingers. *Could it be true?*

He reached for her hand, then hesitated. Waiting.

Davina glanced toward Nan. *She will see us.*

Undaunted, he rested his hands next to hers, palm up. An invitation.

My love. He did not need to say those words. For the sake of their families' reputations, she had no choice but to marry him, and he knew it. Yet Somerled wooed her.

"Sir," Nan said, walking up, "they'll be wantin' ye baith for denner suin." She stood nearby, waiting to follow them up the steep walk toward the castle, a self-satisfied look on her face.

Somerled offered Davina his arm, and she took it willingly. Even Nan could not find fault with that. The couple walked side by side along the wide, graveled walk, through a rectangular door in the garden wall, then upward, past a closely clipped hedgerow and the *lowpin-on stane,* two stone steps used to mount a horse or carriage.

"I have a last tune in mind for tonight," Somerled told her as they paused by the castle door, built when men as tall as Somerled were seldom found. " 'Tis a reel," he said, ducking beneath the lintel. "You'll recognize it from the first note."

Indeed she did.

As the sun was setting and the half-moon was high above Arran, Somerled led them into their final piece, "I Love My Love in Secret." Davina blinked away tears as her bow flew across the strings. She couldn't sing the words, but she knew them. *I gied my heart in pledge o' his ring.* Could she do so? Could she give this man her heart, not just her hand?

Davina finished the reel with her back to Somerled, hiding her feelings, remembering his confession. *I have wronged you in the worst imaginable way.* Aye, he had. The very worst. Yet his remorse seemed genuine. *I truly am sorry, Miss McKie.* Spoken many times. Contritely. Sincerely. *I dare not ask you to forgive me.* But it was not Somerled who asked. *Our Father which art in heaven.* She'd prayed the words aloud as a child and whispered them in her heart every Sabbath. *Forgive us our debts, as we forgive our debtors.* Yet she'd never been so tested. Forgiving her brothers had been easy. She loved them; it was an accident; they were children. But forgiving Somerled required a divine portion of grace. Her defilement was no accident, and Somerled was no child.

The applause round the room crowded out her solemn thoughts as Somerled took her hand. "Bow with me." She felt the warmth of his grip, the solid strength of him. *My love.* Did he mean what he said?

He remained by her side as she stored her fiddle, then followed her down the turnpike stair. When the couple stepped out of doors and tarried at the top of the castle steps, Nan stood a few feet away, waiting to escort Davina back to Kilmichael, the baize bag tucked beneath her arm. Not far to the east Brodick Bay glimmered in the moonlight.

" 'Tis breezy tonight." Somerled caught her shawl before it slipped to the ground and arranged it round her shoulders. "I'm glad you brought something to keep you warm."

Davina blushed, grateful for the cover of night. Did he not know that his voice, his words, warmed her far more than a length of fabric?

She had yet to slip on her gloves, kept in her reticule while she played. As she shook them out, Somerled gently took them from her. "Let me." He fitted each silk glove over her fingers, in no hurry, his voice soft as the night air. "If I cannot hold you in my arms, Miss McKie, I must be satisfied with this." He smoothed her gloves in place and buttoned the pearl at each wrist.

His tenderness took her breath away, even as his entreaty from Monday night pressed on her heart. *I am asking you to forgive me.* Could she extend grace to this man, however grave his transgressions? *As Christ forgave you, so also do ye.*

"What time will you leave for kirk in the morning?" he asked, unaware of her spinning emotions.

She drew the time on the palm of his hand, a figure eight, then touched his cheek as her eyes filled with tears. *Mercy is a gift.* Her father's words, spoken to her. And her words, written to her father. *Will you not do the same?*

Fifty-Three

Here shame dissuades him, there his fear prevails,
And each by turn his aching heart assails.

OVID

Jamie climbed the road heading north from Lamlash Bay, his gait unsteady from too many hours on the open water. Though the night had been clear and moonlit, calm winds were the boat's undoing. The *Westgate* had sailed out of Ayr yestreen, then stalled off the Arran coast. The captain and crew of the packet boat had no choice but to wait until the Sabbath dawned and a fresh wind carried them into the bay. Their only passenger had remained awake through the long night, pacing the deck.

'Twas not the rocking boat that had left Jamie sleepless but thoughts of the daughter he'd brought to Arran's shores. Two days of riding alone on the road they'd traveled together had grieved his heart to the point of breaking. *My darling girl. My precious, innocent girl.* As he'd crossed over Rowantree Hill, he'd imagined the worst—that Davina had scandalized the parish, then fled for Argyll with the Highlander. By the time he'd made his bed on Michael Kelly's cottage floor, Jamie had tamped down such fears, certain he would arrive on the island and find Davina playing for His Grace with her usual carefree spirit and the Highlander nowhere in sight.

Perhaps his ministerial cousin was prone to exaggeration. *It is difficult to say what else may have transpired.* Was Benjamin Stewart the sort of fellow who saw a bogle behind every hillock or warned his parishioners against the evils of modern poetry? Did he observe two talented musicians playing with heartfelt passion and unfairly jalouse the rest?

Jamie turned onto the narrow lane leading to the manse, shifting the traveling bag strapped to his shoulders. Poor Leana, distraught and tearful, had packed his belongings in a matter of minutes. He required little for his journey except her prayers. And her forgiveness. *You were right, Leana, and I was so very wrong.* Why had he not listened to his own wife's counsel and kept Davina home for the summer? Jamie knew the answer and did not like it. *A man's pride shall bring him low.*

The plain manse rose before him, shutters open, doors closed, neither welcoming nor foreboding. Birdsong filled the ruinous old kirkyard, and the eastern sky was bright and cloudless at the break of day. Mrs. McCurdy would be tending her kitchen hearth even if the rest of the household were asleep in their beds.

He knocked, hoping he would not wake them.

The black-haired maid—Mary? Betty?—opened the door, blinking as she did, almost forgetting to bob a curtsy. "Guid mornin' tae ye, Mr. McKie. We've been expectin' ye." She did not comment on the time. Six o'clock at most. "Reverend Stewart's in his study." She deposited his leather bag in the parlor, then knocked on the door to the minister's study. "Ye hae company, Reverend."

He appeared in the hall a moment later. "Cousin Jamie." Benjamin took his arm, a look of dread and sympathy on his face, as if he were about to conduct the funeral of a dear friend. "Join me in my study."

"Forgive the hour," Jamie began, but his cousin brushed off his apology.

"The sea keeps no hourglass. We're grateful to God when visitors arrive at all."

The moment they were seated in the cramped study, Benjamin said without preamble, "I know you must be eager to see your daughter. Though she did not appear at kirk on the Sabbath last, Davina assured me she will be here this morning."

Despite his exhaustion, Jamie clearly heard the dissembling in his cousin's voice. "Why was Davina not at kirk?"

The minister hastened to offer an explanation. "She overslept, apparently. The evening before, she'd returned to Kilmichael rather late."

Jamie narrowed his gaze. "What else have you learned?"

Benjamin did not respond at once, fidgeting with some papers at hand and avoiding Jamie's gaze. " 'Tis difficult to sort out such things, gossip and hearsay being what they are." He shifted his weight, as if trying to get comfortable in a hard-backed chair. "You received my letter, of course, so you're aware of my objection to Davina's music on Midsummer Eve."

Jamie rose to her defense. "My daughter plays with great feeling. As do most fiddlers—"

"Now, now. I know 'tis true." The minister eyed the door, then lowered his voice. "According to her maid, Davina continues to play her fiddle with rather too much zeal. She has, however, been well received by the duke's guests. All gentlemen, I might point out."

Exhaling with some frustration, Jamie leaned forward, hands on his knees. "Cousin, have I traveled all the way to Arran to be told that my daughter has found an appreciative audience?"

"Nae, Jamie." His shoulders drooped, like a man defeated. " 'Tis your daughter's obvious fascination with Somerled MacDonald that prompted me to write you."

Jamie nodded, though he had a hard time picturing such a thing. Davina never flirted with men in the kirkyard, as many young women did. "This Somerled…he's a gentleman, is he not?"

"If you mean is he of good stock, well educated, and of sufficient fortune, then aye."

Most fathers would be relieved; Jamie heard something that was not spoken.

His cousin cleared his throat. "But MacDonald also has a reputation for…ah…"

Jamie's heart seemed to slow, waiting for the rest. Except he knew, even before the minister finished. *Not my Davina. Surely not my daughter.* He could hardly form the words. "A reputation for…"

"Lechery."

Jamie sank against his chair, as if felled by a pistol. "You are certain of this?"

"Apparently 'tis common knowledge round Argyll. As to whether or not MacDonald has ensnared Davina, I cannot say. She has confessed such details to no one."

Jamie heard his words through a fog of pain. *Please tell me it is not so, Davina. Please tell me you are unharmed.*

"Had you not come, Jamie, I would have risked offending His Grace and insisted she remain at the manse this evening rather than returning to Brodick. But now that you are here, I believe things may be resolved and the truth brought to light."

Jamie stood so quickly he almost sat down again, dizzy from the effort. "Benjamin, I must borrow your horse." Whatever had happened, his daughter needed him. At once. "I'll return later this morning," he pledged, "with Davina."

He did not wait for a reply nor greet the rest of the household as he hurried down the short hall and out the front door, grabbing his leather bag en route. Time enough for greetings when he returned. For now, only Davina mattered.

Within minutes the horse was saddled and Jamie was riding north toward Brodick Bay. Though surrounded by verdant glens and rugged hills, he saw nothing but the ribbon of road leading him to his daughter. All the gossips on Arran could not tell him what Davina alone knew. *Have you given yourself to him, lass? Or has he taken you against your will?*

Both possibilities weighed heavily on his heart. If the first, then Jamie had failed her as a father by not teaching her the fear of the Lord and the wisdom of his commandments. But if the second—if this cursed man had violated his daughter—then she could not have cried for help, could not have begged him to stop, could not have pleaded for mercy.

"Nae!" Jamie shouted, bearing down on the horse, sending dirt and gravel flying. Hot tears stung his eyes, and his heart grew hard as a fist.

O God, to whom vengeance belongeth, show thyself.

Fifty-Four

Our wanton accidents take root, and grow
To vaunt themselves God's laws.
CHARLES KINGSLEY

Somerled could still feel Davina's gloved fingertip drawing the number eight on his bare palm. If she planned to leave for kirk at eight o'clock, then he would tap on her bedchamber window at seven and see if she might give him what he longed for.

One kiss. That was all he would ask of her, all he would expect.

Hadn't he behaved like a gentleman for more than a week? Not one untoward touch, not a single improper suggestion. Then yestreen on the castle stair she had brushed his cheek with her hand, a most welcome overture. Surely a kiss would not undo her. *Just one, my love.*

Monday evening at the castle was far too long to wait. He would see her now and know her heart. Aye, she had agreed to marry him, but had she truly forgiven him? One kiss, and he would have his answer.

Somerled crossed the burn that bordered the Kilmichael estate, taking care not to plunge into the cold water swirling round his boots. He neared the bench where they'd met on two very different occasions: a moonless night full of passion and a sunlit day full of tears. *Forgive me, Davina. For both of them.* Once they heard from Davina's father and could proceed with the wedding, perhaps they could meet here again to celebrate.

I shall kiss you then, too, lass. More than once.

Skirting the garden, trying to disappear among the taller plantings, he eyed the house, grandly proportioned, the windowpanes in the upper story sparkling in the early morning sun. One ground-floor window near the rear of the house drew his gaze: the one he'd climbed through on Midsummer Eve. Was Davina a light sleeper? Would she hear his gentle knocking on the glass? At least that detestable Nan Shaw did not sleep in her lady's room, or she'd wake the whole household and cry, "Thief!"

Not altogether without merit, that charge.

He approached the window, feeling his heart beginning to pound, though no servants were in sight. Until this moment he'd have told anyone who surprised him on the lawn that he was joining Miss McKie for breakfast in the music room. But now that his back was pressed against the side of the stone house and he was inching toward the window, that story would no longer be plausible; most visitors entered through the door.

Surrounded by an enormous clipped yew, Somerled turned and faced her window at last, confident he could be heard by her yet not seen by others. He tapped on the glass, then pressed his ear against it, listening. No rustling of bedcovers, no footfalls. He knocked again, more firmly this time. In the hush of early morning, his knuckles on the windowpane sounded dangerously loud.

There. He heard movement within. For a moment his heart caught in his throat. What if this was no longer Davina's room? What if the Fullartons had brought home another guest? *Nae.* There she was, parting the curtains, a look of astonishment on her sweet face.

"Good morning," he murmured, then smiled as he helped her lift the heavy window sash. She'd tied a linen wrap over her long nightgown in haste—inside out, with the seams showing—and her unbound hair cascaded round her shoulders. A charming vision of youth and innocence and beauty.

And all mine.

He had never been a possessive man. Had avoided such entanglements. Davina McKie had changed all that. The man who'd never wanted a wife could not slip a ring on her finger soon enough. Aye, he longed to bed her—properly this time—but his desire ran far deeper than that.

Somerled rested his arms on the windowsill as she knelt to hear his whispered words. "I have come for one thing only. Naturally you are free to refuse."

Davina glanced over her shoulder—was there a sound in the

hall?—then turned back, brushing the sleep from her eyes. She nodded. *Go on.*

"'Tis a kiss I'm wanting. Only one. Chaste and true."

She studied him at length before answering. *Aye.*

"Is the door locked?" he asked.

A shake of her head. *Nae.*

"Will that maid of yours appear soon?"

A slight shrug. *Who can tell?*

Somerled smiled. Already he was beginning to hear the words she could not say but meant. A promising sign for the years to come.

He looked round her at the shadowy room. Did he dare risk climbing inside? The window was broad and the drop to the ground short; he could leap out with little effort if someone knocked on the door. But the coins he'd paid Nan would not be enough to buy her silence if the maid discovered him in Davina's bedchamber, however innocent his intentions.

Davina sat back on her heels. Her hands were folded on her lap in ladylike fashion, her wrap modestly tucked round her. Despite her state of undress, Davina was everything virtuous, everything pure.

Unbidden, a lump rose in his throat. Could it be he'd not ruined her completely? This young woman who'd stolen his heart—might she offer hers in return?

He could not find out across a windowsill. "May I come inside for a moment, Miss McKie? And kiss you there?" When Davina blanched, he held up his hand. "One kiss, I assure you. Nothing more."

She hesitated, eyes closed, as if she was listening. Nae, as if she was praying. At last she scooted back across the carpet, making room for him. Trusting him.

He crawled over the windowsill, dragging his long legs over with caution, aware of sounds elsewhere in the house. Their one kiss would need to be very brief. Since he'd not see her again this day nor much of the next, he would do his part to make it memorable.

"I'll not put my hands on you unless you want me to," he said, kneeling before her.

She shook her head. *Please don't.*

Somerled leaned toward her with care, both of them on their knees, his fingers touching the floor so he would not tip forward and knock her over. "Thank you, my love," he whispered, and then he pressed his mouth to hers.

Time swept backward. To their first kiss, tender and sweet.

And in her kiss he tasted forgiveness. And in his heart he knew his love for her was genuine, a love that would last for all their days together.

Somerled fought to keep his balance, not wanting their one kiss to end. Not hearing the knock at her bedchamber door until it was too late.

Fifty-Five

Know this, that troubles come swifter
than the things we desire.

PLAUTUS

M iss McKie," Nan sang out. " 'Tis yer faither, come tae see ye."
Davina broke their kiss with a gasp, falling backward onto the
carpet as Somerled shot to his feet.

"Sir, this is not as it appears—"

"Appears?" Jamie McKie was shouting, on the verge of exploding, as
he strode into the room. "What right have *you* to speak of appearances?"

Davina was too stunned to do anything but clutch her robe round
her neck as her father pulled her to her feet.

He circled his arm round her, his gaze still pinned to Somerled. "I
will let my daughter explain what has occurred here. Not you, Mac-
Donald."

He knows his name. Davina could not breathe, could not think.
What was he doing here? And why was her sketchbook not at hand
when she needed it so desperately? Out of the corner of her eye, she saw
Nan standing in the open doorway, gloating.

Father turned round long enough to dismiss the maid. "Inform the
Fullartons of my arrival. And see that we're not disturbed."

Davina felt his chest heaving, fury coming off him like steam.
Father, dear Father. She loved him but was terrified he'd found her like
this. With Somerled. *'Twas only a kiss, Father. One kiss.*

Somerled straightened his coat and ran his hand through his
disheveled hair. "Forgive me, sir, but I hardly know where to begin." He
bowed stiffly. "I am Somerled MacDonald of—"

"I ken who you are, lad."

Her father was not looking at Somerled now. Only at her. Searching her face for answers. "Tell me, Davina. What is this man to you?"

She saw the glint of tears in his eyes. And the disappointment. And the fear. *I will tell you, Father. When we are alone, I will tell you everything.*

"Has he hurt you, Davina?" A note of urgency in his voice. "Are you well?"

Davina heard the unasked question: *Are you still chaste?* She swallowed, wishing she might close her eyes and hide the truth from him. Instead she nodded in response, convincing herself she wasn't telling him a lie. *I am well enough.*

Somerled tried again. "May I assume you received our letters, sir?"

Jamie looked at him now, his expression hardening. "The only letter I received was from my cousin, Reverend Stewart, full of concern for my daughter. I came at once. For her sake."

The strain in her father's voice was nothing compared to the tension Davina felt in the arm surrounding her. Shielding her. Protecting her from the man she'd pledged to marry.

Despite her father's anger, Somerled did not back down, nor was he disrespectful. "Mr. McKie, two letters were sent by packet boat on Monday. One from my father, Sir Harry MacDonald of Argyll, and one from me. I regret that you did not receive them before you left Glentrool."

"Whatever the content of those letters, words cannot atone for what I witnessed in this room." Jamie glanced at the floor and then at her hand. "Unless a wedding ring has been placed on my daughter's finger without my knowledge, your conduct...nae, your *presence* here is reprehensible."

"I can explain that, sir, and will do so gladly." Somerled took one step toward them, his hands clasped behind his back, dispelling any threat; he was both taller and broader than her father. "First you must know that a wedding ring awaits your daughter in Argyll. It belonged to my grandmother and is meant to be worn by my wife, the future Lady MacDonald."

Her father stiffened. "Am I to understand that you wish to marry my daughter?"

"I do, sir. Very much. Without delay."

Oh, Somerled. She tried to catch his eye, to warn him. *Do not give us away.*

"You sound...eager." Her father's voice was suddenly cool. "Davina, while you dress for kirk, I shall escort Mr. MacDonald out of doors where we might speak in private." He pressed a firm kiss to her brow. "I'll send in your maid. See that you are ready in half an hour. Then you and I shall have our own discussion, aye?"

Davina trembled as he released her. *He knows.* Was the guilty truth in her eyes? In Somerled's voice? *Without delay.* Her father was astute; he knew an anxious bridegroom when he heard one. *Father, you must agree to this. Please, you must.*

Somerled paused before following him out the door. "Miss McKie, I hope you will pardon my imprudent visit this morning." He wanted to say more—she could see that—but instead he bowed and disappeared into the hall. Somerled did not seem afraid; she was frightened enough for both of them. What would he say to her father? And her father to him?

Nan came sauntering in, then closed the door with her hip. "'Tis the last time I'll be forced tae dress ye," she said curtly, yanking open the wardrobe, then pulling out one gown after another and tossing them across the bed. "Syne I told the Fullartons aboot yer early mornin' visitor, they want ye oot the door suin as yer bags are packed." She shook her head, making her white cap dance. "And aren't I the blithe lass tae do it?"

Davina did not give Nan the satisfaction of seeing her cry. She had far graver concerns than an inexcusably rude maid or a scandalized hostess. Somerled might think it necessary to tell her father the terrible truth, if only to convince him of the need for haste. *You cannot tell him. You must not!* If her father could not forgive the twins for the accident that took away her voice, he would never forgive the man who'd stolen her innocence.

The twins. Davina's skin grew cold. Once her father learned the truth, so would her brothers. Will and Sandy would not ask to speak with Somerled, as Father had; they would leave Somerled battered and bleeding and consider it justice.

She sank down onto the edge of the bed, too numb to move.

Be not far from me; for trouble is near.

Indifferent to her lady's misery, Nan emptied the pitcher of hot water into the bowl, splashing it everywhere, then draped a linen towel over the side. "Here ye are."

Retrieving the towel before the edges were soaked, Davina attended to her bath, not caring if the *ill-scrapit* woman saw her bruises, now faded to a pale lavender. Any trace of color or tenderness would be gone by the time she married Somerled. He had seen one bruise and been chastened; he did not need to see the rest.

As Nan brushed her riding habit with perfunctory strokes, Davina was glad she had no voice; she'd have only harsh words for the maid who'd lorded it over her, punishing her daily for disregarding the rules of good society. She looked away as Nan dressed her, the maid tugging harder than required on her laces, dragging Davina's blouse over her head, jabbing her torso with her sharp thumbs as she buttoned her coat. Davina was afraid to let the woman comb her hair and so did it herself, plaiting her red locks while Nan packed her valise.

Nan scowled as Davina finished her thick braid with a bow. "Ye leuk like a *puir* kintra lass. Mrs. Fullarton's maid would ne'er dress her leddy's hair sae plain."

Davina did a hatesome thing: She turned and flung her braid over her shoulder, swatting Nan Shaw in the face.

Be silent and safe—silence never betrays you.
JOHN BOYLE O'REILLY

"Hizzie!" Nan sputtered, but her abusive comment fell on deaf ears. Davina quit the room without a backward glance and with no intention of returning. She sailed down the hall, buoyed by her tiny victory and driven by a fresh wind of determination, even as tears stung her eyes. If Somerled was fearless, could she not be brave as well?

The hall was empty, but there were servants pressed against each closed door—eavesdropping, no doubt. She heard them shuffling and whispering as she walked by. This house and its inhabitants would not be missed. Davina followed the sound of voices to the music room, where Captain Fullarton and her father were in deep conversation. Somerled had gone apparently. Did that bode ill or well?

Both men stood to greet her with grim expressions.

"Mr. MacDonald has taken his leave," her father said evenly. "As we shall do shortly."

Captain Fullarton looked very ill at ease; she could hardly blame him. Had there not been gossip enough for the last week, now an amorous Highlander had climbed in his guest-room window on the same morning an enraged father had appeared on his doorstep. No wonder the captain's hospitality had come to an abrupt end; the Fullartons were not about to risk their august reputation for the sake of a Lowland fiddler. Though his eagerness to see her leave cut her to the quick, Davina could not fault the man's prudence.

His smile was painful to look at. "Miss McKie, I thought...that is, my wife and I believe that you will feel more comfortable lodging elsewhere." He gestured in the general direction of the bay. "I have taken the liberty of sending Clark to the inn at Cladach to make lodging arrangements for you." He nodded at Jamie. "And for your father, at his request.

'Tis quite close to Brodick castle, which should make things easier for you each evening. I believe you'll find the inn very…commodious."

Davina glanced away, almost feeling sorry for him.

Her father spared him additional false blandishments. "I'm sure it will suffice, Captain. We'd be grateful if you would also send Davina's belongings—"

"Aye, aye, they will follow shortly." The master of Kilmichael had already pressed Davina's fiddle into her hands and was escorting her to the front door, as if anxious to sweep the house clean of her. "We've a horse saddled for you, Miss McKie, that will carry you to kirk and back. Will you require anything else?"

Davina pressed her hands together in thanks—until this moment the Fullartons had been most hospitable—then took her father's arm and walked into the unforgiving light of a Sabbath morning. It was not yet nine o'clock; she'd not had breakfast, not even tea. Perhaps the two of them might stop at the manse before or after kirk, if the Stewarts would still make her welcome. A wretched thing, to be shunned by polite society.

"Up you go, Davina." Her father helped her onto the sidesaddle, then strapped her baize bag in place, knowing she would want her fiddle safely at hand. Jamie mounted Grian with ease, then directed their horses toward the long avenue of firs and beech trees leading toward the bay.

Sunlight dappled the road, and birdsong filled the air, as if nothing had happened, as if nothing had changed since the pleasant Thursday evening she'd bumped along in a farm cart on this same narrow road. A time when life was grand and people were kind and no gentleman had done more than give her an admiring glance.

"Davina…"

She straightened in the saddle as her heart began to pound.

"I had a brief conversation with MacDonald. The explanation for his appearance in your bedchamber was romantic to the extreme. He said he'd climbed in for a single kiss before you left for kirk. Can that be possible?"

She blushed, yet made certain he saw her nod. *Aye. One kiss.*

"His reputation would suggest he came for a great deal more..."

Nae. She could answer honestly, shaking her head. *Not this morning.*

"I'm relieved to hear it, Davina." Jamie shifted in his saddle to look at her more closely. "You realize, I'm sure, that Reverend Stewart has a rather low opinion of Somerled MacDonald." When she affirmed his comment with a slight shrug, he continued, "Aye, well, I prefer to make my own decisions on such things. Since my youthful behavior left much to be desired, I try to be fair in my judgment of others."

Davina adjusted her skirt round the pommel, hiding her surprise. Father had never made such an admission—not to her, at least.

"Somerled is quite resolved that you will be his wife. Is that what you would wish?"

She took a deep breath, then nodded. *Forgive me, Father, but I must.*

His low groan made her heart ache. " 'Tis serious, then, this affection you share."

Aye. Davina longed for her sketchbook. This evening at the inn she would put her thoughts and feelings on paper. Describe Somerled's good qualities. Convince her father that, despite any scurrilous reports he might have heard, the accusations were not valid. *Not anymore.*

They rode on, catching glimpses of towering Goatfell through the silvery branches. After a lengthy silence, he reached over and took her hand. "I did not send you to the Isle of Arran to find a husband."

I know. She touched her brow. *And I did not come here looking for one.*

"I am afraid your mother will be inconsolable at the thought of your living so far from home. And I am not persuaded that you belong with a Highlander."

She did not respond, hoping he'd not pursue that topic further. Family loyalties ran deep among the McKies.

"You are very young, Davina. But then I am reminded that Margaret McMillan is but sixteen." He paused to brush a leaf from his coat, sighing as he did. "The heart does not pay much attention to calendars, I'm afraid."

At least her age would not be a hindrance.

"As for Somerled, he seems well educated, well mannered, well spoken. Not quite the rogue your cousin painted him to be. And gifted musically, I'm told, though the reverend is not enamored of his technique."

Davina pretended to play her fiddle in a highly exaggerated manner.

"Aye, that's the way of it." His smile was slight but welcome. "I've asked Somerled to arrange a meeting for us tomorrow morning. Until I've met with Sir Harry and have discussed their proposal at length, I cannot promise what the future holds."

She touched the instrument strapped behind her, a thought coming to mind. Could Father not come to the castle and hear the two of them perform? His Grace was a generous man; he would not protest one extra plate at his table. And surely if her father heard them play together...

"Would that I had received the MacDonalds' letters before leaving," he was saying. "Your mother's mind would have been greatly eased, and I might have put a stop to the blether making the parish rounds."

Her hand stilled on the fiddle bag. *In Monnigaff?* Davina listened with increasing dismay as her father described the letter Reverend Moodie had received from their cousin, asking the minister from Monnigaff to pray for her moral fortitude.

" 'Twas a most unfortunate choice of words. We will be some time undoing the damage."

Davina stared at the grassy verge, lest her father see her face. *Cousin, you have undone me!* The scandal was no longer contained within Arran's shores. Her disgrace had gone forth, paving the way home with sharp-edged stones cut from lies and innuendos. She could not return to Galloway and hope to hold her head up. Nae, she could not return home at all.

Marry me, Somerled, and save me from my shame.

Tears, held at bay all morning, welled up inside her, spilling down her cheeks.

Her father touched her shoulder. "Dinna fash yerself, lass." Rab's oft-used phrase. "Your mother will mend the parish fences in her own gentle way. And if you do marry, 'twill not matter what's been said."

But your name, Father. Your good name. She sniffed, drying her cheeks with her sleeve. He was being far kinder than she'd expected. Or deserved. But then he did not know the truth about Midsummer Eve. *You must never know, Father.*

He tugged on the reins, pointing Grian south along the coast road. A line of gannets flew over the bay, their white bodies and black-tipped wings conspicuous against the azure sky. Brodick Bay shone glassy smooth and iridescent in the morning sunlight, and boats bobbed along the water's edge, well staked and filled with empty nets. No fishermen were about on the Sabbath; the few cottages nestled along the shore were quiet. On the rutted track ahead were families walking to the kirk, bearing dinner and children on their backs.

"The packet boat that brought me here from Ayr was stalled by calm winds yestreen," her father said, gazing out to sea. "This morning's weather is much more conducive for sailing: a good breeze from the east, dry air, and clear skies. I daresay many a boat will reach Arran's harbors before this day ends."

Davina glanced over her shoulder toward the castle and beyond. Somerled would sail from Lochranza four days hence, when the duke's summer gathering ended and his guests headed for the far corners of Scotland. Some gentlemen had already departed for home days ago, Mr. MacDuff of Fife among them. She was glad to see him leave. The older man had regarded her too closely, with an unnerving gleam in his eye.

"What is it, lass?" Her father must have noted her furrowed brow. "Might you be uneasy about facing the parish? What say we show the folk of Arran you are a gracie lass, despite the *clack* they've heard?"

But I am not virtuous, Father. Given or stolen, her virtue was gone.

Unaware of her musings, he continued, "I did not have time to greet the lasses when I arrived or anyone else at the manse. I ken they'll be relieved to see you. And I've a word or two for an overzealous reverend." Her father gestured toward the Clauchland hills ahead. "Suppose we ask our mounts to climb a bit faster and so give us time for a cup of tea before service?"

She'd not deny her mouth was dry as toast without butter. And a warm embrace from Cate and Abbie might soothe the painful wounds others had inflicted.

Her father urged their horses forward, tipping his hat as they passed a knot of islanders on foot. "The sooner we reach Lamlash Bay, the better, Davina. It's been a trying morning. Who kens what the rest of the day may bring?"

Fifty-Seven

Their rage supplies them with weapons.

VIRGIL

W ill's temper had not cooled in two days of hard travel. Not on
the stagecoach from Edinburgh to Glasgow, jostled to and fro
with fifteen overdressed passengers reeking of onions and whisky and
sweat. Not astride the hired gelding that carried him south to the harbor at Saltcoats, the wet road tossing mud in his face until his visage was
brown. Not aboard the fishing boat that stank of haddock, pitching his
stomach fore and aft as he sailed across the Firth of Clyde toward Arran.

Nor was his anger abating now as he and Sandy stood on a stone
quay on the north side of Brodick Bay with one portmanteau between
them, a thinning purse, and no prospects for their Sabbath meal.

"Gaelic," Will muttered, listening to the men round them helping
passengers disembark. He took off in no particular direction except
away from the foul boat. "How are we to find Davina if we cannot make
ourselves understood?"

"You might have thought of that sooner, Brother." Sandy grabbed
their bag and caught up with him, aiming them toward a row of cottages thatched with heather. Folk of all ages trudged along the coast
road, most barefoot, some carrying shoes. Heading home from kirk, it
appeared, and eying the brothers with frank curiosity.

"Have they not seen twins before?" Will fumed.

Sandy stopped to converse with an elderly couple, their faces round
and wrinkled, like overripe apples. He feigned spooning food into his
mouth, then turned to the cottages, a questioning look on his face.

The couple nodded at each other, then at him. *"Tigh an Sglèat."*

"Och." Will wagged his head. "That's helpful."

This time the woman pointed to the only house with a slate roof
and said again, "Tigh an Sglèat."

Whatever the place was called, Will decided there were enough windows above stairs and below to suggest lodging rooms. And, God preserve them, some supper.

As Sandy thanked the couple with a nod, Will blurted out, "Ask them where we might find Brodick castle."

The woman gestured toward a thick bank of vegetation to their right, then drew a line uphill with her finger. *"Caisteal,"* she said before the couple moved on.

Will looked over his shoulder. Not much to see except a narrow track crowded with firs. "We'll start our search when our stomachs are full," he decided. They hadn't eaten in a full day and hadn't slept or bathed their faces in two. An hour at most and they'd be tracking Davina.

The brothers approached the two-story cottage built of white-washed rubble and found the front door ajar. Will knocked, the sound echoing down the hall, then ventured one step within. An open door was an invitation, was it not? He knocked again, harder this time.

"Aye, aye!" a woman's voice called from the back of the house. She appeared a moment later, drying her hands on her worn apron. Nearly as broad as the lads, she might have been forty years of age. Or fifty. Her gray hair was scraped back from her face, revealing a low brow and a sharp gaze. "Mrs. McAllister's me *nem.* Were ye hopin' tae find denner or ludgin?"

At least the woman spoke English. "We need both," Will told her. *And our sister.*

"I've let the twa rooms below stairs to a faither and his dochter just this mornin'. They've yet tae arrive, though I'm leukin' for 'em onie time. But I've a room above the stair. Wull that do?"

"Aye." Will nodded at Sandy. "My brother is in charge of the silver."

"We've meikle time for that. This way, sirs." As they followed her up the stair, she blethered on about the old inn. When Sandy tried to pronounce the Gaelic phrase the old woman had used, Mrs. McAllister snorted. "Ye haven't the tongue for it, lad. It means 'hoose o' slate.' "

Their lodging was as plain as her apron and as colorless. Two bed-steads, two chairs, an unsteady table, and a washstand. But the room was clean, and the inn stood near the castle where they hoped to find

Davina. MacDuff had said she played her fiddle for His Grace each evening. Surely she wasn't residing at Brodick with all those men…

"Is there another inn nearby?" Will asked.

Mrs. McAllister's expression hardened. "Doesna this suit ye, lad?"

"Oo aye," he quickly said. "We're to meet a certain lady and wondered where else she might be lodging." He dared not give away their sister's identity, not until they knew how things stood with her.

"Thar's not anither proper inn for miles," she said with a shrug. "I canna think *whaur* else the leddy would stay."

"Is the parish manse far?"

"Aye, 'tis in Lamlash Bay, aboot five miles south o' here."

Will nodded, trying to piece things together. Davina wouldn't make the long trek up the shore road to the castle every evening. Unless she had a horse. And a braisant Highlander to escort her.

"I'll leave ye tae get settled." Mrs. McAllister stepped back from the door. "Thar'll be a plate o' cock-a-leekie soup waitin' for ye in the kitchen parlor. 'Twas hangin' o'er the fire afore *midnicht*. I've not broken the Sabbath, ye ken."

The moment she left, Will opened their portmanteau; his belongings were on one side, Sandy's on the other. They'd packed in such haste he couldn't remember what they'd brought, let alone determine what they'd forgotten. He looked up to find his brother gazing out the window as if Davina might wash in with the tide.

"We'll find her, Sandy. And take her home."

"But what will Father say when the three of us show up at Glentrool?"

"He doesn't know what we know," Will snapped, exhaustion and hunger sharpening his *birsie* mood. "Father didn't overhear what this… this cur did to our sister." He'd had nightmares about those bruises.

His brother turned round, pinning him with a hard gaze. "What should we do about the Highlander?"

Will had been asking himself the same question since they'd fled from Edinburgh. He knew what he wanted to do, what MacDonald deserved, what justice required. But 'twas an *ill-deedie* notion. And they'd brought no weapons, only their anger.

He finally told Sandy the truth. "I'll know when I see Davina. When I see her eyes and can tell whether or not MacDonald has truly hurt her. And if he has—"

"We shall hurt him," Sandy finished.

"Aye, won't we just?"

After Mrs. McAllister delivered a pitcher of hot water to their room, the twins took turns at the washstand. Clean shirts and scraped chins made them more presentable but no less hungry and no less determined.

"If and when we meet this Highlander, we must not give our intentions away," Will cautioned as they prepared to go down for supper. "Who knows what lies he employed to beguile our sister."

"Are you asking me to be cordial to a man—"

"Nae, nae," Will murmured as they started out the door. "I'm asking you to hold your tongue."

The twins were halfway down the stair when Will froze, hearing voices in the kitchen parlor. One very familiar voice in particular. *Father.* He took the rest of the steps in a bound, Sandy close behind him.

When Will rounded the corner leading into the sunlit room, he stopped in his tracks as a red-headed lass turned in her chair.

"Davina!"

In an instant she was on her feet and in his arms, pressing her face into his neck, her tears wet against his skin.

"My bonny wee fairy." Will fought for control, squeezing her tight. "How I've missed you."

Mrs. McAllister stood with a plate of soup in each hand and a look of astonishment on her face. "D'ye ken ane anither?"

"Aye," Sandy explained. " 'Tis our father and sister."

"Is that richt?" The innkeeper put down her soup plates. "Then tak yer time visitin' while I tidy the rooms." She grabbed her broom and was gone, leaving the four McKies to their unexpected reunion.

Will found it hard to let go of his sister, so ardent was his resolve. *He will never hurt you again, lass. Never.* When he finally released Davina so she might embrace Sandy, Will turned to their father, who did not look at all pleased to see them.

"Has Lammas come early this year?" Jamie McKie folded his arms across his chest. "Or did your professors decide you needed a holiday on Arran?"

Will caught Sandy's eye over Davina's bright hair. The truth? Or a fabrication yanked from the salt-tinged air? "Father, we are here to do what we've always done: protect Davina."

"That is what brought me to Arran as well." His father's eyes narrowed. "But I was alerted to a particular situation by means of a letter from Reverend Stewart. I cannot think that he wrote to you as well."

"Nae, Father, he did not." Will pulled him aside and kept his voice low. "However, I suspect the…ah, situation is the same. 'Twas another man's revelation that prompted us to come. A stranger in John Dowie's tavern."

"A *stranger*?" His father slowly unfolded his arms, as if he might have need of his fists. "Can you identify this man? At Dowie's, I mean?"

"His name is Alastair MacDuff."

Davina's head snapped in his direction.

Will kept talking, though his gaze was now locked with his sister's. "He's a Fife man. Part of the duke's fishing party at the castle. He left Arran early and found his way to Dowie's."

"And?" Jamie demanded.

Davina was as white as Mrs. McAllister's linen sheets. Her lips moved, a single word. *Nae.*

Will took her hand and drew her close, wanting to assure her, wanting to help her. "And he made some…comments about the fiddler at Brodick castle. A bonny Lowland lass with red hair. He suggested she might be…in trouble."

Davina's eyes fluttered closed, and she collapsed in his arms.

Fifty-Eight

For, dark and despairing, my sight I may seal,
But man cannot cover what God would reveal.

THOMAS CAMPBELL

M iss McKie? Wull ye drink a wee sip o' water noo?"
Davina swallowed the cool water from the tin cup Mrs. Mc-
Allister pressed against her mouth, finding it hard to meet the gaze of
anyone in the kitchen parlor. Her father looked stricken, her brothers
distressed, and the innkeeper, though helpful, regarded her with a wary
expression.

"Are ye the lass wha's been playin' her fiddle for the duke?" A thread
of censure was woven through Mrs. McAllister's voice. She'd heard the
gossip, then, and not realized her female lodger's identity. Until now,
when Davina fainted in her kitchen and had to be revived.

Davina shuddered, remembering her brother's words. *She might be
in trouble.* What did Will know that Father did not? Too much, it
seemed. She had Alastair MacDuff to thank for that.

"I believe we can take care of things here." Jamie lifted the cup from
the innkeeper's hands. "If you'll find your seats, lads, I'll bless the meal so
we can eat our soup while it's still hot. That will be all, Mrs. McAllister."

With a jerk of her treble chin, the woman retreated to the far end
of the long kitchen, then pretended to stir the contents of her kettle
while she kept a watchful eye on her lodgers.

The McKies ate their soup in silence and in haste, her father's gaze
often drifting toward the door. The moment their plates were empty
and their stomachs full, he offered a blessing once more, as was the custom, then suggested a walk along the bay. "The sea air will do us all
good," he said rather loudly, aiming his voice toward the hearth.

While the men waited in the entrance hall, Davina stopped by her
room to collect her sketchbook, knowing she would have need of it.

Nervous about the discussion to come, she tarried at the washstand—scrubbing her face and hands, shaking the dust from her riding habit—until Will knocked on the door. She could not keep them waiting any longer.

"Here's our lass." Her father's greeting belied the creases in his brow. "I've nicked a blanket from the bed, thinking we might find a dry place where we could sit. 'Twould make it easier to write out your thoughts for us, aye?"

Aye. But whatever would she write, except the truth? *I must marry, and soon.*

They set out for the coastline four abreast, with Will and Father flanking her and Sandy dutifully carrying her sketchbook. Not far from the inn they found a grassy expanse sheltered from the prevailing winds by a copse of trees.

Once they were settled on the wool blanket, Jamie wasted no time getting to the heart of the matter. "Davina, 'tis clear something happened here of which I am not aware. You alone know what that is." He glanced at Will and Sandy, then looked at her, his expression as gray and stony as the mountains rising behind him. "If you are in trouble, as Will said, then we must know what that trouble is." He took her sketchbook and pencil from Sandy and pressed them into her hands. "Please write for us."

Davina had never opened her book more slowly nor turned the pages with greater care, pinching two together to hide her May Day sketch of Somerled. She paused to show them a few of her Arran drawings with the names written below each one. *Holy Isle* on this page and *Standing Stone* on that one. When she turned to the carving of *Fir God*, her father gently laid his hand on hers. "Forgive me, Davina, but this is not why we've come." He slipped his finger between the remaining pages and turned them over, revealing a blank one. "Why not start by telling us what happened on Midsummer Eve?"

Her hand trembled as she pressed the charcoal tip to the paper.

I played my fiddle for the Duke of Hamilton at Kilmichael. Somerled MacDonald, my dinner escort, surprised me by accompanying me on the violoncello.

She looked up and tried to smile. *See?* she wanted to say to them. *'Tis not so bad as you think.*

"Davina, we already know that." Will grimaced. "MacDuff said as much."

Jamie moved closer, reading over her shoulder. "Reverend Stewart's initial concern was the unrestrained nature of your playing. Davina, we've seen you nigh to dancing with your fiddle. Was that all it was that night at Kilmichael? Our wee fiddler being exuberant?"

Nae, that was not all it was. Davina could not bring herself to tell even one McKie man the truth, let alone three of them looking at her with such concern, such trust—her brothers, with their dark eyes, and her father, with his moss-colored ones, waiting for an answer.

She finally wrote what she could. *We kissed by the burn.*

"He kissed you that night?" Jamie frowned at the page. "What sort of chaperon permitted that?"

She gripped her pencil so hard that her fingers ached. *We were not far from the house. No one was with us.*

His scowl darkened. "Your mother and I made it very clear; you are never to walk anywhere with a gentleman unchaperoned."

Knowing full well she was dodging his reproof, Davina nodded at her brothers, then wrote, *Will and Sandy were always my chaperons.*

"Exactly!" Will banged on the ground with both fists. "None of this would have happened if we'd been here. Or if you'd been here, Father. Don't you see? Davina is not to blame. We are."

Her father groaned. "We've had this argument before, Will. 'Tis not the point of this evening's discussion."

"I thought the point was to help Davina."

"So it is." Jamie lowered his voice when a fisherman and his children ambled by. "What you lads do not ken is that Somerled Mac-Donald has asked for your sister's hand in marriage."

"Marriage?" Will cried, a look of horror on his face. "Father, you cannot allow it."

Please, my brother! Davina leaned toward him, imploring him with her eyes. *Do not interfere.*

"Why would you protest his suit?" Jamie demanded to know. "Because he is a Highlander?"

"Nae, Father. Because he is a—"

Please, Will! Davina muffled his words with her hand, then scrawled on the page. *Rumors. Not the truth.*

"I've heard those rumors," Jamie was quick to say. "Reverend Stewart accused MacDonald of being—in his words—'a lecher.'"

Will threw up his hands. "Well, there you are! Father, how can you possibly approve—"

"Aye, aye." Jamie brushed away his concerns. "I, too, feared the worst. But when I met MacDonald, and he assured me of his genuine regard for Davina and his desire to marry her, I saw no evidence of lechery. Infatuation, to be sure. Impatience. But nothing unseemly."

Davina's pencil slipped from her fingers, so great was her relief. She did not need to defend Somerled; her own father would.

"Few gentlemen come to the bride stool without apology," Jamie cautioned his sons. "MacDonald is ashamed of his past actions and freely confessed them to me." He spread out his hands. "I am a man who has been forgiven much. So must I forgive others."

"Oh, must you?" Will's face was a storm cloud. "Well, you have chosen the wrong man to forgive." He was on his feet in an instant and striding toward Cladach, not looking back even when their father called after him.

"Och," Jamie groaned, then took off in the same direction. He caught up with Will and matched his stride as they continued walking, both shaking their heads and talking with their hands.

She watched them for a moment, with Sandy by her side, quieter than usual. Finally he spoke. "Davina…" His neck began to redden. "Do you know why Will is so upset at the thought of you marrying MacDonald?"

She tapped the word on her page. *Rumors.*

"Aye, but the truth is more *ill-kindit* than anything Father mentioned. MacDuff told us…well, he told his friend, but we overheard it…"

Davina felt a chill move over her—not a salty breeze from the bay or a fresh wind from the west, but an icy sense of foreboding. She retrieved her pencil and forced herself to write on the page. *What did Mr. MacDuff say?*

Sandy was a long time answering. "He said that you and Somerled MacDonald played a duet of sorts. For the horses." He swallowed. "In the stables."

Her sketchbook slid from her lap.

"Forgive me, Davina." Sandy's voice was low, urgent. "I am not saying it is true. You could never do such a thing."

I could. I did.

"MacDuff also said…" Sandy was beside himself, thrusting his hand through his unruly hair. "Oh, dear sister, he intimated that…well, according to your maid…"

Davina was on her feet before he finished, leaving her sketchbook behind, lifting her skirts above the grass. Running after her father and brother, running from the truth.

Please, Will. Please don't tell Father!

Fifty-Nine

Alas! how easily things go wrong!
GEORGE MACDONALD

Will turned round just before Davina reached him. He could hardly have missed her panic-stricken approach. "What is it, lass? Did you fear we'd left you?"

Nae. She fell against him, breathless. *I feared you'd betrayed me.*

"Your brother believes he knows what is best for you," Jamie said. "And I believe it's time we returned to the inn." Judging by the dogged look on their father's face, nothing convincing had been said. He motioned impatiently to Sandy, who'd already gathered up the blanket and her sketchbook and was heading their direction, looking even more agitated than before.

Davina stepped into his path, holding out her hands, knowing she could not stop his movement, praying she might stop his mouth. *Don't, Sandy. Please don't tell him.*

He frowned at her, shaking his head, before addressing their father. "Has Will persuaded you that our sister must not marry this Highlander?"

"He has not, nor will he." Jamie's voice brooked no argument. "Nothing will be decided until I've met with the MacDonalds tomorrow."

"But MacDuff said…"

"Who is this MacDuff to you? A reliable companion? Nae, a stranger in a tavern, who had no business discussing your sister." Father took the blanket from him and shook it hard, sending bits of grass flying. "I've heard quite enough meanspirited gossip since I arrived on this island. The only person we can trust on this matter is your sister."

Oh, Father. Though his words eased her fear, guilt rushed in to take its place.

Jamie folded the blanket over his arm, looking at her all the while. "If your sister believes Somerled MacDonald is a worthy husband, and we find no evidence to the contrary—factual evidence, mind you, not hearsay—then I will be forced to consider his proposal of marriage."

Sandy persisted, "But her maid at Kilmichael—"

"Och! You'll not find a more *ill-fashioned* excuse for a servant in all of Scotland. Five minutes in her presence and you'd see for yourselves what a contemptuous gaze and slandering tongue the woman possesses." Their father's voice lost its strident note. "Davina has shared with me a few of her abuses. I'd not give that maid's blether any credence whatsoever."

"But, Father—"

"That is enough, Sandy." Jamie started for the inn, pulling them along in his wake. "This is a decision Somerled's father and I shall make. Not you, nor Will. You may both join me at tomorrow's meeting only if you agree to behave like gentlemen."

"Oh, we'll be there," Will promised him, "for we'll not abandon our sister again."

Davina walked between them, her emotions in turmoil. Was withholding the truth the same as telling a lie? Would her father's trust, his support—aye, even his love for her—be shattered if he learned what had truly happened? And what of the twins, who'd come to rescue her, armed with facts she dared not affirm, even knowing them to be true. Would they ever forgive her disloyalty?

Mrs. McAllister was waiting for them in the entrance hall, a sealed letter in her hand and a gleam in her eye. "A certain Hieland laddie was jist here. He left this for ye." She handed the letter to Jamie. "*In trowth!* I thocht he might *greet* whan he learned ye were not here, miss."

Davina did not acknowledge the woman as she edged past her. Somerled MacDonald would not cry over so slight a thing. Though *she* might, remembering their tender morning kiss.

The four McKies convened in her father's room rather than open the letter with the innkeeper looking on. " 'Tis from both gentlemen," Father informed them, "requesting our presence at the castle at ten o'clock tomorrow morning. His Grace will provide a room for us while the rest of his party engages in a morning of hill climbing."

Will's eyes narrowed. "Is that so?"

"Aye." Jamie nodded toward the window. "The path to Goatfell is just beyond our door and through the castle grounds. If our business goes well in the morning, perhaps you and your brother can make the ascent after our noontide meal. As I recall, the view from the summit is breathtaking."

When the men turned toward Jamie's room, intent on continuing their discussion of hill climbing, Davina plucked her sketchbook from Sandy's grasp, though he seemed reluctant to let go of it. "Will you not join us, lass?"

She closed her eyes and tipped her head down, certain he would understand.

"A full night's rest would do us all good," he agreed. "Sleep well, dear sister."

A moment later Davina sagged against her closed door, eyes brimming with tears born of exhaustion and relief. Her father had discredited the scandalous rumors; Lord willing, her brothers would not persist in discussing them. Perhaps by noon tomorrow—if Somerled continued to impress her father and if Sir Harry kept his pride in check—she would find herself betrothed and her family's reputation spared without anyone knowing the truth.

Please, Lord, please. She mouthed the words over and over while she prepared for bed, pulling her nightgown over her head, then brushing the tangles from her hair. The sun hung low in the sky, filling her room with amber light, as she closed her eyes and folded her hands and pleaded for the strength to do what she must. *In the morning will I direct my prayer unto thee, and will look up.*

Davina had not paid a morning visit to the castle before. It was cool and a bit gloomy, though the duke had been generous with candles; beeswax tapers brightened the center of their oak table and each corner of their fifteenth-century meeting room.

Seated on her left, Somerled was resplendent in his double-breasted tail coat. Sir Harry sat at one end of the narrow, rectangular table and Father at the other. The twins were across from her, black eyebrows slashed across their foreheads, underscoring their displeasure. Poorly attired in wrinkled cravats and sullied waistcoats, her brothers wore their resentment like beggars' badges pinned to their lapels. Eying them, Davina remembered poor Jock Robertson being pummeled by the twins on May Day. They would not find Somerled so easily vanquished.

She scooted back in her chair, the seat high enough that her feet barely rested on the floor. Dressed in a blue gown embroidered by Leana's own hand, Davina smoothed the polished cotton across her lap. *You are here with us, Mother. I am certain of it.* After tea was offered but declined, the McKies and MacDonalds were left alone in the high-ceilinged chamber, with its red sandstone walls and peat-darkened beams.

As the servants' footsteps faded down the stair, Davina prayed once more. *Thou hast been my defence and refuge in the day of my trouble.* No one else, only the Almighty. *God is my defence, and the God of my mercy.* She'd never needed his strength more than now.

Sir Harry began the meeting, his gaze aimed at the other end of the table. "You will no doubt find our letters waiting for you when you return to Glentrool, Mr. McKie. I regret that you came to Arran not knowing the situation."

Somerled's father sounded rather formal, Davina thought. And quite restrained. She'd seen an occasional hint of Sir Harry's temper at the duke's dinner table, but not this morning. At least not yet.

"I arrived with very little information in hand," her father acknowledged, his tone neither hot nor cold. "It seems our children have found each other rather quickly."

"Aye." Sir Harry glanced at Somerled, then settled his gaze on Jamie. "My son has not expressed any interest in marriage before, yet it appears Miss McKie has captured his heart. On his behalf, I would ask that you give your daughter to Somerled as his wife."

Davina swallowed her surprise. He'd wasted no time in getting to the point.

"*Give* her?" Will muttered under his breath.

Sir Harry eyed her brother. "Despite speaking out of turn, your son is quite right. A gentleman does not make so great a request without offering something substantial in return. I've prepared a list of the Mac-Donald holdings. Perhaps you'd care to review them."

A sheet of fine stationery traveled from one patriarch to the other—on Will's side of the table. Sir Harry was no fool. Both brothers took their time as the paper was passed to them. Even from where she was sitting, Davina could read the bold hand in sweeps of black ink. The income in pounds and the property in acreage were impressive, though of little importance to her.

Davina turned to Somerled as the tally sheet reached her father, and she faintly shook her head. *That is not why I agreed to marry you.*

Beneath the table Somerled wrapped his hand round hers.

"As I have no other sons," Sir Harry was saying, "nor any living brothers, the first male whom Davina bears can be assured of his inheritance." His smile was almost genuine. "Think of it, McKie. A Lowlander laying claim to a Highlander's lands."

"Or think of this, MacDonald,"—Jamie's expression matched his in guile—"a Highlander laying claim to a Lowlander's daughter."

Davina's gaze darted from one man to the other. Were they in agreement, then? Or throwing down their gloves?

"What say you, Somerled?" Her father looked down the table, pinning him with a sharp gaze. "What will you offer for my only daughter? For I'll not give up such a treasure easily."

"As well you should not, sir." Somerled released her with a gentle squeeze, then folded his hands above the table, a display of good will and of supplication. He looked first at her father and then at both her brothers. "I ask only for your blessing. If I am the husband you favor for this woman, then you are free to set the bride price. Whatever you say, I shall give."

"Somerled!"

He ignored his father's outburst and made his offer clear. "You may ask for as much as you wish if you'll give me Miss McKie as my wife."

Jamie leaned back in his chair, patently bewildered. " 'Tis generous."

"And foolish," Sir Harry grumbled.

Davina stared at her future husband, a bit dazed. *As much as you wish.* She would not doubt the sincerity of his commitment again.

Gazes were exchanged among the men, though no one broke the weighty silence.

Finally Will leaned across the table toward Somerled, his chin like the prow of a ship. "No gentleman would offer so much unless he felt an obligation. A need to make recompense—"

"Will." Jamie cut him off. "Do not offend the MacDonalds with your accusations. Somerled's offer is meant to demonstrate his affection, not appease his guilt." His stern look softened. "Young man, your liberality speaks well of you. I'll not take advantage of it. What say you to a bride price of one thousand pounds?"

"Nae!" Sandy cried out. "*Fifty* thousand, for the man must pay—"

Jamie was on his feet. "Not another word, lads. You have insulted your sister and the gentleman she wishes to marry."

" 'Tis not an insult if the gentleman can afford it." Somerled's voice poured over the room like cool water, dousing their ire. "Miss McKie is worth fifty thousand and more. What say you, Father?"

"I'd say you are paying too much for damaged goods."

The earlier silence was nothing compared to this. Davina could not move, could not breathe. *Damaged.* No word better described her.

Somerled looked as if he'd been struck by a caber.

Jamie remained at his end of the table, but the heat from his anger radiated through the room. "How dare you suggest that because my daughter cannot speak she is of lesser value!"

" 'Tis not her impaired voice that concerns me." Sir Harry's chuckle was low, coarse. "What husband would not prefer a silent wife? Rather, it is your daughter's—"

"Father!" Somerled grabbed the man's sleeve. "We agreed—"

"Nae, *you* insisted." Sir Harry wrested his arm free. "The plain truth is, McKie, your daughter has already given herself to my son. And without costing him a shilling, let alone fifty thousand pounds."

Davina stared into a dark void. *I did not give… I did not…*

"Given herself?" Jamie leaned toward her, lowering his voice as he did. "Daughter, whatever does he mean?"

"I'll tell you what he means." Sandy pulled Davina's sketchbook from beneath her limp hands and dragged it across the table.

Sixty

Arm thyself for the truth!

EDWARD ROBERT BULWER, LORD LYTTON

N ae!" Somerled lunged across the table to retrieve her sketchbook. "You *cannot* do this. Not if you mean to protect your sister."

Will blocked his arms, then shoved him aside. "She is ours to protect. From you."

Before Somerled could protest, Sir Harry pulled him back by the scruff of his neck. "Enough, lad. You cannot save her now."

"On the contrary." Somerled shook free of his grasp. "I am the only one who can."

He sat down and turned his chair toward Davina, with her sorrow-filled eyes and her trembling chin. "My bonny wee girl." He took her cool hands in his. "Do not be afraid. Whatever is said here, you and I know the truth."

"We shall all know the truth shortly." Sandy was leafing through the book. "I only caught a glimpse of it yestreen. No more than a sentence, written at the top of a page, but 'twas quite enough."

"Sandy, that is not your property." Jamie's voice held a warning, though he did not stop his son from turning the pages as he reclaimed his seat.

Desperate, Somerled tried another tack. "Will you not let Davina write out what she wants you to know?" He released her hands so she might face them herself. "She is sitting right here, though you seem to have forgotten that. Or would you rather steal her secrets?"

Will glared at him across the table. "You're a fine one to speak of robbery, MacDonald."

"Here." Sandy pointed to the page, empty except for a single line written across the top.

Somerled knew very well what it said. Only a blackguard would reveal such a thing. *And only a blackguard would have done such a thing.*

Now that Sandy had found what he was searching for, he seemed reluctant to read it, his hand resting on the page.

"Go on," Will told him. " 'Twill be easier on Davina if you do this."

Sandy wet his lips, then looked down as he read her words. "What is to become of me now that I am ruined?"

"Ruined?" Her father yanked the sketchbook closer and read the truth for himself. "Davina, surely you have not…" He swallowed audibly, staring at the page. "Please tell me this is not…that it means… something else."

Somerled could wait no longer. "Mr. McKie…"

His hand shot out. "*You* will say nothing."

Hands trembling, Davina reached for her sketchbook, then wrote these words beneath the others. *My heart and my body belong to Somerled. We must marry at once.*

"God, help me." Jamie's features twisted in pain. "Davina…how could you do this?"

"Do not blame our sister." Will's gaze fixed on Somerled. "No woman sins alone. He seduced her, Father. In truth, MacDuff said—"

"The drunkard from Fife?" Sir Harry scoffed. "What does he know?"

"He knows what her maid saw," Will shot back. "Isn't that so, Davina? However willing you might have been, MacDonald bruised you, did he not?"

Somerled had heard enough. He gently took the sketchbook from Davina's hands. "Trust me in this," he murmured, looking into her ravaged face. He then turned back one page, to the rest of her questions. The ones her brothers apparently had not seen. The ones he alone could answer.

"I care not what you think of me," Somerled began. "Any names you call me are well deserved. But I'll not have you thinking ill of your daughter, Mr. McKie. She is in no way to blame for her ruined state. I am."

"Hech!" Sir Harry said, a rude sound in a quiet room. " 'Tis as her brother said: No one sins alone. Who is to say the lass did not entice you?"

"Miss McKie knows differently. And I know differently." Somerled pushed the sketchbook into her father's hands. "After I took… That is, the following afternoon these are the questions she asked of me."

Jamie scanned the page, blinking hard, as if he could not believe what was written there. " 'Why did you not stop…' 'Did you intend to hurt…' Davina, did this man…did he *violate* you?"

Somerled knew she would turn to him, and she did. Searching his face. Wanting to be sure. "Miss McKie, I am grateful you accepted my offer of marriage. But your family must know the terrible truth of how it started. Please answer your father's question."

Davina took a deep breath and nodded.

"Nae!" Jamie shoved his chair behind him and stormed round the table, his sons close on his heels, all of them shouting.

Somerled stood, unafraid. He was strong enough to take their blows.

Then Davina leaped to her feet, arms spread, blocking their advance.

"Lass, whatever are you…"

She pressed her back against his chest and would not budge. A wee fairy of a shield, protecting him.

"Davina!" her father roared. "Has this man bewitched you, that you defend him?"

She firmly shook her head, then pressed her hand against her heart and held it out as a gift.

Somerled was undone. *My beloved, my bride.*

"You *cannot* forgive such a crime!" Her father's expression was utter anguish.

Sir Harry answered for her. " 'Twould seem that she has, McKie."

"How is that possible?" Her father's voice was strained to the point of breaking. "He…*defiled* you, Davina. Can you truly want him for a husband?"

Her crown of red braids slowly bobbed up and down. Somerled did not need to see her eyes to know what he would find there. *Aye. I do.*

Jamie McKie and his sons saw her answer as well and backed away, though their faces remained stony, their hands clenched.

"You've raised quite a daughter, McKie." Sir Harry eased into his chair. "Far better than my son deserves."

Somerled would not dispute that for a moment. "My offer still stands, sir. Whatever bride price you ask, I will gladly pay. This is the woman I love and will have as my wife."

"We'll see about that, MacDonald." Her father glowered at him, then retreated with his sons to the far corner, where they huddled in a tight circle, dark heads bowed.

As the trio murmured among themselves, Somerled whispered in her ear, "I believe your family is coming round." Though he could not hear their words, the intent expressions on their faces gave him cause for hope. Better a conversation than a brawl.

When the McKie men finally resumed their seats, their private discussion over, Somerled and Davina sat down as well, inching closer together before she retrieved her sketchbook. To think she had stood up to her father on his behalf. Had he ever known a braver woman?

After much clearing of throats and scraping of chairs, Will was the first to speak, though he waited for a nod from Jamie first. "Whatever our sister's wishes may be, MacDonald, we cannot simply give her to a man who stole her virtue and disgraced our family name."

"Will—"

"Please, Father. We agreed on this." Will looked round the table, his expression resolute. " 'Tis not ready silver our family needs but an assurance that our sister will be provided for, since she may even now bear the MacDonald heir."

A hush fell across the room. Was that still a possibility? Somerled stole a glance at her. Aye, judging by the faint blush on her cheek.

Will continued, "Why not bestow on Davina the right to inherit your income and property now, at your betrothal? 'Twill not cost you any silver yet guarantees the welfare of your son from this day forth."

Somerled eyed the men at the table, his father in particular. The plan was a sound one. What if, when he and Sir Harry sailed home to Argyll, their boat sank in a storm? Would he not want to provide for Davina? And for their son, if his seed had already taken root?

"What do you make of it, Father?" Somerled turned to the head of the table. "Is it not a reasonable request? After all, it will cost us nothing. Unless we die." He shrugged. "And then we'll not mind so much, eh?"

Sandy took up the cause. "We are only asking that she be protected by your name and fortune sooner rather than later." He folded his arms across his chest. "If you refuse, we'll take our sister home at once."

"*I* will take her home," Jamie admonished him. "My sons have well stated our terms. What is your decision, MacDonald?"

Sir Harry nodded his silvery head. "'Tis fair. The duke's steward, Lewis Hunter, can easily draw up such a letter of intent, allowing a certain annuity for my wife." He looked at Davina with begrudging respect. "Miss McKie, it appears you've stolen my son's heart and my holdings without a single word. My hat is off to you and to your family."

"And so is mine." Somerled pushed back his chair, mystified by how the negotiations had proceeded. Could the McKies be satisfied with so paltry a bride price—nothing more than paper? Lest they change their minds and demand further satisfaction, he'd not tarry in fulfilling their request. "Father, we must see the agreement penned this very morning."

"Aye, 'tis best not to delay such matters." Sir Harry grunted as he rose, then settled his gaze on Somerled. "We will sign away our land and silver. And pray good fortune attends us."

Sixty-One

Who thinks that fortune cannot change her mind,
Prepares a dreadful jest for all mankind.

ALEXANDER POPE

As Sir Harry took his leave, Davina rested her hand on Somerled's arm. *Don't go.*

He gazed down at her, the row of brass buttons on his coat catching the light. "What is it, milady?"

She heard the confidence in his voice, saw the assurance in his blue eyes. If only she might follow him down the castle stair, rather than face her father and brothers, whose brooding countenances could not be ignored. Somerled did not know them as she did. The McKie men were far from appeased, no matter what bargain had been struck.

Anxious for some reason to detain him, Davina wrote across the sketchbook page. *What of tonight?*

"I shall ask His Grace to include your family at his table." Somerled's expression softened as he added, "Practice your Gow tunes, Miss McKie. I've arranged a surprise for you." He bowed, then wisely kissed her hand rather than her cheek; the slightest provocation, and her brothers would surely bolt from their chairs and wrestle him to the floor. "I will count the minutes 'til I see you again," he promised, then was gone.

The sound of the iron latch falling into place echoed across the silent room. Davina stared at the door, her vision clouding. *I will count them as well.*

"Davina, look at me." Her father was beside her now. Kneeling. "You do not have to marry him."

Oh, Father. He'd misconstrued her tears. She turned to her sketchbook and started to underline what she'd written earlier—*My heart and my body belong*—but he stopped her pencil.

"That is not true," he said, the strain in his voice evident. "Until you are wed, Davina, you belong to me. It is my responsibility to care for you—"

"And ours to protect you," Sandy insisted. "I cannot fathom what poor Mother will think when she learns what this miscreant did to you."

Hampered by her father's grasp, Davina could not write and so stamped her foot in protest. *I have forgiven him.* But she could not expect that her family would do the same.

"We shall weather the scandal in Monnigaff," Father said, releasing her hand, "and raise MacDonald's bairn, if it comes to that. But I'll not see you married to a brute."

Davina quickly reclaimed her pencil to respond. *Father, I have made a vow—*

"Vows can be unmade." Jamie rose from his knees and began to pace the room, ignoring the rest of her written declaration. "We shall depart for the mainland this very afternoon."

Depart? Her heart leaped into her throat. Did he mean to abscond with her? Somerled would never allow it, nor would she.

"Why wait?" Will countered. "Escort Davina to the harbor this morning. When the MacDonalds reappear, Sandy and I will bid them good riddance, then sail for Saltcoats." He leaned across the table, his dark eyes snapping. "Leave at once, Father. Before the Highlander returns and convinces our sister otherwise."

Jamie eyed the door. "You may be right, lad. He has her quite spellbound."

Och! Determined to be heard, Davina wrote across the page in letters too large to ignore. *I accepted Somerled's proposal of marriage willingly.*

"There! Do you see, Father?" Will's face was ruddy with rage. "MacDonald has stolen more than Davina's virtue. He has robbed her of all reason as well."

Nae! She stamped her foot, then pushed her sketchbook at them, pointing to her last word. *Willingly.* Even if that was not so at first, it was now.

The twins bristled but held their tongues, staring at the irrefutable truth.

"All right, lass, all right." Her father's sigh was heavy, a fitting punctuation. "You have accepted his proposal, and the MacDonalds have agreed to our terms. I suppose if honor is to be served—"

"Honor?"

"He *debased* her, Father!"

Jamie ignored his sons. "Given the unfortunate circumstances, perhaps a wedding is inevitable."

Davina's racing pulse began to slow. *Aye, 'tis.*

"We shall pocket their letter of agreement," Jamie finally said, "and tarry until Wednesday afternoon. That is when His Grace sails for the mainland and the MacDonalds take their leave." He shrugged, his face filled with resignation. "Who can say? Three days spent together at table and at sport may blunt our fury toward these Highlanders."

Will snorted. "My anger will burn far longer than that."

"Aye, and so will mine." Sandy's features were sharp as razors.

Davina cringed at their harsh words. Clearly the twins had no mercy for the man who'd ravished her. But might their father come round, as Somerled had said? She slowly closed her sketchbook and pressed it to her heart. *Please forgive him, Father.*

Jamie stood before her, his broad shoulders sagging as if sensing what she was asking of him. "Give me a moment with your sister, lads."

Davina's throat tightened. After such a morning, her courage was waning. *Remember me, I pray thee, and strengthen me.*

Her father waited until Will and Sandy were halfway down the stair before he spoke again, his voice raw with emotion. "Davina, had I known from the first…had I realized that this man…that he…"

Jamie looked away but not before she saw the tears in his eyes.

Nae, Father. Her fingers tightened round the frayed edges of her sketchbook, her nails digging into the cloth. *Please, I cannot bear it.*

"The thought of him hurting you…forcing you…" His words dissolved into a groan as he pulled her into his arms.

Davina collapsed against him. *I did not know… Oh, Father, I did not understand.*

He nearly crushed her in his embrace, whispering ragged phrases in her ear. "Forgive me. For bringing you here. Abandoning you here."

She tried to shake her head. *'Tis not your fault. I wanted to come.*

"Nae, Davina." His voice was taut with pain. "Do not excuse me so easily."

She pressed her sketchbook to his heart and her wet cheek against it. *But I must.*

They remained there, father and daughter, with only the sandstone walls to witness their grief. For all that was lost and could never be regained.

After many minutes, her father released her with a tender kiss to her brow. "I see forgiveness in your eyes, Davina, though I hardly deserve it." When she started to protest, his answer was firm. "This would never have happened had you spent the summer at home. Your brothers are right to be furious with Somerled. And with me." He glanced toward the door. "I will see what can be done to change their minds, though you ken the twins: slow in mercy and plenteous in anger…"

As his voice trailed off, he touched her elbow and guided her toward the stair. "Perhaps this evening's music will temper their wrath." Even though he smiled, the sadness never left his eyes. "Yet I fear 'twill take more than a few merry tunes to convince your brothers this Highlander is worthy of you."

Sixty-Two

No man likes to be surpassed
by those of his own level.

TITUS LIVY

Davina gripped her fiddle, praying for a miracle. Candlelight within and daylight without illumined the room where she'd dined with a dozen gentlemen. How extraordinary to find three dear faces among them. *Father. Will. Sandy.* She missed her mother and Ian all the more, having some but not all of her family present.

The Duke of Hamilton had made the McKies welcome at his table, introducing them to his guests, announcing the betrothal, and praising Davina's talents. His flattery had pleased her father but incensed her brothers, who'd grumbled about their sister being forced into the role of an entertainer. Her father, engaged in conversation with Sir Harry, had eaten little of the roast grouse; her brothers had eaten much and barely spoken, least of all with Somerled.

Now it was her turn to mollify Will and Sandy. Might music accomplish what food and conversation had not?

Dressed in pale green muslin—the twins' favorite color—she stood with the castle hearth at her back, eying the duke's guests. Somerled's promised surprise had yet to materialize, and the gentleman himself was nowhere to be seen. Should she begin without him? She'd dutifully rehearsed all the Niel Gow tunes in her repertoire that afternoon while her brothers had climbed Goatfell. They'd returned drenched with sweat and breathing hard, with barely enough time to dress for dinner, wearing expressions as hard as the granite they'd traversed.

Lifting her bow, Davina prayed her instrument might be like David's harp, soothing their spirits. *Please, Lord.* She began with a familiar Gow strathspey, "Highland Whisky," driving her bow across the strings with even more vigor than usual, attacking the dotted quavers.

When she finished the opening measures, a second fiddler joined her for the repeated phrase, matching her spirited bowing. *Somerled.*

He was smiling as he walked across the room, playing all the while, his tail coat a fitting match for her darker green sash. Wherever had he located a fiddle? The duke's guests applauded his entrance; her brothers did not join them. Refusing to be discouraged, she segued into another strathspey in the same key, "Miss Stewart of Grantully." Somerled kept pace with her, letting her add the many grace notes that enlivened the tune, communicating only with his eyes and with his bow.

Mind the G natural. That's the way. A bit faster this time? Perfect, my love.

Davina looked away, overwhelmed by her feelings. Somerled understood her. Nae, he heard her. And spoke in a language meant for her alone.

As they finished the tune, the duke called out, "Have you a jig for me, Miss McKie?"

Davina nodded to assure him that, aye, she did: one with a blithe melody yet a sobering name, "The Stool of Repentance." She could not imagine climbing the dreaded wooden stool of old, sitting before the pulpit for an entire morning service, then openly confessing her sins to the congregation. Had the *cutty stool* not gone the way of tricorn hats, Somerled would surely have been sentenced to *compear* for many Sabbaths in a row. The notion would no doubt please her brothers.

Their dark eyes were fixed on the Highlander as he played, their mouths unsmiling, their chins jutted out. Even the energetic reel "Dunkeld Bridge," to which the twins had often danced on Glentrool's lawn, did not set their feet tapping or erase the furrows in their brows. Davina kept to the melody, allowing Somerled to embellish the tune, and still her brothers seemed unimpressed by him.

As the hour grew later and drams of whisky were poured round the room, the lads did not imbibe but sat straighter in their chairs, defying those who were beginning to list. Davina had one final Gow tune to offer, a gentle air written for Lady Ann Hope. Somerled lowered his fiddle, giving her the stage. She missed hearing his notes intertwining with hers, yet was grateful for his perceptiveness. If she played alone, the twins might sense her affection for them and put aside their need to punish the man who'd changed her life in a single night.

The tune swept up and down the scale in graceful phrases, even as her hands moved up the ebony fingerboard to reach the higher notes. She looked directly at Will and Sandy as she played, hoping they might read her thoughts as Somerled often did. *You will always have my love, dear brothers. Nothing could ever change that.*

Did she note a sheen in Sandy's eyes, or had the flickering candle fooled her? Davina took one step toward them, pleading her case with music. *Can you not see that we must marry? And that I have forgiven him?* Will shifted his posture but not the firm line of his mouth. *Please, Will. He is not so different from us.*

Somerled accompanied her on the final chorus, playing not in harmony but in unison, strengthening the power of each note. The McKie men joined in the crowd's lengthy ovation, though her brothers' applause ceased when she nodded toward Somerled, inviting him to take a bow as well. He clasped her hand as together they acknowledged the audience's enthusiastic response, his grip strong and warm as ever. If the twins unnerved him, it did not show.

The duke's guests rose to their feet at last—some more steadily than others—and ambled off in several directions toward their sleeping chambers. Her father reached her first. "You've never sounded better," he told her, paternal pride shining in his eyes. "Don't you agree, lads?"

"The last tune especially," Will said, looking only at her.

Somerled squeezed her hand before releasing it. "I concur with you, Will. Your sister fares very well without my accompaniment."

"Indeed she does." Sandy folded his arms across his chest, like a bird ruffling its plumage to appear larger to its rivals.

Davina was glad when Sir Harry joined them; three McKies to one MacDonald felt less than sporting. She slipped her hand through the crook of Somerled's arm, making her allegiance clear to her brothers. *Though I am proud to be a McKie, I will soon become a MacDonald.* A tremor ran through her at the thought of all the changes ahead. A new name. A new home. A new life.

"So, lads." Sir Harry's booming voice, soaked with whisky, filled the quiet dining room. "Your father tells me you spent the afternoon on Goatfell."

"We did." Will exchanged glances with his twin. "Have you been to the summit yet? It offers an incomparable view."

"So we've been told, though Somerled and I have yet to make the ascent."

"Really?" Sandy arched his brows with marked disdain. "Surely you'll not leave Arran without mastering Goatfell?"

Sir Harry rose to her brother's challenge. "Nae, we will not."

"Have you forgotten, Father?" However smooth Somerled's delivery, Davina heard the underlying tension in his voice. "Tomorrow we journey on horseback to Machrie Moor for a look at the stone circles. With His Grace."

"Aye, aye." Sir Harry rubbed his chin. "Still, if the weather holds, we might climb Goatfell on Wednesday before we take our leave."

An uneasiness stirred inside Davina. *Goatfell.* Somerled had lodged a fortnight in the jagged mountain's shadow with no desire to mount its heights. Yet if he did not climb, the twins would brand him a coward.

"My brother and I would be willing to guide you," Will offered. "What say you, Father, to a scramble up Goatfell?"

"Alas, I cannot join you," Jamie admitted, though it clearly pained him to do so. " 'Tis difficult for me to get a decent footing on the steeper hills." He shrugged in Sir Harry's direction. "I once wrenched my leg crossing a tidal burn at night."

The older man frowned. "A pity, that."

"Sorry you cannot join us, Father." Will sounded more compassionate than usual. "Suppose you keep Davina company while Sandy and I take the MacDonalds climbing. Other than some loose stones and gritty slabs of granite near the summit, Goatfell is none too daunting."

"See that you descend along the same path," Jamie cautioned, "for there are dangerous precipices to the west."

Sir Harry drew himself up. "You forget, McKie, that my son and I are Highlanders. We've climbed many a *ben* and will hardly be bested by this one."

"Let us hope for fair weather on Wednesday, then." Somerled rested his hand on Davina's; she nearly jumped at the coolness of his skin. "As for this evening, with your permission, I should like to escort Davina to your lodging at Cladach."

"By all means." Will stood back, gesturing toward the door. "We know what a gentleman you are, MacDonald. 'Tis why my brother and I will stay close on your heels 'til the very hour you depart this isle."

Sixty-Three

When the mind is in a state of uncertainty
the smallest impulse directs it to either side.

TERENCE

Leana knelt beneath her dining room window and pressed the sharp blade of her garden knife against the thorny stem. She winced as the first bloom from her Apothecary's Rose gave way, feeling her heart break with it. *I should never have let her go.*

She held the deep pink flower to her nose, hoping its sweet fragrance might ease her anxious thoughts. Would her husband come riding up with Davina in a day or two, rescued from the Highlander's embrace? Or had Jamie already sent a letter, assuring her their daughter was well and in no danger?

Leana had little hope for either outcome; her heart was too heavy, her spirit too restless. She'd lived with a sense of dread from the moment Arran had been mentioned. Then Sunday at kirk the phrase "moral fortitude" had flown round the sanctuary like a trapped wren. *What has Davina done? Who is she with? What will become of her?* Between services Leana had remained in the pew with Ian rather than face the gossips in the kirkyard belittling her daughter.

Please, Lord, let none of it be true. Leana hastened for the door of the house, as if she might outrun her fears, breathing in the rose's fragrance once more when her foot touched Glentrool's threshold.

"Och! Thar ye are." Eliza closed the drawing room door behind her, then hurried to Leana's side, keeping her voice to a whisper. "Ye've a visitor, jist arrived. I've taken the *leebeertie* tae serve him tea." She relieved Leana of her apron and plucked the rose from her fingers. " 'Tis Mr. Webster o' Penningham Hall, mem."

Leana had taken note of him on the Sabbath: seated alone in his pew, his auburn head bowed, his shoulders sagging as if he bore a heavy burden. She'd longed to speak with him, but he'd slipped out the door when the morning service ended. Away to the Penningham kirk, perhaps. Away from the blether, to be sure.

Had he come to inform her he no longer wished to court Davina?

Moving toward the library, she told Eliza, "I'll speak with Ian briefly and then greet Mr. Webster. You say he has tea?"

"And honey cakes baked fresh this morn."

"Well done. Do tell our guest I shall join him presently."

She found Ian sitting at his father's desk, surrounded by books. "Graham Webster is here," she informed him, then rinsed her hands at the washstand and patted her face, grown moist beneath the sun. "You are free to join us, but it might be best…"

"Aye," Ian was quick to agree. "You should meet with him alone, for 'tis a private matter. Do send Jenny for me if I'm needed."

"Ian…" She dried her hands on the fresh linen, then carefully placed it by the bowl. "Might you pray for our conversation? I can only imagine how upset Mr. Webster must be, yet I've so little information to offer him."

"Consider it done, Mother." His smile was Jamie's. His blue gray eyes were hers. But his heart belonged to God, and for that she was abundantly grateful.

Leana crossed the entrance hall, with its polished floors and gleaming mirror, and opened the drawing room door, mustering what confidence she could. "Mr. Webster, how good of you to come."

He was already standing, his hat and gloves on the table, his tea poured but apparently untouched. "Your housekeeper was kind enough to usher me in, Mrs. McKie. Pardon me if I've chosen an inconvenient time to call."

"Not at all. You are always welcome at Glentrool."

He murmured his thanks, then sat, though he looked uncomfortable, as though he might spring to his feet at any moment.

She took her cup and saucer, hoping he might do the same. "Were you expecting to find my husband at home? I know Mr. McKie has five-score sheep set apart for you come Lammas. The very best of his flocks."

"I am pleased to hear it, but…" He spread out his large hands, as if they might express what he could not. "'Tis your daughter…'tis my concern for Miss McKie that brings me to your door."

"Of course." Leana put down her teacup before it began rattling in her hands. *Give me wisdom, Father. And strength.* "In truth, I meant to speak with you on the Sabbath last."

His hazel eyes brightened. "You have news, then? From Arran?"

Leana hesitated, knowing her answer would disappoint him. "Not yet," she finally admitted. "Later in the week—Thursday or Friday, perhaps—I may receive word from my husband."

Graham sighed, his gaze settling on the window facing the loch. The morning sun poured through the glass, decorating the carpeted floor with yellow squares. "Might he bring her home?"

"I confess, Mr. Webster, that is my hope. I will gladly tell you what I know." She briefly described Davina's Midsummer Eve performance for the Duke of Hamilton.

Graham blanched. "His Grace?"

"Aye." Leana still could not comprehend it herself. "It seems one of his guests, a young Highlander from Argyll, accompanied Davina on the violoncello."

"I see."

"Do not imagine the worst," she hastened to add, noting his downcast expression. "Mr. MacDonald is the heir of Sir Harry MacDonald, a gentleman of some standing. I feel certain his son has made no inappropriate, ah, overtures toward our daughter."

Heat rose up her neck. She had no such assurance, and Graham Webster knew it.

"But wasn't Reverend Moodie asked to pray for her—"

"Aye." Leana could not countenance hearing the phrase again. "I beg you not to condemn our daughter on such slender evidence."

"You can be sure I will not," he said firmly. "Until you or your husband informs me otherwise, I'll assume Miss McKie remains chaste and above reproach."

May it be so, Lord. She waited until her cheeks cooled before she broached the delicate subject of his suit. "Then you'll not withdraw your offer to court our daughter?"

"By no means."

Leana could not contain her relief. "I am very glad to hear it, Mr. Webster." All was not lost. Not if a gracie man such as he could ignore the gossips and trust his own heart. "The moment Davina is home, we'll join you for dinner at Penningham Hall, as you requested."

"I shall look forward to it, Mrs. McKie." He smiled as he reached for his hat and gloves. "The sooner I may begin courting your daughter, the better."

Before Leana could rise to bid Graham Webster farewell, voices sounded in the hall. More company on a quiet Tuesday morning?

She heard Ian greeting a visitor. John McMillan, judging by the bold sound of him. As a child, Davina had drawn a sketch of their neighbor, then titled it "The Giant of Glen Trool." Even Ian, the tallest of the McKies, barely reached John's mammoth shoulders.

Moments later Ian escorted him into the drawing room; John's black hair brushed the lintel as he strode beneath it. Both men were smiling. "Look who's come bearing news, Mother."

Dressed in the simple attire of a gentleman farmer, their neighbor looked perfectly at ease in the richly furnished room. He and Jamie had been friends since they were lads. Very little intimidated John McMillan.

"Mrs. McKie." He offered her a cordial bow, then produced a bulky letter from his coat pocket. "You'll be wanting this, I imagine. Courtesy of yestermorn's mail coach. By way of Reverend Moodie." John grinned at her. "Best I can tell, he did not break the seal."

"My husband will be sure to reimburse you." Leana grasped the letter with both hands, noticing its thickness. Two pages or more. "Gentlemen, I…" She knew it would be rude to open the post and read it as if they were not present. Yet her heart would burst if she did not soon learn the contents. Though the handwriting was not familiar, the postmark was: Arran.

John came to her rescue. "Truly, madam, we are as eager as you are for news. Read your letter. We'll entertain ourselves with honey cakes, aye?" The others nodded, dutifully piling their plates with the round sweets.

"Bless you," she murmured, already sliding her finger beneath the wax seal. A separate letter waited inside, addressed in a different hand. She laid that one aside and began reading the first, her eyes widening at the sender's name: Sir Harry MacDonald of Brenfield House.

> To Mr. and Mrs. James McKie of Glentrool
> Monday, 27 June 1808

The date gave her pause. *More than a week ago, yet soon after Mid-summer Eve.*

> Pardon me for conducting such important business by post. We will no doubt meet in the near future, when I may better express myself in person.
>
> To state things succinctly, my son and heir, Somerled MacDonald, desires to marry your daughter, Miss Davina McKie.

Marry? Leana dropped onto the nearest settee. *But they've only just met…*

> I confess, I was taken aback by the brevity of their acquaintance. I am certain you are both surprised as well. When you see the two of them together, I believe you will be convinced, as I am, that Somerled and Miss McKie are meant to be husband and wife.

Davina…a wife? And wed to a Highlander?

Stunned at the news, Leana did not know how to think, where to look, what to say. Despite the honey cakes in their hands, the three gentlemen in her drawing room were not eating; they were watching. And waiting for some explanation.

Struggling to maintain her composure, she scanned the balance of the letter.

> My son and I wish to arrange a meeting at your earliest convenience—on Arran, if that is your preference, or at our estate in Argyll. I trust the enclosed letter will convince you of my son's sincerity and eagerness to proceed.

He closed with an elaborate signature, as impressive as his title: *Baronet*. Meaning his son would one day be Sir Somerled MacDonald.

Leana stared at the page. *And Davina would be Lady MacDonald.*

However could Jamie refuse this titled man and his wealthy heir? Indeed, he'd be hard pressed to do so if Somerled was deemed worthy. And if Davina truly desired him for her husband.

She looked up to find Graham Webster's gaze pinned on her. Had he guessed the subject matter? Could she bring herself to tell him?

"There's a second letter," she said faintly, reaching for it. Breaking the seal, she unfolded it to discover only a few lines. Yet they were most convincing.

> My very soul has cleaved to your daughter. Though I speak
> five languages, she has taught me the sweetest language of
> all: silence. Though I am a skilled musician, her talent is far
> superior to mine. Though I have traveled the continent, I
> have yet to meet her equal in cleverness and beauty. Might
> I be so bold as to ask for your daughter's hand in marriage?
> My father and I earnestly await your reply.

With slow, deliberate movements, Leana folded both letters. She did not need to read them again.

"Mr. McMillan…" She rose, giving him an apologetic smile. "I am afraid this news cannot be shared until my husband returns."

His shaggy brows knotted in a mock scowl. "Can you not at least tell us if the winds on Arran blow fair or foul?"

She hesitated, for Graham's sake. "Fair," she said at last.

"Good." John deposited his empty plate on the tea tray. "My wife and daughter will be relieved to hear it." He clamped a meaty hand on Ian's shoulder. "The McKies are nigh family to us now. If there's anything I can do…"

"Thank you, John." She offered their old friend a grateful curtsy. "Ian, please see our neighbor to the door while I have a word with Mr. Webster."

Didn't Graham deserve to know something? Even as she tried to convince herself, Jamie's admonition came to mind: *I have asked Graham to wait, Leana. I'm asking you to do the same.* Could she send this anxious suitor out the door uninformed, knowing what she knew? Alas, she could not.

Leana resumed her place on the settee. "Do join me, Mr. Webster."

Though he did as she asked, she saw the stiffness in his posture, the reluctance on his face.

Waiting until he met her gaze, she then held out the folded letters so he might see the masculine handwriting on each address and know that she spoke the truth. "These are from Sir Harry MacDonald and from his son, Somerled," she began.

Graham glanced at them, then sighed. "I assume he wishes to marry your daughter."

His perceptiveness made the answer all the more difficult. "Aye."

"Does your daughter wish it as well?"

" 'Twould appear she does." Leana pretended not to see his eyes water. Was there no solace she might offer? no word of comfort? "Mr. Webster, nothing has been decided." She held up the letters as proof. "We have only these few words on paper…"

Graham shook his head, defeated without a skirmish, then rose and pulled on his gloves. "Forgive me, Mrs. McKie, for hoping too much."

"You've no need to apologize, sir." She stood and touched his coat sleeve. "We were honored by your offer of courtship. Perhaps if…"

"Nae. 'Tis clear this is not meant to be." Graham was already moving toward the drawing room door, his expression resolute. "Good day to you, Mrs. McKie. Kindly convey my regards to your husband. And to your daughter."

Moments later he was riding west toward Penningham, no doubt trampling his dreams into the ground. Watching from the window, Leana saw him disappear among the pine trees skirting the loch. "Godspeed," she whispered, wishing things might have turned out differently. If Davina had known, if she'd been told of Graham's interest… Ah, but there was no use contemplating such possibilities now.

Ian came up behind her, lightly resting his hands on her shoulders. "Now will you tell me the news from Arran?"

Leana sighed as she moved toward the settee. Needing to sit. Needing to think. "I fear 'tis most unexpected."

As Ian read both letters, his expressions mirrored her own: shock, concern, and disbelief. "Mother, how can this be? They've known each other but a fortnight."

"Far less, when the letters were written." She swallowed, trying to stem her tears. "And who can say what has transpired since then?" Despite her best efforts, her voice grew thin. "Your father may have already given their marriage his blessing."

"Come now. They will not make such plans without you." Ian drew out his linen handkerchief and placed it in her hands. " 'Tis clear, I must escort you to Arran."

Arran? Leana's spirits began to lift. "Oh, Ian, can we manage such a thing?"

"I well know the road to Ayr," he assured her. "And Father told me much about his journey with Davina. Where they lodged en route. How they acquired passage across the firth. 'Tis less than a two-day journey from our door to the Kilbride manse if the winds are favorable."

She pressed his handkerchief against her heart, looking about the room. "But what of Glentrool?"

"Rab and Eliza are more than capable. I'll ask them to manage things in our absence." The confidence in his voice dispelled the last of her fears. "If we make haste, we'll be away by eleven."

Bethankit! She would see her precious daughter in a matter of days and be reunited with her dear husband. "Ian, you are your father's son." She leaned forward and kissed his cheek. "However can I thank you?"

He smiled. "By packing our bags, since that is decidedly your gift and not mine."

"With pleasure." Leana began mentally sifting through the contents of her clothes press. And from Davina's room she would include a yellow silk gown with matching slippers. A costume fit for a bride.

"Shall we post a letter to the twins?" she wondered aloud. "Unless your father has found time to write them, they know none of this. I would hate for them to return home and find all of us gone."

"But they'll not depart Edinburgh 'til the end of the month," Ian reminded her. "Wouldn't it be better to write them from Arran once we know the situation?"

"Aye, indeed." When had he become so wise, this handsome son of hers?

Ian stood, then helped her to her feet. " 'Twill be an adventure, Mother." He steered her toward the door with a sure hand. "And think of the view we'll have from Rowantree Hill."

Sixty-Four

Approach the verge
Of that dread precipice; with care approach.

DAVID LANDSBOROUGH

Somerled gazed out the castle window at a world made of pewter: gray skies, gray water, gray pebbles along the shoreline. Though one could never be certain on Arran, heavy cloud cover usually boded hours of intermittent rain.

"'Tis a poor day for hill climbing." Somerled tried not to sound hopeful.

Sir Harry, nursing his morning dram of whisky, merely grunted in response.

Far below them a curl of smoke rose from the chimney of the old inn at Cladach, barely visible among the trees. When he imagined Davina, dressed for the day and spooning her porridge, Somerled regained his sense of purpose. He would climb Goatfell whatever the weather. 'Twould not do to appear weak before his future brothers-in-law. Or his future wife.

I will do this for you, beloved. He would tell her as much when she arrived to send them off. *I am not afraid.*

A manservant appeared at his elbow. "Yer valet is waitin' in yer bed-chamber. Says he's bound for Lochranza harbor at yer biddin'."

Somerled nodded his thanks, then strode across the dining room, where only a handful of visitors remained, tarrying over their breakfast plates. His Grace had sailed for the mainland at dawn, taking half a dozen guests with him and leaving his servants to attend the rest. Somerled bade each man farewell in turn; after more than a fortnight together, they'd become well acquainted.

"Will it be a Highland or a Lowland wedding for you and the wee fiddler?" Stuart Cameron asked as the two men clasped hands.

Somerled shrugged. " 'Tis the bride's prerogative to choose. I imagine we'll sort that out when we return to Brenfield House." He would leave such details to his mother and to hers. All that concerned him was Davina: marrying her, loving her, creating a life with her.

"Safe journey," Cameron said, lifting his dram in a parting salute. " 'Twill be good to be home, aye?"

Aye. Somerled had not slept well yestreen, so eager was he to quit the Isle of Arran. He longed for his own tester bed, his many musical instruments, and a menu that did not feature salmon or trout at every meal. Yet it was more than that: He'd grown restless and ill at ease since the McKies had arrived from the mainland. The twins' disapproval was understandable—had he not debauched their sister?—but their blatant distrust continued even after the two fathers had signed a generous agreement in the steward's office. Perhaps today's outing would put their suspicions to rest.

Somerled headed for his castle bedchamber, reviewing the hours to come. Even with the climb up Goatfell, they would be back at Brodick by early afternoon and bound for Lochranza on horseback for an evening sail home.

"You have us packed, Dougal?" He greeted the valet with a smile. "Well done, man. Have you had enough of Arran as well?"

"Aye." Despite his stooped posture, Dougal had wrestled their trunks to the bedchamber door. "I ride in cart on coast road." He pointed toward the window. "*Tuath*...north."

"That's right. If you depart the castle at ten, you'll reach Lochranza well before us and can arrange a boat for Claonaig." Somerled filled the servant's coat pocket with silver. "This should secure our passage."

Dougal's gnarled hands reached up to straighten Somerled's collar, then produced a comb to tame his waves. "Nighean," he said simply.

Somerled laughed. "And Miss McKie appreciates your grooming efforts, I assure you. She's to arrive with her brothers at eight." He checked his watch, then bolted for the door. " 'Til this evening, Dougal."

Still smoothing back his hair, Somerled returned to the dining room to collect his father, who would not be deprived of his last few sips of whisky. "I'll meet you at the lowpin-on stane by the castle door," Sir Harry grumbled. "Ten minutes at most."

Somerled wouldn't argue, not if it meant a longer visit with Davina. He bounded down the turnpike stair and through the broad doorway into the murky light of day. Moisture in the air deadened the sound; even the birdsong seemed muted. He circled round the castle and started downhill toward Cladach, then spied the McKies emerging from the border of firs at the edge of the lawn.

Davina scampered ahead of them, more like a child than a woman. *Nae.* He grinned. *More like a fairy.* She was breathless and pink cheeked by the time she reached him, her hair turned to wisps, the hem of her blue gown drenched with dew. When she turned her face toward his, Somerled did not hesitate for a moment, claiming a kiss he'd imagined for days. *So sweet, my love. So pure.*

"That's enough," Will barked as he and Sandy drew near.

Somerled kissed her once more, not caring if he irked the lads, then murmured in her ear, "The day will come, Miss McKie, when I'll have you all to myself. And then we shall see what 'enough' is."

Davina's face turned so red her freckles disappeared, though he noted a slight smile as well.

Her brothers marched up, dressed for a day on the hills: coarse woolen clothing, sturdy boots, and flasks of water on their hips. "Where's your father?" Sandy asked, looking about with obvious irritation.

"You'll find him in the vicinity of the lowpin-on stane. If not now, momentarily." Somerled waved his hand in that direction, already weary of their company. James McKie seemed decent enough, but his sons left much to be desired. "Wait for me there," Somerled told the twins, "while I bid your sister farewell."

When she touched his watch, he assured her, "I shall meet you at the inn six hours hence. Then, alas, we truly must part." He turned to meet Will's narrowed gaze. "Well, lads?"

"We'll not be far," Will warned him. The twins crossed the lawn but did not round the corner, stopping instead to watch the couple from a distance.

Somerled turned his back on them, ignoring their belligerent stances. "I fear your brothers' trust will not be easily won." He gazed down at her, memorizing her delicate features. "But if I have yours, Miss McKie, that is more than sufficient."

She touched her heart, then his. Slowly, tenderly.

Oh, lass. He swallowed hard. To imagine that she would trust him. Care for him. It was almost more than he could grasp on that cool, gray morning.

But Davina was not finished. Her blue eyes shimmered as she reached up to cradle his face in her small hands, then stood on tiptoe to kiss him.

My love, my bride. He pulled her into his embrace.

Somerled did not care if her brothers were consulting their watches. Did not care if the servants gaped from the castle windows or whispered in the halls. Davina McKie had forgiven him. Nothing else mattered.

"Make up your mind, Son." Sir Harry's gruff voice carried across the lawn. "Will you spend the day wooing Miss McKie or climbing Goatfell?" He strode toward the couple, a determined look on his face. "You've already conquered the first. Come show these McKies you can handle the second."

"Aye, Father." Somerled did not take his eyes off Davina as he released her. "I'd much rather remain by your side, Miss McKie. But if 'twill convince your brothers I am worthy of you, I will gladly climb any hill on Arran."

She stepped back, tears swimming in her eyes, then pressed her hands together. *Thank you.*

"Where is your sire?" Sir Harry demanded to know when the twins strolled up. "Will he not see you off this morning? Or does he leave such duties to your sister?"

"Our father departed for Lamlash Bay an hour ago," Will informed him, chewing on each word. "Arrangements must be made if he and Davina are to sail for Ayr in the morning."

"And what of the two of you?"

"We sail for Saltcoats this afternoon," Sandy said, glancing toward Brodick Bay. "Almost the moment we return."

"Time we started, then." Sir Harry led the way, walking stick in hand.

With its filigreed handle wrought in silver, the ebony stick was more ornamental than useful, but Somerled did not begrudge his father a prop if it pleased him. For his own footing on the hills, he would count on his leather boots and a careful eye. And Davina's prayers; no man could wish for greater support than that.

Will turned to his sister, a stern expression on his face. "'Tis not far back to the inn. Will you be all right on your own?"

She nodded, though her eyes still bore a faint sheen.

"Father promised to return by three o'clock," Sandy reminded her. "We'll arrive a bit sooner. I've asked Mrs. McAllister to look after you until then." Having attended to their sister's welfare, the brothers trailed after Sir Harry.

Somerled hung back, clasping Davina's hands once more. "Pray for us, aye?" He kissed her cheek, then released her, difficult as it was, and sent her in the direction of the inn, waving farewell before he turned toward the woods where the others stood waiting.

"Besotted," Sir Harry said, shaking his head as Somerled walked up. "The lass will still be here when you return. For the moment, we've a hill to climb."

Since the well-trod path accommodated two abreast, Somerled joined his father with the McKies close behind them. "How high is Goatfell?" he asked as they struck out. Though he dreaded the answer, a bit of conversation would calm his nerves more readily than silence.

"'Tis high enough," Will said bluntly. "Nigh to three thousand feet."

The path was not steep, but the incline was noticeable, more so after they passed through an old gateway in a low dry stane dyke. Somerled kept his gaze to the ground, watching where he planted his feet, though a quick glance upward revealed a thick mantle of clouds. "Are you not worried about the weather, lads?"

"Nae." Will slapped his shoulder from behind, rather harder than necessary. "The clouds are so low, we may climb above them before we reach the summit."

"You've been on the isle longer than we have," Sandy chided him. "Do the skies not alter without a moment's notice?"

Somerled could not deny that Arran's weather was changeable. "'A cloudy morning bodes a fair afternoon,' eh?" He could only pray the Scottish proverb proved true. He'd not felt a drop of rain yet, and the ground was moist but firm. Bracken and heather covered the area round them, with scattered stands of birch on the slopes. He had yet to feel the change of altitude in his lungs or his legs. They'd only ascended a few hundred feet, he imagined. 'Twould be a different story by morning's end.

As they started up the east ravine of a hilly stream, Will said, "I've heard this called 'Knockin' Burn,' though I cannot fathom why they chose such a name."

"'Tis *Cnocan* Burn," Somerled corrected him, spelling it out. Did these Lowlanders know nothing of Gaelic? "It means 'hillock.' 'Stream of the little hill,' as it were."

And a fine streak of water it was, falling down rocky gorges and forming deep pools along the way. From the branches of the rowan and birch trees framing its banks, willow warblers sang a plaintive tune, descending the scale in a fall of liquid notes. Somerled listened carefully, wondering how he might mimic their song on his flute.

When Cnocan Burn veered to the west, the twins guided them north instead. Somerled asked over his shoulder, "You are certain of this route, Will?"

"My brother and I took this same path two days ago," he said, not bothering to hide his impatience. "'Tis the fastest way."

"We need to be off this mountain by two o'clock," Sir Harry insisted.

"Oh, have no fear of that," Sandy told him. "You'll be off even earlier if the weather cooperates."

They trudged through a wet, grassy moorland strewn with boulders as Goatfell's slopes loomed closer, the summit draped in clouds. No wonder they'd not encountered other walkers on the route.

An hour or more had passed since they'd left the castle. With

Davina's father busy in Lamlash harbor, Somerled wondered if she would remain at the inn, immersed in reading *The Lay of the Minstrel,* or go walking with her sketchbook in search of some view she'd not captured. He only knew that he missed her and wished he'd had the courage to stay behind.

Or was this the braver thing, to face what he feared?

Somerled knew the answer. *I will do this for you, beloved.* He'd neglected to tell her so, but the canny lass knew. Though her tongue was silent, those charming ears of hers missed nothing, not even words left unsaid.

"Climbing a bit more now," Sir Harry observed, a slight wheeze to his voice.

Somerled eyed him askance. Despite the man's silvery crown, Sir Harry was far more fit than most men his age. Would his father manage the climb without mishap? Would he?

As the gradient increased, their vista widened, encompassing more of the mountain fastness that was north Arran. Somerled spotted a red deer amid the heather. To his right a peregrine, flying high in search of prey, swept down suddenly on its unsuspecting victim.

"Heaven knows why 'tis called 'Goatfell,'" Will groused, "when there are no goats to be seen."

Somerled kept his irritation in check. "'Tis from the Gaelic word for wind: *gaoth.* It must be a windy hill."

"Not today," Sir Harry muttered, "or why have the clouds not lifted?" He began puffing harder as they ascended a much steeper slope, then turned west, directly toward Goatfell. "It seems we'll have no view at all."

Will turned on his heel. "Would you quit here, gentlemen, so close to the summit?"

"Quit?" Sir Harry shook his walking stick at him, his face red. "Indeed not. Shall we, Son?"

"Nae." Somerled paused to catch his breath, gazing up at the formidable granite peak. Just as well he'd not eaten much breakfast; his stomach was tied in a knot.

"The last bit is the roughest." Sandy pointed to the gritty surface of the granite, worn down by the moist westerly winds. "Mind the loose stones beneath your boots, or you'll lose your footing."

Will gazed at the summit. "'Tis about six hundred feet up. The path is winding and not easily tracked." He turned round, a hard look in his eye. "You'll have to follow Sandy and me."

"Aye," Somerled said grimly, knowing he had no other choice. "Lead the way."

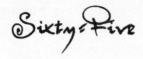

Sixty-Five

Deep vengeance is the daughter of deep silence.

VITTORIO ALFIERI

Fear not, Somerled. I'll lead you where you need to go.

Will clambered up the bare granite bedrock, leaning into the rugged slope, his hands outstretched, ready to grasp at anything to keep his balance. Sandy was close at his heels, the MacDonalds straggling well behind them. So much for Highland superiority on the hills.

The weather was ideal. Rain or high winds might have put an end to their plans; a solid bank of clouds would make things far easier.

Conversation among the men had ceased, which suited Will. He wanted them to reach the summit in one piece. Wanted their confidence bolstered, their heads swollen with pride. What was the verse Father often harped upon? *Pride goeth before destruction.* Aye, that was it. Will grimaced, remembering the rest. *And an haughty spirit before a fall.*

He gripped the rocks beneath his hands, steadying himself, no longer able to walk upright; the ascent was too steep. A ridge of rock struck a jagged, vertical line toward the summit. Had he and Sandy veered to the right of it last time or to the left? Too late for such questions; they had already started up the grassier left side. Tempting as it was to secure his footing using the boulders scattered round them, Will had learned such footholds could give way. On Monday's climb hadn't he nearly clobbered Sandy with a rock the size of his head? He could not afford a single misstep this morning, not of any kind.

Three days they had waited. Three days they had stilled their tongues and plotted their revenge.

When he heard a sudden cry from below, Will's heart stopped. "Sandy?"

A quick glance down, and his heartbeat steadied. His brother, without meaning to, had sent a shower of loose gravel raining down on the MacDonalds. "Careful," Will called out, though his admonishment was unnecessary. His brother was being as cautious as he, their two minds thinking as one since they'd learned the truth.

Somerled MacDonald had violated their sister. Treated her like a common harlot. Such a man deserved no mercy. And they would show him none, nor his arrogant father. Never mind that the McKie brothers had fled from Edinburgh without sword or pistol. The mountain would be weapon enough.

"Ravens," Sandy cried, drawing his attention upward. Two birds came tumbling through the clouds, their wings folded, their solid black bodies diving and rolling, showing off their wedge-shaped tails.

Will looked away, refusing to acknowledge the superstition: Two ravens foretold a wedding. He was relieved to glance up a moment later and see another pair of birds gliding through the air with the others. Four ravens meant death, a more timely portent.

Will lodged his feet against an outcropping of rock and waited while the others caught up. Whatever Sir Harry's claims, his golden-haired son had no gift for hill climbing. Will almost felt sorry for Somerled, watching him scramble upward, his long arms and legs working against him, as if he might fall through the air like the ravens.

"Do you need a rest?" Will called down, exchanging glances with his brother, who was not two feet below him.

"Nae," the Highlanders answered in unison.

Will resumed his ascent, beginning to shiver from the cold and the dampness of the clouds that crept round the summit. Could it possibly be July when it felt more like October? Monday's clear skies and bright sun had warmed the rocky slopes; they had no such advantage this forenoon. His breath came in steamy puffs, and the wind had picked up, smelling of the sea. Not a straight blow that would chase away their cloud cover, but a whirling, chilling wind that stirred the pebbles round his feet and whipped his hair into his eyes.

"Another hundred feet," he hollered, not knowing if they could hear him or if the wind had carried his voice off to the mainland. He'd not remembered Monday's ascent being so perilous; they must have climbed on the right side of the ridge after all. They would surely come down that way, he and Sandy.

All at once Will was swallowed by a cloud; thick, white mist wrapped him like a burial shroud. He could not see the summit above or his brother below. Refusing to panic, he pressed on, one foothold at a time, cursing the weather and Somerled and granite slopes and anything else that stood in his way.

He would have his revenge, if only for Davina's sake. *My bonny wee fairy.* She did not love this Highlander, could never love him. He'd bewitched her, as Father said. That would end very soon. He and Sandy would not let this man ruin Davina's life as he'd ruined her virtue. Furthermore, they would claim his silver and gold, his property and lands, as payment for her loss.

But first Will and the others with him had to climb this wretched mountain.

He heard Sir Harry's voice below. Strained, anxious. Then his brother's voice. Calm, encouraging. "Not much farther," Sandy told them. "Just keep coming."

Will's hand touched a broad expanse above him, and he pulled himself onto the bare table of rock. Even through the cloud cover, he could see several large boulders, precisely where he'd remembered them. Monday they'd spent a good deal of time on the summit; now that knowledge would be put to use.

He turned and reached down for his brother, helping Sandy scramble over the edge before clutching him in a brief but fervent embrace. "We're here, lad," he whispered. "'Tis almost done."

A moment later Somerled vaulted himself over the top, his brow slick with sweat, his breath coming in gasps. "Did you...not say...'twas none...too daunting?"

"Aye." Will pointed to the far side of the vertical ridge. "We came up the left side when we should have come up the right. The error is mine, I'm afraid."

Somerled turned to help his father climb onto the summit. The older man's skin was blanched as white as his hair, and his legs were far from steady as he dropped onto one of the flat-topped boulders.

Still on his feet, Somerled blotted his face dry with his coat sleeve. "I trust we'll not make the same mistake going down?"

"Depend upon it," Will told him.

The foursome fell silent, taking in their colorless surroundings. They might have been adrift on a raft, so unchanging was the scenery. No peaks to the north, no peninsula to the west, no bays to the south, no firth to the east. Nothing but moist white clouds, growing thicker by the minute.

Will knew what lay out there; two days earlier he had seen the panorama. Now, except for the cold and the wind, any sense of elevation was lost. As if he could easily step beyond the precipice and find solid ground beneath his feet instead of thin air and sharp rocks below.

"So this is Goatfell's incomparable view." Sir Harry threw up his hands. "At least you cannot call us cowards, lads. We climbed your hill. That we did."

"Aye," Will mumbled, his mind racing. If he could not see what lay beyond the summit, how could he steer the MacDonalds in the right direction—right for him but very wrong for them? How could he be sure of their demise? And how would he and Sandy find their way down the steep slopes when they could barely see the rocks beneath their feet?

Suddenly their cunning plan seemed an impossibility. Yet they dared not abandon it, or Somerled would sail for home and the wedding plans would proceed.

Nae. There would be no better time, no other time but now.

Will took a turn round the summit, walking closer to the edge than was prudent, hoping to appear confident and worthy of their trust. He had no fear of heights, but this was unnerving, knowing how sheer the drop was yet being unable to see it. Stopping for a moment, he stared into the endless sea of clouds. Was *this* the spot they'd chosen? The west face of Goatfell overlooking Glen Rosa was a descent even the most experienced climbers avoided.

Steeling himself, Will turned to face them. "Since it appears the clouds are not likely to lift, suppose we start down and take a different route back to the castle."

"In which direction?" Somerled's eyes narrowed. "Did your father not warn you to descend along the same path?"

Will tried to shrug, though it felt more like a nervous tremor. "My father has not climbed Goatfell in thirty years. Sandy and I were here on Monday and tested this descent ourselves." He swiveled toward the precipice, if only to mask the heat climbing up his neck and no doubt staining his cheeks. He'd lied before, but not with such murderous intent.

When he turned back, Somerled was beside him. Alarmingly near.

Without thinking, Will took a step back. Closer to the edge. He could feel the winds sweeping up the precipice and over his shoulders.

Somerled eyed him. "Careful, Will." Almost a threat.

Surely the Highlander had no scheme of his own? He was taller, if not stronger, and half a dozen years older. Will would not forget that when the time came. He stepped round him, then motioned to Sandy. "Join us, Brother."

Sir Harry came along as well, his color restored and his breathing even. "Any route we take will be slow going in this weather." He scanned the cloud cover. "We'd best begin before the rain does."

Will nodded, grateful for the baronet's unintentional support. "Here is what Sandy and I had in mind." Using terms known only to veteran climbers, he described the route, carefully chosen to start with ease. "Sandy and I will descend on either side of you so we can easily maintain contact. And assist you, should your foot slip."

"Send me down first," Sir Harry demanded. "I've spent the better part of my life on hillsides."

Will heard the bravado in his voice but would not dispute the man's claim. Not when his foolhardy offer so thoroughly suited his own needs. "As you say, sir."

Somerled was not so quick to agree. "Might it not be best if I went first?"

Sir Harry scowled at him. "And risk losing my heir? Nae, 'tis a father's duty to go first." He straightened his woolen coat and stamped the grass from his boots. "On with it, gentlemen."

Will walked the precipice with Sandy once more to be certain—very certain—of their starting point. He caught his brother's gaze. *Are you sure? Any doubts?* They'd be jeopardizing their own safety in the process. If Sir Harry grabbed one of their arms in desperation… If Somerled had seen through their ruse and formulated a plan of his own…

Nae. The scoundrel did not know Goatfell. His ignorance would be his downfall. *Quite.*

"Sandy, if you'll start to the right." Will watched his brother gamely lower himself over the edge, then he did the same, half a dozen feet away. Jamming his boots into narrow crevices, Will rested his arms on the summit and looked up at their adversaries. "Sir Harry?" He nodded to the gaping spot between them. "The place of honor is yours."

With a grunt, the man lowered himself over the precipice and started downhill. "Aye, 'tis an easier path," he said, a look of relief on his broad face. "Follow my lead, Somerled. I'll have you back in your lassie's arms before noon."

The man hadn't looked at his pocket watch of late, Will decided. It was already noon.

Sir Harry continued moving downward with Sandy's encouragement. "There's a solid ledge there, sir. Have you found it?"

"Aye, aye. Come along, Son."

Somerled crouched over the summit, looking down at the three of them. Will could not read his expression. Fear, hidden behind a firm jaw? Resolve, locked inside his unblinking gaze?

"Have a care, Father. For I do not trust these hills. Nor this weather."

Nor us. Will caught Sandy's gaze across the stony expanse. *Be on your guard. He suspects something.*

With his long legs, Somerled was soon lower than they were, with his father directly below him, barely visible in the cloud. "How goes it, sir?"

"Well enough," he called up. "Are the lads coming, or have they abandoned us?"

"We're on our way, sir." Will and Sandy moved as one, easing down only a few steps. The terrain would soon take care of things without any assistance from them.

Somerled inched farther down as well, his countenance a fair match for the granite.

"Och!" Sir Harry fumed. "'Tis my hand you're stepping on, lad."

When Somerled shifted his leg in search of another toehold, his father began to lose his footing, with nothing but loose gravel beneath his boots. The sound of rocks tumbling into a vast cavity of air was wrenching. The older man's urgent cry for help was worse.

"Father!" Somerled shouted. "Take my leg. The lads will hold me."

Will heard Sir Harry's anguished groan. Saw Somerled's body jerk as his father latched on to his boot. Watched them both slide farther down, almost beyond reach. Felt his stomach heave as Sir Harry lost his grip and went the way of the rocks, his heavy frame not falling into thin air but hitting the jagged mountainside with sickening thuds, his screams fading into the cloudy abyss.

A deep and terrible silence descended on Goatfell.

"Father…" Somerled was weeping. Pressing his forehead against the rocks.

Will could not bear to look down. Could not bear to think of what he had done. Could not bring himself to do it again. For any reason.

"Somerled. We're coming." He started down, ignoring the risk. "Sandy, please…help him."

His brother did not protest. Yet even moving another foot lower, the twins were barely able to grasp Somerled's coat sleeves. "We'll have to continue down," Will insisted, knowing what it could mean. "One more foot, Sandy."

"Will…" His brother's eyes were wet with tears, his body trembling. "I cannot go farther."

But I can.

"Somerled! Are you able to move this direction?" Will reached into the wind. "Take my hand."

Somerled looked up at him, his face ravaged. "Did you mean this to happen?"

Will swallowed. The time for deception was over. "We did."

"Then how can I trust you?" Somerled struggled to pull himself up, fighting for a toehold.

"I give you my word." Will clamped onto his forearm. "As a brother." He dragged him toward the summit, straining to keep his balance. "Get your footing," he yelled, sensing the pull of gravity. "Sandy! Can you reach him?"

He could not.

Somerled slipped from his grasp, a look of terror on his face as the rocks beneath him gave way. "Will…help me!" he cried before disappearing into the cloud.

Will grabbed for him nonetheless, nearly falling himself. "Nae!" He choked on the word as he clung to the hillside, wishing he could cover his ears.

Sixty-Six

When the day gaed doon ower Goatfell grim
And darkness mantled a'.
THE SIGNAL OF THE BRUCE

They'll not come hame onie faster, Miss McKie, nae matter how lang ye leuk oot the *windie*."

Davina kept her nose pressed to the glass, even as the innkeeper's nagging voice grated against her ears. Mrs. McAllister had fussed at her when she'd had no appetite at noon, then complained when Davina had put aside her book of poetry to stare out the kitchen window, watching the road to Brodick castle and imagining Goatfell beyond it.

Will and Sandy had asked her to wait for them at the inn. Could she not honor their simple request? Perhaps her loving obedience might build a bridge between the twins and Somerled. They were soon to be related by law; she prayed the McKies and MacDonalds might someday be true brothers.

Mrs. McAllister leaned closer and squinted through the glass. "Hoot! Whan did the sky turn sae *mirksome*? 'Tis dark as nicht oot thar."

Davina had spent the last hour pretending not to notice how thick the clouds had become—so dark they almost shut out the sun. She knew enough about climbing hills to realize that clouds ruined the view and rain showers made for slippery footing on grass and granite. Still, the men should be long off the summit by now.

My brave Highlander. Somerled had climbed Goatfell for her.

She was already thinking of ways to show her appreciation: learning a tune from his repertoire; sketching him as he played his wooden flute; fashioning a *waddin* sark for him, as marriage customs of old required, though she'd need her mother's help. Sewing an embroidered shirt to fit Somerled's broad shoulders would be no easy feat, yet the thought of him wearing it warmed her heart.

Hurry home, lad. She expected him shortly, but without the sun's position to guide her, she could not be sure of the time. Might the innkeeper know? Davina drew an imaginary clock on the pane, marking the hours, adding the hands.

" 'Tis nigh two o'clock," Mrs. McAllister said before returning to her soup kettle. "Yer brithers told me tae leuk for them onie time noo."

Davina turned away from the glass. She could not speed their journey by fretting. Only by praying for guidance and protection. *God is our God for ever and ever.* A comforting verse, that. *He will be our guide even unto death.*

Davina eyed the table in the kitchen parlor, plates and spoons already in place for the hungry sportsmen. She was certain Somerled and his father would join her brothers for a plate of barley broth before riding north to Lochranza. It was unlikely they'd find a meal waiting for them at the castle; a steady stream of guests had departed Brodick all morning, bound for the stone quay.

She'd paused to straighten one of the horn spoons when the front door opened and closed so quietly she knew it could not be her boisterous brothers. Was Father home early? Or was Somerled playing a trick on her? She smoothed back her hair and pinched her cheeks, then started for the entrance hall, the innkeeper not far behind.

A soft knocking sounded on one of the hall doors. "Davina? 'Tis Will."

Nae. That thin, weak voice could not possibly be his.

Alarmed, she turned the corner and found the twins sagging against the door to her lodging room, arms limp, as if the wooden panels were their only support.

With a soundless cry she ran up and clasped their hands, only to discover their palms bruised and bleeding.

"What's this?" Mrs. McAllister demanded, her sharp gaze roving over their disheveled clothes and filthy boots. "Ye didna return from Goatfell in sic a state on Monday."

"Nae, we did not." Will and Sandy straightened with obvious effort. "If you might fetch us two pitchers of hot water, Mrs.—"

"Aye, and weel I maun, or ye'll have *bluid* on me linens." She was already bound for the kitchen.

Davina opened their hands, staring at the torn skin. *Poor lads.* Had they not worn gloves?

" 'Tis nothing," Will said, pulling free of her grasp, then lightly brushing his fingertip along her chin. "You are safe. That is all that matters, lass."

Safe? When she turned to Sandy, he nodded but made no comment. His hand in hers was limp.

The innkeeper returned promptly, holding up two pitchers. "I'll tak these tae yer rooms, for yer hands dinna leuk as if they'll grip the handles." She headed for the stair, calling over her shoulder, " 'Twas fearsome on the hills, aye?"

Sandy did not look at her when he answered. "It was."

Davina followed them up to their room, unwilling to let the lads out of her sight. Something was very wrong. Had the men quarreled? Lost their way? And where was Somerled? Surely he'd not departed without bidding her farewell.

To her relief, Mrs. McAllister poured the steaming water into the bowl yet did not tarry. "If ye need oniething, I'll be doon the stair."

Davina helped her brothers remove their coats, then gave them room to bathe, dismayed to see them wincing in pain as they splashed hot water over their cuts and bruises. *Whatever has happened?* she asked them with her eyes, touching her lips with trembling fingers. *Speak to me.* When they did not respond at once, Davina tugged at their shirt sleeves, her desperation mounting. *Look at me. Please, for I can bear it no longer.*

At last her brothers turned to her. Their hands were dry, but their faces were wet with tears.

Her throat tightened. 'Twas even worse than she'd feared.

"Davina...oh, my dear sister." Will took her hands in his, squeezing them until they ached. "Sir Harry...fell."

Fell? Her eyes widened in shock.

"From the summit...," Sandy said, his voice breaking.

But did he…was he… As if by rote, she pulled one hand free to pat her forehead. *I don't understand.*

"Davina, he did not…survive the fall."

Nae. 'Tis not possible. She shook her head, slowly at first, then harder. *Not Somerled's father. Not Sir Harry.*

"We are so very sorry, lass."

The room began to spin. *He cannot be dead. Cannot, cannot.*

"Somerled tried to rescue him…" Will's voice was raw, painful to listen to. "He did everything he could, Davina."

"Everything." Sandy took her free hand, numb as it was. "Somerled was very brave."

"And he…" Will choked on a sob, then looked down at the floor.

He what? Davina tried to mouth the words but could not. She wrenched her hands from their grasp and pressed them to her brow. *What? Somerled what?*

They did not answer her. They could not look at her.

And then Davina understood. *He fell too.*

She sank to the floor. A faint groan, low and deep, came pouring forth like blood from a wound. *Not my betrothed. Not my Somerled. He cannot be dead.*

He had kissed her. That morning. And she had kissed him. That morning.

He cannot be gone. Davina began to rock back and forth. *Nae, nae, nae, he cannot.*

Will knelt beside her and gathered her in his arms. "Davina, you must believe me." The words sounded bruised, like his hands. "We tried to save Somerled. Truly, we did. We wanted him to live. We wanted him…for you."

For me, Somerled. You did this for me. Tears flowed from the well of her heart, from the place where sorrow had its source. *'Tis my fault. My fault completely. If not for me…oh, Somerled, if not for me…*

Sixty-Seven

See, sons, what things you are!
How quickly nature falls into revolt.
WILLIAM SHAKESPEARE

Jamie leaned forward on his borrowed mount, urging the mare on, even as he cast an eye to the darkening skies. The inn at Cladach was only a mile hence. Might he escape the coming storm?

One plump drop of rain hit his cheek, then another.

Pulling the brim of his hat more firmly over his brow, Jamie rode hard for the inn where his daughter waited for news: They would indeed sail in the morning. Home to Glentrool and to Leana, who would be shocked to learn their daughter was betrothed to a Highlander.

I had no choice, dear wife. She was already his.

The rain was slowly increasing by the time he reached the small settlement. Doors were still propped open, and folk stood about in twos and threes, engaged in their endless gossip. At the sight of him the cottagers bent their heads together, making no attempt to conceal their scorn or lower their voices.

Circulating among them was Mrs. McAllister, Cladach's leading purveyor of clack. Jamie would not miss her meddlesome ways or her thin mattresses or her thinner broth.

"Thar ye are, Mr. McKie!" Despite her girth, she hastened toward him with surprising speed, her visage more ominous than the clouds overhead. "Ye maun see tae yer family wi'oot delay." She waved toward the inn. "Mak nae mistake. 'Tis a tragedy what's come."

"My *family*?" Jamie had already dismounted and was running for the door, dragging his horse and the innkeeper with him. "Tell me what's happened, woman!"

Breathless, she managed a single sentence. "Sir Harry MacDonald *tummled* from the *heid* o' Goatfell and didna survive the *fa'*."

He stopped as if struck. "Sir Harry is…dead?"

"Aye." She dabbed at her moist brow with her apron. "MacDonald's son tried tae save him, they said."

Jamie stared at her. "Who told you this?"

"Aye, weel…" Her cheeks grew ruddy. "I *hearkened* near yer sons' door. From the landin' on the stair, ye ken."

Disgusted, he thrust the reins into her hands. "'Tis nothing but blether you're peddling. See it travels no further 'til I learn the truth." Fueled by anger, by grief, by fear, Jamie marched through the inn door and up the wooden stair, grinding his teeth when he turned on the landing and heard voices from above. *How dare the woman eavesdrop on my sons!*

Jamie took the rest of the steps two at a time, then knocked on the door out of habit before flinging it open. "Lads?" He found them pulling on their coats while the storm unleashed its fury on the slates above them. "Can it be true?"

The twins looked at each other, then at him. Their hands stilled, and their faces grew ashen. "You know?"

"Aye." He gestured toward the stair, then closed the door behind him. "Mrs. McAllister tarried on the landing and jaloused some of your conversation."

Sandy's shoulders sagged beneath his unbuttoned coat. "Goatfell was covered in clouds. We should ne'er have climbed it."

"Then why did you?" Jamie regretted his sharp tone; Sandy was clearly in enough pain. "Did Sir Harry insist upon it?"

"The four of us struggled to reach the summit," Will admitted. "Once there, 'twas difficult to find our bearing."

Jamie slowly nodded, imagining the harrowing scene. *Poor Sir Harry.* To have lost his life for no good reason. Somerled must be suffering as well, having witnessed his father's deadly fall. And Davina would be inconsolable.

His heart stopped at the realization. "Where is your sister?"

"We left her not a minute ago," Will said, "in her room down the stair, curled up on the bed. She is…" He paused, struggling to find the words. "Grieving. Terribly."

"And no wonder." Jamie shifted his weight, torn by his responsibilities. Davina needed him; so did his sons, who'd beheld a grisly sight. Mindful of the need for prudent action, Jamie pressed the twins harder than he liked. "I assume you've reported Sir Harry's death to the duke's steward."

Sandy was attempting to button his coat without much success. "We've told no one. Yet."

Jamie's hands went cold. "You were witness to a death and did not report it?"

"We've been on Arran only a few days," Will reminded him, "and didn't know where to turn."

His son's words chafed at his conscience. *I should have been here. Nae, I should have been on that mountain.*

Jamie leaned against the door with a weary sigh. "Finish dressing, for I must comfort your sister, then take you directly to Brodick castle. I met the steward on Monday, you ken. He also serves as Arran's justice of the peace. You'll be prepared to answer his questions, aye? About how Sir Harry fell?"

"Father…" Will bowed his head. "The news is far worse than that."

Jamie straightened, even as the hairs on his neck rose.

"When Sir Harry slid down the north side of Goatfell, Somerled tried to reach him and…fell…onto the rocks."

"Somerled is dead as well?" Horrified, Jamie stared at his sons. At their stubborn jaws and their averted gazes. "Did you do nothing to prevent this?"

"We tried to rescue Somerled," Sandy murmured at last.

"He slipped from our grasp, Father. I promise you, we did everything we could."

Jamie remembered another of Will's promises. *My anger will burn far longer than that.* Had his sons done the unthinkable?

Two strides and Jamie was face to face with them, his hands clenching their collars. "Tell me this was an accident and not an act of vengeance."

Will flinched when Jamie tightened his grip. "We did not murder them, Father."

"That is not what I asked you." Jamie shook them both, even as his heart began to break. "Did you deceive these men and then allow them to die?"

"We tried to rescue Somerled." The same answer from Sandy, which was no answer at all.

Jamie wanted to shout at them. Wanted to throttle them. He could do neither in a public inn, but he would not let go of them without knowing the truth. "Did you want these Highlanders dead? *Did* you?"

"We did." Will yanked free from his grasp and stepped back. "From the day we arrived on Arran. But we did not murder them. They fell. Both of them." His voice was ragged, as if scraped across granite, and his dark eyes shone like glass. "We could not save Sir Harry, because he was too far down the hillside. But we did everything possible to save Somerled. I risked my life—"

"He did," Sandy interjected. "Will climbed down and tried to reach him."

"But you did not succeed. You watched him die and his father before him." Jamie released his grip on Sandy, then backed away, clenching his fists in frustration. "What am I to do with you? Let the justice of the peace probe and question until he has enough evidence to hang you both? What will I say to your mother? And—God, help me—how will I comfort your sister? You have torn apart Davina's life. Twice."

"Please, Father." Will begged him with his eyes, with his hands, with his tears. "Help us do whatever must be done. To make things right."

Right? Did they think such a travesty could be mended with words? "Two men are dead because of you. Never forget that. You can be sure I will not." Jamie turned away with a groan, unclenching his hands, releasing some of his anger, if only for the moment. There was too much to be done. Too much to be explained. And a daughter who needed him.

"Make yourselves presentable," he ordered them, "while I attend to your sister. Do not tarry, for tongues are already wagging round Cladach."

Jamie did not remember walking down the stair, turning at the landing, reaching the entrance hall. Shock and disbelief numbed his mind, dulled his senses. *We did not murder them.* The men were nonetheless dead, and his sons were in some way responsible. *God forgive them.* No one in Scotland would be so merciful.

Standing before his daughter's door, he lifted his arm as if a sack of oats hung from his wrist, then knocked twice. "'Tis your father." Jamie gave her a moment to compose herself, then eased open the door of the small room with its single, flickering candle and rain-soaked windowpanes.

Davina was sitting on the side of her bed, her hair unkempt, her cheeks chapped from crying. The handkerchief Leana had embroidered for her was clutched in her hands.

Undone at the sight of her, Jamie simply held out his arms.

She leaped into them with a sob, knocking him back on his heels, then clung to his shoulders and buried her face in his chest.

My poor child. He held her for a long time, saying nothing. Smoothing back her tangled hair. Drying her tears, though they would not stop.

"I am sorry," he whispered at last. "So very sorry."

She touched the handkerchief to her heart again and again.

"Aye." Tears tightened round his words. "Somerled loved you very much."

Davina's features crumpled as she nodded her head.

Searching for some word of comfort, Jamie finally said, "I will take you home to your mother. Before the week is out, Lord willing." He could think of no greater solace to offer her. Leana would know what to do, what to say to help their daughter, an innocent young woman who'd lost her virtue and then her only hope of redeeming it. *God, help us. What is to be done?*

Footsteps in the hall, then a tapping at the door announced her brothers. Jamie gently stepped back, making sure she could stand on her own. "Forgive me, Davina, but I must take Will and Sandy to the castle. We've some business to attend to." He did not burden her with details. "I'll ask Mrs. McAllister to remain withindoors, should you need her, and will send for Reverend Stewart. We'll not be gone more than an hour."

When he guided Davina toward her bed, she did not protest but stretched out on the narrow mattress and let him slip off her shoes. He located a clean handkerchief in her valise and tucked it into her hand, then pressed a kiss to her freckled brow. "Rest if you can."

She nodded, though he was sure she would not sleep.

Jamie met his sons in the hall rather than usher them into her room. Who knew what fabrications they'd told Davina? Or how she felt toward them now? He would not upset her further. Time enough for reconciliation later. Davina, like her mother, had a great capacity for mercy. He did not.

Mrs. McAllister was hard at work scrubbing the floor in the far corner of her kitchen, her manner less vexing than usual as she stood to address them. The innkeeper agreed to look after Davina, then offered to take her a cup of tea.

"Better that she rest," Jamie told her, wanting to spare Davina the woman's ill-fashioned company. "We will be at the castle should we be needed. In the meantime, send a messenger to the Kilbride manse on my behalf." He wrote a terse note of explanation to Benjamin Stewart and sealed it firmly. Two hours earlier he'd galloped north after a pleasant visit with his cousin, never imagining how soon the minister's services would be needed.

With his note and a few coins in the innkeeper's hands, Jamie directed his sons toward the door. The sky had lightened considerably, and the rain was reduced to a fine mist as they strode uphill toward Brodick. "Choose your words with care," he warned the twins, keeping his voice low. "Mr. Hunter has a sharp eye and a keen mind. Speak the truth, yet take heed where your words might lead you."

"Father." Will had not met his gaze since they had left the inn. "Sandy and I made arrangements with a fishing boat sailing from Brodick quay at four o'clock. Might we still—"

"You may not," Jamie snapped. "Only guilty men flee. Unless you would brand yourselves as criminals, you'll remain on Arran until the justice of the peace deems you innocent."

Sandy's eyes grew round. "How long might that take, sir?"

"I cannot say." *Too long, I fear.* His own plans to sail in the morning were dashed as well. He'd at least see a letter placed on board, marked for Glentrool. Much as he dreaded committing the words to paper, Leana had to be informed of all that had transpired.

Your daughter lost her innocence and her betrothed. And your sons watched two men die.

Jamie was to blame for all of it; he could not pretend otherwise. Not with the gruesome evidence lying battered and broken on Arran's hills. And with a daughter, also battered and broken, watering her pillow with her tears.

The maidservant who met them at the castle door shrank back when she saw the twins. Mrs. McAllister's gossip had traveled quickly. "This way," she said in a shaky voice, directing them to Lewis Hunter's office on the ground floor. Had it been only two days since Jamie was there signing the marriage agreement?

"Gentlemen." The steward rose as they entered. He walked round a desk littered with papers as he removed the spectacles perched on his nose. "I've been expecting you."

"Pardon our delay," Jamie hastened to say. "I was riding home from the manse when my sons returned from their climb. They were distraught, of course—"

"Of course," Lewis Hunter said evenly.

"And being new to Arran, they did not know whom to tell or what to do concerning the accident on Goatfell."

"Then they are fortunate to have their father with them."

A man of perhaps fifty, Hunter still had most of his black hair, straight and thin as it was, and gray eyes that were ever alert. As justice of the peace, he was charged with trying minor civil cases and examining persons accused of serious crimes. Jamie prayed his sons would not fall beneath the man's talons, for they appeared very sharp indeed.

"Please be seated." Hunter pulled three chairs close together, then sat behind his oak desk, a silent reminder of his authority. "Mr. McKie, if you will allow your sons to answer my questions." He motioned to an efficient-looking young man across the room, who joined them at once, pen and ink at the ready. "My clerk will be taking notes, but do not let that alarm you. We simply need an accurate record of the day's events."

Hunter asked for their full names, which Will and Sandy provided. Jamie could tell the lads were nervous, but their confident postures and steady voices served them well. He sat back, resisting the urge to intervene for his sons as a barrage of questions were fired at them. Some were merely a request for information—the time of their departure, the ages of the climbers, the condition of their boots—but other inquiries were more pointed.

"In light of the heavy cloud cover, why did you not turn back?"

Will looked genuinely remorseful. "I wish we had, sir. When we approached the last six hundred feet, I asked the MacDonalds if they preferred to quit. Sir Harry in particular was quite winded. But he said, 'Quit? Indeed not.'" Will hung his head. "Then he shook his walking stick at me."

"Ah." The steward tented his hands, nodding. "I confess, in my brief acquaintance with the baronet on Monday morning, his pride was *kenspeckle,* as my mother used to say."

Jamie well knew the Scots word—*conspicuous*—but did not gloat over the observation. If pride alone could kill a man, he would have perished long before these sons of his were born.

As the questions grew more difficult, Will and Sandy did not make excuses for their behavior, nor did they incriminate themselves. Their facial expressions were open, their comments seemingly honest and sincere. Might they be innocent after all?

"I've already dispatched a party of men to retrieve the bodies," Hunter informed them. "Once I've determined the cause of their deaths and have ruled out foul play, you will be free to leave Arran. I assume that is your desire."

"At the earliest possible hour," Will confessed, looking at Sandy as he spoke. "My brother and I long to put this sad incident behind us and return to our studies in Edinburgh."

It was then Jamie realized what talented actors he had for sons. The twins had no desire to resume their education; they simply wanted to escape from Arran before Lewis Hunter deduced the ugly truth.

Sixty-Eight

Hope, withering, fled—
and Mercy sighed farewell.

GEORGE GORDON, LORD BYRON

Leana's first steps on the Isle of Arran were less than agile.
"Dinna fash yersel'," Ian said gently, guiding her along the coast
road, carrying their bulging valise. "By the time we reach the manse,
you'll be walking as gracefully as ever."

"I pray you are right." She carefully put one foot in front of the
other as they headed north from Lamlash harbor. Their packet boat
captain had spoken of passengers having "sea legs," which Ian had
quickly developed, as if born for sailing the main.

He'd arranged for everything, this capable son of hers. They had
reached Maybole yestreen, far sooner than anticipated, then sailed at
noontide from Ayr with the wind at their backs and a storm brewing
overhead. Last hour's drenching rain was the only disappointment of
their journey.

Leana shook out her wet skirts as they walked, starting to regain her
balance. Would they find Jamie and Davina at the manse? Or at Brodick castle with the MacDonalds? She and Ian were not expected—not
by the Stewarts and certainly not by her husband and daughter. "I do
hope our visit will be a welcome surprise," she murmured, "and not an
imposition."

"You could never impose on anyone," Ian assured her, then gestured to the right. "This way. Past the old kirkyard, the captain said."

When Leana glimpsed a tidy garden to the rear of the manse, her
apprehension eased; Elspeth Stewart was a kindred spirit.

A black-haired maidservant answered their knock, agape when she
saw Ian. "Ye maun be the son o' Mr. McKie! I've niver seen a lad wha
mair favored his faither."

Ian smiled down at her. "You've a good eye, lass. Are the Stewarts at home?"

"Mrs. Stewart is, aye. She'll be pleased tae see ye baith." The maid ushered them in, eying Leana all the while. "Ye're Mrs. McKie, I jalouse."

"I am." Leana held her dripping hem away from the hall furnishings. "Might my husband be here? Or my daughter, Davina?"

"Nae, mem." Her cheeks took on a rosy hue. "They're at the inn at Cladach. And here comes Mrs. Stewart tae greet ye." The maidservant dipped a brief curtsy and was gone.

"Can this be Cousin Jamie's wife and son?" When Leana nodded, Elspeth Stewart let out a happy cry, then drew them into the parlor. "Finally we meet! Oh, but do change your gown at once, Mrs. McKie, for I'll not have you catching cold. Betty will escort you to our bedroom."

Leana descended the stair a few moments later, grateful to have freshly combed hair and dry linen against her skin. Ian had donned another coat and was comfortably settled in an upholstered chair. By the look on his face, Elspeth had not ceased talking since they'd arrived.

"Your husband was here this very morning," Elspeth explained, "making arrangements to...oh!" Her eyes widened. "Thank heavens you did not sail a day later, or you would have missed them altogether." She fluttered her hands round her face as if quite shaken by the notion. "You'll want to meet the MacDonalds, I trow."

Leana nodded. They'd been right to come after all, and none too soon. "Betty mentioned that my husband and daughter were staying at...an inn?"

"Did she?" Elspeth frowned in the direction of the kitchen. "You must think me a poor hostess. But after the Fullartons..." She cleared her throat. "Well, the inn at Cladach is much closer to Brodick and..."

After an awkward pause, Ian asked her, "Are the MacDonalds lodging at the inn as well?"

"Nae!" Elspeth looked startled at the suggestion. "They're guests of His Grace at the castle. 'Tis all a bit...complicated." Never had a woman looked happier to see a tea tray arrive. "Look, here's Mrs. McCurdy's shortbread to tempt you."

"Many thanks," Leana murmured, trying to collect her thoughts.

Complicated. Jamie would explain things, of course. But it was disconcerting to know so little. "Your household is rather quiet, Elspeth. I'd hoped to meet Cousin Benjamin. And your daughters…"

"Dear me, the lasses are with their father, visiting Mrs. McCook at Kingscross." Elspeth looked most disappointed. "They're to return at four. Can you not tarry 'til then?"

Leana put aside her empty cup, then caught Ian's eye. "Pardon us, but we're anxious to see Mr. McKie and Davina. Might you point the way to their lodging house?"

Elspeth sighed, as if resigning herself to their hasty departure. "You'll need to borrow our horse, for 'tis five miles north o'er a steep hill."

Moments later Leana was seated on Grian's sturdy back, their valise strapped behind her, while Ian led the horse on foot, headed toward Cladach. Davina's letters had aptly described Arran's majestic hills. But it was her daughter and husband Leana longed to see most.

"What do you make of it all?" Ian asked, turning to look up at her. "Our cousin was hardly forthcoming."

"Nae," Leana agreed, "yet had Somerled's wedding plans fallen apart, Elspeth would not have suggested meeting the MacDonalds."

"Some comfort there."

For two days she'd imagined the bloom of love on Davina's face: her freckled blush, her elfin smile, her twinkling eyes. *My sweet daughter. I do hope you are happy.* Leana would have her answer soon.

A scruffy lad riding a piebald pony slowed at their approach, wearing a mystified look on his face. "Is that not Reverend Stewart's horse?"

"'Tis." Ian smiled at the boy. "Borrowed with Mrs. Stewart's permission."

"Weel…" He held up a letter, folded and sealed. "I'm tae deliver a message tae him."

"He's not home at present but due shortly," Ian told him, then tugged their mount forward as the lad rode off, frowning to himself. Ian glanced over his shoulder. "Whatever the tidings, I pray the minister won't miss his horse."

Brodick Bay came into view, the water as gray as the sky. Yet the shoreline boasted a pleasing curve, and the mountain that dominated the scene was impressive. *Goatfell,* Davina had called it in one of her letters. *A grand giant of a hill.* Elspeth's directions were quite detailed, bringing them round the wide bay to a small settlement and its slate-roofed inn.

When a large woman with a scowling countenance answered their knock, Leana tried not to peer round her shoulder. "Good day to you, madam. I believe my husband and daughter are lodging here."

"Aye." The woman's eyes narrowed. "Along wi' yer sons."

Confused, Leana gestured toward Ian. "This is my son, aye."

"I mean the lads ludgin here. The twins. Are ye not their mither as weel?"

"I…" Leana's voice faltered. "I…am." *William. Alexander.* Whatever were her sons doing on Arran? And where was Davina?

"Mrs. McAllister's me nem," the woman said, motioning them inside. "Yer man and the lads are gone tae the castle. Yer dochter's in her room, thar at the foot o' the stair…"

Leana hurried past the innkeeper, her gaze fixed on Davina's door. "In here, you say?" Two taps, the slightest of pauses, and Leana opened the door. "Dearie? 'Tis your mother. And Ian."

Standing behind her on the threshold, he touched her elbow. "Mother, let me press on to the castle and see about Father. And the twins."

Leana was torn, needing to be in two places at once. "Davina will want to see you," she whispered.

"She'll want to see you more. Lord willing, I'll not be long." He nudged her inside, then softly closed the door.

Leana blinked, letting her eyes adjust to the dimly lit room where her daughter lay sleeping. Images came into focus: spare furnishings; one candle, nearly spent; an oft-mended curtain; Davina's fiddle on the dresser. Tiptoeing across the rough pine floor, Leana flattened her hand to her heart as if that might calm its frantic pace.

Oh my sweet child. She knelt beside the bed, hesitant to wake her daughter yet longing to see her face, hidden in the folds of her pillow. She smoothed her hand over Davina's hair, barely touching the loosened strands, then brushed a single finger across her cheek. How raw her skin felt! Had she been crying? When she realized the pillow was damp, Leana sat back on her heels in dismay. *Whatever has happened? Is this why your brothers are here?*

Her daughter's eyes fluttered open, unfocused for a moment until their gazes met. *Mother.* She saw the word on her lips, formed but not spoken.

"Aye, lass." Leana smiled, tears pooling in her eyes.

Davina held out her arms, welcoming her embrace.

"Precious one," Leana murmured, pressing their cheeks together, holding her as tightly as she dared. "How warm you are! I hated to wake you…"

Davina held her closer still.

At last Leana eased her daughter back onto the bed, then sat beside her and clasped her hands, relieved to feel those delicate fingers inside hers once more. "Ian and I have both come," she began, certain the news would please her. "He left for Brodick castle to find your father. And the twins."

The flicker of light in Davina's eyes went out, as if a sharp wind had blown through the room. She stared dully at her shoes, abandoned beside the bed; the hands inside Leana's grew cool.

Praying for wisdom, Leana veered in a different direction. "Davina, I have…so many questions. Why you're no longer staying with the Stewarts nor with the Fullartons. Why the twins have come to Arran. But 'tis only fair you know first why *we* have come." Leana pulled two letters from her reticule, touching them to her heart with affection. "I've read these many times on our journey. Now 'tis your turn, for I know their words will mean more to you than to anyone."

She presented her with Sir Harry's letter first, astonished to find Davina's hands trembling as she unfolded it. Did she not guess its contents and know the words were heartsome?

From the moment she began reading, fresh tears rolled down the girl's cheeks. Davina brushed them away, but they would not stop. She held the letter upright, as if to avoid smearing the ink, and still she wept. When Leana tried to retrieve the letter, fearing she'd done more harm than good in sharing it, Davina turned away, gripping the paper.

Surely Sir Harry's recommendation of marriage was not news to her?

When Davina finished reading, she folded the letter with utmost care, rubbing her fingers across the broken seal before slipping the letter beneath her pillow. She eyed the second letter with obvious trepidation, which Leana now shared.

"Perhaps I might save this for another time. When you are stronger."

Davina plucked the letter from her hand, then held it to her heart, eyes closed, her lips forming a single word. *Somerled.*

"Aye, 'tis from Somerled. Are you certain…"

Davina already had it open. Whether she'd read one sentence or the whole of it, Leana could not tell, but she'd read enough. Davina collapsed on top of the letter with an expression of anguish so profound, Leana's own heart broke.

"Davina! Please, can you not tell me what has happened?" Distressed, Leana looked about the room for Davina's sketchbook, hating to leave her side yet desperate to help her.

Then she heard voices in the hall, each one of them dear to her.

Jamie. He would tell her what she needed to know.

Leana draped herself round Davina like a blanket, comforting her, protecting her, as the four men in her life walked into the room, filling it with their presence.

Jamie was beside her first, kissing her brow. "I'm glad that you came," he said softly. "Your daughter needs you."

Leana nodded, too overcome to speak.

The twins knelt to look at her as well, their faces stark with pain.

"Mother…," Sandy began but could not continue.

"We need you too," Will said, shocking her with such an admission.

As her family gathered round her, Leana clung to her daughter, giving Davina every bit of strength she possessed. When Ian rested his hand on her shoulder, offering his support, Leana laid her cheek upon it, catching his father's gaze.

Jamie. She implored him with her eyes, praying he might explain all she did not know.

He rose to his feet, slowly pulling her up with him. "Ian can comfort his sister for a moment," he said, leading her toward the door. "We must speak, Mrs. McKie. In private."

Once she saw Davina well ensconced in her brother's arms, Leana followed Jamie across the hall. His room was a mirror of Davina's and every bit as gloomy. As there was only one chair, they stood near the window so they might see each other's faces.

"Ian told me about the letters from Sir Harry and Somerled," he began, his voice low, as if someone were pressing an ear to the door.

"Alas, I let Davina read them," Leana confessed. "As you saw, they upset her greatly. Are she and Somerled not to marry after all?"

Jamie's gaze met hers. "There was an accident on Goatfell this morning. The twins went climbing with the MacDonalds. When they reached the summit, both of the Highlanders...fell."

Leana felt as if she were standing on the packet boat once more, the boards beneath her feet unsteady, the horizon ever swaying. "They've been injured?"

"Nae." Jamie swallowed. "They've been killed."

She closed her eyes, shutting out the pain—not her own but Davina's. *It cannot be. Must not be.*

Jamie caught her by the elbows, holding her steady. "Now you know why 'tis good you've come."

"Aye." Leana opened her eyes, remembering Somerled's words. *My very soul has cleaved to your daughter.* "Did he truly love her?"

"I believe he did."

"Oh, Jamie..." She sank against him, grateful when he circled his arms round her. "I cannot fathom her pain."

After a long pause he said, "Her suffering goes deeper still." Jamie sought her gaze once more, then held it. "Though Somerled was honorable in pursuing her hand in marriage, he...dishonored her at the start."

"You mean when he accompanied her...when they played together?"

"Nae, Leana."

She looked away, frightened by what she saw in his eyes. But still he said the words.

"I mean when he violated her."

Leana shook her head, as if she might dislodge the dreadful image of a man forcing himself upon a woman. Upon Davina. Their innocent daughter.

"Nae," she insisted. Somerled's letter was too loving. His words were too kind. " 'Tis not true," she said firmly, though tears were already gathering in her eyes.

"Leana, listen to me…"

She tried to pull away from him. Needing to breathe, needing to run, needing to scream. *Not…our…daughter!* Her words came out in broken pieces. "He cannot…he cannot have done that. Not to Davina."

"I'm afraid he did. On Midsummer Eve…"

Leana touched his mouth, stopping his words. But she could not stop the memory of a June evening alone at Glentrool. A breathless letter from her daughter. A request for prayer…

" 'Tis all my fault." She struggled free from his embrace. "Davina needed her mother that night…and I was…not here…"

Jamie held on to her arm. "None of us were here, Leana. That is my fault, not yours."

"Nae!" she cried, refusing to listen. "I should have been here. To… help her…to…"

"Leana, do not torture yourself."

She looked at him through a blur of tears. "How can I not?" *Forgive me, Davina. Please, please forgive me.* "Don't you see? She needed me here. She needed her mother."

"She still does." Jamie gently released her, then brushed away her tears. "Go to her, Leana. 'Tis never too late."

Sixty-Nine

Whene'er I meet my mither's e'e,
My tears rin down like rain.
ROBERT BURNS

Davina heard her mother's footsteps in the hall. Heard her open the door and send the lads off with their father to dine on plates of barley broth. Heard her close the door and tiptoe across the room, the silence as palpable as the mist that followed the day's rainstorm.

Please, Mother. She held her breath, stifling her pain. *Help me.*

"My darling daughter." Leana quietly drew a chair next to her bed, then smoothed her hand across her brow. "I love you so."

Davina had cried more tears that day than all the days before. But still the well had not run dry. With a sigh she let them fall, trailing across her cheeks and onto her bed linens. She touched her heart and then her mother's. *I love you too.*

Leana clasped Davina's hand, holding it tight as she inched her chair closer to the bed. "Your father shared some things with me...I did not know."

Poor Mother. Davina squeezed her hand a little. There was so much she had not told her. Could not tell her. Not in a letter.

"When I arrived, I did not realize...I had not heard about the accident. I am so sorry, Davina." She brushed a kiss across her fingers. "So very sorry."

Slipping her other hand beneath the pillow, Davina felt the two posts hiding there. Too painful to read now but in the months to come, salve for her wounds.

"Your father also told me about Midsummer Eve." Leana began to stroke her hair, speaking so softly Davina had to strain to hear her. "How terrible for you. To be here alone. To endure such a thing. And then have no one to console you."

She trembled beneath her mother's touch, undone by her sympathy.

Leana leaned closer, her voice breaking. "I am here now, dearest. Come, let me hold you."

Davina lifted her arms as her mother drew her onto her lap. She no longer fit there, but it did not matter. Her mother smelled of lavender and rain, like the gardens of Glentrool. Like home. Wrapping her arms round her neck, Davina rested her cheek against her mother's breast and wept.

In the quiet stillness, the only words she needed were the ones she remembered from long ago. *Come unto me…and I will give you rest.*

She could not guess the hour. Was it still Wednesday? So much had happened, all of it painful. Her body was in pain too, and she dreaded discovering the reason. But it could not be postponed. Davina sat up, meeting her mother's gaze, then pointed to the chamber pot beneath the bed.

"Of course," Leana murmured, helping her stand. She crossed the room to gaze out the window and give her daughter a moment's privacy.

Just as Davina had suspected, her courses had begun.

Guilt pressed down on her. Had she not prayed for this on Midsummer Day? *Please, Lord. Not a child. Not his child.* Yet here she was a fortnight later, clinging to one hope, like a thread pulled taut between life and death. *Let me bear his child and redeem his name.* Aye, and assuage her guilt, if only a little.

But, nae. No child was nestled in her womb.

As she attended to her needs, Davina had difficulty concealing the evidence from her mother.

"Oh, lass." Leana dried her tears, then discreetly slipped the chamber pot out of sight. "Whether you're disappointed or relieved, I'll not judge you for either. Not after all you've been through." Her mother kissed her cheek, then drew her close. "Children are a gift of God in any circumstance. But if 'tis not to be, then that is from God's hand as well."

They sighed as one.

Two taps at the door, and Ian was in the room with them, bearing a cup of tea. "I thought you might have need of this."

Davina took his offering, embarrassed when the teacup clattered in her hands.

Leana placed it on the table for her, then reached inside her reticule. "Perhaps this will bring a wee bit of comfort." She pulled out a lumpy napkin and unwrapped its contents. "Shortbread from the manse."

Davina sat down on the chair rather abruptly, bumping the table and nearly spilling her tea. Had she ever known such heartache? Yet here were the people she loved most, offering what they could to encourage her. A fragrant cup of tea. Mrs. McCurdy's shortbread. She consumed them both, surprised she could even swallow, while her mother and Ian exchanged vital news.

Assuming Reverend Stewart was able to borrow a mount, he was expected shortly. The family would gather for prayer and retire early, building their strength for the difficult day ahead. At noon they were to meet with the justice of the peace, a gentleman named Lewis Hunter.

The thought of it all made Davina slump in her chair, pressing the empty teacup into her mother's waiting hands. Tomorrow she would have her sketchbook and pencil ready. To answer questions and to ask them. To make very sure the truth was known and Somerled's memory honored.

"The men have had supper." Leana inclined her head toward the kitchen. "Would you like something else to eat? Barley broth? Bannocks and cheese?"

Davina waved away even the mention of more food. She pressed her hands together, then placed them beside her cheek.

"A wise choice, Davina." Leana shook out her bedcovers, then smoothed them in place. "'Tis the best remedy for sorrow. 'For so he giveth his beloved sleep.'" She turned over Davina's pillow, careful not to disturb the letters beneath it. "Ian, 'tis time we gave your sister an hour's peace."

"Aye." Ian leaned down as she stretched out on the bed. "And if you're still resting when 'tis time to pray, I will pray on your behalf." He brushed a kiss across her forehead. "Sleep well, my sister."

Davina watched them leave, her eyes drifting shut as the door latched closed.

Blessed silence. But not for long.

In the recesses of her heart an imaginary bow was drawn across the strings of a violoncello. She responded at once, pressing her unseen fiddle against her shoulder to join him in a lament. Hearing every note he played. Feeling every breath he took. Regretting every day she would live without him.

Seventy

Davina bowed her head, disheartened to find herself sitting once more in the room at the top of the turnpike stair in the oldest part of Brodick castle. The room where Somerled had offered all he owned in exchange for her hand in marriage. *Whatever you say, I shall give.*

He could not have imagined what his love would cost. *Everything.*

"Miss McKie?" Lewis Hunter's voice forced her to look up. He knew of her impediment and so did not press for a verbal response. "Pardon me for asking you to join us. You have my sincerest sympathy. Alas, 'tis imperative that I have the entire McKie family present for this formal inquiry."

She acknowledged him with a slight nod, then looked across the table at the twins, sitting in the same chairs they'd occupied on Monday and wearing the same clothing. Her father as well. Ian was by her side, as Somerled had been, and her mother to her right. Mr. Hunter did not begin to fill Sir Harry's seat, though that was the chair he'd claimed at the head of the table.

"You should know that Lady MacDonald was informed of their deaths sometime overnight. When our messenger returns, we shall ascertain her wishes concerning her family members' remains."

Davina's heart sank at the thought of this woman she had never met answering her door in the dark of night, learning the worst news of her life. Her dear husband. Her only son.

"And now, if you will, Peter." Mr. Hunter gestured to his clerk, who occupied a small desk in the corner. "At twelve twenty on Thursday, the seventh of July, a formal inquiry commenced regarding the deaths of Sir Harry MacDonald and Somerled MacDonald." The steward listed those present, carefully spelling out each name for the record. "I will direct my questions primarily to William and Alexander, though I may call upon their father or Miss McKie for verification of certain facts. Mrs. McKie, you and your eldest son are welcome to offer silent support but no other."

Leana responded, "Then I am free to pray."

"You are indeed. Man's laws are no more than a fumbling attempt to make God's laws sovereign. 'Thy will be done.' As justice of the peace, that is ever my prayer, Mrs. McKie."

"And mine," she murmured. "Let thy mercy, O LORD, be upon us."

Mr. Hunter cleared his throat. "I shall begin with the results of our medical examination of the deceased, the bodies having been recovered with some difficulty early last evening."

Davina stared at her hands, fearing she might be sick. *The deceased. The bodies.* No longer Sir Harry and Somerled. *Sown in dishonor. Raised in glory.* She would cling to that promise and remember them as they were. Strong men with stout hearts.

After shuffling his papers, Mr. Hunter found what he was looking for. "The duke's surgeon conducted the inspection of the bodies. His report indicates he found no evidence of foul play."

The room seemed to exhale, the red sandstone walls expanding and contracting with their collective relief. Oddly, Will and Sandy showed little reaction to the news, though of course they already knew foul play was not involved. Vengeful as the twins might be, they were not murderers. Not the brothers who'd doted on her from the time they were children.

"Furthermore," Mr. Hunter continued, "we have determined that no weapons were employed, neither blunt nor sharp, and no bullet wounds were found. Their injuries suggest a struggle only with the mountain itself." He paused, as if considering whether to elaborate. The paper before him clearly listed further details.

Davina pleaded with her eyes. *No more. Please.*

Though he did not look up, the steward honored her wishes nonetheless, moving to the next item. "Since both MacDonald men were older and physically larger than the McKies, it is unlikely that

William and Alexander could have overpowered them. We also found no indication of a scuffle having taken place on the summit. No torn bits of clothing, freshly scraped rocks, or traces of blood."

Davina had barely come to terms with Somerled's being gone from her life. She had not yet begun to think of him as truly dead. But she could not bear to envision him dying. Crying out in pain. Injured, bleeding. Fighting for his life and losing. *Nae, nae.* A tear slipped down her cheek. *I pray it was swift. O Father, I pray you were with him.*

Beneath the table an embroidered handkerchief was placed in her lap.

"I have reviewed the many questions posed yesterday, gentlemen, and am satisfied with your answers. For the record, William, please state once more the exact sequence of events that led to both deaths."

Will squared his shoulders as if preparing for battle. "While standing on the cloud-covered summit of Goatfell, Sir Harry MacDonald inadvertently stumbled over the western precipice, falling several feet beyond our reach. His son, Somerled MacDonald, made his way down the slope in a valiant attempt to save his father. Unfortunately, Sir Harry slid farther down the steep hillside and was lost to us. Since he'd grasped his son's boot in the process, Somerled's safety was compromised as well. My brother and I climbed down on either side of Somerled and did everything in our power to reach him. To save him."

"You wanted him alive."

"Very much, sir. For our sister's sake. And for his."

"Almost the very words we recorded yesterday," Mr. Hunter murmured. "Either you are well rehearsed, or 'tis the truth."

"You may depend upon it, sir," Will said evenly. "I did not rehearse my testimony."

"As it happens, we found a piece of your brown woolen coat, snagged by the granite, in the very place this rescue attempt of yours was said to have occurred. 'Twas quite far down. You took a great risk, William."

" 'Tis a difficult thing, sir, to watch a man die."

"I am sure that is true."

Davina had not considered the grim scenes that must haunt Will and Sandy. Hearing the men's desperate cries. Watching their torment. *My dear brothers.* She would pray for their peace of mind.

"There is one final matter that concerns me." Mr. Hunter leaned back in his chair. "The marriage agreement prepared in this office on Monday states that, upon the death of both Sir Harry and his heir, all but a small portion of the MacDonald fortune is to be awarded to Miss McKie."

Her mouth fell open in dismay, only now remembering the terms of their agreement. And Somerled's offhand remark. *After all, it will cost us nothing. Unless we die.*

Mr. Hunter pointed his knife-sharp gaze at her brothers. "All our current evidence notwithstanding, such an agreement, newly signed, provides a strong motive for murder."

Davina stared at him in horror. *Nae!* Her brothers loved her. They could never have…not possibly…

"But 'tis our sister who is the beneficiary," Will reminded him, his voice cool. "My brother and I had no incentive whatsoever to kill these men."

"Unless Miss McKie promised to divide the spoils with you."

Will's eyes narrowed. "My sister is not capable of such a devious plot."

"I am not suggesting that it was her idea."

Only half listening, Davina wrote furiously across the page of her sketchbook. *I do not want or need the MacDonald fortune. See that Lady MacDonald retains the whole of it.* Satisfied, she presented her sketchbook to the steward, certain her bold statement would put their discussion to an end. There could be no motive for murder if there was no reward.

Mr. Hunter read her words, then peered at her over his spectacles. "I am afraid 'tis not so simple as this, Miss McKie. The wishes of Sir Harry and his son were clearly stated: You are the sole beneficiary of the MacDonald holdings. Those rights were irrevocably assigned to you by the deceased."

Davina turned to her father. Though he had not officially been called upon, perhaps he might come to her defense. *Please, Father. Say something.*

He did not disappoint her. "Surely the law would allow my daughter to accept and then reassign these same holdings to Lady MacDonald."

Mr. Hunter pursed his lips. "While such generosity is admirable, if you mean for it to resolve the problem of an obvious motive for William and Alexander to commit murder, I am afraid you have not persuaded me."

Davina reached for Ian's hand, at a loss for what else she might do to convince Mr. Hunter their twin brothers were innocent.

The steward looked down the table, folding his hands over his notes. "Now I have a question for you, Mr. McKie, regarding this unusual marriage agreement. 'Tis uncommon enough to name a wife as sole beneficiary, entrusting her to provide for her offspring rather than allowing one's heir to inherit his fortune directly. But to visit such riches upon a young woman to whom a gentleman is merely betrothed"—he spread out his hands—" 'tis unprecedented. In light of that, I am curious to know if Sir Harry made such an offer of his own volition. Or was it someone else's suggestion to pursue such a course?"

Davina knew the answer. *The twins.* She had watched them huddling in the corner that day. Had seen her father shake his head, even as Will shook his finger. Recalled Will saying to her father at the table, "We agreed on this." But Will had presented the idea. Not her father.

Would Jamie say as much? Build a gallows for his sons with mere words, however truthful?

Her father hesitated only a moment. " 'Twas my idea."

"Oh?" Mr. Hunter's black brows arched. "Then if I may ask, why were you so eager to see your daughter provided for, even before her wedding day? You are a wealthy gentleman in your own right, Mr. McKie. Was there some concern that has not been voiced here?"

Davina quietly retrieved her sketchbook. And prepared her heart.

If her father confessed that Somerled had violated her, Mr. Hunter would have an even stronger motive for murder at his disposal. Not only greed but also revenge.

So she wrote the words herself. And spared her father the dilemma.

I am no longer a maid. We were allowing for the possibility of a child.

Her mother gasped when she read the words over her shoulder, but Davina resolutely placed her sketchbook in Mr. Hunter's hands. She did not care what the man thought of her. If her words—truly written— saved the twins, her pride was well sacrificed.

Mr. Hunter did not tarry over her confession. "I see. Well." He pushed her book away with a faint look of disgust. "That explains your need for haste. If the agreement was your father's suggestion, and he was at the manse at the time of the accident, he can hardly be implicated, nor does he stand to gain from the deaths of these good men. As to your own gain, Miss McKie, I leave that up to you."

I have gained nothing. I have lost everything.

Davina closed her sketchbook, grateful he had not glanced through the other pages. She, too, had recorded the truth.

A sudden knock at the door made them all jump.

Mr. Hunter bade the person enter: a kintra man of thirty-odd years. His clothes looked slept in, his chin needed shaving, and his eyes were bloodshot from lack of sleep.

"I'm jist back from Argyll and thocht ye'd want tae hear the news wi'oot delay." When the steward nodded for him to proceed, the man shuffled from one foot to the other as he told his sad tale. "I found Leddy MacDonald at hame. 'Twas four in the mornin', and the sun weel up, though I fear I stirred the puir woman from her sleep." He hung his head. "She did greet for a lang time, and I canna say I blame her. She asked tae have their kists delivered tae her hoose in Argyll and for a piper tae *fallow* them from Brodick castle tae her door." He shrugged. "'Tis not me place tae say, but it seems a fair request."

"We'll take care of things, Fergus." Mr. Hunter stood, ending the inquiry. "Ladies and gentlemen, I must attend to these details on behalf of Lady MacDonald. Miss McKie, do you have any desire to see your betrothed before…"

Nae. Davina pressed her hand to her mouth, imagining his broken body, then shook her head.

"In that case, you and your family are free to return to the inn. You are not at liberty, however, to leave Arran. Not until I review my records on this case and make a final decision on whether or not the deaths were accidental."

Jamie stood as well. "Might I ask when that will be, sir?"

Mr. Hunter's gray eyes bore no hint of his verdict. "You shall have my ruling in the morning."

Seventy-One

Could he with reason murmur at his case,
Himself sole author of his own disgrace?

WILLIAM COWPER

C ousin, will you not sit and have some breakfast?"
Jamie did not object to Benjamin Stewart's company or Mrs.
McAllister's tea; he simply could not remain seated for very long without bolting to his feet to pace the floor. The justice of the peace had promised an answer by morning. *'Tis morning, sir.* How much longer would the man make them wait? Perhaps Lewis Hunter took delight in making the accused suffer. Or perhaps he had no notion of the misery he inflicted.

Whatever the official verdict, Jamie did not doubt for a moment the twins' guilt.

His wife and daughter both refused to consider the possibility. Ian was a gracie lad, like his mother, and slow to find fault. But Jamie knew the twins were fashioned out of the same black cloth God had used to make him. Thievery and deception were woven through his past; the same threads ran through the fabric of his brutish sons.

Forgive them, Father, even as you have forgiven me.

But until the twins sought God's forgiveness, until they repented and were divinely changed, Jamie could do nothing but look in the mirror and heap their guilt on his own shoulders.

"Good morning," Leana said softly, joining them at table. The shadows beneath her eyes belied her greeting; she had not slept well. None of them had, judging by the bleariness in Ian's gaze, the tenderness round Davina's eyes, the slump in Benjamin's shoulders.

The twins had yet to make an appearance. According to Ian, they were still in their beds. Sleeping soundly, no doubt, and proud of themselves for avenging their sister. Their lies made Jamie grind his teeth, yet he'd spoken a falsehood in order to protect them. *"'Twas my idea."* He deserved such sons.

While Jamie sat in troubled silence, the others spoke quietly round the table. Remarking on the weather, which was cloudy and warm. Commenting on the porridge, served with fresh cream. Safe, comforting words on an uncertain morning.

High above Cladach a lone piper's drone floated down from Brodick castle.

Davina's porridge spoon stilled. The sadness in her eyes was beyond bearing.

Jamie offered her his hand, and she took it, though her attention remained fixed on the kitchen window and the unseen funeral procession slowly moving their direction.

Yestreen Davina had pleaded with them to let her follow the kists along the coast road, bargaining with her parents on paper. *Just to Sannox Bay? Then only to Corrie?*

Leana had finally persuaded Davina that her mourning was best done in private. "The inclusion of a McKie in the funeral procession might compound Lady MacDonald's grief when she learns of it," was his wife's gentle reasoning. In truth, the McKies had become anathema on Arran. People avoided them on the street, looked the other way if they walked by, threw a litany of words at them in passing. *Ill-deedie. Meschant. Wickit.* However Mr. Hunter ruled, the folk of Arran had deemed the family guilty of murder, fornication, deceit, and a host of lesser sins.

As the minutes passed, the procession drew closer. The tune was appropriately mournful and skillfully played. When the piper reached Cladach, Davina pushed back her chair, beseeching her parents as she pointed to the door, then to her eyes. *Just to the front door? Just to see them pass?*

Jamie could not refuse his grieving daughter. "Aye, aye. But only to the threshold."

Leana stood at the open front door with her arm round Davina's waist as the notes from the chanter filtered through the entrance hall. Jamie watched from the kitchen doorway until his resistance wore thin, then joined his wife and daughter, with Ian and Benjamin not far behind.

Plain coffins made of pine and covered with black *mort-cloths* were balanced on the shoulders of six men in service to the duke. Another half-dozen men walked behind them, ready to take their turns when backs grew sore on the long climb to Lochranza harbor, since custom did not allow kists to travel on wheeled conveyances. The piper, kilted in a length of faded tartan, brought up the rear, walking with a steady, solemn gait as he played a lament to honor the dead.

Silent as ever, Davina slipped down the hall to her room. She returned a moment later with her fiddle and cradled the instrument against her heart as she watched her betrothed make his last journey home.

The funeral party turned north on the coast road and disappeared from sight not far beyond the quay as the piper's notes lingered in the moist air. Gazing off in the distance, Jamie did not see Lewis Hunter until he was nearly at their door.

"A sad picture," the duke's steward said, eying Davina in particular. "Might I come in?"

The knot of people at the threshold quickly unraveled. Jamie directed Hunter toward his room—an unsuitable meeting place but the only one at their disposal—then sent Ian for the twins. He ushered the rest of them into his cramped quarters, his patience sorely tested as they waited to hear the verdict.

When the twins arrived, hastily dressed and unshaven, Jamie begged for Hunter's indulgence and prayed the man had sons.

"I'll not keep you waiting this morning," the steward began. "You've no doubt agonized enough. After a thorough review of the facts in hand, I have ruled the deaths of Sir Harry and Somerled MacDonald accidental."

Relief and guilt washed over Jamie in tandem. Two men were dead, yet his sons lived. It was not God's justice; it could only be man's mercy. And his own unwillingness to convict them.

No one shared his dilemma, it seemed; round the room all were smiling. Leana kissed Sandy's brow as Davina buried herself in Will's embrace, though he freed one hand long enough to extend it to Hunter.

Despite his rough appearance, Will at least sounded respectable. "We are both in your debt, sir."

The justice of the peace removed his spectacles and polished them on his sleeve. "In truth, this is not the first incident of summer visitors perishing in ill weather. 'Tis a risk all men assume when they take to the hills."

Benjamin offered a grave nod, looking properly ministerial. "The hand of the LORD was heavy upon them."

His words from the Buik took Jamie aback. Did his cousin think the MacDonalds deserved to die so brutally? 'Twas hard to see the hand of the Almighty when the hands of Will and Sandy loomed far closer.

"You and your family are free to sail to the mainland," Hunter was saying. "I'd encourage you to take advantage of this morning's auspicious winds."

Jamie heard what was not said: *Go at once. Your family is no longer welcome.* He would heed the man's advice, much as it rankled.

Hunter took his leave a moment later, as if to facilitate their swift departure. "I'm certain Reverend Stewart can make your arrangements. The forenoon packet boat sails from Brodick quay, mere steps from the inn. I wish you all a safe passage." With a tip of his hat, Lewis Hunter was gone.

Benjamin followed him out the door, intent on his duties, while the McKies commenced with a hurried hour of dressing and packing. Leana calmly oversaw her family's efforts, while Jamie settled their account with the innkeeper. Mrs. McAllister's tally of their expenses, scribbled on a half sheet of paper, was offered with a smug expression. To her credit, she held her tongue. Jamie imagined she wanted his silver more than she wanted to dismiss her lodgers with a caustic word.

"I'm most obliged, sir," she said, dropping his coins into her deep apron pocket.

No sooner had Jamie lightened his purse than Benjamin returned from the bay with unfortunate news. "We've a problem with the packet boat captain." As the two men stood in the entrance hall, doors opening and closing all round, Benjamin explained, " 'Tis a Friday, which sailors consider unchancie enough. But to include women among his passengers and two young men whose moral character is in question…" The minister sighed, shaking his head. "I'm afraid the crossing to the mainland will cost you dearly."

Jamie paled at the sum but could not argue.

"Forgive me," his cousin said, accepting the coins. "I did what I could to bargain with the man. At least the weather appears favorable. And you'll be the *Isabella*'s only passengers." Benjamin colored when he said it; 'twas likely no one else had agreed to sail with them. "May I carry your bags to the quay? You're to embark at half past eleven."

Jamie checked his pocket watch. "We've not much time. If you would, kindly take Leana's bag and mine, along with the captain's silver." He hesitated yet knew he could not send the man off without an apology. "Alas, what began as a blithesome visit has ended on a distressing note."

"Regrettably, it has." Benjamin's sincerity could not be denied. "I apologize again for not caring for Davina properly. In a parish of this size…"

"Say no more, for the fault is not yours; it is mine." Jamie clasped his hand warmly. "Please convey my deepest thanks and sincerest regrets to Elspeth, Catherine, and Abigail, who made us most welcome."

Benjamin pressed his mouth into a firm line and shook his hand. "'Twas our privilege, Jamie." A moment later the minister headed for the quay, two more bags in hand.

Jamie was still watching from the door when Leana came up and slipped her hand round his elbow. With a furtive glance up the stair, she whispered in his ear, "Have you spoken to the twins yet this morning? They feel your judgment most harshly, Jamie. 'Tis why they've been avoiding you, hiding in their room."

His jaw hardened. Did they mean to turn his own wife against him? He followed her gaze to the second floor. "I will speak with them now. Have Davina and Ian bring their bags to the door. We must leave for the quay in mere minutes."

Jamie took the stairs two at a time, trying to release his anger. But when he arrived at the twins' door, his ire had climbed with him. He marched into their room unannounced—was he not their father?—and found Will and Sandy neatly dressed, their closed portmanteau waiting on the bed.

Sandy stepped forward. "Did Mother ask you to speak with us?"

He could not have said anything worse.

Jamie struck him with words of steel. "Do not demean your mother by asking her to serve in the role of messenger." He slammed the door behind him, perfectly willing to feed Mrs. McAllister all the gossip she could swallow, now that they were leaving. "If you wish to speak to me, come to me directly. You will no longer write to your mother; you will write to me. If you need money, I am your only resource."

Will tried to intervene. "Father, we just wanted to say how grateful we are for what you did yestermorn."

"Do you mean when I spared your thick necks from the gallows?"

Both their faces reddened.

Jamie moved closer and lowered his voice but only because he was almost growling. "The people who live on this island consider our family *rubbage*. Because of you. They hold their noses and murmur ill-scrapit words. Because of you."

Sandy's voice was thin. "But, Father, the verdict—"

"Do not fool yourselves that Mr. Hunter's decision changes the facts. You are brothers in cruelty, ruled by anger and driven by revenge."

Will rose to his challenge. "But, Father, Somerled treated our sister like a—"

Jamie slapped him hard. "Your sister? Your sister has no hope for the future. Because of you."

Now they were silent. Almost sorry, by the look of them.

Jamie outlined his sons' future in no uncertain terms, grinding out each word. "We will go to the quay. We will sail to the mainland. You will proceed by coach to Edinburgh with due haste and resume your classes."

"But, Father—"

"Do not come home at Lammas. Nor at Michaelmas. You will not find yourself welcome in our parish. Nor at Glentrool."

Sandy's eyes were swimming. "May we never come home again?"

Jamie did not have a ready answer and so gave them none. "We sail at once for Ayr."

Seventy-Two

It is not in the storm nor in the strife
We feel benumb'd, and wish to be no more,
But in the after-silence on the shore,
When all is lost, except a little life.

GEORGE GORDON, LORD BYRON

Leana nearly wept when her foot touched the stone quay at Ayr. Aboard the *Isabella* since noon, the McKies had been tossed round a choppy sea, rained on for endless hours, then stranded without wind in the packet boat's sails for much of the evening.

" 'Tis midnight," Captain Dunlop said gruffly, squinting up at the full moon high overhead. "Ye'll find the King's Arms on the High Street. I dinna ken if they'll hae onie ludgin for ye."

Jamie threw the last of their traveling bags onto the quay, then disembarked, bidding the captain good night in a sea-roughened voice. He was exhausted; they all were.

Leana longed to be rid of her shoes, to unlace her stays, to stretch out on a mattress and sleep until dawn. Her gown, still damp from the rain and crusty with salt, chafed her neck as they walked toward the town center. The younger men carried their belongings, and Davina clutched her fiddle, safe in its baize bag.

With both hands free, Leana slipped one hand round her husband's elbow and the other round Davina's. "Let us pray the King's Arms has enough beds to accommodate us. Though I believe a length of wool carpet would do our tired lads."

"Aye," they groaned, trudging not far behind her.

Will had hardly spoken during the long crossing, and Sandy even less. Their silence grieved Leana, for she knew its source: She'd heard Jamie's tirade at the inn at Cladach. His words did not travel through the pine floor, but his wrath did, leaving her trembling for the twins' sake. Lewis Hunter had pronounced the lads innocent. Could her husband not do the same? Before their sons headed northeast by coach in the morning, she would do what she could to appease them and pray Jamie's parting words would be less strident.

At that late hour the High Street was deserted. The breeze had died down, and few sounds were heard except the occasional cry of a gull sailing over the harbor. When the sun rose in a few hours, fishermen and tradesmen would be about their work, and Ayr would come to life. For now, sleep was all anyone had in mind.

The proprietor of the King's Arms greeted them with bleary eyes and dismal news. "I've no rooms to let. But there's a parlor through that door with sofas and the like. None of the guests will be about just now. I can have a maid bring you some blankets—"

"Fine." Jamie yanked out his purse. "Two of my sons will be needing seats on the morning coach to Glasgow."

"Aye, sir. I'll sort that out for you. Ten o'clock."

The McKies awakened long before ten. Sunlight crept round the shutters at four, and the clamor of vendors arranging their stalls for Saturday's market soon followed. When guests wandered into the parlor, expecting to be served coffee, Leana roused her family and helped straighten their rumpled attire.

"We've company," she murmured. "'Tis a new day."

Breakfast was oatcakes, fresh strawberries, and tea. Davina sat quietly poking her berries with a spoon, while Jamie downed his tea in gulps and Ian glanced at a week-old copy of the *Glasgow Journal*, left on his chair by another lodger.

Sandy was the first to finish his breakfast. "Once we arrive in Glasgow, there'll be an eastbound coach to Edinburgh." He stole a quick glance at his father. "That means we'll be in attendance for Professor Gregory's lecture on Monday, having missed but one week of our studies."

"Had you remained in Edinburgh," Jamie said evenly, "you'd not have missed one day. And the MacDonalds would still be alive."

"Jamie!" Leana stared at him, aghast. Their daughter looked nigh to fainting.

"He is right, Mother." Will brushed the crumbs from his waistcoat. "Father thought it necessary for us to become better acquainted with the MacDonalds—"

"Och!" Jamie cut him off. "Climbing with the Highlanders was your idea, not mine."

Leana sighed. Her prayers for reconciliation had hardly been answered.

"Nothing can be gained by this discussion," Ian said, the gentle voice of reason. "The duke's steward made his ruling and blames no one for the accident. Davina's grief should be our foremost concern."

"Well said," Leana agreed, "though I'll not send my younger sons to far-off Edinburgh without the assurance of our concern for them as well." She looked at Will and Sandy in turn, meaning to encourage them, and instead was troubled by what she found. Dark eyes clouded with distrust. Jaws hardened by conflict and scarred from brawling. Mouths turned down, their expressions sullen, resentful.

A foolish son is the heaviness of his mother. How the weight of that truth grieved her.

She had given birth to her twin sons but did not recognize them. She'd raised them, yet they'd not matured. Had her own father's ill temper come back to haunt her? Had Evan McKie, Jamie's birsie twin brother, somehow influenced them from afar? Or had she failed her sons as their mother?

Leana clasped her hands in her lap and pressed her mouth closed, lest a cry escape her lips. *Please, may it not be so, Lord!* She had loved them, cared for them. And yet they were not loving, like Davina, nor caring, like Ian. Tempted though she might be, Leana would not blame Jamie, as the twins did, or she would sin as they sinned. *Honour thy father.* But when she had her husband to herself, she would ask him where things stood with their headstrong sons.

Jamie rose, eying his watch. "Coaches do not wait for their passengers. 'Tis time, lads."

The twins strode toward the inn door as if glad to be on their way and eager to put their family behind them. Once they reached the crowded stables where the Glasgow-bound coach was loading its passengers, Sandy tossed their portmanteau up to the driver to be strapped in place for their journey. The lads began greeting the other passengers, barely acknowledging the family members who tarried behind them on the street.

Davina looked stricken. Her face mirrored Leana's own concerns. *What is to become of them?*

When Will finally turned round and took his sister's hands, he was dry eyed, but she was not. "We'll not forget you, lass."

Though Davina's mouth was trembling, Leana could read the words she formed. *Come home.*

But Will shook his head. "Father has asked us to remain in Edinburgh." His voice softened a little. "Do not fret, my bonny wee fairy. We shall see you again."

Davina wriggled free of Will's grasp, then threw herself against her father's chest, pressing on it with her small fists, as if to punish him.

Remain in Edinburgh? Leana could not guess what that meant. For a month? For a year? For good? *Oh, Jamie, I trust your judgment, but I pray for your wisdom.*

Holding their daughter, Jamie addressed the lads over her knot of red hair. "I believe you have what you need for the upcoming term." When Will did not respond, his father continued, his emotions well in check. "A safe journey to you both."

Ian's parting sentiments were brief. Though her sons did not embrace, their words to one another bore no ill will, and for that Leana was grateful.

At last her turn came to bid the twins farewell. She had done so in May, certain of seeing them in a few months. Now she had no such hope.

Though they stood in a crowded street, theirs were the only faces she saw. "My dear sons..." Her voice faltered as she cupped their rough chins, her hands shaking. "I will always love you." For a moment their dark eyes cleared, and she caught a glimpse of the lads she'd cherished from their first breath. "Remember that your father's discipline is meant for your good. 'For what son is he whom the father chasteneth not?'"

"Aye, Mother." Will's voice was low, rough. "We will remember."

"I shall…write to you." Words came harder now. She felt her sons drawing away from her. "And I shall pray for you both. Always."

"Mem, they'll be needin' tae tak their seats," the driver cautioned, reins in hand, his team of horses restless. "We've fine wather and a fu' day *aheid*. Dinna keep us waitin', lads."

Leana watched her sons climb on top of the coach, their eyes already scanning the road ahead. "Godspeed," she called up to them, brushing away her tears so she might see their faces. "Mercy and truth be with thee…" The rest of her benediction caught in her throat.

The horses took off with a noisy jolt before the twins had a chance to answer her. Gripping the iron rails beside them, Will and Sandy could only nod over their shoulders as she trailed after their departing coach, waving good-bye.

Seventy-Three

Trouble rides behind and gallops with him.

NICHOLAS BOILEAU-DESPREAUX

Jamie shifted in his saddle, the new leather uncomfortably stiff and his new mount even more so. Ayrshire folk usually purchased their steeds at Quarter Days fairs; convincing Watson's livery stable to part with two horses had tried his purse and his patience mightily. In the end, Jamie had paid too much silver for too little horseflesh.

"Father, suppose you take Magnus tomorrow." Ian trotted up beside him on his favorite black gelding. "That mare may be docile, but she has an uneven gait."

Jamie grunted in agreement. "Better suited to a plow, I'd say."

The evening sky was the color of his daughter's eyes washed with tears: dark, watery blue. She followed a few lengths behind them on a dappled gray of dubious conformation. Lithe as she was, Davina managed her unfamiliar mount with ease, yet her countenance was lined with sorrow. Had he ever seen her so despondent?

Leana rode beside her on dun-colored Biddy, her wide-brimmed hat askew after a long day on horseback. She'd hardly spoken since bidding the twins farewell, though her troubled expression said enough. How much of their sons' treachery could his wife bear to hear? More, perhaps, than he could bear to tell.

"Where might we spend the night?" Ian wondered aloud. "We've yet to see many farmhouses tucked among these hills. The weather is mild enough, but a valise makes a poor pillow and the ground a hard bed."

Jamie scanned the countryside, marked by steep fells and moss-edged burns. They'd traveled but fourteen miles, and already the gloaming was upon them. Michael Kelly had not been at home when they'd knocked on his cottage door an hour earlier, leaving them no choice but to press on. "Ian, do you recall passing Drumyork on your journey north?" When his son nodded, Jamie continued, " 'Tis a small steading, hard against Drumyork Hill. Pray they can accommodate us."

The southbound road dipped and curved half a dozen times before the signpost for Drumyork appeared at the end of a rutted track. Greeted by the lowing of cows in the byre, Jamie led his family toward the clay farmhouse and nodded to a laborer making the most of the Sabbath eve's waning light.

"Jamie?" Leana touched his arm before he dismounted, her voice thin with exhaustion. "Might Davina have a bed to herself? She did not sleep well yestreen."

"Nor did you," he reminded her gently. "I'll see what can be done."

His knock was soon answered by a man his own age, though taller and whip thin, as if he'd never sampled the rich cream his dairy cows produced. "Guid evenin', sir." The farmer dipped his chin in greeting. "Ebenezer Morton's me name."

Jamie responded in kind, introducing himself. "Might my family and I find shelter here for the night?"

"Och, o' course." The farmer opened the door wider still. "Oor parlor is yers, Mr. McKie. I'll tell me *guidwife* ye'll be needin' supper."

"Much obliged." Jamie motioned the others to join him, then followed the farmer inside. The floor was made of rough pine, the painted walls had no adornment, and meager rushlights served as candles. But as in most Scottish homes, every room had its bed, and this parlor had two, more than he'd expected. Mother and daughter would each sleep soundly, with father and son not far below them, stretched out on the thick plaids now stacked in the corner. "The Lord bless you for your hospitality, Mr. Morton."

"Aye, weel." He shrugged his narrow shoulders. "Be not forgetful tae entertain strangers."

Davina sank onto the heather mattress so quickly that Jamie feared they might not rouse her for a plate of broth. Indeed, by the time the farmer's wife hastened from the kitchen to welcome her unexpected guests, Davina's head lay on the pillow, and her eyes were drifting shut, though she still held her fiddle bag.

"Yer puir dochter." Mrs. Morton clucked her tongue. "I've niver seen sic a *wabbit* lass in a' me days."

"We're all weary," Leana admitted, "and exceedingly grateful for a warm supper and dry beds."

The older woman bobbed her graying head. "Yer plates are waitin' on the table, mem."

An hour later, their stomachs full of broth and the Scriptures duly read aloud, the McKies joined slumbering Davina in the parlor. Leana perched on the edge of her daughter's borrowed bed and lightly stroked her cheek. "Sleep is more necessary than food," she said softly. "The sun will rise before we will, and we've a full day of riding ahead."

"Twenty miles." Jamie stood aside as their hostess gathered the woolen plaids and unrolled Ian's makeshift bed close to the hearth, then discreetly placed Jamie's blankets on the floor next to his wife's low bed.

"We're up the stair if ye need oniething," Mrs. Morton said before leaving them in peace.

Rushlights were extinguished and good-nights spoken. Tired as he was, Jamie lay for some time holding his wife's hand against his heart and praying for the courage to say what he must.

"Leana," he whispered when he was sure their offspring were both fast asleep.

She slowly lifted her hand, beckoning him upward. "Come."

He climbed onto the narrow bed never meant to hold two. Side by side, fully clothed, the couple touched from head to toe. He kissed her and was gratified by her immediate response. Enfolding her in his arms, he held her close, lest she draw back in dismay when he told her the truth.

"We must speak of Will and Sandy," he began, his words more air than sound.

"Aye, we must," she said, softer still. "What angered you so on Arran?"

He closed his eyes, summoning a last ounce of strength, then touched his mouth to the curve of her ear. "I am not sure that what happened on Goatfell was unintentional."

When she gasped, he tightened his embrace. "I am sorry, Leana."

"That cannot be true!" Her fingers clutched the loose fabric of his shirt. "Mr. Hunter said the twins were innocent."

"He ruled the deaths accidental. But our sons are far from innocent."

"Did they make some...confession?" The strain in her voice was unmistakable.

Jamie knew he could put it off no longer. "I asked them if they wanted the Highlanders dead. Will admitted that they did. From the day they arrived on Arran—"

"Nae!" She buried her face in his neck and bathed his skin with her tears.

He held her for a long time, finding it hard to swallow, harder to breathe. It was unfathomable that such ill-kindit sons could come from so gentle a woman.

"Please..." She pressed in harder. "Please tell me...our sons...are not murderers."

"They insisted the men fell and were not pushed." That much he could offer her. "You heard their testimony: They tried to save the Highlanders at their own peril."

She lifted her head. "Do you believe them, Jamie?"

God, help me. He could not lie to his wife. Nor could he break her heart. "I am not sure what to believe."

Leana's sigh was laden with a mother's sorrow. "Whatever they've done, Jamie, they are still our sons."

"Aye." Her mercy humbled him, nae, amazed him. Had any woman ever loved her children more than Leana McKie?

She fell silent for a bit, then finally asked, "How long must the twins remain in Edinburgh?"

"'Til Yuletide." He'd decided that much. "Sufficient time to repent of their sins, while my anger runs its course."

"And while Davina grieves her loss." Leana turned to look across the room at their sleeping daughter. "She must never know of your doubts, Jamie."

"Aye," he agreed, "for they are only that. Not certainties." If Davina thought for a moment that her brothers were to blame for Somerled's death, her grief would be compounded beyond any hope of recovery. Nothing would be gained by telling her; the lass had suffered enough.

He kissed Leana's brow and then her lips once more. "I'm afraid your bed is too small for us both, and you need your rest." Reluctantly he eased away from her, then lowered himself onto his bed of blankets. "Sleep well, my love."

After a lengthy silence Leana reached down and touched his cheek. "I am glad you are my husband."

"And I am grateful you are my wife." Of that he had no doubt.

Seventy-Four

And silence, like a poultice, comes
To heal the blows of sound.
OLIVER WENDELL HOLMES

Davina ran her fingertips down the strings of her fiddle, from the rosewood pegs to the thin maple bridge and then back up again. No music came forth, only the faint whisper of skin against string.

An hour ago she'd tucked her fiddle beneath her chin, wondering what melody she might play now that she was home again, sitting by her bedchamber window. But no notes rang in her heart. No song asked to be heard. The last tune she'd played was with Somerled, a tender air in the key of G.

Practice your Gow tunes, Miss McKie.

Somerled's music was silent now. And so, it seemed, was hers.

Davina touched the back of her hand to her cheek, catching the tear before it landed on her fiddle. The supply was limitless; the reservoir never emptied. When the four McKies had arrived at Glentrool yestreen on the Sabbath, bone weary from riding over the hills of Ayrshire, Davina had washed the scent of Arran from her skin and crawled into bed, too tired to think. And still she'd soaked her pillow.

She could not always name the source of her tears: sorrow one moment, guilt the next, and a pervasive sense of loss that she feared might never lift. If not for Somerled, she would still be a maid. If not for her, Somerled would still be alive.

No sooner had a fresh spate of tears threatened to spill over her cheeks than her mother's voice floated through the open doorway. "I've always loved this room."

Davina dabbed her eyes, then turned to find Leana gazing at the turret walls that formed a perfect circle.

"You and your brothers learned to walk here. Ian took his first steps right where you're seated." She crossed the room and stood behind Davina's chair, smoothing a hand over her long braid. In a low voice she added, "Perhaps this is where you will learn to walk anew."

Davina nodded for her mother's sake, though the idea of beginning again overwhelmed her. She'd planned a new life in Argyll. Now that life was no more than a memory.

Leana reached over her shoulder and rescued the silent fiddle from her lap. "Not every day is meant for music." She placed the instrument on the dresser and reached for Davina's sketchbook. "Is your mood better suited to drawing?" Her mother held out her book only as a possibility, Davina sensed, not as a demand. "Or might you prefer a conversation?"

Aye. She'd not had her mother all to herself since they'd boarded the *Isabella* on Friday last. Davina accepted the sketchbook, then remembered that only a handful of blank pages remained.

Her mother drew up the chair from her dressing table and sat next to her. "I'll ask your father to purchase another for you when he visits the bookbinder in Dumfries."

Earlier that morning Davina had wrapped a broad ribbon round the front portion of the sketchbook, tying all the old pages closed, leaving the few untouched pages free. Newly sharpened, the charcoal pencil was too short for drawing but adequate for words.

Now all she needed was the courage to write them. Again.

What is to become of me now that I am ruined?

After reading her question, Leana sighed. "My precious girl. How I wish I had an herb in my stillroom that might restore your innocence." She slipped an arm round her shoulders, then put aside the sketchbook to draw her closer and rested Davina's head against her shoulder. "What I can offer you are words. Not my own, but the words of One who loves you even more than I do."

Beneath her cheek Davina felt her mother's heartbeat and the warmth of her body, a healing comfort like no other. Could the Almighty truly love her more than this?

For a long time, they simply breathed together, mother and daughter. Sounds from the entrance hall below and the steading out of doors were muted. Glentrool seemed to hold its breath.

When Leana spoke, her voice was as gentle as a lullaby. "Heal her now, O God, I beseech thee. Let thy tender mercies come."

Davina's throat began to tighten. If there was no other way to heal, then she would weep until she could weep no more. Tears pooled in her eyes, then flowed down her cheeks and onto her mother's breast.

Leana spoke again, softer still. "Yea, I have loved thee with an everlasting love. I have seen thy tears. Behold, I will heal thee of thy wounds."

Davina pinched her lips tightly together. *Do you see me, Lord? Can you heal me, truly heal me?* She waited for an answer. She did not wait long.

"Daughter, be of good comfort," Leana whispered. "Thy faith hath made thee whole."

Whole. She clung to the promise of that word. To be whole and not broken, to be full and not empty, to be complete and not half. *I will praise thee with my whole heart.* Aye, she would.

Once again Davina and her mother sat, listening to the silence. When Davina groped for the handkerchief she'd left in her lap, only to find it soggy and of little use, her mother righted her long enough to stand and pluck a fresh one from her open valise, then tucked the handkerchief in Davina's hands. "I am happy to embroider more of these. A lass can never have too many."

Davina noticed the sleeve of her damask gown protruding from the jumble of dresses. There was no better time than this. She rose on unsteady legs and tugged on the gown until it pulled free, then sat and held the soiled fabric to her breast, ashamed.

"Ah, your ivory gown." She heard no hint of disappointment in her mother's voice. But she did hear sadness. "You wore it on Midsummer Eve, aye?"

Davina slowly nodded, unfolding the wrinkled dress for her mother's inspection.

Seated next to her once more, Leana ran her fingers over the embroidery. She studied the worn places, rubbed the stubborn stains, and turned the fabric this way and that until she'd examined every inch. " 'Tis not ruined."

Davina's stared at the soiled gown. Was it possible?

"Linen is a very tough fabric," her mother explained. "It can be washed again and again and withstand the hottest iron in the laundry." Leana touched her cheek. "I have a daughter much like fine linen. Resilient, her faith tried as in a furnace. Yet she, too, is not ruined. In truth, she is whiter than snow."

Davina closed her eyes and let the truth sink in. Her dress could be made good as new. And so, by God's mercy, could she.

When she opened her eyes, there was her gracie mother, carefully folding her gown as if it were freshly cleaned and about to be slipped inside her clothes press.

Davina's sketchbook lay open at her feet, her one question finally answered. But now she had another. Though her body and her soul could be healed and made new, her heart still grieved for her golden prince. She'd known the man only a fortnight, yet the loss of him was almost more than she could bear. Might her mother understand? With some hesitancy, Davina picked up her sketchbook and wrote a second question. *When Aunt Rose died, did you suffer for a long time?*

"Ah, dearie, I mourn her still." Sympathy shone in her blue gray eyes. " 'Tis a long journey, grieving. I was numb at first and did not quite believe my sister was gone. I expected any moment to turn and see her on the stair."

Davina looked away. *Aye.* Had she not imagined Somerled standing at the quay as they sailed from Arran's shores?

"The day will come, Davina, when sorrow and mourning shall flee away. Until then, let your heart mend. And let those who love you bind your wounds as best we can." Leana stood, the linen gown in her arms. "Will you come to the dining room for your noontide meal? Or might you prefer a tray in your room?"

Davina patted the book in her lap. *Here.*

"A tray, then." Leana paused at the door. "Solitude can be a fine remedy, and silence an even better one." Her mother's voice was infused with love, more restorative than any herb. "I am here if you need me, lass. And we'll be glad to have you at table whenever you're ready."

O summer day so wonderful and white,
So full of gladness and so full of pain!
Henry Wadsworth Longfellow

D avina did not venture down the stair until Friday. And then only
for Ian's sake.

"You will join us for dinner with Margaret…with Miss McMillan?"
Ian's expression had been so earnest when he'd asked her, Davina could
not refuse him.

Aye, dear brother. I will join you.

At nine Davina donned her freshly pressed blue gown, then wandered about the house, feeling at loose ends. A walk out of doors? Alas,
the grass was still drenched from yestreen's rain and would soak her cotton hem. A book? Davina found it hard to read; her mind wandered
easily, often down disheartening paths.

Come midmorning her brother discovered her studying grandfather's atlas in the library. Davina abruptly closed the *Geographiae Sco-
tiae,* lest Ian take note of the particular page she was examining. The
map was dated, yet the necessary details were there: two crescent-shaped
bays, an isle within an isle, a stalwart castle, and a fateful mountain.

If Ian recognized the outline of Arran, he did not mention it.

"Miss McMillan will be along shortly," he reminded her, crossing
the room. "But if I may, I need to speak with you before she arrives."

Davina knew what he was going to say.

As they sat by the window where Mother and Father often had tea,
Davina prepared her heart. *Let me not be selfish. Let me share his joy.*

Ian leaned forward in his chair, elbows resting on his knees as he
took her hands in his. "Davina, I will officially announce this at the end
of our meal, but I wanted to tell you privately first so you would not be
surprised. Miss McMillan and I are engaged to marry."

Help me, Lord. Please help me be happy for him. She squeezed his hands and tried to smile.

He looked relieved. "You are glad, then?"

I am. Davina pulled one hand free to touch her heart and then his. *I love you, Ian.*

"I love you too, lass." He swallowed, his eyes watering. "But I cannot imagine how…difficult this must be for you."

Davina held up her palm, putting a stop to his words. *I am fine,* she mouthed. *I am delighted for you.* Then she tried to clap her hands, expressing joy. But she could not. Her hands refused to move. *Nae.* She could not clap. She could only choke back tears.

"Och, lass." He took her mutinous hands in his. "Forgive me. We should have waited. 'Til autumn, perhaps."

Davina shook her head. *Not for my sake.*

"We were hoping to wed at Michaelmas. But perhaps Yuletide…"

Nae. She pulled free from him long enough to reach for her sketchbook, pressing one of the remaining pages into service as she wrote furiously across the paper.

> Please do not wait. Marry at Michaelmas. And forgive me
> for weeping yet again.

Reading over her shoulder, Ian brushed a kiss against her hair. "Never apologize for tears, lass. They are so precious to God, he stores them in a bottle for safekeeping."

A very large bottle. Davina released a shaky sigh.

Two light taps at the door, and Eliza was standing in the room. "Mr. McKie, your guest is here."

Blotting her cheeks with a handkerchief, Davina followed Ian into the entrance hall, where Mother waited with their fair-haired, brown-eyed neighbor.

The lass stood practically on tiptoe with anticipation as Leana said, "Margaret, I believe this is the young gentleman you are looking for."

"He is indeed." She turned as pink as her rose-colored gown when she curtsied and whispered his name. "Mr. McKie."

His color matched hers as he bowed. "Miss McMillan."

Father was waiting for them at the dining table. "Grace before meat," he said simply, calling them to prayer. The servants tarried while he offered thanks, then resumed their duties, filling the glasses with claret.

Davina had not sat at table with her family since they returned home. The chair felt familiar yet strange. The twins were noticeably missing. And in their place next to Ian sat a lovely young woman, glowing more brightly than the candles in their polished silver stands.

Kippered salmon and a host of cooked vegetables crowded their china plates, but no one paid much attention to the food or to Davina, for which she was grateful. Having every eye fixed on her grew tiresome. Margaret and Ian had eyes only for each other; Father and Mother were busy watching the two of them, no doubt aware of what was to come.

The instant their plates were cleared, Ian clasped Margaret's hand—above the table, in full view of everyone. "Father, I am pleased to announce that I have asked Miss McMillan of Glenhead to be my bride." Ian gazed down at her radiant face. "And she has consented."

"Has she indeed?" Her father succeeded in looking surprised. "This is most welcome news."

"Indeed." Leana smiled across the table as she secretly clasped Davina's hand.

Bless you, Mother. Davina was the only one with tears in her eyes.

Margaret, meanwhile, was beaming. "Shall our banns be read come the Sabbath?"

Her parents exchanged glances, easily read. *Nae. Not this Sunday.* Her father spoke for both of them. "Miss McMillan, I'm certain Ian has apprised you of the difficulties we endured while on the Isle of Arran."

Davina looked away as Margaret's face dimmed.

"A little, sir."

"Because this will be the family's first Sunday at kirk since our return, it might be prudent to wait before announcing your wedding plans. Perhaps a month or two."

Margaret's entire body sagged in response.

"Come September," he continued, "the news of your engagement will be welcomed by our parish neighbors. But just now…" He looked at Leana for support, and she nodded.

Seventy-Six

As the yellow gold is tried in fire,
so the faith of friendship must be seen in adversity.
OVID

Davina started down the aisle of the kirk, her heart pounding. *I will not be afraid what man can do unto me.* But what man could do was far worse than Davina had imagined.

She'd sensed a collective intake of air when the McKies entered the kirk at ten, stepping from the bright Sabbath sunshine into the shadowy light of the preaching house. Heads swiveled in their direction. Then the whispers began. A low hiss at first, gradually increasing in volume until she distinctly heard what they were saying as she walked by.

Limmer. Hizzie. Tairt.

She winced, hearing the shameful words mumbled by neighbors she'd known all her life. McWhaes and Herons and Patersons. They had danced to her fiddle tunes on May Day and welcomed her into their homes at Yuletide. She'd held their bairns and listened to their stories and cried when they'd buried loved ones. Now they jerked their chins at her and would not meet her gaze.

Please look at me. She could not beseech them with words. Only with her eyes. *I am still Davina.*

Her mother walked behind her, so close that her toes brushed the hem of Davina's skirt. Leana was whispering too. "The LORD is the strength of my life; of whom shall I be afraid?"

Davina bowed her head, hiding her dismay.

When they reached the McKie pew, her mother and father sat on either side of her, their backs straight, their eyes clear. They knew the truth about their daughter; so did the Almighty.

The gathering psalm began, calling them to worship. All round her, parishioners sang the words of the sixth psalm in *run-line* manner, with the precentor singing each line and the congregation repeating it in tuneless unison. Davina knew the verses, having memorized them long ago and having lived them for the last fortnight at Glentrool.

I water my couch with my tears. And her pillow and her handkerchiefs and her gowns. She'd grown accustomed to the sad face that gazed back at her from the looking glass: her eyes rimmed in red, the skin round them swollen.

Mine eye is consumed because of grief. Everything she saw reminded her of Somerled: her fiddle hanging on the library wall, undisturbed; her sketchbook brimming with memories that even a wide ribbon could not hide; Ian's long-legged gait, so like her braw Highlander's.

When she thought of Somerled in a pine kist, buried in the hard soil of Argyll, a coldness swept over her. He had once been a dream and now was nothing more. She closed her eyes while her family sang and imagined Somerled's voice among them. A sweet tenor, wending its way through the air and through her heart.

For the LORD hath heard the voice of my weeping.

Davina squeezed her eyes shut. *Do you hear me, Lord? In the dark of night, when no one else does?*

During the long sermon, the parishioners kept their comments to themselves. But in the kirkyard the McKies were treated as if they were *fremmit*. Strange, foreign. Spoken of but not spoken to.

One family stood by them: the McMillans.

"I'm ashamed of my own parish," John grumbled under his breath, glaring at anyone who dared narrow their eyes at him. "They assume the worst and ask no civil questions."

His wife, Sally, frowned at the neighbors who frowned at them. "Why does the minister not preach against gossip? For 'tis the sin his flock most commits."

Reverend Moodie was not unaware of the problem. He sought out the family the moment the service ended, assuring them he would do what he could to stem the rumors by telling others the truth.

"Alas, gossips prefer savory lies to dry facts," John said when the minister was out of earshot.

The household had gathered not far from the door facing east among the oldest graves in the kirkyard. Moss-covered and crumbling, the gravestones stood about like sleeping guards, their once-broad shoulders drooping with age. Margaret and Ian flanked Davina on either side, deflecting the brunt of the parishioners' stares. Even Janet Buchanan of Palgowan avoided her, standing a safe distance away with her father.

Davina touched Margaret's hand, silently thanking her for her friendship.

The girl's brown eyes turned glassy. " 'Tis wrong, what they are doing. I am glad to stand by you, Davina."

Glancing in the direction of the old yew, Davina glimpsed a familiar face bearing a sympathetic expression. *Graham Webster.* A brave soul indeed, to be willingly counted among their friends. Though he was not wearing the armor of a knight nor bearing a sword, he courageously walked toward them, leaving no doubt of his allegiance.

Mr. Webster offered her father a cordial bow. "Mr. McKie." The man's voice was warm and his gaze kind. "I was grieved to hear of your family's trials on Arran." The widower greeted her mother with equal decorum and then Ian.

When he turned to Davina, Mr. Webster not only bowed; he also looked into her eyes, as if unafraid of the sorrow he would find there. "Miss McKie."

Fresh tears welled up, then spilled over. Chagrined, Davina looked down, letting the drops fall to the ground, then drying her cheeks with her sleeve. When she lifted her head, Graham Webster was still there. Waiting for her. Offering his handkerchief.

"I'm sorry the unkind behavior of our neighbors has compounded your suffering." He aimed a cool gaze at Mrs. Paterson, who tarried closer than necessary, one ear cocked. "The words of a talebearer are as wounds," he murmured. When the woman moved along in a huff, he returned his attention to Davina. "I'm honored to bear this burden with your family. If there is anything else I might do…"

The bell announcing the second service clanged over their heads. When he stepped back, giving her room, she pressed her hands together,

Seventy-Seven

The perfection of art is to conceal art.

QUINTILIAN

Graham dipped his sable brush into the porcelain saucer of paint, then tapped the brush to remove the excess water. In his haste he'd neglected to mix the colors as evenly as he liked. The small, hard cakes of pigment and gum were far easier to work with than grinding his own colors from natural pigments, but the combination had to be just right. Too much water, and the paper cockled; too little, and the paint would not brush on smoothly.

There. The consistency was perfect. He held the paintbrush with a steady hand as he leaned over the drawing board to apply a thin line of color near the center.

Paint touched paper.

A bell tinkled outside his study door. "Yer denner is het, sir."

He groaned under his breath, leaning back. "Thank you, Mrs. Threshie."

Graham swirled his brush in a shallow dish of water, then wiped the silky marten hairs dry with a *clootie.* Once again, time had slipped away from him. He'd meant to keep an eye on the mantel clock, but the landscape before him had so captured his attention that an hour had passed without his noticing.

Graham glanced at the clock as he strode toward the door. *Nae, two hours.*

Not until he stretched out his hand to grasp the doorknob did he remember the dried pigment on his fingertips and the color-stained apron protecting his suit of clothes. If he meant to keep his paintings a *saicret* from his canny housekeeper, preventive measures were in order. A hasty visit to the washstand and a folded apron tucked into a desk drawer solved the problem for the moment.

He was not embarrassed by his efforts as an amateur artist, because his paintings were not meant for the public; they were for Susan. He'd painted the first one the day of her funeral, watering the pigment with his tears. His journey through grief was measured by watercolors, each progressively smaller, yet more detailed; softer, yet more colorful. As he'd learned to paint, he'd also learned to live without the woman he loved. Painting brought him joy, and grieving brought him sorrow, yet he'd found strength in both. Both were gifts from the same loving hand. *From sorrow to joy, and from mourning into a good day.*

Mrs. Threshie had been instructed not to enter his study uninvited, and for two years she'd honored his request. Had she outwitted him, Graham soon would have known: The woman could not keep her opinions to herself. "Leuk at a' yer *paintrie*, Mr. Webster!" she would say. "Hae ye been aboot yer *wark* for a lang time? Ye've a real *airt* for it, sir. That's a richt guid likeness o' Garlies castle." His talkative housekeeper was a welcome fixture at Penningham Hall, but she was not one for keeping secrets.

She stood waiting for him now in the dining room, her black dress styled for a matron, her red hair not unlike a certain fiddler's, though fading with age. "I've a *gustie* dish for yer Wednesday denner," she announced as he sat at the head of his table. "Rabbit curry, jist the way ye like it. Wi' mushroom and celery and onions."

"But not with fresh coconut," he teased her, knowing she would bristle. He'd once been served a tasty mild curry with coconut on a London visit and had never let Mrs. Threshie forget the fact.

"Och! Whaur would I be findin' a coconut in Scotland?" she said with a flap of her hand, then returned a moment later with his piping-hot dinner.

"I am sure this rabbit would have no use for tropical nutmeat," he told her, nodding toward the aromatic dish. "My compliments to you for a fine meal. Though it appears you've cooked enough to feed two people."

"Beggin' yer pardon, Mr. Webster." Her ruddy coloring heightened. "I dinna mean tae forget."

After a dozen years of cooking for Penningham Hall, Mrs. Threshie sometimes neglected to halve her recipes; the additional serving was a poignant reminder of his late wife. "Mrs. Webster would have enjoyed your curry very much," he said lightly, wanting to put her at ease. "I am sufficiently hungry to consume a second portion. You can be sure 'twill not go to waste."

"Ye're the kindest o' men, sir," she said with a curtsy, then disappeared into her kitchen.

A woman of sixty years, Mrs. Threshie had a temperament well suited to her descriptive name; she would soundly flail anyone ill-disposed toward her master. Had *he* been the subject of parish gossip for the fortnight past, Mrs. Threshie would have stood beside him in the kirkyard and thwacked naysayers with her broom. Indeed, if Miss McKie continued to suffer from their neighbors' cruelty, Graham would extend his housekeeper's services to the lass, complete with a new besom.

As he tasted a forkful of curry and rice, he recalled Davina's first Sabbath after returning from Arran. The good people of Monnigaff did not bother to inquire if the rumors about her had any merit. Had they asked her father or consulted Reverend Moodie, as he had, they would have learned the terrible truth: The innocent Miss McKie was violated by Somerled MacDonald, then forced into a betrothal, only to have him fall to his death. A tragedy by any reckoning. And for this they scorned her? Insulted her with callous names?

He jabbed his fork at the stewed rabbit, remembering how infuriated he'd been, watching tears stream down her freckled cheeks. The poor lass! He'd had to clasp his hands behind his back to resist taking her in his arms and shielding her from thoughtless onlookers. Or taking folk by the neck and throttling them until they apologized.

On Sunday last, the furor had died down a bit. Still, he'd tarried in the kirkyard in case the family required his support. However polite, Davina had not paid him particular attention. Apparently the McKies had never informed their daughter of his interest in courting her. A blessing, that. Otherwise Davina might feel awkward in his presence, and he in hers. Instead he could befriend her family. Offer encouragement. Continue to do business with her father.

Oo aye, and find every excuse to be near Davina. Have you forgotten that part?

He gulped down a goblet of water, ashamed of his thoughts. Toward Somerled MacDonald, whom he did not mourn. And toward Davina McKie, whom he could not put out of his mind. She would have no interest in marriage, not for a very long time. And she might never have an interest in him.

Drowning his frustration in rabbit curry, Graham finished the second serving, then rang for Mrs. Threshie to bring the last course.

"Ye leuk flushed, sir. Was the curry too flavorful for yer taste?"

"It was delicious," he assured her, letting her refill his water goblet while his face cooled.

"I hae burnt cream wi' orange rind for a sweet." She smiled when she said it, knowing it would please him. "Wull ye hae yer coffee noo, sir?"

He nodded toward the front corner of the house. "I'll take it in my study later."

Mrs. Threshie paused, her thinning eyebrows arched. "I'd be glad tae serve ye thar."

"And have you discover what a mess I've made of the room this week?" he chided her. "Indeed not. When it's ready for you to clean, I'll throw open the door, I promise."

She looked downcast, though he knew it was for show. "Whate'er ye say, Mr. Webster."

A quarter of an hour later he carried his steaming cup of coffee into the study, considering how he might enhance his current painting. A solitary human figure would give the scene perspective.

Donning his apron—a poor fit for a man's chest—he then wet his brush, working the hairs into a fine point. He dipped a cake of dark brown watercolor in water, then rubbed the color into a clean porcelain saucer until he was satisfied with the consistency. After barely touching the fine hairs to the paint, he lifted the brush above the woven paper pinned to his drawing board and held his breath as paint met paper. Tiny strokes. Minimal detail.

There. Davina was in his painting now, if not truly in his life.

Come Lammas, when the shepherds of the parish gathered for their annual festivities, he would have a sound reason for visiting Glentrool: to arrange for delivery of his fivescore sheep and to see the bonny fiddler he'd captured in watercolor.

Seventy-Eight

The music in my heart I bore,
Long after it was heard no more.
WILLIAM WORDSWORTH

'Twill not be Lammas wi'oot yer fiddle, Miss McKie."

With the patience of a shepherd and the stubbornness of a red-headed Scot, Rab Murray had shadowed Davina all through July, pleading with her to reconsider providing the music for Lammas. In the end, Rab had accepted her decision: Her memories were far too fresh and far too painful. She'd yet to lift her grandfather's fiddle from the library wall, waiting for her music to return. Perhaps by Ian's wedding at Michaelmas. Perhaps then she could find the courage to play again.

The first of August dawned clear and bright—fine weather for a day of festivities, despite her misgivings. By midafternoon the shepherds from neighboring farms would begin arriving and the lasses of the countryside as well.

Vowing to do what she could to celebrate, Davina chose a gown in white Brussels lace; browns and burgundies could wait until autumn settled over the hills. With a wide blue sash round her waist and a braid of hair circling her crown, she was dressed to greet their visitors.

"Aren't ye the bonny lass?" Eliza exclaimed when Davina wandered into the drawing room, where gleaming furniture and a well-swept carpet awaited their guests. "The herds wull miss yer fiddle, but they'll be pleased tae see yer loosome face." She waved her dusting cloth toward the door with a cheery smile. "If ye're leukin' for yer mither, she's in the gairden jist noo."

But Davina did not find her mother snipping herbs in her physic garden or pinching withered flowers among her ornamentals. Instead she came upon the servants setting up tables for the food and Robert attending to his duties, pulling the weeds choking his radishes and peas.

The moment he spied her, the lanky gardener stood and tipped his cap. "Mrs. McKie is round the hoose, miss, prunin' yer aunt's rosebush."

Davina nodded her thanks and headed in the direction of the Apothecary Rose, a spreading shrub her mother nursed through summer's heat with particular care. When she turned the northeast corner of the house, she spotted Leana kneeling by the plant, her hands full of faded blooms and her eyes full of tears.

Feeling like an intruder, Davina waited until her mother noticed her, then walked to her side, lifting her white hem above the freshly cut grass.

"How nice you look." Leana dabbed at her eyes with the corner of her apron, then stood, depositing the roses in her pockets. "For potpourri," she explained, though Davina knew she saved the petals for sentimental reasons too.

Davina stood beside her mother in companionable silence, admiring the rosebush. The robins had started singing again, a sure sign of summer on the wane. Warmed all morning by the August sun, her aunt's Apothecary Rose perfumed the air.

"My sister would have been thirty-five today." Leana drew her closer, nestling Davina's head beneath her chin. "We cannot control the seasons, dearie, and we have far less control of our lives than we imagine. Yet the Lord reigns. 'He healeth the broken in heart, and bindeth up their wounds.'" Her mother kissed her hair, then gently released her. "'Tis what he did for me, Davina, and what I believe he is doing for you."

Aye. She still soaked her pillow at night. Still had little appetite. But the sharpness of her pain had eased a bit. She could smile from time to time without a sense of guilt washing over her.

Hearing voices on the hill, her mother turned, taking her round with her. "Here come our lads." Both women shaded their eyes to see the herds descending through the purple expanse of heather, their arms bearing dried branches for the Lammas bonfire. "The others will not be far behind. Will you help me attend to the food?"

Davina was glad to keep her hands occupied, for then her mind stayed busy as well. Aubert's kitchen staff had already delivered the food out of doors; her mother's task, by happy choice, was to arrange the dishes in some artful fashion.

Working side by side, they soon had Glentrool's storehouse well displayed. The first of the season's apples and pears waited to be plucked from willow baskets, while scones and oatcakes beckoned from pottery plates surrounded by cream, butter, and cheese. Smoked ham and boiled eggs were stacked in several places along the table, and glass pitchers of Eliza's cider and black currant wine sparkled at each end.

Davina was beginning to think she might be hungry after all.

Her father joined them, eying the feast appreciatively. "The fiddlers are here," he said, his voice free of any censure, then turned and waved for two young men to join them. "They hail from Newton Stewart. Reverend Moodie says they play a lively reel." He leaned down and added in a whisper, "Rest assured, they cannot hold a candle to my daughter's talents."

Davina nodded to each lad as they were introduced. *Tam Connell. Joseph Dunn.* Both in their twenties, bright eyed and leanly built. Apprentices to a joiner in Penningham parish, they'd learned to play by listening to an old fiddler in Newton Stewart whose name Davina did not recognize.

Tam shuffled his feet, looking somewhat embarrassed. "Miss McKie, we heard ye're the best fiddler in South West Scotland."

"Aye, and that ye performed for His Grace," Joseph added, clearly in awe. "I howp ye'll not judge us too harshly, miss." He looked at Tam askance. "We've been playin' *thegither* nae mair than a twelvemonth."

Jamie brushed off their concerns. "'Tis only a Lammas gathering, lads. My daughter will be happy to have the day free, I'll warrant."

As they tuned their fiddles, Davina's emotions swung back and forth like a clock pendulum: relieved she was not expected to play, disappointed she would not have the joy of doing so. The lads must have come early, for not many guests were standing about yet. None, really, except Glentrool's own shepherds.

Then Ian walked up with Margaret McMillan on his arm and her smiling parents not far behind.

"John!" Jamie called out, waving them over. "You'll remember Lammas days here when we were lads."

"Indeed I do." He laughed, showing off his back teeth. "A fine crowd of folk came, as I recall. And a piper walked round the bonfire when darkness fell."

A piper. Davina's stomach tightened at the thought. She could manage hearing another fiddle played, but not a bagpipe. Not so soon.

Her mother, as always, read her expression. "We've no piper coming, dearie. And should you decide to play your fiddle, I'm sure the lads from Newton Stewart would gladly sit at your feet."

On cue, they struck up a tune for the few herds standing round the garden, bringing smiles to their faces, while the McMillans filled their plates at the tables. If there were more neighbors on foot, making their way to Glentrool, they would no doubt hear the music and quicken their steps.

As each minute passed without a new face to welcome, Davina became more concerned. When her father pulled out his pocket watch, she checked the time as well. *Four o'clock?* Surely so many folk were not delayed. The skies were clear, the main road to the village was dry, and the paths surrounding Loch Trool had not seen rain in a week.

Platter upon platter of food remained untouched. A dozen herds stood about, rubbing their necks and shifting their weight, patently eager to dance but not with one another. Where were the lasses? the dairymaids and the laundresses? the laborers' daughters and the maidservants? None of the gentry had come either. Not the Carmonts or the Galbraiths or the McLellans.

The two fiddlers made a valiant effort, sawing away at their instruments, spinning out strathspeys and reels, but the garden of Glentrool remained almost deserted.

Davina sank onto the nearest bench and did not hide her tears. *Because of me. They've not come because of me.*

Her mother was beside her at once. "Do not blame yourself, Davina. Not for a minute. Our neighbors have chosen to observe Lammas elsewhere, it seems. So be it." Leana tugged her to her feet. "We shall have our own celebration, the McMillans and the McKies. Beginning with a dance."

Nae, Mother. Davina gazed at the forlorn knot of shepherds. *Not dancing. Not like this.*

Gentle as she was, Leana would not be dissuaded. "We have a fine group of lads, any of whom would be honored to serve as your partner. Not landed gentry, yet well mannered, to be sure, and very capable dancers. What say you, Davina? Shall we make the most of an unfortunate situation since the day is so fair and you are so bonny?"

A male voice drew her ear. "Do I understand Miss McKie needs a partner?"

Davina turned to find Graham Webster striding toward her, his face flushed from riding. His auburn hair, pulled back in a longish tail, had come loose, and the ends brushed against his bearded chin. She had a fleeting realization that Mr. Webster was as tall as Somerled, though they had nothing else in common.

He surveyed the garden, then turned to her and smiled. "I see I have the good fortune of being one of the first to arrive. I'd hoped to hear you play your fiddle this afternoon, Miss McKie, but as you've hired two lads from my own parish, I must be content."

"You've come at the perfect time, Mr. Webster." Leana motioned Jamie and the others to join them. "We were about to form our lines."

Though Davina's feet—like her hands—were not inclined to music that day, if Mr. Webster wished to join the others, he would need a partner. She curtsied to signal her willingness, avoiding his gaze.

"Pardon me, Mrs. McKie. But I am not certain your daughter cares for dancing just now." His response surprised Davina, as if he'd seen past her artifice. "Perhaps she prefers to sit and have a cup of cider."

She looked up in time to see the warmth in his smile. *He understands.* Though her mourning was private, she was not ready to dance in public. Food, however, held some appeal. She gladly took his arm and let him lead her to the tables, where victuals sufficient to feed an entire parish waited to be sampled. As befitted a hostess, she prepared a plate for each of them. Uncertain which foods he might choose, she settled on a taste of everything, covering his plate with Aubert's best selections.

Mr. Webster cocked an eyebrow at her. "Is the afternoon's entertainment going to be watching me consume all this?" When she nodded, he put on an impressive show. Between bites he chatted amiably about the pleasant weather, the beauty of the heather in bloom, and his plans for her father's sheep. "I expect Rab Murray will deliver them to Penningham Hall one day next week."

Had he come on business, then? And not, as he'd said, to hear her music? Davina tried not to mind too much. Still, she did think Mr. Webster a trustworthy gentleman, unlikely to say one thing and mean another. He fell silent as they watched the other three couples dance in longwise fashion.

All at once the rear door to Glentrool flew open, and a bevy of maidservants appeared, headed directly for the shepherds. It seemed Eliza had decided her staff would be of more use on their feet than in the house. A shout rang out when the herds saw them coming. Maids were swept into the reel before they could catch their breath, and the fiddlers from Newton Stewart nearly joined the dancers on the flagstone, so sprightly did the lads play.

"Lammas at Glentrool is well begun," Mr. Webster said, as amused by the spectacle as she.

The herds had few inhibitions, kicking up their heels like Michael Kelly dancing round his loom, while the maids in their matching uniforms took care not to get stepped on and laughed at the lads' antics. After several reels Davina found herself smiling and tapping her foot. How could she not when "The Stuart's Rant" was so ferlie?

Mr. Webster brought her a fresh cup of cider. "Even seated, Miss McKie, you are full of music."

She looked up to find his hazel eyes trained on hers and felt her cheeks warm, though she could not say why. He was merely a friend of the family—though a good friend of late—and there was nothing unseemly about his gaze.

"Tell me, O May Queen, when will I have the pleasure of hearing your grandfather's fiddle?" He sat down, placing her cider before her, then lightly touched his gloved hand to hers. "I confess, I have wished to be in your audience for some time now."

Flustered, Davina sprang to her feet without thinking. *Please...don't.*

Graham stood at once. "Miss McKie?"

I cannot... I am no longer... She tried to curtsy, then fled for the door.

Seventy-Nine

And every door is shut but one,
And that is Mercy's door.

WILLIAM COWPER

Y e've a visitor at yer door, sir. Mr. McKie o' Glentrool."
Graham frowned, the ledgers and receipts on his desk forgotten.
Jamie McKie had delivered his new flock? *Nae.* Mrs. Threshie must
have misunderstood. Rab Murray was the one expected. Not the man's
employer. *Not Davina's father.*

And why was there no bleating of sheep?

Graham closed the study door behind him, then strode down the
entrance hall and turned left into the drawing room, as light and femi-
nine a place as his study was dark and masculine. The comparison had
always intrigued Susan.

Standing before the marble mantelpiece was the laird of Glentrool.
"Mr. McKie. It *is* you."

Jamie smiled, returning his bow. "I rode on ahead. Rab will be
along shortly with two other herds and your flock of sheep." He walked
toward a west-facing window, brightened by the afternoon sun. "The
day was well chosen, Graham. Suitably dry but not as hot as August can
be. You'll find your sheep no worse for the journey." He peered through
the glass. "Is that your pasture?"

Graham heard a thread of doubt woven through the man's words.
"The forage is quite rich and the dry stane dyke newly built. My new
herd is inspecting the soundness of the dyke. You'll see him out there."

"Aye." Jamie knitted his brow. "Well drained, is it?"

"All round, sir." He reminded himself the man was a seasoned sheep
breeder; any questions he raised were for the good of his flock.

Jamie turned away from the window at last and nodded. "Well
done, Graham. Shall we see your fivescore safely home?"

Relieved to have his approval, Graham walked Jamie through the house and out the east-facing door by intent. "Most properties of this size have a garden in the rear. Penningham Hall has a river." The Cree flowed behind his house, slower and broader here than farther above and below stream. "I'd be pleased to have you join me for smelt fishing next March. Mrs. Threshie thinks they taste like rushes."

Jamie laughed. "Your housekeeper has a discerning palate." Dodging the bracken as he walked, he said, "You've a fine stand of trees, though you'll not want your flock wending their way here. Sheep have an aversion to water and boggy land."

At the sound of bleating, Graham's chest swelled. *My flock.* Guiding his visitor round to the front, he saw the sheep some distance north, being herded along the road.

"Sheep don't move with particular speed," Jamie warned him, "but they do like to stay together. You'll find they prefer moving from lower to higher ground, from darkness to light, and any direction that takes them toward food."

"On that subject, sir, I hope you'll accept my invitation for supper."

Jamie smiled, lengthening his stride. "As long as you're not serving baked smelt."

Graham matched the man's gait as they neared the flock moving in one fleecy mass toward his enclosed pasture. Rab managed the sheep with ease, walking behind them with his long crook. Two young herds and a pair of black and white collies kept the flock from straying as they guided the sheep through the gate and into their new home.

"Is this your first flock?" Jamie asked.

Graham looked straight ahead, hoping he didn't appear foolish. "Aye, it is."

"The men I most admire are shepherds," Jamie said simply, then closed the gate as the last sheep scurried through. "If Rab or I may be of service, you ken the road to Glentrool. Come anytime, Graham."

The sheep huddled in the corners, as if afraid of the pastureland. "They'll not stay like that?" Graham asked.

"Not once they realize their water troughs are in the middle," Jamie assured him. "Give them time. Sheep hate change. Almost as much as people do."

Graham took advantage of the open door. "Mr. McKie, on the matter of change…" He inclined his head toward the house, and they both began walking. "Am I correct in assuming you've not informed your daughter of our June conversation?"

Jamie was slow in answering. "I…have not."

Just as he'd suspected, Davina knew nothing of his interest. No wonder she'd jumped at the mere touch of his hand on Lammas. "Was there some reason for not telling her, Mr. McKie? I know her age was a concern for you."

Jamie had a ready answer. "Initially I thought it best to wait until she returned home from Arran so that her mother and I might advise her in person."

The idea of their keeping the news from Davina rankled, yet Graham held his tongue. He was not a father; he did not know how a man informed his daughter of such things. Perhaps face to face was best.

Jamie continued, "In light of all that has happened, we could not bear to add to her misery."

"Her *misery*?" Graham stopped in his tracks. "Would my interest so grieve your daughter?"

"By no means," Jamie hastened to say. "But telling Davina that she might have been courted by such a fine gentleman…" Jamie groaned, shaking his head. "Surely you can see how that would make matters worse for her."

Now he understood. "You mean if she compared courtship with a gentleman to her own experience of being violated and then forced into a betrothal."

Jamie gazed back toward the pasture, squinting into the sun. "That was not quite the way of it, Graham. Sadly, you are right on the first count. The Highlander confessed as much. But my daughter was not forced to consider marriage. Pressed upon by her circumstances, perhaps, but not by Somerled MacDonald. He did not insist on marriage. Rather, he wooed her until he won her heart."

Graham dragged a hand over his beard to hide his dismay. *Wooed her? Won her?* 'Twas not the story Reverend Moodie had shared. But who knew better than her own father? "You are certain this rake had some genuine affection for her? And she for him?"

Jamie McKie's gaze was steady and his voice sure. "I have loved my wife for twenty years, and I know of what I speak. Somerled MacDonald loved my daughter, for however brief a time afforded him. And I believe she favored him in return."

Graham began walking toward his house. To make sure that his body still moved, that his heart still beat, even though he felt numb, lifeless. He'd cherished an innocent woman from afar. Then a grieving victim from near. But this was a different Davina McKie.

He'd thought she was mourning her lost virtue.

Now he knew she was mourning her lost love as well.

"I can see this does not sit easily with you." Jamie sighed. "Frankly, I cannot blame you, Graham. Though she is still very much our sweet daughter, she is not the same lass who sailed with me to Arran at the end of May."

"Nae, she is not the same," Graham agreed. "For if she truly cared for him, then her heart is with him still."

"I fear you may be right."

He sighed heavily. "I know I am, sir." Hadn't he grieved for Susan two long years? Only this summer did he once again see the sun shining through the trees over the Cree. And hear children laughing in the village on market day. And dip his paintbrush in yellow more often than black.

They'd reached the front door, though Graham tarried outside, wanting to finish their discussion beyond Mrs. Threshie's listening ears.

Jamie spoke, his voice low. "I must be truthful with you, Graham. Though I was initially taken aback by your proposal, I would have welcomed you as a son-in-law."

"*Would* have? Has your opinion of me diminished, sir?"

"Not at all." Jamie looked at him evenly. "But I can hardly hold you to an offer made before…well, when the situation was very different. Most gentlemen of your stature…"

Graham held up his hand. "My heart has not changed, Mr. McKie. Nor has my offer of marriage."

Jamie stared at him in disbelief. "Can you mean that?"

"Depend upon it. She is an extraordinary young woman to forgive so completely and care so deeply. I would be honored to call your daughter my wife someday."

Jamie shook his head, as if trying to make sense of things. "Shall I tell her, then?"

"Nae, for she may conclude I'm acting out of pity or prior obligation and so think less of herself."

Jamie clasped his hand. "Your kindness and mercy are exemplary."

"The example was set by One far greater than I, sir. Centuries ago." They shook hands, their agreement made. "Understand, 'tis not a marriage of convenience I am seeking. I endeavor to win her heart on honest terms. For I'll not have Miss McKie marry me for any reason other than love."

"You are certain?" Jamie asked. "Considering what my daughter has been through, such a transfer of her affections may take some time."

"So be it." Graham pushed open his front door. "I have learned how to wait."

Eighty

From henceforth thou shalt learn that there is love
To long for, pureness to desire, a mount
Of consecration it were good to scale.

JEAN INGELOW

You know what Robert says?"

Davina looked up from the calendar on her father's desk to find her mother smiling at her from the doorway.

"Fair on September first, fair for the month."

Davina turned to gaze out the library windows facing the loch. The weather was indeed fair, with a cloudless sky and brilliant sunshine.

Her mother was beside her now, looking down at the calendar with a single word written across the twenty-ninth: *Wedding.* "I do hope our gardener is right. If we have such a fine day on Michaelmas, 'twill be an answer to Margaret's prayers." She laughed softly. "And mine. Because if it rains, as it often does in late September, we'll have to roll up the carpets or scrub out mud for weeks to come."

Weddings were traditionally conducted at the bride's home. Aware of Glenhead's modest size, Leana had quietly offered the McMillans the use of Glentrool's drawing room. Sally McMillan had leaped from her chair and thrown her arms round Leana's neck. "God bless you! For I declare, our wee house could not hold even our two families."

"I believe we will need every inch of space," her mother admitted, "now that the parish realizes we are the same family we've always been." She touched Davina's cheek. "And that you are worthy of their compassion and not their judgment."

Davina nodded, grateful that it was so. When she went abroad to market or to kirk, sympathetic gazes had begun to replace dubious stares. On the Sabbath last, Janet Buchanan had finally spoken to her, full of apologies. "We did not understand, Davina, what had truly happened. Och, you poor lass! Such a terrible thing."

The unfortunate business with the marriage agreement had at last been settled. After a flurry of papers came and went from Galloway to Argyll, each affixed with Davina's signature, Lady MacDonald's fortune belonged to her once more.

Davina treasured the brief note she had received from her only last week.

> To Miss Davina McKie
> Saturday, 20 August 1808
>
> Dear Miss McKie,
>
> You have my deepest sympathies, for I understand your loss, even as I share it. My only solace through this most difficult of summers has been knowing what an honorable young woman my son chose for his bride.
>
> Your kindness and generosity in releasing your claim on my family's estate will never be forgotten. May you find comfort in knowing that your benevolence honors both my beloved son's memory and your abiding affection for him.
>
> Ever grateful,
>
> Lady MacDonald of Brenfield House

The treasured letter lived between the pages of her new sketchbook, to be removed and read often. *His bride.* With Ian's wedding on the horizon, it comforted Davina to know that someone had desired to marry her once. That she, too, might have been a bride and not merely the young woman chosen to serve as witness.

When Margaret had asked her, Davina could hardly refuse, not when the lass had been so supportive. She would gladly stand beside Margaret and pray her tears looked joyful.

"Come, dearie." Mother tugged gently on her arm. "I've a new gown for you to try on. Since Margaret is wearing blue, this yellow one should be a fine complement."

Standing in her bedchamber moments later, Davina slipped on the new silk dress, luxuriating in the feel of it against her skin. The color was rich, like butter freshly churned, with ecru lace along the neckline.

As Leana tied the generous sash round her waist, she met Davina's gaze in the mirror. "I confess, I brought this gown with me to Arran but did not have the heart to show it to you until now."

Dear Mother. Always so sensitive.

When Leana held up matching silk slippers, Davina clapped with joy. How like her to think of everything.

"Without you here, I had to guess at the measurements." She pinched the excess fabric at the waistline. "I'll need to take this in, I'm afraid. Unless you might be willing to eat a bit more."

Davina had lost weight since returning home—half a stone, judging by the loose fit of her garments. 'Twas not an improvement. Gazing in the full-length mirror, she realized her small body looked younger now. More boyish.

Aye, she promised her mother, nodding emphatically. She would eat more.

The following Tuesday, Davina awakened to the sweet aroma of treacle scones. Aubert had baked them especially for her, knowing she could not resist them fresh from the oven. Once seated at table, Davina spread a dab of rich butter across the crumbly surface, then sank her teeth into the warm scone and was, for a few seconds, in heaven.

Ian smiled at her across the breakfast table. "I've not seen that look on your face in a long time, my sister. We must feed you scones more often."

Davina ducked her head, then promptly took another bite.

"Father, you've arranged for the banns to be read on the Sabbath next?"

"I have." His teacup clinked on the saucer. "The *cryin siller* has been duly paid. You and Margaret must tarry in the kirkyard while the session clerk calls out your names before the service."

Folk considered it unchancie for a couple to hear their own banns read. Even in the new century, old customs remained. Three Sundays in a row their banns would be cried, with the wedding to follow on Michaelmas, the twenty-ninth of September. A Thursday boded well, Davina thought; Friday would have been better, but Saturday worse. According to her father's copy of *The Gentleman's Diary*, the moon would be waxing the night of their wedding and would shine full and bright on Ian's birthday a week later.

Would their brothers come home for the wedding? Father would begrudge the twins their missed lectures, of course, but might he allow them to attend?

Earlier, when Davina had posed the question to Ian on paper, he'd promised to ask Father. She aimed a pointed gaze at him now, eying the empty chairs next to him to prompt his memory. Good brother that he was, Ian immediately responded.

"Father, I wonder if we might include the twins in our wedding plans. They would miss less than a week of lectures—"

"Nae. 'Tis your day and Margaret's. I'll not have your brothers disrupting this household nor stirring up rumors in the parish."

Davina watched her mother's chest rise and fall in a sigh as soundless as her own.

Her father must have noticed as well, for he abandoned his breakfast plate. "I am sorry to distress you, Mrs. McKie. And your children as well." His acknowledgment, though brief, showed the sincerity of his appeal. "'Tis no secret to anyone at this table that the twins and I did not part well in July. Since nothing would be gained by sharing the particulars of our conversations on Arran, I will tell you only that my anger was justified, and my insistence that they remain in Edinburgh for a time was prudent."

"He that covereth a transgression seeketh love," Leana said softly.

Her father's features did not alter, but his eyes bore a faint mist. "Aye, just that."

Whatever transgression her brothers had committed, Davina knew it was not against her. And in any case, she would forgive them. Hadn't she written them weekly since returning home? They'd not answered her letters, but that was easily explained: They might have worried that

Father would see their incoming posts and rekindle his anger toward them, poor lads.

"Your brothers will return at Yuletide," Leana promised. Nothing more was said of the twins.

Her breakfast finished, Davina tucked her sketchbook under her arm and made for the loch. High, thin clouds covered the better part of the sky, sparing her any need for a broad-brimmed hat. She'd worn a plain braid that morning; the family was not expecting company, and she'd been too eager for Aubert's scones to let Sarah do more than plait her hair. Her gown was not fancy either—unadorned blue linen— though Sarah declared the fabric matched the color of her eyes.

Ensconced at the end of the pier on one of its broad stone seats, Davina opened her sketchbook with pleasure. On Father's last trip to Dumfries, he'd located a larger book for her. Splayed across her lap, the edges extended well past her legs on both sides. The paper was of better quality, too, more suitable for drawing. Davina took her sharpened charcoal pencil in hand and turned to a fresh page, feeling very much as she had in Septembers past, seated in the library under Mr. McFadgen's tutelage about to learn a new subject.

She moved her hand across the paper in short, light strokes, sketching the plants that rimmed the loch. Mother would know their names; Davina knew only their shapes and colors. Were they stiff? Did they droop? Might those be leaves? Or green flowers? Some names, because they were musical, were easier for her to remember—willowherb, loosestrife, starwort, brooklime—though Davina could never sort out which name accompanied which plant. She simply sketched them.

"What might you be drawing, Miss McKie?"

She acted as if she'd not heard Mr. Webster, remaining hunched over her page, her pencil busy and her pink cheeks out of view.

"You cannot fool me, miss, for I know your hearing is very keen."

Davina smiled, in spite of her embarrassment. Though he'd not made her feel foolish about bolting from his presence on Lammas, the memory still lingered. They'd seen each other at kirk half a dozen times since; the awkwardness between them was slowly beginning to ease.

She scribbled a few words in the margin as he sat down beside her, then returned to her sketching.

"And good morning to you," he murmured, responding to her brief notation. "I see you've been keeping something from me."

Her hand stilled as she looked up.

"You are a far more talented artist than I realized," he said, smiling down at her. "But then, you've not shown me your work."

The kindness in Graham's eyes was like nothing she'd ever experienced. There was no sense of pity—she could not abide that—nor did he make her feel like a child. His gaze was warm but not heated. Deeply interested yet not probing.

He cares for me.

Just that. *He cares.* Such awareness came effortlessly, as if she'd known for a very long time.

"Since this is a new sketchbook," he was saying, looking over her shoulder now, "perhaps you'll allow me the privilege of paging through an older one."

She dipped her head, making no commitment. *A much older one, perhaps.*

"I've not come about sheep today," he told her, glancing toward the hills.

On his last two visits Davina had been forced to hide her smile. The questions he'd asked her father! Did sheep not see well behind them? Apparently he'd startled a few. Would he need a herding dog? Aye. Might his flock recognize his voice, distinct from his herd's? They would. Father was very patient with Mr. Webster, though she could not imagine why the man had developed a sudden interest in sheep.

Though she liked them. Lambs especially.

"I've come to extend an invitation to the McKie family," he explained, "for dinner at Penningham Hall. On the fourteenth of September, if the day suits everyone. 'Tis a fortnight before your brother's wedding. Perhaps an outing with just the four of you might be of some value."

Thoughtful. If anyone asked her to describe Graham Webster, that would be the first word that came to mind.

She wrote her answer across the page. *I am sure my family will be pleased.*

"And what of you, Miss McKie? Will you be pleased?"

He was teasing her now, which she did not mind in the least. A man with no sense of humor was hardly worth engaging in conversation.

She dashed off a quick response. *So invited, I'm delighted.*

"I cannot provide the sort of entertainment you might offer, Miss McKie, but I do promise you a memorable evening."

On impulse, Davina wrote down a promise too. *And I shall bring a surprise.*

Eighty-One

A grace within his soul hath reigned
Which nothing else can bring.

RICHARD MONCKTON MILNES, LORD HOUGHTON

Graham pretended not to notice Davina walking through his front door, holding something behind her back. Her new sketchbook? A bread offering sent by Aubert? Cut flowers from her mother's garden?

He would have to wait to find out. And wasn't he very good at waiting?

Davina did not test his abilities for long, revealing a baize bag.

"I'll tak yer fiddle," Mrs. Threshie offered, which Davina politely declined, cradling the instrument as if it were a newborn and she its proud mother.

The image unnerved him, because when Davina crossed the threshold of his home, Graham knew she belonged there. Was meant to live there, raise a family there. The house suited her. Even an amateur artist could see the warm shades complemented her coloring, and the smaller rooms were a good fit for her diminutive form.

"Mr. Webster?" Leana McKie peered at him. "Are you quite all right?"

"Quite." He smiled, stepping back with a sweep of his arm. "Welcome to Penningham Hall."

While they found seats in his drawing room, Mrs. McKie declared the peach-colored upholstery and ornate ivory-and-gold furnishings "charming," while Jamie and Ian looked out of place, like stags that had wandered in from the moors. Davina, dressed in a lighter shade of the same golden pink, appeared to have been part of the room's original décor.

He directed his attention to her fiddle, if only to keep from staring at her lovely face. "I am honored by your surprise, Miss McKie, and commend you for your courage." Graham had some inkling of what lifting her bow would cost her. Not unlike lifting a paintbrush and deciding that life must be lived, that it must continue, however great the sorrow.

When their gazes met, he hoped his thoughts might show on his face. *Tonight will be the hardest, lass.* However tentative her playing, he would applaud fervently. *'Twill become easier over time, I promise you.*

Mrs. Threshie stood at the drawing room door, grinning like an old cat handed a wee mouse. Graham had not spoken a word about his feelings for Davina; the woman had jaloused everything the moment she'd answered the McKies' knock.

"Denner is served, sir."

As the housekeeper stepped back, allowing them to enter the hall, Graham said sotto voce, "Make haste to the table, my friends. We've oysters on the menu, and the only way to eat them—"

"Is verra het." Mrs. Threshie nodded her approval, shepherding them into the dining room. No sooner had Graham offered the blessing than she rang a bell, bringing forth two kitchen maids with steaming plates of soup. "Have a care," Mrs. Threshie warned, "for the bree—"

"Is verra het." Graham lifted his spoon but not before she saw him smile.

With guests to educate, Mrs. Threshie was in her element. "The saicret tae guid oysters is thus: Oysters. Salt." She served the mutton, then confessed she'd purchased the meat from a flesher. "Me puir master couldna bear tae part wi' onie o' his wee sheep."

"Och, Graham," Jamie lightly chided him, "you'll be breeding your ewes next month and soon have more sheep than you have land. Your flock will not suffer if you cull one now and then for your table."

"I'll remember that," he said, chuckling.

When the maids served roast red grouse, Graham couldn't resist taking credit for hunting the game birds on his own land. "Well done," Jamie told him, "and well cooked, Mrs. Threshie."

One word and Jamie McKie had won the woman's heart. On all subsequent visits, the laird of Glentrool would surely command the largest portions from the kitchen.

Graham smiled at his guests, enjoying their company at his table. Over the summer both Jamie and Leana had become good friends. Ian was a bright young man, deserving of his heirship. And Davina brought nothing short of light and life to his home. Her animated features and expressive hands gave the lass a voice all her own. He could hardly wait for the final course to be served, for the joy of seeing her face and then hearing her music.

With much fanfare from his housekeeper, a large glass compote was ushered into the dining room and placed on the sideboard for all to admire: Naples biscuits soaked in wine and heaped with the richest concoction imaginable. Butter, eggs, almonds, loaf sugar—it made Graham's teeth hurt to look at it.

"Fairy butter," Mrs. Threshie announced, flourishing her serving spoon.

Davina's reaction was all Graham had wished. Her blue eyes widened, her sweet mouth fell open, and her freckled cheeks turned pink.

"Our wee fairy is impressed," Ian told him, the gratitude in his eyes apparent.

"My pleasure," Graham murmured. He could think of no better way to spend his days than loving this woman and her family.

When the rich pudding was consumed and their plates cleared, the party moved to the drawing room. Davina hurried in ahead of them, no doubt to tune her instrument. Or perhaps to collect her thoughts or calm her nerves. For a seasoned fiddler, she did seem anxious.

Yet Graham was as nervous as she was. He prayed from the psalms for her comfort and his own. *God shall help her, and that right early.*

The gloaming fell over Galloway well before seven o'clock now. Davina stood before the darkened windows, which framed her like a stage. *Nae, like a painting.* Graham folded his hands, covering up a stray dot of blue watercolor he'd neglected to find earlier.

"Whenever you are ready," Leana said, smiling at her daughter, a mother's love in her eyes.

Davina lifted her bow with a slight tremor in her hands until the moment the taut horsehairs touched the strings. Her shoulders relaxed.

A faint smile appeared. And music, smooth as fairy butter, poured over the room.

Graham had never imagined such a voice as hers. Singing to him. Speaking to him. They were not notes; they were words, and he heard every one.

Lord, what must I do to deserve this woman?

He knew the answer—*wait*—but he did not know how long. He was thirty now. Would he be another year older when she was ready? Two years older? Could he bear it if he waited and she married another?

I will wait, Davina. And pray that my waiting will not be in vain.

He was ashamed of his tears until he saw her family dabbing at their eyes.

Each tune, like the first, was played lovingly, reverently. No reels and jigs to set their feet tapping, but pastoral melodies, tender airs, slow laments. Graham could not name the titles or composers. Was not certain of the keys or tempos. He only knew that Davina McKie had been given a gift. And that he would give her a small one in return.

Not until she lowered her bow did her audience break the spell she'd cast. Applauding. Standing. Leana embraced her, and then Ian, and then her father, holding her so tightly Graham feared she might be crushed. 'Twas only envy; he longed for the day when he might do the same.

After her family finished showering her with praise, Graham offered his arm and an invitation. "Miss McKie, I wonder if you might join me in my study."

Jamie's brow darkened. "Webster?"

"Nothing untoward, sir. I will leave the door open, and Mrs. Threshie will stand inside the room as chaperon." An impromptu decision but proper. "I'll have a maid bring you coffee and nuts. We'll not be long."

Davina was still holding her fiddle when she took his arm. She seemed willing to go with him, Graham thought, though her eyes did not tell him why. Curiosity? Interest? Amusement? He escorted Davina to his study, then left her there only long enough to make arrangements with Mrs. Threshie.

"Coffee for yer guests, aye. But stand wi' ye in the study? Jist stand thar?"

"I've not required a chaperon for more than a decade, but that time has come." He returned to the study with Mrs. Threshie close on his heels.

When they stepped inside the room, she hung back, her face flushed. "I've nae need tae hear yer quate *wirds* wi' Miss McKie."

"You do not need to listen," he murmured, leaning toward her. "You need only to watch from a distance. To be sure I behave like a gentleman."

The older woman patted his arm. "Sir, ye couldna behave onie ither way."

Leaving her at her post, Graham walked through the cozy room with its dark wood panels and book-lined shelves, its broad desk and shuttered windows. Davina had taken the chair beside his desk. Her fiddle lay across her lap, her hands idly plucking the strings.

"Bless you for waiting, Miss McKie." He'd almost called her by her Christian name. Much as he loved the sound of "Davina," such familiarity was not fitting.

Where to begin? He opened the oversized bottom drawer of his desk and began lifting out his supplies: his paints and brushes, his papers and sponges. Beneath them in a shallow box were the paintings themselves, well hidden from prying eyes.

Davina quickly became engrossed, examining each of his supplies with care before putting one down to study another. He had yet to open his paintings, his growing self-consciousness making him wish he had never proposed such a foolish thing. But Davina had played for him. Trusted him. Revealed her soul through her music. Could he not show his paintings to her? trust her? open his heart and let her inside?

Graham placed the unopened box of paintings on his desk, his hands resting on top. "One April, Susan and I visited London and discovered an exhibition of watercolors on Lower Brook Street. Hundreds of works were on display, all done by master painters. Having seen only oils—portraits, mostly—I'd never imagined such a thing. Still lifes and landscapes, bold colors and muted ones, all created with nothing but water and cubes of pigment. I came home with this…" He splayed his hands. "And with grand dreams of teaching myself to paint. But then my wife fell ill…"

The words stopped. Trapped in his throat. Lodged in his heart.

When Davina touched his hand, they broke loose.

"She was so…sick, Miss McKie." He hesitated, not wanting to continue.

I know, Davina's eyes said. *I am listening.*

"Yet I could not help her…" He ground his teeth remembering. "I could not…save her."

A mist of tears. *Somerled.* Aye, she understood.

"When Susan died, my heart died with her. On the day of her funeral, I came home to an empty house, not knowing what to do with the endless hours. And so I began to paint."

He slowly opened the wooden box, embarrassed when his hands shook. One by one he laid his watercolors in front of her, beginning with the first he'd painted. A hillside, dark and desolate. A hawthorn tree, bent with age. A winter garden, reduced to sticks.

Graham had not remembered there being so many. But when he tried to hurry past them, Davina tugged each painting from his hands, her gaze roaming over the thick paper with its wavy edges. The longer she looked in silence, the more uncomfortable he became. 'Twas hard enough to show them to her, but not to know what she might be think-ing, to fear she might be laughing at his lack of talent.

Nae. He'd not painted them to impress anyone. He'd painted them to find his way home. By the look of her, Davina understood. She ran her finger along the wide border, well away from the watercolor, as she eyed the wildflowers, painted on a happier day. The geese, sketched on a wind-swept morning. The Cree, rippling beyond his door.

Finally he showed her a watercolor he knew she would recognize: Loch Trool with her standing on the pier. A tiny figure against the fastness of the glen. Half a dozen touches of brown paint. A suggestion of Davina, no more than that. But she knew who it was and why she was included.

Davina lifted her head and looked straight into his heart. Her eyes said the only words he needed to hear. *Aye. Wait.*

Indeed he would. "Lord bless you, Miss McKie."

"Och, Mr. Webster!" In the far corner of his study, Mrs. Threshie threw her apron over her head and wept.

Eighty-Two

Endurance is the crowning quality,
And patience all the passion of great hearts.

JAMES RUSSELL LOWELL

M r. Webster often appeared at Glentrool unannounced. But this time he'd given her notice.

"I will come on Thursday afternoon," he'd promised, his hazel eyes hinting at secrets. "If the weather is fine, we'll go boating on the loch. Oh, and do bring your sketchbook, Miss McKie."

Thursday had come. The weather was ideal: clear skies, warm autumn sun, a gentle breeze off the loch. She waited for him on the pier, sketchbook in hand. Not her new one, full of blank pages, but her last one, full of memories. Honest soul that he was, Graham deserved to know the truth; she would hold nothing back.

Davina watched him approach the pier and lifted her hand in greeting as soon as she thought he might notice. He hailed her but did not urge his mount into a gallop. Graham Webster did things at a steady pace. Not in a hurry, yet never late.

"I am honored to find you waiting for me." He dismounted with the practiced ease of a gentleman well acquainted with horses, then handed the reins to a waiting stable lad. "May I greet your parents before we climb into the skiff?"

She shook her head and pointed east toward Glenhead.

"Visiting Ian's future in-laws, is that it?" He brushed the dust from his coat and knocked it off the brim of his hat. "Only one week to the wedding. I cannot imagine how harried your mother must be."

Harried? Davina smiled at the description, then slowly walked about the pier, trying to imitate her peaceful mother, who often worried but seldom showed it.

"Ah. She has my temperament, then."

Davina paused her steps. Graham *was* much like her mother. Gracie. Generous. Patient beyond measure. Impossible not to like.

He'd already steadied the boat by the pier. "Will you feel uncomfortable without a chaperon?"

She thought he was teasing until she glanced at his face. To think, he would endeavor to protect her reputation! Davina gestured toward the property round the house, where Robert and some of the hinds were busy about their work, then extended her arm to include the wide open glen.

"I see your point." Chuckling, he climbed into the skiff. "There's little privacy in the middle of a loch. But there are also few interruptions." He offered his hand to help her aboard. "I look forward to the time alone with you, Miss McKie."

After gingerly taking their seats inside the wobbling boat—Graham in the center, Davina nearer the front—he soon had the oars working in a steady rhythm, and they left the pier behind. She tipped back her head as they glided across the water, reveling in the sensation of the sun warming her face and the wind teasing her hair. According to the calendar, summer had taken wing. Perhaps the two of them might hold it captive a bit longer.

When they reached the center of the loch, Graham pulled in the oars and fit them inside the boat, careful not to brush the wet blades against her gown. "Might we both sit in the middle?" He inched over, minding his balance. "There's room next to me. And I believe 'twould make it easier to page through that intriguing sketchbook of yours."

Davina handed him her book first, the stub of a pencil still attached. Then she moved toward him with slow, cautious steps, crouching all the while. Safely settled beside him, she reclaimed her sketchbook with the fleeting wish that she'd not been so brave and had brought her new one instead.

Nae. A gentleman who painted exquisite watercolors in the loneliness of his study knew what it meant to be troubled on every side, yet not distressed; cast down, but not destroyed. The contents of her book would not frighten away such a man.

He held out his hands. "May I?"

Davina placed her sketchbook there, like an offering.

The first pages were from early spring: drawings of birds' nests and catkins and blackthorn blossoms. "You have a fine eye for nature and a skilled hand." Graham eyed her drawings more closely. "Softly tinted with watercolor, these would be worthy of framing, Miss McKie. Would you let me teach you?"

She felt an odd fluttering inside as she wrote along the margin. *I would enjoy that very much.*

He continued studying each sketch. Later in the spring her drawings turned to her mother's garden. And then to hawthorn newly in bloom. And to May Day. She held her breath when he turned the page that revealed Somerled.

"A braw lad." He stared at the sketch. "Though I cannot say I recognize him." Graham looked at her, his brow creased. "Did he come to Glentrool on May Day?"

In a manner of speaking. She found herself loath to mar the drawing and so leaned across him to write on the opposite page. *Good-morrow, good-morrow, fair yarrow.* Would he know what that meant?

"Come, tell me before tomorrow," he recited, "who my true love shall be." Graham touched the paper, following her pencil lines. "Did you dream of this man?"

When she nodded, then touched her barren ring finger, Davina saw that Graham understood the rest. *Aye. 'Tis him.*

However uncomfortable she felt, there was no turning back now. She showed him her drawings of Arran, knowing where the pages of standing stones and wooden bridges would lead. When they came to the list of difficult questions she'd asked Somerled, Davina covered them with her hands and looked into Graham's eyes. *Are you certain?*

"I want to know everything there is to know about you."

She lifted her hands, then hid her face. *Please, let me not be ashamed.*

Graham studied her questions at length without saying a word. After he turned to the page Sandy had found and read aloud, Graham closed her sketchbook and returned it to her, a sheen in his eyes. "I am sorry that Mr. MacDonald hurt you. In all the ways that he hurt you. Yet 'tis clear that you forgave him. Such grace, Miss McKie. Such unmerited grace." His eyes searched hers, longer than he'd looked at the page. "As to the question of what will become of you…"

Davina felt the boat shift beneath her. Or so it seemed.

"A week before Midsummer Eve, I asked your father permission to court you."

Stunned, she could only gape at him.

"Your parents chose not to inform you while you were on Arran, preferring to tell you in person." Graham's voice was even, though it seemed their decision grieved him. "When you returned home, after all you'd suffered, they thought it best not to mention my interest."

Davina rubbed her brow, trying to make sense of it. Had her parents meant to spare her because Graham had changed his mind? She found a page that was not covered and wrote in the margin, *What are your intentions now, sir?*

"Honorable," he assured her. "I do not, however, wish to be your suitor." He waited until she looked up at him. "I wish to be your husband."

Her heart rose and sank at once. *My…oh, Graham…'tis too soon.*

He spoke gently yet firmly. "Such games of courtship are for children who do not know what they want. I am very sure what I want."

But I am not sure… I am not ready… Davina pleaded with her eyes, too distraught to write down what she was feeling.

Graham knew. And answered her question before she could ask. "I am willing to wait, Miss McKie. A very long time."

You would wait for me?

Aye, he would. Davina saw it in his eyes, in the set of his mouth. Though her body had been bruised and her life stained with scandal, this kind, intelligent soul—a gentleman of means who might have any lass in Galloway—this handsome widower had chosen her for his bride. And would give her time to heal.

You would wait for me? She wrote two words with some effort. *How long?*

Graham took her free hand in his. Not grasping, merely resting it in his palm. "I will wait until your heart is whole."

Aye. That day will come. A sense of peace fell over Davina as she carefully wrote, *And when my heart is whole, it will be yours.*

"As mine is yours, Miss McKie." Graham kissed her hand. "Always."

Author Notes

But though the beams of light decay,
'Twas bustle all in Brodick-Bay.
SIR WALTER SCOTT

I sailed into Brodick Bay on a blustery autumn afternoon, buffeted by strong winds and a chilling rain, the water gray green and choppy with whitecaps. The Caledonian MacBrayne ferry did not make another crossing that day or the next, so foul was the weather—more akin to early March than mid-September. Arran was lost in the sea spray, as my photographs taken from the boat deck attest. But once I drove down the ramp and turned north onto the two-lane shore road that rings the island, I found Davina's bonny Arran amid the heather-carpeted hills, hidden beneath the mist.

My first stop was the Arran Public Library; my second, the local bookshop. Research via the Internet has its rewards, but nothing can compare to holding a book, especially a used one: the leathery scent of the binding, the rough texture of the paper, the realization that others have clasped that same volume in their hands.

Several books from Davina's time period are mentioned in the novel. She carries Sir Walter Scott's *Lay of the Last Minstrel* (1805) in her valise. Had Jamie not been dripping wet in that Edinburgh bookshop, he might have looked for Scott's *Marmion* for her, published a few months before his visit, as was Elizabeth Hamilton's *The Cottagers of Glenburnie*. My copy of *Cottagers* is a third edition, also from 1808, printed for Manners and Miller. The author's comment in the preface of her book perfectly expresses my affection for Scotland: "A warm attachment to the country of our ancestors naturally produces a lively interest in all that concerns its happiness." Aye, it does, lass.

Like Jamie, I also held in my hands (but could not afford) Reverend James Headrick's *View of the Mineralogy, Agriculture, Manufactures and*

Fisheries of the Island of Arran, published in Edinburgh in 1807. More affordable and exceedingly helpful were John McArthur's *The Antiquities of Arran* (1861), the Landsboroughs' *Arran: Its Topography, Natural History, and Antiquities* (1875), and W. M. MacKenzie's *The Book of Arran,* Volume 2 (1914). Two modern books that provide a wonderful introduction to Arran are Hamish Whyte's *An Arran Anthology* (1997) and Allan Wright and Tony Bonning's photographic gem *Arran* (2002)—both ideally suited for armchair travelers.

Even more than books, music is at the heart of *Grace in Thine Eyes.* James Hunter's text *The Fiddle Music of Scotland* (1988) was seldom far from reach, and I kept an old fiddle and bow on hand so I might hold them to my heart whenever Davina was preparing to play. I also own an embarrassing number of CDs featuring traditional Scottish music. Jean Redpath's series, *The Songs of Robert Burns, Volumes 1–7,* stands without peer. References to nine songs by Burns (1759–1796) are featured throughout the novel. In Michael Kelly's cottage, his neighbors sing "To the Weaver's Gin Ye Go"; aboard the *Clarinda,* the sailors belt out "Rattlin, Roarin Willie"; Cate and Abbie sing in the rain "There's News, Lasses, News"; at Kilmichael House, Davina plays "Highland Laddie"; at Brodick castle, Somerled croons "Farewell, Thou Stream" and "Highland Lassie, O" and plays "I Love My Love in Secret." He also sings "Lady Mary Ann" to distract his seasick father, and on the night he meets Davina, the ribald Burns song Somerled hums for his own amusement is, appropriately, "Wantonness for Evermair."

As for fiddle music, Alasdair Fraser's *Fire and Grace,* recorded with cellist Natalie Haas, inspired me as I wrote the scene with Davina on fiddle and Somerled on violoncello (shortened to *cello* around 1875). 'Tis no surprise our heroine favored the compositions of Niel Gow (1727–1807), Scotland's most beloved fiddler. Even Robert Burns sang his praises:

> Nae fabled wizard's wand, I trow,
> Had e'er the magic airt o' Gow.

Pete Clark's *Even Now* is an all-Gow collection of tunes played on Gow's own fiddle at Blair Castle. The disc closes with "Niel Gow's

Lament for the Death of His Second Wife," performed on fiddle and—ah, serendipity—cello. Gow's fourth son, Nathaniel, composed "The Fairy Dance" for the Fife Hunt in 1802. Played twice in our story by Davina, the spirited reel remains popular among fiddlers today as "Largo's Fairy Dance."

Grace in Thine Eyes includes more figures from history than my previous novels, simply because the histories of Arran and of the Dukes of Hamilton are inseparable, spanning three hundred years. Good Duchess Anne is remembered for her many improvements on Arran in the mid-seventeenth century: Schools were started, churches were built, and a small town was established near her harbor built in Lamlash Bay. My description of Archibald, the ninth Duke of Hamilton, was based on portraiture. For John Fullarton, family records call the captain of the *Wickham* a "dashing naval officer," and so he is described as such here.

Kilmichael House was built in the summer of 1681 by Alexander Fullarton and Grizel Boyd, his wife, buried in the ancient Kilbride cemetery. Recently the house has been lovingly restored and expanded by owner Geoffrey Botterill to create the Kilmichael House Hotel. I stayed in the stables behind the house—yes, *those* stables—significantly upgraded since they were built in 1716. My heartfelt thanks to Geoffrey, who provided invaluable assistance on the history of Kilmichael and the Fullartons.

One evening while seated in Kilmichael's second-floor drawing room, I met Brian and Tracy Thompson of Devon, England, who'd braved Goatfell that day and kindly shared their experiences with me. My daughter, Lilly, cleverly suggested the suspicious accident on Goatfell. Imagine my horror when I discovered that a murder occurred on Goatfell in the summer of 1889 with frighteningly similar details. Allan Paterson Milne's *Arran: An Island's Story* describes the death of Edwin Rose at the hands of John Laurie. Mr. Rose was last seen alive standing with Mr. Laurie at the summit of Goatfell. "But mist enshrouded the hill top, so that none saw where they went." The prosecution later stated, "Two young men went up a hill together and only one came down." Rather too close for comfort, that grisly tale.

Reverend Benjamin Stewart is fictitious, but three generations of

Stewarts ministered under the patronage of the Dukes of Hamilton for more than a century. James Stewart came to Kilbride in 1723; his son, Gershom, stepped into the pulpit thirty years later; then Gershom's son, John, served Kilbride until 1825. Imagine one family holding sway over a parish for more than a hundred years.

My research efforts on Arran were greatly aided by several exceptional women. Diana McMurray greeted me at the Brodick castle door and pointed me to Eileen McAllister, head guide at the castle, who patiently answered my many questions about the state of the castle in 1808, since in 1844 the tenth Duke of Hamilton greatly expanded and transformed the castle into a splendid year-round residence.

Mrs. McAllister wisely directed me to the Arran Heritage Museum. Grace Small, a very knowledgeable volunteer in the genealogy section, and Jean Glen, her able assistant, slipped white gloves on my hands and presented me with a stack of rare books to peruse to my heart's content. For their enthusiasm, endless photocopying, and assistance via e-mail, I am most grateful. And in Ayr, Elaine Docherty of the Carnegie Library was especially helpful in the local history section.

Once again, antiquarian bookseller Benny Gillies served as my on-site editor and cartographer; you'll find his handcrafted maps at the front of the novel. Benny is particularly keen on birding and has tramped across Arran's hills on many an occasion. His thoughtful input on those subjects and others helped *Grace in Thine Eyes* ring as true as possible. If you enjoy Scottish books and maps, please visit his bookshop online at www.bennygillies.co.uk.

Benny is one of many whose hands touched the manuscript long before it was typeset. My deepest thanks to my editorial team: Sara Fortenberry, Dudley Delffs, Carol Bartley, Danelle McCafferty, and Paul Hawley. I'm also grateful for proofreaders like Laura Barker, Leesa Gagel, Nancy Norris, and my own dear husband, Bill, who searched diligently for typos. Our son, Matt, offered his stargazing talents to plot the constellations for the Midsummer Eve sky, Verna McClellan made sure our Crosshill weaver used his loom correctly, Barbara Wiedenbeck of Sonsie Farm checked my shepherding references, and Ginia Hairston provided horseback-riding expertise.

As you may have surmised, *Grace in Thine Eyes* is based on the story of Dinah from Genesis 34—a difficult chapter in the Bible and in history. Several questions may have come to mind while reading Davina's story, particularly if you know the biblical account. Why, for example, is Davina mute? When I did my biblical research before plotting the novel—a detailed process involving fourteen translations and forty commentaries—I realized that Dinah has no spoken words recorded in Genesis, nor do we see or hear the story from her viewpoint. Davina's literal silence through laryngeal trauma echoes the figurative silence of her biblical counterpart.

A second concern for readers—and certainly for me as a writer—is the rather abrupt change in Somerled, from rapacious rake to besotted suitor. The Scriptures indicate that's precisely what happened. "And when Shechem the son of Hamor the Hivite, prince of the country, saw her, he took her, and lay with her, and defiled her" (Genesis 34:2). The stark succession of Hebrew verbs paints a clear picture of the tragic scene. Yet the very next verse reads, "And his soul clave unto Dinah the daughter of Jacob, and he loved the damsel, and spake kindly unto the damsel" (verse 3). Not a typical postrape scenario, to be sure. Furthermore, Shechem is described as "more honourable than all the house of his father" (verse 19). Hence we have the chameleon-like character of Somerled, who "both intrigued and repelled" my editor in chief, and rightly so.

Finally, please know that the biblical parallel ends with chapter 71. The closing lines of that chapter are meant to approximate Jacob's caustic comments to Simeon and Levi—"Ye have troubled me to make me to stink among the inhabitants of the land" (verse 30)—to which his sons responded, much as Will did, "Should he deal with our sister as with an harlot?" (verse 31). In the biblical account, Dinah's story is left unfinished; we are not told what happened to her after she was taken out of Shechem's house by her vengeful brothers. Because Dinah's ending is uncertain, *Grace in Thine Eyes* has a *hopeful* ending rather than the typical *happy* ending. I could not in good conscience stage a wedding when the Bible does not do so, but I certainly could give Davina hope for the future and a secure faith in God.

If you care to explore further the biblical story of Dinah, please visit my Web site: www.LizCurtisHiggs.com. You'll find a free Bible study guide examining Genesis 34, as well as additional historical notes, readers' comments, a listing of my Scottish resource books, links to my favorite Scottish Web sites, a discography of Celtic music, some tempting Scottish recipes, and Davina's sketchbook featuring scenes of Arran.

I'm truly honored to hear from readers. If you would enjoy receiving my free newsletter, *The Graceful Heart*, printed and mailed just once a year, or would like free autographed bookplates for any of my novels, please contact me by post:

Liz Curtis Higgs
P.O. Box 43577
Louisville, KY 40253-0577

Or visit my Web site:

www.LizCurtisHiggs.com

If you've not read my Scottish trilogy that introduced Leana, Rose, and Jamie, I hope you'll consider a return visit to Galloway with *Thorn in My Heart, Fair Is the Rose,* and *Whence Came a Prince.* And if you've already read that series and wondered why *Grace in Thine Eyes* featured a pair of twins named William and Alexander—the same names used for another pair of twins in *Whence Came a Prince*—I've not lost my Scottish marbles, I promise! You will find the answer in this novel, hidden in chapter 8. (Don't you love a treasure hunt?)

Meanwhile, I'm thrilled to be working on a new Scottish historical series for you. Please watch for *Here Burns My Candle* in spring 2008. Until we meet again, dear reader, you are a *blissin*!

Liz Curtis Higgs

Grace in Thine Eyes

READER'S GUIDE

That is a good book which is opened
with expectation and closed with profit.
AMOS BRONSON ALCOTT

1. Davina's inability to speak does not hinder her ability to communicate. How would you describe her "voice," her personality? In what ways does her muteness shape the story? Consider the crucial events in *Grace in Thine Eyes:* If Davina had been able to speak, how might that have changed things? What is your response to the explanation in the author notes for Davina's silence?

2. Are Will and Sandy justified in their overprotective attitude toward Davina? Are they to blame for what happened a decade earlier, or was it simply an accident? In the early chapters did you see the twins as misguided but well meaning, or did they appear cruel? As the novel unfolded, how did your opinion of the twins and their motives change?

3. Jamie McKie has a hard time forgiving his sons. Is his reasoning valid? If you've faced a similar situation—being asked to forgive a person who deeply wronged someone you love—how did you handle it? Were there moments in the story when Jamie's behavior angered you? Others when he earned your sympathy? How would you characterize Jamie as a husband? as a father?

4. Unlike her spouse, Leana is patient and grace-giving. In what ways do you admire Leana as a wife? as a mother? How might you identify with her struggles in letting go of her grown children? When does Leana demonstrate her greatest weakness in *Grace in Thine Eyes?* And when is her greatest strength evident?

5. Leana tells her daughter, "Have I ever seen a fairy? Only when I look at you, lass." According to Eve Blantyre Simpson in *Folk Lore in Lowland Scotland* (1908), a learned Scotsman was asked if he believed in fairies. "The Highlander replied as gravely as if his confession of faith had been challenged, 'Of course I do.'" How do you reconcile people with strong religious beliefs also embracing fairies, kelpies, brownies, and the like? Did you find the fairy lore in this novel fascinating or unsettling? How might such references to the wee folk serve the story and the characterization of Davina in particular?

6. The epigraphs that open each chapter are meant to prepare the reader for what's to come. How might the words of Samuel Coleridge at the start of chapter 22 describe what follows with the twins? Select an epigraph that you particularly like. Why did it capture your fancy, and how does the quote suit the chapter it introduces?

7. Somerled MacDonald shows his rakish side from the moment we meet him in chapter 28. Describe your initial impression of Somerled. In what ways did your assessment of his character change as the story progressed? Did he ever win your heart, as he does Davina's? Why or why not?

8. Is the tragedy on Midsummer Eve inevitable? Davina blames herself as well as Somerled. Is she right in doing so? Do you see her as naive, flirtatious, foolish, or the sad victim of a crime? Sir Harry claims, "In a plight such as this, society punishes the woman far more than the man." That was so in 1808. Is it still true today? What emotions did those harrowing scenes evoke for you?

9. The aftermath is painful to witness. What circumstances make those first hours especially difficult for our dear Davina? If you'd been there as her mother or her friend, how might you have counseled or consoled her? If you'd been Davina, given all the limitations of her situation, what might you have done the next morning?

10. Grace—often defined as "unmerited favor"—is not only part of the title but also the theme of *Grace in Thine Eyes*. What do you make of Davina's eventual willingness to extend grace to Somerled? Is her mercy commendable or appalling? Contrast Jamie's stubborn attitude toward forgiveness with Davina's generous one. Must a person be worthy of forgiveness before receiving it? How does accepting the gift of undeserved mercy change people?

11. Chapter 65 shows us Will's nature at its basest. Do his efforts at the last redeem him in your sight? Why or why not? What do you make of Sandy's actions in the final, harrowing moments? Despite the clear foreshadowing, were you hoping for a better outcome on Goatfell? How did you feel when Somerled slipped from Will's grasp?

12. Jamie is furious with himself and with his sons, clenching his fists and shouting, "What am I to do with you?" Who is truly at fault for the Goatfell incident? When the family meets with Mr. Hunter, Jamie lies to protect them. As a parent, would you do the same in such a situation? When Will and Sandy return to Glentrool at Yuletide, what do you think should happen to them?

13. Though Davina leaves Arran behind, she cannot escape the judgment of others. If you've ever been wrongly accused, as she was, how did you feel? What did you do? In what ways does gossip still have the power to wound and isolate us? Other than seeking the support of friends, how might one rise above such false accusations?

14. Graham Webster has many heroic attributes, yet Davina is not initially attracted to him. Why might that be so? How does his personality compare to Somerled's? What qualities does Graham have to recommend him? Can you imagine his making Davina happy? How long might it take for her heart to be truly whole?

Scottish Glossary

Except where noted as Gaelic, all italicized words listed here are Scots.

a'—all
aboot—about
aflocht—in a flutter, agitated
aften—often
aheid—ahead
ahint—behind
airt—art, skills
amang—among
ance—once
ane—one
anither—another
ashet—oval serving plate
auld—old
awa—away, distant
ayeways—always
bairn—child
baith—both
baloo—used to hush a child to sleep
ben—mountain
bethankit!—God be thanked!
birsie—hot-tempered
bleeze—blaze
blether—jabber, gossip
bliss—bless
blissin—blessing
blithesome—cheerful
bluid—blood
bogle—ghost, specter

bothy—small cottage
bowie—bucket
brae—hill, slope
braisant—shameless
braw—fine, handsome
bree—soup, broth
brither—brother
buik—book
Buik—the Bible
burn—brook, stream
byre—cowshed
bystart—bastard
cabbieclaw—dish of salt cod
caisteal—castle (Gaelic)
clack—gossip, idle chatter
cladach—shore, beach (Gaelic)
clootie—piece of cloth, rag
cloots—clothes
close—passageway, courtyard
cnocan—hillock (Gaelic)
coble—ferry boat
compear—appear before congregation for rebuke
couthie—agreeable, sociable
cryin siller—coins required for the marriage banns to be read
cutty stool—stool of repentance
deasil—sunwise or clockwise
denner—dinner

dochter—daughter

doocot—dovecote

doon—down

douce—amiable, sweet

dreich—bleak, dismal

droondit—drowned

dry stane dyke—stone fence without mortar

dummie—mute

e'e—eye

elf-shot—having a sickness thought to be caused by fairies

ell—linear measure, just over a yard

Embrough—Edinburgh

Erse—Scottish Gaelic

etin—giant

evermair—evermore

fa'—fall

faither—father

fallow—follow

fash—troubled, vexed

fee—engage, hire

ferlie—superb, wonderful

ferntickles—freckles

firsten—first

flindrikin—flirtatious

flooer—flower

fowk—folk

fremmit—strange, foreign

fu'—full

gaed—went

gairden—garden

gallus—rascally, bold, mischievous

gane—gone

gaoth—wind (Gaelic)

gardyloo—warning call that waste water was about to be poured into the street from an upper story

garitour—watchman on a tower

gart—made

gentrice—gentry

gie—give

glent—shine, gleam, sparkle

glessie—toffee

glib-gabbit—gossipy

goun—gown

gowan—daisy

gracie—devout, virtuous

green—young, youthful

greet—cry, weep

guid—good

guidwife—farmer's wife

gustie—savory, tasty

hae—have

halie—holy

hame—home

hatesome—hateful

haud—hold, keep

hearken—eavesdrop, listen

heartsome—merry

hech!—expression of contempt

heid—head

heidie—headstrong, impetuous

heirship—inheritance

herd—shepherd

het—hot

Hieland—Highland

hind—farmworker

hizzie—hussy

hochmagandy—fornication

hoose—house

hoot!—pshaw!

howp—hope

ilka—each, every

ill-deedie—wicked

ill-fashioned—ill-mannered

ill-faured—ugly, unattractive

ill-kindit—cruel, inhuman

ill-scrapit—rude, bitter

inneal ciùil—instrument, musical (Gaelic)

in trowth!—indeed! upon my word!

ither—other

jaicket—jacket

jalouse—imagine, presume, deduce

jillet—flighty girl, flirt

jist—just

ken—to know, recognize

kenspeckle—conspicuous

kintra—of the country, rustic

kirktoun—village in which parish church is situated

kist—chest, coffin

lang—long

Lawland—Lowland

leddy—lady

leebeertie—liberty

leuk—look

limmer—prostitute

loosome—lovely

losh!—lord!

lowpin-on stane—leaping-on stone, used to mount a horse or carriage

luckenbooths—locked stalls

ludgin—lodging

mair—more

mak—make

maun—must

meikle—great, much

mem—madam

mercat—market

meschant—wicked, bad

midnicht—midnight

mirksome—dark, gloomy

mither—mother

mony—many

morn's morn—tomorrow morning

morrow—tomorrow, future

mort-cloth—pall covering a coffin

mowdiewort—mole

nem—name

nicht—night

nighean—young woman (Gaelic)

niver—never

noo—now

nor—north

och!—oh!

onie—any

oniething—anything

oniewise—in any way

onless—unless

oo aye!—yes! (from the French *oui*)

oor—our

oot—out

ower—over

paintrie—paintings

paisg—wrap, fold, pack (Gaelic)

parritch—porridge

plumpshower—heavy downpour of rain

posy—term of endearment for a child

preesed—pressed

puir—poor

quate—quiet, private

raik—journey, trip

rant—lively tune for an energetic dance

rantin—uproarious

reekie—smoky, misty

richt—right, authentic

rin—run

rubbage—rubbish

run-line—singing one line of a psalm at a time

sae—so

saicret—secret

sang—song

sark—shirt

sclaff-fittit—flat-footed

scriever—writer

seanchaidh—tradition-bearer, storyteller (Gaelic)

sic—such

siller—silver

simmer—summer

sith—fairy (Gaelic)

sithean—fairy hill (Gaelic)

slaoightear—rogue, villain (Gaelic)

slitterie—messy, sloppy

sonsie—substantial, appealing

spurtle—porridge stick

stane—stone

stracht—straight, without delay

stupit—stupid

suin—soon

syne—ago, thereafter, since

tae—to

tairt—tart, promiscuous woman

tak—take

tàlantach—talented, gifted (Gaelic)

tattie—potato

teinntean—hearth, fireplace (Gaelic)

thankrif—grateful

thar—there

thegither—together, concerted

thocht—thought, believed

thrashel—threshold

Tigh an Sglèat—house of slate (Gaelic)

timorsome—timid, fearful, nervous

tongue-tackit—dumb, mute

toun—town

tuath—north (Gaelic)

tummle—tumble

twa—two

ugsome—gruesome, horrible

unchancie—unlucky, dangerous, risky

unco—strange, eccentric, odd

verra—very

wabbit—exhausted, weary

waddin—wedding

walcome—welcome

wark—work

warld—world

washerwife—laundress

wather—weather

wauken—awaken

weatherful—stormy

weel—well

westlin—western

wey—way

wha—who

whan—when

whatsomever—whatever

whaur—where

wheesht!—hush!

wi'—with

wickit—wicked

widdershins—counterclockwise

windie—window

wi'oot—without

wird—word

wranglesome—quarrelsome, contentious

wull—will

wynd—narrow, winding lane

yestermorn—yesterday morning

yestreen—yesterday evening

A new series begins...

Here Burns My Candle

Spring 2008

WaterBrook
PRESS